GOD'S GONNA CUT YOU DOWN

BRANDON GILLESPIE

Hardback ISBN: 9780998749952
Paperback ISBN: 9780998749976
Ebook ISBN: 9780998749969

September 2025 (1.6.0b)

Author
Brandon Gillespie

Development & Line Editors
Amy Guam
Christina Crosland
Colin Murcray

Contributing Editor
Colin Murcray

Cover
Margaret Faro

Interior Art
Brandon Gillespie

Riders of the Stars

There is another dimension beyond our own—a reflection of the familiar, subtly altered. A realm where the golden age of the atom takes center stage, and the stars themselves serve as the canvas for humanity's boldest dreams. Riders of the Stars recounts tales not of our earthly past, nor our future, but of a universe both recognizable and markedly different.

Unveiling a new setting entails a delicate balance in revealing just enough information without burdening the narrative with excess details. For those seeking deeper insights, consult the appendix or explore the website:

https://**RidersOfTheStars**.com

Furthermore, each chapter's heading corresponds to actual song titles, providing additional layers of connection to the events within, either through the song's lyrics, or simply the title itself.

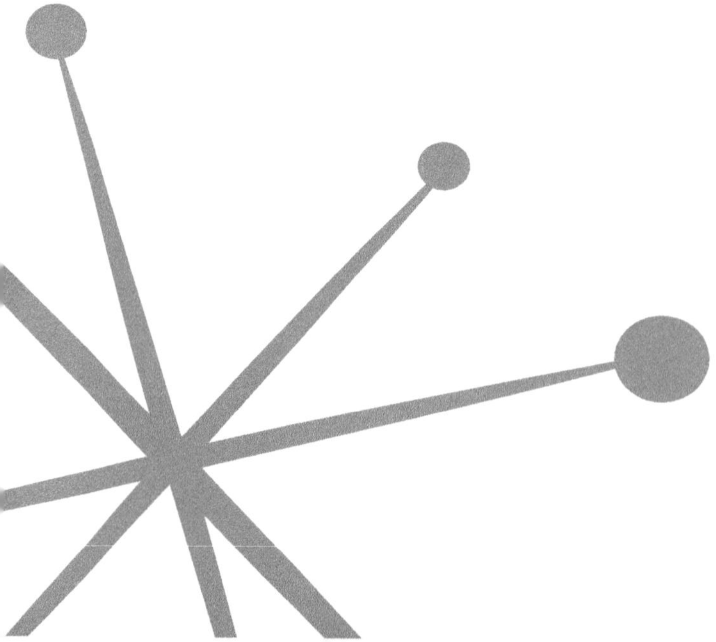

Depression and Suicide

This story includes themes of Depression and Suicide.

Depression distorts the way you see yourself and the world. It traps you in a cycle of self-critical, destructive thoughts that feel true but are not. They are *not* how the world sees you. They are *not* who you really are.

If you are having thoughts of self-harm, suicide, or are struggling with a similar darkness, please reach out to someone. You are not alone, and there is no shame in feeling this way.

The first and most important step is to talk to someone—a friend, a loved one, or a professional. There is always someone who cares and is ready to help.

In the U.S., you can call 988 to connect with someone who will listen, any time, day or night.

Remember: you are **not** your darkest thoughts. You are so much more. Please, reach out. Make the call.

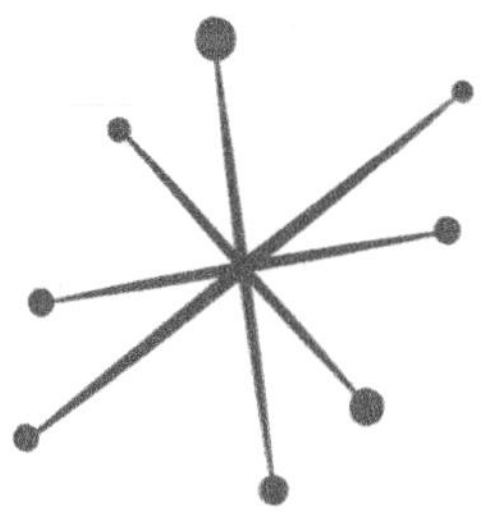

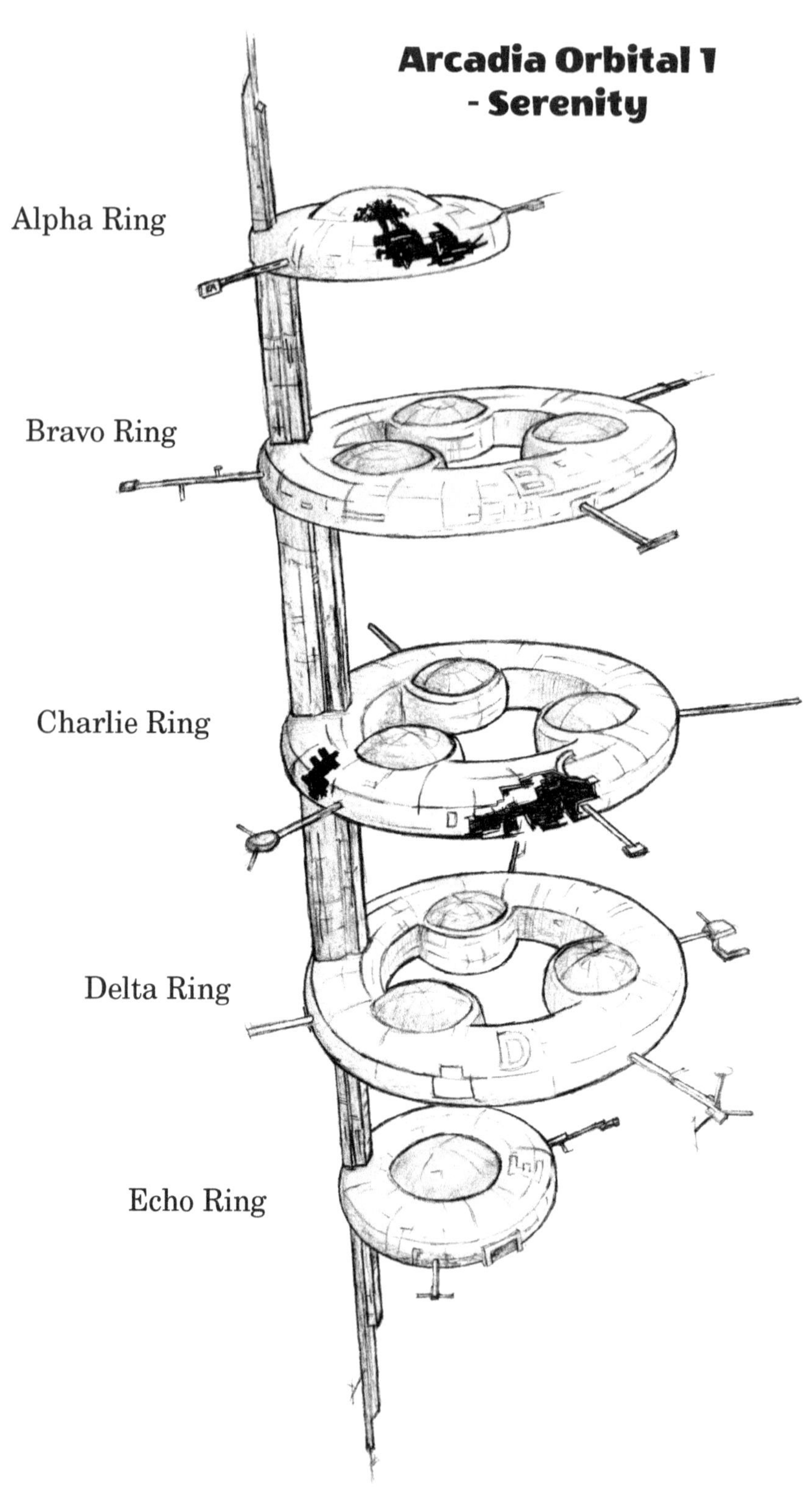

Arcadia Orbital 1
- Serenity
Alpha Ring
Bravo Ring
Charlie Ring
Delta Ring
Echo Ring

Delta Ring

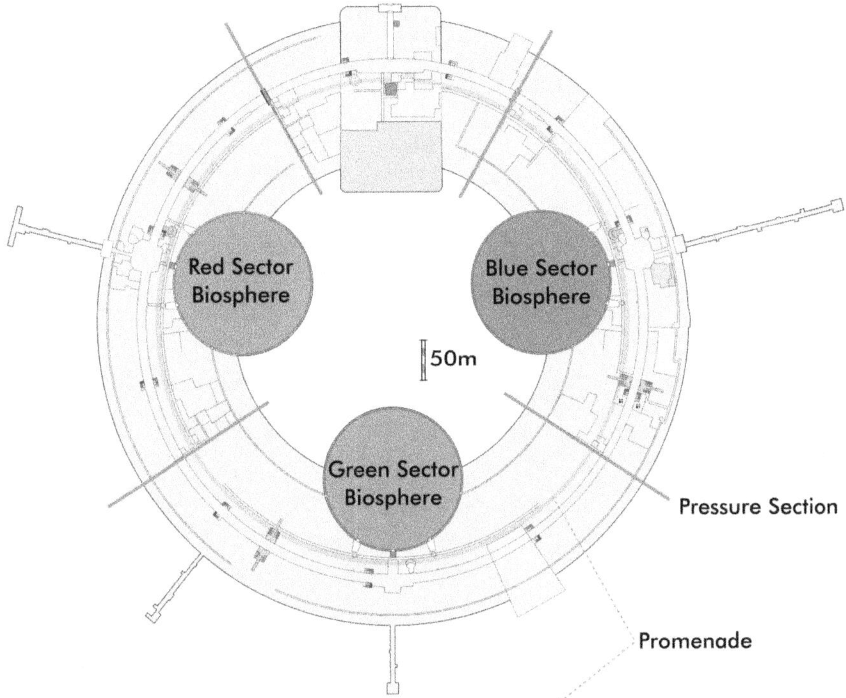

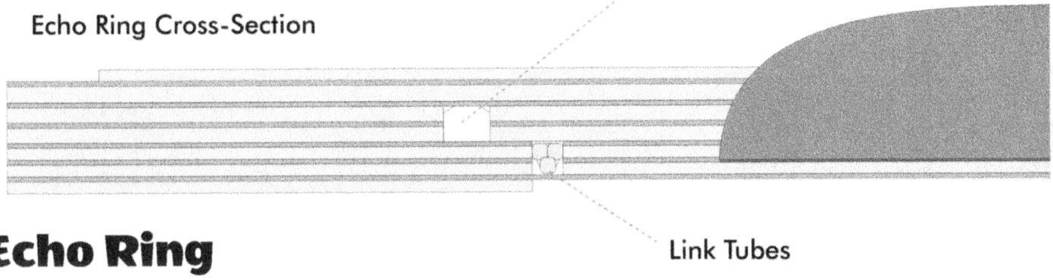

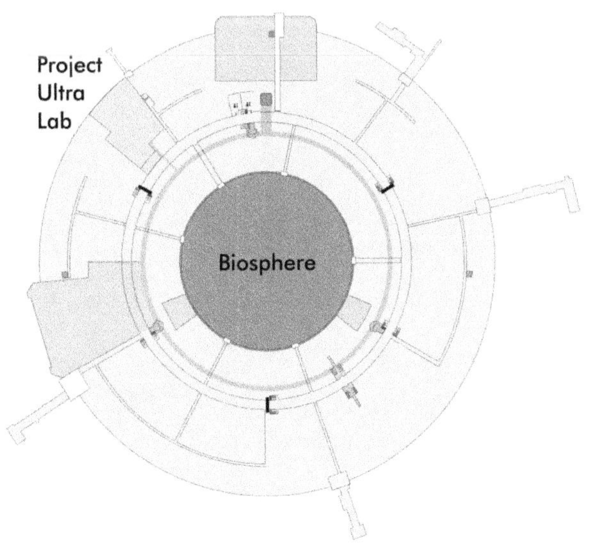

Echo Ring

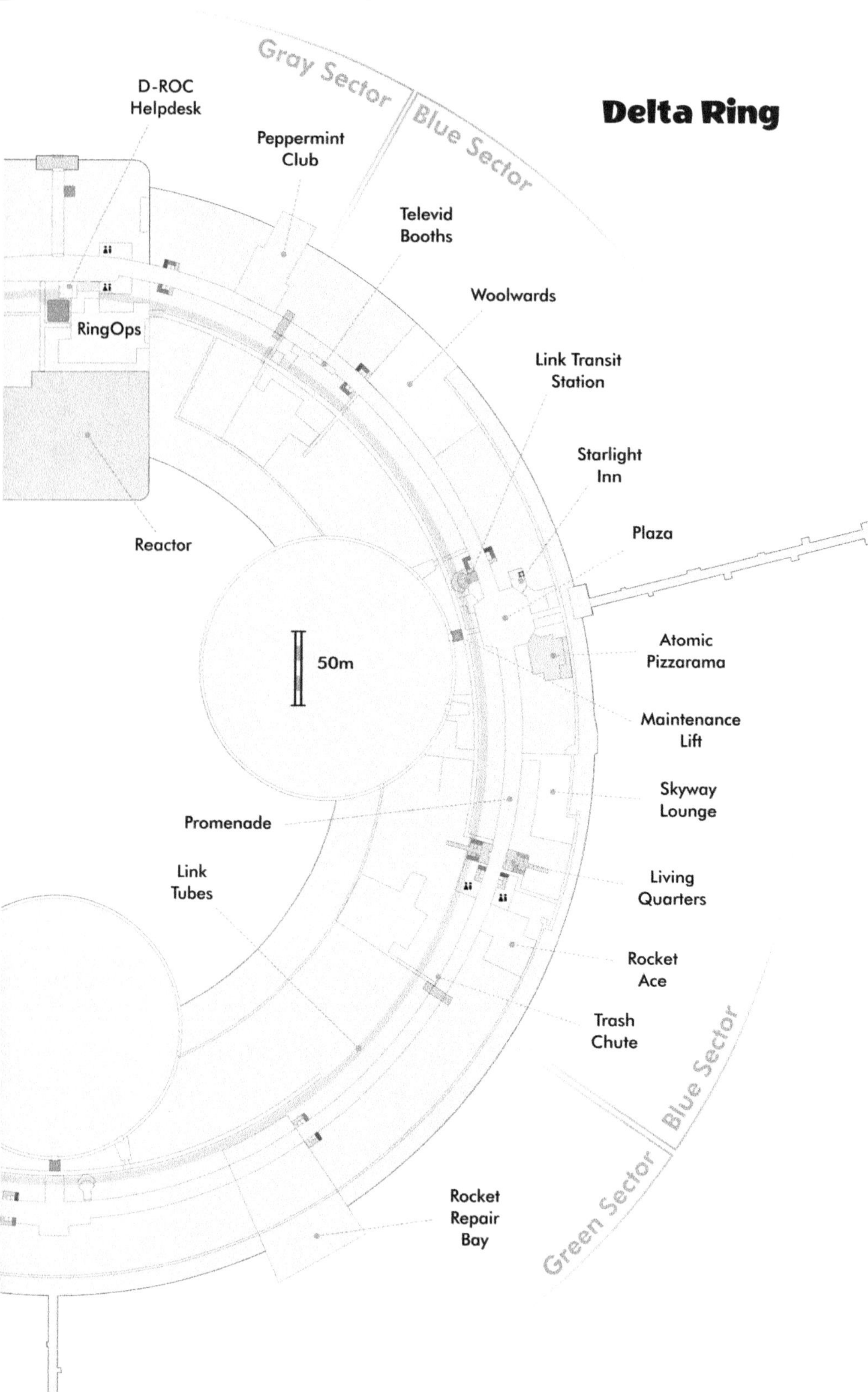

Delta Ring
Gray Sector
Blue Sector
D-ROC Helpdesk
Peppermint Club
Televid Booths
Woolwards
Link Transit Station
Starlight Inn
Plaza
RingOps
Reactor
Atomic Pizzarama
Maintenance Lift
50m
Skyway Lounge
Promenade
Living Quarters
Link Tubes
Rocket Ace
Trash Chute
Rocket Repair Bay
Green Sector
Blue Sector

Act 1

It's A Sin To Tell A Lie

Diego's feet tangled and he crashed to the station's deck, scraping his palms raw. Evacuees shoved past in blind panic, desperate to escape the extra-dimensional horror that had shuddered in from beyond time and space. His mother stepped forward to shield him, arms spread wide, her voice cracking as she shouted, "Run!"

Unbearable light flooded the corridor in oscillating colors that held no meaning. Colors that didn't belong in the world Diego knew. His stomach twisted and churned. The space station's walls, the floor —his mother's silhouette—all flared and faded in sickening waves that bent the edges of reality. He gritted his teeth, forcing himself upright on wobbly legs.

"Come on, Maria!" his father yelled, grabbing her arm.

But it was too late.

Pins of searing light lanced from the Kraal, striking his parents. Their bodies dissolved into pulsating, orange matter, the edges blackening and curling into vaporous ash. The air carried the last remnants away, leaving only their clothes in a lifeless pile on the ground.

Diego couldn't breathe. He couldn't think. His mind screamed at him to move. To run. But his body remained frozen. No matter how hard he tried, he couldn't comprehend the Kraal's shape. Its shifting form and tendrils of light stretching from every corner defied all reason.

His heart beat once. Deafening. And then the Kraal's mind seared into his skull. He doubled over, retching, and his legs gave out. The world tilted, and he collapsed into darkness.

*   *   *

Diego came to with a jolt. Blaring alarms cut through the fog in his mind. Red emergency lights pulsed overhead, sending flashes of color across the corridor.

He coughed and spat, wiping his mouth, bile burning his throat. Pushing up on shaky arms, he avoided the mess he'd made and staggered to his feet.

The Kraal was gone, the hallway empty. His parents' clothes lingered in piles where they'd last stood.

The deck shuddered, sending him stumbling into the wall. A distant roar from an explosion somewhere deep in Charlie Ring rattled Serenity Orbital's structure.

Diego ran, legs unsteady, his breath ragged. A primal instinct to survive drove him toward the crowded Serenity Link Transit station. There, bodies crushed in from all sides, everyone shoving and clawing for space as they waited for the next Pod to arrive. The Link system was their lifeline—an elevator-like transport capable of moving in any direction through the station's five rings, from Alpha to Echo.

Diego pushed through the crowd, knowing he'd be left behind if he didn't. The deck jolted, drawing a scatter of screams from the packed transit station. A chime played, followed by a robotic voice crackling over the public address system. "Please allow passengers to exit the Pod before boarding."

Doors opened, and Diego moved with the surging throng. His smaller frame helped him when everyone pressed into the cramped Link Pod. Ducking under an outstretched arm, he squeezed through the narrow gap and stumbled inside, only moments before the door hissed shut.

It was crammed beyond capacity, holding twice, perhaps three times the number it was designed for. The air hung thick with fear and the sour tang of sweat. People gasped to catch their breath and quietly muttered to each other. In contrast to the chaos and horrors they had barely escaped, The Ink Spots' tune "It's A Sin To Tell A Lie" played softly overhead.

Diego rubbed his scraped palms as he scanned the faces around him. His stomach lurched—not from the Pod's motion but from the familiar face glaring at him through the crowd.

Raphael.

Of all people, it had to be Raphael.

Their eyes locked, and Rafe's expression twisted into a scowl of open contempt. Leaning toward his parents, Raphael muttered something, and both adults turned his way.

Diego's mouth went dry. He swallowed hard, hands curling into fists. Glancing around, he hoped for an ally but only saw eyes narrowing in recognition. Low whispers rippled through the Pod filled with sharp words: "Is that him?" "He did it."

The passengers shifted—subtly but deliberately—until a small bubble of space formed around him. Maybe just an inch or two, but it was there. In a habitual gesture he'd developed to hide his disfigured face, Diego tugged his hair forward and stared at the floor. His heart pounded. A cold knot tightened in his chest.

Accusations had shadowed him for all of his thirteen years. Claims that he was a growler—one of the twisted, mutated abominations born from the void storms. The walking dead that had once been human. Everyone believed he was some kind of void terror, capable of speaking with the growlers. Others whispered that he was something far darker, claiming he could commune with the eldritch Kraal.

But Diego's scars weren't from any void storm. He was born with the mottled patterns twisting across his face and arm. Worse yet, his left eye was entirely black and held sparks of purple with an unsettling violet shimmer that only deepened their fear.

His parents had always denied the accusations, but the rumors weren't entirely without merit. Diego had a gift, one his mother called *tu sentido dotado*. By stretching his senses, he could detect the void terrors lurking nearby and even nudge them away. He could also use that same gift to vanish from their awareness—they didn't even register he was there. His father had found this fascinating and dubbed it "masking."

Over time, Diego refined this technique and even figured out how to extend it to others. Despite being shunned, he'd secretly been their guardian, keeping the void terrors on the space station at bay whenever he could.

But he couldn't stop this last Kraal attack.

The Kraal first appeared nearly twenty years ago, emerging from beyond the universe in an event known as the Arrival. Their coming shattered intergalactic society, leaving only scattered survivors clinging to life across the ruined worlds—including those aboard Serenity Orbital-1. Once a bustling transit hub above Arcadia, Serenity had remained free of the Kraal for decades... until now.

The Link Pod moved through the troubled space station, heading toward Bravo Ring.

Diego gritted his teeth, trying to still the tremble in his chin as images of what just happened burned through his mind.

His mom. His Dad. Standing there one moment. And then... and then... No—he couldn't even think about it.

A numbing wail tightened in his chest. The loss crushed in on him with the pressure of a collapsing star. His heart thudded slow and heavy, every beat an aching toll as he struggled to face what had just happened.

They were gone.

And he couldn't stop it.

He fought to keep the hot tears from falling as his throat tightened.

Shoving his hands into his pockets, Diego squeezed his eyes shut, desperate to shift his thoughts. His fingers brushed against the soft fabric of Donna's scarf. He had spent the entire morning clutching it, his emotions tumbling in free fall as he rehearsed the words he'd wanted to say to her until he'd finally mustered the courage.

But his resolve had shattered the moment he saw her in the plaza with her friends. He had lingered to the side, clenching the scarf, suddenly unable to approach her in front of everyone else. Shame and self-loathing had twisted in his chest, sending a storm of emotions surging through him.

It was one thing for Donna to be friendly to a freak like him when they were alone, but in public? And to be sweet with him? What was he even thinking?

The Pod lurched, its doors hissing open. A wall of noise crashed over them. The transit terminal outside churned as survivors flooded in from Pod after Pod.

Bravo Ring.

His parents had often voiced concerns about the zealous religious group controlling this ring of the station. They didn't trust La Familia's prophet and leader. Diego could still hear his father's voice, thick with conviction: "Beware of a man who promises salvation yet demands everything for himself. Carlos twists the words of the good book, using people's faith against them, erasing who they are until they believe his way is the only way. Anyone who questions him disappears. That's not a prophet, Diego. That's a tyrant."

The warning faded beneath the chaos pressing in around him— cries for lost loved ones, the shriek of a child, and barked orders from Carlos's flock as they scrambled to impose order over the evacuees.

Much like on Charlie Ring, traces of Serenity's old Art Deco grandeur remained. Decorative columns adorned with boxy patterns were even the same—perfect for handholds. He'd once climbed them on Charlie Ring, earning him a stern reprimand from a patrol bot.

Here, though, La Familia had left its mark. Religious iconography dominated the space. Shrines to various saints filled niches around the walls. Each was elaborately adorned, showcasing hand-painted images lit by the soft flicker of candlelight.

Men in drab jumpsuits worked alongside women in equally plain dresses, shouting instructions and guiding the evacuees into queues. Others sat behind makeshift desks, scribbling notes or typing commands into green-lit terminals.

Diego stepped out of the Pod with the other evacuees, hoping to disappear into the flood of people. Edging toward a far corner, he wondered how long it would be until he could return home when a sharp voice called out.

"You! Boy!" A stern-faced man pointed sharply at a table where a new line was forming. "Over there!"

Diego froze, heart pounding. On instinct, he reached for the gift he loathed, thinking he could use his masking and slip away—but the thought of becoming the very thing they feared twisted in his gut, stopping him cold. He never wanted to use it again. Not here. Not ever.

Obeying the direction, he shuffled into the line, hoping to avoid attention. When his turn finally came, he approached a woman seated at the table, keeping his head down and letting his bangs fall over his face.

"Name?" she snapped, then quickly added with a scolding tone, "Did nobody teach you to look up when speaking to your elders?"

Diego reluctantly straightened. The woman's eyes widened, and she let out a startled sound.

"N–Name?" she repeated, her tone thinner than before.

"Diego." His voice cracked, as it had done more often lately. He clenched his fists, praying this would end quickly. The last thing he needed was a scene.

She glanced around the room. "And your parents?"

The question came as a punch to the gut. Diego's throat tightened, the words of an answer refusing to form.

The woman's pen hovered mid-air, her brow furrowing. "Well?"

Diego shook his head, lips pinched tight. His vision blurred, and he knuckled his eyes.

"Hold that boy!" a voice bellowed.

The plaza stilled as heads turned toward the shout. The crowd parted, revealing an immaculately dressed man in a tailored blue suit striding forward.

Alcalde Carlos Garcia.

Deep lines etched the man's sienna-toned face, giving him the look of someone who had faced a long and hard life. His cold, unsettling eyes demanded attention. Long, gray hair flowed down his back, and a silver mustache, twisted into perfect handlebars, adorned his upper lip. The whole image was one of wisdom—but it wasn't a comforting aura.

At his side, Raphael's father jabbed a finger toward Diego.

"That's him!" he shouted. "He's the one who called in the Kraal! He's a growler!"

All eyes turned on Diego, the weight of their stares a cold knife twisting in his gut. Accusations swept outward, driven by a need to find a scapegoat for the horror that had descended on them. "He brought it here!" "It's all his fault!"

Diego wanted to protest, to shout a denial—but he knew he only had moments to act. He lunged for the folding table, papers scattering as he climbed onto it. The woman screamed and stumbled back.

Hands clawed at his clothes as he gripped the column and scrambled upward, slipping free. At the top, he swung a leg over the railing and rolled onto the balcony, ignoring the cries for his capture.

His eyes darted around, heart pounding, searching for an escape. Fabric rolls and weaving frames littered the space. There—an archway at the far end.

Diego bolted for it, veering to pull a fire alarm at the last second. Sirens blared, red lights flashed overhead, and a bulkhead door began to drop in the archway—exactly what he'd hoped for.

Shouts rang out as members of La Familia rounded the corner and spotted him.

He sprinted for the narrowing gap and dove under the door, sealing his pursuers behind. The fire alarms still blared, and he kept running. Serenity had once hosted tens of thousands, but now sheltered only a few hundred. Surely, somewhere within its maze of empty corridors, he could disappear.

He ventured deeper, the knot between his shoulders tightening. Serenity's rings had started as identical in design, but decades of modification had given each a distinct personality. So, while Bravo Ring's halls echoed the familiar layout of Charlie Ring, the subtle differences only put Diego on edge.

Memories of Miguel's hideout in an abandoned cargo bay on Charlie Ring lingered in his mind. And he hoped that maybe, in some forgotten corner here, he could carve out something of his own.

He'll Have to Go

After more than a day of running and hiding, Diego had reached his limit. He wedged himself behind a support beam, legs trembling as he pushed into the narrow space. Each breath came ragged and uneven, and his limbs weighed heavily, refusing to move—he had nothing left to give.

Each time he thought he'd found a safe place to rest, the distant echoes of his pursuers' voices drove him to take flight again. He just couldn't hide from all the cameras. Food and sleep were distant memories. His pounding head was a reminder he had overused his gift. He wouldn't be able to mask himself again anytime soon—not even if his life depended on it. Footsteps echoed along the corridor, growing louder with each beat of his heart.

Serenity was the only home he'd ever known. Orbiting high above Arcadia, Diego had often gazed down at the planet, imagining what life on the surface might be like. The adults warned that Arcadia was a far worse place to be than the station. That it was a hostile world plagued by void storms, with savage raiders and abominations prowling its wastelands.

"There he is!" came a shout, followed by a flashlight sweeping into the corner. Diego lifted his arm to shield his face, blinking against the glare.

"Bring him to the lift," someone commanded. "We'll send him down immediately,".

Rough hands grabbed his arms, yanking him upright. Diego's thoughts spiraled. Down? Down where?

An announcement crackled over the station's intercom. "He has been captured."

The cold words wallowed in Diego's gut as they dragged him to the central plaza. A crowd quickly gathered. Diego's gaze darted across each person, searching desperately for Donna, but found only glares.

She has to be here. She has to be alive.

There—a friendly face. Miguel stood near the front. Relief flickered in Diego's chest, but it was snuffed out just as quickly when Miguel's eyes darted away without meeting his gaze. The gesture cut deeply.

There was no one to defend him.

No one gathered here would even dare. Their judgment weighed on him. He could see it in their eyes—there were no looks of compassion. No doubts about his guilt. They had already decided his fate. They weren't here for justice. They were here for punishment. To watch "the boy who had summoned the Kraal destroyer" get what he deserved.

Anger simmered among them, a volatility on the edge of exploding. Jeers erupted—"Monster!" "Murderer!"—and small objects began to fly: a crumpled scrap of paper, a discarded cup, bits of old food. A spanner clanged loudly at his feet, making him jump.

Alcalde Carlos stepped forward, a rosary dangling from one hand. He raised his arm high, and the crowd stilled. The devotion etched into their faces made it clear how deeply his influence ran. In a matter of days, he had consolidated control over all of Serenity Orbital, and now La Familia's compound was the station's seat of power.

Standing next to Carlos, Diego looked utterly ragged. His standard-issue blue jumpsuit was smudged, rumpled, and torn after days of fleeing and hiding.

"Diego Roberto Alvarez. You are hereby banished to the lower rings," Carlos's gravelly voice resonated across the plaza.

Diego's breath hitched. The crowd, the noise, the scowling faces —they all blurred into a distant hum as the sentence sank in. The lower rings? They were off-limits—a death sentence for anyone sent there.

Carlos held out a kitchen knife barely four inches long. "Take this for your protection, son," he said. "Your fate is in God's hands, now. Find and destroy the Kraal. I've received a revelation that you can do this for us. We believe in you."

Diego stared at the knife. The gesture, the sentence—it was all too much. Slowly, mechanically, he reached out to take the cold Bakelite handle, glancing back to the crowd, hoping for at least one sympathetic face.

Miguel wasn't there. Hiding or he left—it didn't matter anymore.

Carlos clamped a heavy hand on Diego's shoulder, leaning close as he whispered, "We don't need you going full-on growler, my boy, so it's best you use this to finish things quickly." His breath was hot against Diego's ear as he added, "Do the honorable thing, you hear me?"

The words slithered into Diego's mind, burrowing deeper until he grasped their real meaning, and his stomach churned in a cold, unsettling disbelief. Surely, Carlos wasn't suggesting he should end himself, was he?

The lower rings—God help him—were overrun with growlers and abominations. This small knife would be of no help against them, so what else could it be for? It was a joke... It had to be, right?

Carlos straightened and adjusted Diego's collar with fatherly care. For one fleeting moment, Diego dared to hope this was some twisted ruse, that Carlos might send him to the brig instead. But then, with a quick flick of his wrist, Carlos snatched Diego's passkey.

Diego's heart lurched, and he lunged for the card. But the old man moved with surprising speed, slipping the passkey into his pocket with an infuriating smirk. Diego's fate was sealed without it—he'd be locked out of nearly every part of the station. He'd be lucky to survive a day.

A seething storm of anger, frustration, and a crushing sense of betrayal all threatened to erupt at once. Diego longed to cry out, to demand justice. His throat tightened. He wanted to scream that it wasn't his fault, but the words lodged in his throat.

Running had given him plenty of time to think—too much time. The accusations that he had summoned the Kraal to the station spun in his mind on an endless, maddening loop. The worst part?

He wasn't sure they were wrong.

Even still, he reeled at the sentence. They were actually doing it —they were sending him down there.

"—God be with you," Carlos finished, the last of his words lingering as he stepped back from the lift.

The door rattled closed in a grinding clatter, sealing Diego inside.

A mechanical clank shook the floor, and the lift lurched into motion, beginning its descent into the depths of Serenity's lower rings.

Diego pressed his back against the wall, the knife trembling in his hand.

What do they expect me to do?

But he knew that answer.

The knife slipped from his grip, clattering to the floor.

Earth Angel

The lift descended, and with every passing second, a cold, leaden worry tightened around Diego's spine. After what felt like an eternity, the metal doors cycled open in layers, revealing the abandoned corridors of Delta Ring. Fear drove Diego to reach down and retrieve the knife. His grip tightened on the handle until his knuckles turned white. While it wasn't much, it was something.

He lingered at the lift's threshold, his chest heaving with rapid breaths that formed faint white puffs in the chilled air—a reminder of the vacuum of space beyond the orbital's walls. The environmentals were set at bare minimums down here, leaving the temperature noticeably colder than the habitable rings.

With slow steps, he ventured out, his senses on high alert for any hint of danger. The rattling of the lift's doors closing behind him carried loudly through the still air. Startled, Diego whirled around and hammered at the button, but the doors remained sealed.

He needed a passkey.

Then he heard it—a distant grunt, the cry of a growler echoing through the back halls. Diego's pulse spiked. He instinctively reached for his gift, and a sharp, white flash shot through his mind—exhaustion made using el sentido dotado almost unbearable.

And, of course, nothing happened.

Whether from too long on the run without sleep or just another symptom of adolescence, his gift had become as unreliable as his voice. Straining for it now only led to splitting headaches.

He hurried down a short hall, emerging into a plaza. His eyes darted around, scanning for a hiding spot. The growlers could arrive any second.

A few dim lights flickered weakly, illuminating dust floating in the air. The plaza was filled with scattered metal benches, abandoned kiosks, faded advertisements, piles of clothing, and the skeletal remains of trees in planter boxes.

Where to hide? He immediately dismissed several options—like climbing on top of a kiosk. Without being able to mask his presence with his gift, the growlers would see him. His eye caught on a trash can tipped on its side. Diego prayed it would be enough and dove in, pulling ancient garbage over himself, heart hammering.

The cold air seeped through his lightweight jumpsuit, sending shivers rippling along his arms and down his spine. The standard attire, ideal for Charlie Ring's steady 21 degrees Celsius, offered little protection against the biting chill down here. Diego would need to find something warmer—and soon.

He waited, and his mind wandered despite the danger. How many growlers could be down here? Hundreds? Thousands? The uncertainty only gnawed at him. Before the Arrival, Serenity had been home to so many. Were they all still down here as growlers?

Every time a void storm hit, terrors from the lower decks somehow made their way back up to the occupied levels. From the stories Diego had heard, growlers were so vicious that even a single one could take down several soldiers if it got too close. Rather than risk a fight, the defense squads had learned to herd them into maintenance lifts, then send them back to the lower rings.

Where he now was.

He slowly began to realize that the steady rattle of the station's environmental systems was the only sound in the air. No growlers.

His pulse slowed. A twinge of embarrassment crept in—was he just jumping at shadows? Resigned to venturing out without using his gift to sense danger, he pushed the trash aside and crawled out.

At the plaza's center stood a dry, tiered fountain, its mint green and pale pink tiles fractured and crumbling. Once-polished chrome accents were dulled by layers of grime and dust. Tattered storefronts bordered the space, their windows shattered, signage broken and dark.

A balcony wrapped the plaza, reflecting the desolation below. The promenade extended beyond in both directions, forming a mall-like corridor that ran through the heart of each of Serenity's rings.

Faded advertisements from before the Arrival clung to the walls and kiosks. One depicted a sleek starship soaring through space, accompanied by the tagline: "Embark on an Interstellar Journey with Quantum Quest Travel Agency." Another featured a beaming teenage girl in a plaid skirt, playfully leaning forward with her hands on her knees, proclaiming, "Buy Tomorrow's Fashion Today at Bobby Soxers!"

Diego paused to consider his options. Nowadays, the residents of Serenity Orbital inhabited the Alpha, Bravo, and Charlie Rings. They'd made many alterations and changes through the years. Stores were gutted, diners repurposed, and offices converted into makeshift homes.

But down here in Delta Ring, everything had remained untouched. The plaza's shops offered various pre-Arrival amenities, including a café, a convenience store, a Starlight Inn, and even a Serenity Link Transit entrance. But what held his attention was the Atomic Pizzarama directly across the plaza. Its dusty sign depicted a stylized mouse, electric guitar in hand, striking a rock-n-roll pose.

Diego paused, remembering the hours he and Miguel had spent huddled in their hideout, flipping through old comics—especially the ones with Atomic Pizzarama's iconic mascot, Remy, and his intrepid friends on their galactic escapades.

A memory surged up.

"I'm not joking," Miguel had said, face lit only by the lamplight. "I saw the faded logo on a wall in Nando's Workshop, behind a cabinet! That place *had* to be one."

Diego's eyebrow lifted. "Just 'cause you saw an old logo, you think there's a real Atomic Pizzarama still out there. Like, untouched?"

Miguel had grinned. "I'm saying there could be. Somewhere out there. Delta Ring, Echo Ring, I dunno—one of those places they never let us into. We just gotta find it."

A flicker of warmth stirred in Diego's chest as the memory faded. But that was quickly smothered by the image of Miguel in the crowd, looking away—refusing even to acknowledge him.

Diego swallowed hard. Nostalgia wouldn't help him now. Food, water, shelter—those were all that mattered. Not some rat in a space-suit.

Rubbing his hands for warmth, Diego studied the promenade curving off in both directions. Every shadow looked like a potential hiding spot for growlers. He glanced around, unable to shake the feeling of being watched, as if unseen eyes followed his every move.

A pile of clothing nearby caught his attention. Similar heaps were scattered around the plaza. His eyes snagged on a jacket tumbled in with other dusty attire.

He reached for it with fingers stiff from the cold, and then stopped. Memories of the Kraal's attack surged through his mind. People fading away at its touch, leaving behind only the clothes they once wore. Glancing around, Diego realized he stood in a graveyard. How many had died here?

A wave of cold, heavy sorrow clenched his heart. These were silent memorials of those who had once walked the orbital's halls and would never be seen again.

Like his parents.

No matter how hard he tried to forget it, that final, horrific moment only days before remained seared into his mind—followed always by the crushing weight it carried. While running from La Familia, he'd struggled against the urge to stop and cry, but no more. The dam broke. The sorrow overcame him, and he let go.

Hot tears streamed down his cheeks as he sank to the floor, huffing, struggling to keep from wailing. He couldn't stop thinking about them.

The sound of his father's guitar as they sang together at night. His mother's quiet humming while she made breakfast.

No more.

Never again would he hear her gentle laugh. Never again would she pull him close after another rough day, gently stroking his hair and whispering the soft words that somehow made it bearable.

It hollowed him out, leaving behind an ache he couldn't ignore and had no idea how to fill.

Was it true? Had he summoned the Kraal that killed his parents? The thought clawed at his mind. But he couldn't go there. He slammed the door on it, locking it away. The possibility was too much to bear.

Even drowning in sorrow, Diego knew he couldn't afford to lose himself too much—not now. Any noise could draw unwanted attention. Sniffling and huffing, he fought to recover his composure. Wiping tears from his eyes, he glanced at the jacket again.

Despite his desperate need for warmer things, grief rooted him in place. While these weren't his parents' clothes, knowing they had once belonged to someone who was once cherished and loved made it too hard to sort through them.

He remembered Donna's scarf, still tucked in his pocket. She would love it; he was sure of that. But she'd also understand if he had to use it. She'd want him to use it. With that thought, he wrapped it around his neck, feeling a slight warmth spread through him. Not much, but better than nothing.

Someday, after all of this, he'd finally give it to her.

She had to have survived. He was sure of it.

*   *   *

Two Years Ago

Diego's heart grew heavier with each dreadful step he took toward the classroom. It was time again for mandatory community service—a monthly ordeal where groups of youth were assigned tasks to help maintain the station. But it wasn't the work weighing his feet down; it was Raphael.

Now, as he neared the classroom, the walls seemed to close in, and his stomach turned to ice.

This morning, he'd tried to get out of it, pretending to be sick—but his mom had seen right through the act. "Please. After running Serenity's schools for two decades, I've heard and seen it all, rocketboy. Now get moving."

Raphael's voice echoed down the hallway, freezing Diego mid-step. "Hey, Donna, check this out!"

Just hearing it sent an icy stab through him. A loud crash followed, accompanied by laughter.

Diego took steady breaths, trying to calm his churning stomach, but it was useless. Resigned to the day ahead, he clenched his fists and stepped into the classroom.

Raphael lay sprawled on the floor amidst a tangle of overturned chairs. A cheeky grin was plastered on his face as if the chaos were his crowning achievement. His stout, well-fed sidekick, Julian, offered a hand to help him up.

Only a few of his schoolmates were selected for each day of service, and the rest of this group included a girl Diego had only seen in passing—Donna—and a boy, Miguel, whom Diego vaguely recognized from a shared class but had never spoken to.

Raphael's eyes locked onto Diego, his grin twisting into a dark smirk. "Well, well, well," he drawled. "If it isn't *El Duende*, the void terror! Beware, folks—a growler walks among us! Better clear the way!"

Julian chimed in. "El Duende, you ever look in the mirror? Or are they all broken in your house?"

Diego's ears burned. He looked around the room for support, but the others avoided his eyes. Their silence cut as deeply as the taunts.

With gritted teeth, he forced himself to ignore Raphael. He'd get through this day like he had countless others before. Miguel straightened the chairs into a circle as they waited for their advisor to arrive.

Diego reached for an empty seat, but Raphael's foot shot out, kicking it away.

"Sorry, amigo," Raphael sneered. "Chairs aren't for growlers."

Diego turned away, chest tight, eyes stinging.

Donna's voice cut through the air like a divine proclamation, and with just a few simple words, she wielded more power than all of Raphael's actions ever had. "You know what, Rafe? You can be a real jerk."

The room fell silent.

In that moment, Donna became an avenging angel in Diego's eyes.

Raphael's smirk faltered, his bravado crumbling. "Hey, what do you mean, doll?"

Donna's expression darkened, her gaze pinning Raphael in place. "Why do you always have to pick on Diego?"

Raphael gave a dismissive wave. "It's all in good fun. Diego knows I'm not serious, right?"

Scowling, Diego clenched his fists, swallowing the retort burning on his tongue. Mercifully, their instructor arrived, ending the exchange.

But fate took a turn for the better that day when Diego was paired with Donna. He braced himself, expecting her to refuse—plenty of other service days had passed with him working alone. But instead, she stepped forward with a smile.

They worked in relative quiet, sorting through bins of worn-out parts in a maintenance bay. Their task was simple but tedious: separating components that could be refurbished from those that were too far gone. Diego welcomed the silence—it spared him from the awkward conversations that so often came with his schoolmates.

But Donna surprised him. She didn't flinch when he came near, as if he were something to fear. Now and then, she gave him a thoughtful look, but there was no malice in her expression—only curiosity.

There was something almost surreal about her soft presence, and he couldn't quite figure it out. Just being near her was a soothing balm. And if that wasn't enough, a delightful scent of flowers and strawberries trailed in her wake.

Diego kept stealing glances, trying to figure her out. Why was she acting like this? Everyone else treated him with fear and scorn. So what was her deal?

He was halfway through prying apart a casing when his tool slipped, slicing his palm. He hissed, jerking his hand back. The part clattered to the floor, and blood welled up as he clenched his fist.

"Diego!" Donna cried, rushing to his side. She caught his wrist and gently pried his fingers open.

"It's nothing," he mumbled, pulling his hand away.

"No, it's not!" she growled, holding it firmly. With a tug that left little room for argument, she led Diego to a nearby first-aid kit, retrieving bandages and antiseptic.

He winced, sucking in a sharp breath as she dabbed the wound. "It hurts when you mess with it," he mumbled. "I'll be fine!"

But he didn't pull his hand away. Her fingers were warm, and he didn't want her to let go.

Donna smirked, her dimples sending his heart into a tailspin.

"Oh, stop whining, ya baby. It's just antiseptic." She wrapped his hand in a bandage. "There. Good as new."

"Thanks," Diego muttered, drawing his hand close and avoiding her gaze.

"Why do you do that?"

"What?"

"Look away," she said.

He instinctively tugged his long hair over the scars on his face. "Just... 'cause."

Donna let out a sharp huff. "Right. So it's easier to ignore everything? To let the guys treat you like that?"

Diego froze, caught off guard by her directness.

"What?" he squeaked.

Donna's expression softened. "Everyone treats you like you're—I don't know—something to be afraid of. But I haven't ever seen that. You're just... you."

He shrugged, his shoulders curling inward. "It's easier if I don't fight back. Gives them one less reason to make things worse, maybe."

"That's stupid," she said, crossing her arms.

Her words stung, but when he glanced at her, there was no scorn in her expression—just a soft smile. If anything, she looked concerned.

"I'm serious," she said, stepping closer. "Don't let them treat you like that. And you shouldn't hide your face."

She hesitated, then added, "You have nice eyes. They're... different. In a good way."

Diego blinked, heat creeping into his cheeks. "They're ugly," he muttered, knowing the black and violet of his left eye made people uncomfortable.

"They're not ugly," Donna said, fingers toying with the edge of her sleeve. "They're... mysterious. Kind of intense. But not ugly."

Diego stared at the floor, at a loss for words.

"Also—your eyelashes? Unfair." She shifted her weight, then planted a hand on her hip. "And I mean...the eyes, the lashes, the whole 'you' thing? It's kinda cute."

Her eyes went wide, and a flush crept up her cheeks. She looked away, voice dropping. "Wow. Did I say that out loud?"

His heart lurched, disbelief and confusion floundering in his chest. He turned abruptly, retreating to the bin of parts. "We have work to do, I think," he said, the words barely audible as he fumbled through the contents.

Donna let out a soft giggle. "Right."

Diego grabbed a worn circuit board, staring at it without really seeing it. Her words bounced around in his mind on an endless loop. *She thinks I'm cute?*

He kept his head down for the rest of the day—not to avoid her gaze, but to hide the small, flustered smile he just couldn't shake.

Wayfaring Stranger

Diego's stomach rumbled. He needed food, water, and shelter—the essentials for survival. Scanning the plaza, his eyes landed on the Quasar Grill. He'd heard about diners before but had never seen one in person.

Its darkened sign hung precariously. Tables, chairs, and other debris clogged the entrance. He scrambled over a toppled cigarette vending machine and picked his way through the dining area, but there wasn't anything useful. Nothing that would satisfy those three essential needs.

The kitchen was no better. Dishes and empty soda bottles littered the counters and floor. Whatever food had once existed was long gone, leaving behind only brittle crumbs and greasy stains. Even the taps refused to give up water.

Diego frowned at the faucet. This was an orbital space station, not somewhere planetside—surely the water just needed to be turned on somewhere, right?

He returned to the plaza, his mind drifting back to Charlie Ring's layout—specifically, where to find the Ring Operations Center. If he made it there, could he turn on the heat and water? A spark of hope flared—only to fizzle just as quickly when he remembered who ran Ring Ops: robots. His archnemeses.

They were relentless snitches, always watching, and always telling his parents what he'd done. No matter how sneaky he tried to be, they inevitably caught him in the middle of whatever fun he was having. "Mischief," as they called it. Down here, they might even report to Carlos.

He hated all the different types. The spider-like repair bots were mildly entertaining to antagonize. But their many spindly legs made them far too creepy, and they always skittered just out of reach. Besides, spiders weren't exactly one of his favorite creatures.

Then there were the spybots: silent, floating vulture drones that saw everything, reported everything, and rarely said a word. But the worst of all, by far, was the perky "Officer Chip" model—all rolling around with forced cheer, acting like everyone's best friend.

Thank you, no.

Diego had long since learned to steer clear of robots. So yeah, maybe it was best to start with the biosphere. At least there, he wouldn't have to deal with fake smiles and a tin can programmed to think it was your *compa*.

Biospheres were vital to Serenity's recycling and environmental systems—lush havens that supplied fresh produce and enhanced the station's air processors. Although given Delta Ring's current condition, Diego wondered if the biospheres even worked at all.

It didn't matter, he realized. The biospheres could only be entered through an airlock—electronically secured with a passkey. And Carlos had taken his.

Struggling to put that disappointment aside, he decided that he would scavenge for emergency rations and preserved food—at least until he could muster the courage to face the robots in Ring Ops.

His dry throat led him to a public drinking fountain, only to find the button stuck from disuse. A hard slap broke it free, and he watched with mixed feelings as black, sludgy water oozed out. He eyed the murky liquid swirling down the drain, the flow slowly beginning to clear. Running water was a good sign—but was it safe to drink? For now, he decided against taking a sip. There had to be better options somewhere.

His gaze wandered across the plaza and settled on the Serenity Link Transit Station. Back on Charlie Ring, you could take a Link Pod to Alpha and Bravo Rings without issue—but access to Delta and Echo had always been restricted. Was that lockout only meant to stop people from coming here? Or could he actually just take the Link back to Charlie Ring?

He had to find out. Hope smoldered in his chest as he approached the station, his mind already two steps ahead. How bad were things on Charlie Ring? Had there been time for anyone to make repairs? Was his home intact?

Diego was so used to automatic systems doing their job that he walked straight into the doors when they didn't slide open. For a moment, he just stood there, glaring at the unyielding metal panels embossed with an "S-Link" logo.

Tightening his jaw, he wedged his cold fingers into the seam running down the center of the doors, slowly working them deeper until he had a solid grip. Then he pulled hard, grunting as the doors shifted ever so slightly—until finally, the system engaged, and they rattled the rest of the way into the wall.

A single, feeble light flickered just inside, doing little to push back the shadows cloaking the far end. It looked the same as any other Link station he'd visited. Benches lined the walls, and a bank of lockers ran down the center. He didn't need more light to know the far side widened into a platform with three sets of doors, one for each Pod.

Diego crept forward, crouching near an open locker while his eyes adjusted to the gloom. A duffle bag rested inside, and he was just about to reach for it when the station doors clattered shut behind him. He froze, fighting the urge to bolt. Something about this dark room put him on edge.

If only he had a flashlight.

He considered the dark platform beyond. Faint glowing lights on the Pod door turnstiles suggested they might still work. Two were yellow, while the third flashed red. If anything, the darkness near the red-lit turnstile looked deeper—was that door stuck open?

Then he heard a faint skittering of claws against the floor. Glimmering purple eyes flickered and bobbed in the darkness, sending his pulse racing.

Void rats.

Diego scrambled back, dashing to the exit, worried he'd have to force the doors again. But they opened just in time. He didn't stop until he reached the dry fountain in the plaza, dove over its edge, and crouched out of sight. He struggled to calm his breathing, keeping an eye locked on the station entrance.

Time seemed to thicken. It wasn't easy to stay still. Even the slightest of movements set the broken tiles beneath him scraping and clicking, their soft sounds unnervingly loud in the stillness.

He should have known the rats were near—his gift should have warned him. But now, with his exhaustion leaving it out of reach, everything felt dulled. It was like his ears were stuffed with cotton. At least the rats hadn't followed him—small mercies.

Being in the plaza brought back the memory of the Kraal attack. He'd lost control of his gift—it had surged up, feral and thrashing, unraveling him from within. He couldn't even remember what had happened afterward—only that he'd come back to himself in a scene of chaos, his father dragging him along as people screamed and scattered from the Kraal.

He could never lose control again. But as much as he hated his gift, he couldn't risk stumbling into a void terror. Like it or not, he needed it—even as exhausted as he was.

Time for a different tactic. Remembering how carefully he had to approach the skittish sugar gliders in the biospheres, Diego drew in a calming breath, then gently extended his mind. His gift was slow to respond, reluctant, like when his mom woke him too early, and all he wanted was just a few more minutes of sleep.

He shut his eyes, braced himself for the inevitable headache, and carefully leaned into his gift.

Sharp, hammering stabs radiated through his skull, the pounding amplifying with each passing second. But he clamped down on it, refusing to let go. Pushing through the pain, he extended his senses. It was rough and uncertain, but he could just barely feel the twisted presence of void terrors clustered more to the left, fewer to the right.

A ghostly, keening whimper reached his ears—only then did he realize it was his own, coming through his clenched teeth.

His gift shuddered and then slipped completely from his grasp. He sucked in a quick breath and clenched his fists hard enough that his knuckles ached. It had failed him again, barely giving him enough time to sense even what he had. He exhaled slowly, waiting for the pounding in his head to ease.

When ready, he turned toward the path with fewer void terrors and darted between alcoves, hugging the shadows. Most of the storefronts along the promenade were sealed up tight. But, a few places remained open: forgotten offices, a dim chapel, and a handful of ravaged stores.

Diego slowed. The thought of traveling beyond Serenity stirred something deep within him. He'd often dreamed of leaving—going somewhere, even as close as Arcadia or as far as one of the distant stars he'd spent his entire life staring at.

He just wanted to get away. To escape everything he couldn't fix. *But I can't escape myself.*

The bitter thought twisted in his gut. Not everything broken on Serenity was mechanical.

Diego shuffled to the windows of the travel agency. One poster advertised a theme park called Astro World. Another urged travelers to grab tickets before they ran out, for an "upcoming" Z-ball tournament at the Intergalactic Atom Games—scheduled twenty-five years ago. It didn't matter. None of it existed anymore.

He let out a frustrated sigh and turned toward a nearby convenience store, hoping it might have something he could eat. But he found only books, racks of yellowed magazines, and items like headrests, thin travel blankets, and earplugs. No food.

Still, he wrapped himself in a few small blankets, which helped take the bite out of the cold. Among the scattered supplies, he uncovered a notebook, pencils, and pens. His mom had long encouraged journaling as a way to help process his emotions—and, to his surprise, it had helped. If there was ever a time to put that advice to use, it was now.

Diego scanned the magazine rack, the faded covers hinting at a time long gone. Comics peeked out from behind periodicals, and he yearned to pull them free, but hunger gnawed. This stuff wasn't going anywhere, and survival came first.

Back on the promenade, cans of paint lay strewn across the floor leading to a promising storefront: Rocket Ace Hardware and Sports.

He stepped carefully around the loose cans, knowing they might rattle if disturbed. Inside, the place was a mess of toppled shelves and scattered inventory. Rummaging through the aisles, he discovered countless items that might prove useful, even if it wasn't food: A multitool with a sharp knife, a backpack to carry his gear, and even an entire shelf of flashlights—all without batteries.

Moving on, he sorted through a rack of denim utility overalls and searched for a pair that might fit his boy-sized frame. But everyone was made for adults. Brow furrowed, he grabbed the smallest set and pulled them on over his jumpsuit. They swallowed him whole, with the straps slipping off his shoulders, the midsection sagging below his waist, and the legs bunching around his feet in a pile.

Refusing to give up, he let the straps dangle at his sides and fashioned a length of twine into a belt. Cinching it around his waist to hold the overalls in place, he used his new multitool to hack off the excess pant legs. It wasn't perfect, but it would do. With the overalls added to the travel blankets around his shoulders, warmth slowly began creeping back into his limbs.

Resuming his search, he finally stumbled upon a box of emergency rations, and his stomach immediately growled. Snatching a brick of instant noodles, his hands trembled as he scanned the instructions, which called for boiling water—a luxury he didn't have.

Tearing open the package, he bit down. The noodles crunched loudly between his teeth, and his dry mouth made chewing a struggle. But he worked up enough saliva to swallow, even if he had to cough as the jagged mass scraped its way down his throat. He ripped open the powdered seasoning packet and dumped it into his mouth—an act he instantly regretted as the saltiness only made him thirstier. Once his mouth wasn't as dry as a desert, he continued, chewing through two more packages of noodles, this time setting the flavor packets aside.

With the hollow ache in his stomach easing, Diego resumed his search through the store. In the sports section, he stumbled across relics he'd only heard about in stories: unwieldy leather gloves, deflated balls, and odd plastic disks—all enigmatic and useless to him.

He passed a shelf labeled "Athletic Supporters," eyed the bizarre gear with a frown, and decided he didn't want to know.

A pile of white game masks lay beneath a faded sign that proclaimed, "The best Z-ball players choose Blammo!" Now that was a game he actually recognized, because teams still played it on Serenity's three occupied rings.

A long, rounded wooden stick brought him to a stop. It was polished smooth and branded with "Top Slugger—the best bat around!" Gripping the handle, he considered how well it might do against void rats. It was for a sport he didn't recognize, but that didn't matter—he could use it as a weapon.

The clatter of an empty paint can rolling across the floor echoed through the store, sending his heart racing. Gripping the Top Slugger, he cautiously peered over the shelves.

Two growlers entered, twisted and burned-looking, one male and one female.

"We're coming," the man hissed through gnarled lips.

"Run!" the woman added, moving in Diego's direction.

Panic surged within him as he scrambled back, quietly making his way around the store, only to realize he was trapped. His gift had always helped him to keep a safe distance from growlers—until now. Their presence pressed nauseatingly in his mind.

He braced himself and reached inward for his gift, but it slipped away with each attempt. Furious at his lack of control, Diego started moving, desperately hoping to find an escape route. The growlers closed in quickly, herding him until he was trapped in an aisle, one growler blocking each end.

Clenching the Top Slugger, he muttered to steady his nerves, "It's just two of them. How bad can they be? I can do this."

He dropped his pack and tightened both hands around the bat, weaving it back and forth to feel the balance.

When the growlers lunged, he swung with everything he had. The blow landed solidly in the first one's ribs.

But before it could react, the second grabbed a fistful of his jumpsuit and yanked him back, hurling him into the shelves. He hit spine-first, momentum flipping him over the top before he crashed into the next aisle. His head smacked the floor, sparks burst across his vision, and the impact knocked the air from his lungs.

Diego gasped and struggled to breathe. The throw had hurt something fierce—but it also might have saved him. The growlers scrambled in the other aisle, unsure where he'd landed.

Staggering to his feet, head spinning and heart pounding, he spotted the stockroom and forced himself forward. The doors slammed open as he barreled into a space cluttered with dusty shelves and broken inventory. Sprinting to the back in search of an exit, he ran straight into a dead end.

Behind him, the growlers crashed through the doors, scanning the dim room. He ducked behind a shelf, hoping they hadn't seen him.

A wave of helplessness pressed down on him. The futility of it all was absurd. He was just a worn-out kid facing two growlers—they were going to kill him. Worse, they'd eat him. Panic clawed at his mind as he struggled to think of an escape.

But there was nothing left he could do.

Except try to use el sentido dotado.

His gift that was out of reach, having failed him time and again.

That didn't matter now.

Clenching his fists, he forced his hands to stop trembling. It was time to focus. To try harder. He swallowed and braced himself. This was going to hurt. He didn't have time to take it gently.

Closing his eyes, he forced his mind to zero in. There—it flickered just out of reach, faint and shuddering. He stretched for it, and immediately a sharp, searing pain seared through his skull.

His jaw clenched as tears leaked from his tightly shut eyes. He could hear the growlers closing in. It felt like his head was about to split open, but the fear of being eaten kept him steady.

With every ounce of concentration he could muster, Diego seized a few threads of his gift, holding tight as they flailed and fought against him. Pulse thundering in his ears, he yanked on the threads, pulling in more and more until—he had control again. How long would it last?

Before another heartbeat passed, he activated his masking. Colors shimmered and faded, leaving the world dim and muted. A sensation that left him feeling like he was shrouded in murky water. Never before had he been so happy to use his gift.

He'd been so focused that he'd lost track of the growlers. He peeked around the edge of the shelf, just as one staggered into view. Its gnarled face twisted in confusion at the seemingly empty aisle, and it hissed, "Escape!"

Diego pressed himself flat against the shelf as it shuffled closer, its head jerking left and right. Every instinct screamed at him to run, but he stayed rooted, barely daring to breathe. His heart pounded so hard he feared it might give him away. The thing's stench almost overwhelmed him—a putrid reek that cut through even the shallow breaths he dared take.

It had been a man once, though whatever humanity it had ever possessed was now buried beneath layers of filth and decay. Its tattered clothing hung in grimy, shredded rags that swayed with each lurch.

Once it shuffled past him, Diego edged around the corner, one agonizingly slow step at a time. With his masking in place, they might not be able to see him, but noises or sudden movements would shatter the illusion.

Reaching the main aisle, he broke into a quiet, controlled jog toward the stockroom doors. His heart raced faster with every step. All the while, the strain of maintaining his masking pulled on him. His control was slipping again, and he needed to get away before it failed.

He prayed for silence and pulled on the stockroom door. Of course, it let out a long, shrill squeal that reverberated through the air. A quick glance over his shoulder confirmed the growlers were scrambling into the main aisle.

Needing no further urging, he bolted out. The pounding in his skull was unbearable, and he had to hold desperately to keep his masking in place, stopping only to grab his scavenged gear before escaping.

When he reached the promenade, he finally released his gift, gasping as the hammering in his head subsided. But the reprieve was short-lived—behind him, the growlers' rapid footsteps sounded closer than ever.

His head throbbed, and he fought waves of nausea as he sprinted forward, relying solely on his eyes and ears to detect dangers. It wasn't long before a barrier loomed ahead, blocking the entire promenade. His steps faltered—he was trapped.

He pressed a hand against the cold steel of the barrier, pausing to catch his breath as he fought against the rising panic gripping his chest. Doubling back wasn't an option—the guttural cries of the growlers came from that direction, growing louder with each passing moment, and it sounded like more had joined in on the fun.

Diego spotted the bulkhead controls on the wall and darted toward them, only to hesitate—fingers hovering over the buttons. Was the space beyond compromised? He had to risk it. But he had no idea how to work the panel. He stabbed a few buttons at random. Nothing happened. The panel didn't even light up.

"Run!" cried a growler when it saw him.

A nearby trash disposal hatch drew his attention. His dad's warning about the dangers of the orbital's recycling system echoed in his mind: "It can just as easily recycle children as any other biological matter."

But Diego pushed the warning aside. There was no other choice. He hoped his parents had been wrong and he could escape somewhere deeper in the system. Yanking the square hatch open, he dove through the narrow opening, dragging his pack behind him.

The orbital's systems reacted instantly—a red warning light flashed and a door further down the chute snapped closed, leaving him barely any room to fit. Outside, an automated warning repeated: "Emergency—living biological detected in the recycler."

"Mierda," he hissed, using his father's favorite curse. The alarm would draw every growler within earshot.

The door rattled and Diego fumbled with the hatch, desperate to find something to keep it shut. But there were no handles inside, only short, stubby screw posts. He gripped them with the tips of his fingers, hands trembling.

The growlers continued to pull on the hatch, and he held tightly. He could hear them outside, their numbers growing. This was it. Nowhere left to run. His gift? Useless. It was only a matter of time before they had him.

Run For Your Life

A cheerful voice came from outside the chute. "Hello, peaceful vagrants! Please vacate the area. We wouldn't want anyone to get hurt, now would we?"

The unnervingly bright tone set Diego's nerves on edge—but at least the pressure on the hatch door eased. He drew a shaky breath. Outside, commands to disperse rang out, punctuated by the snap of electric zaps and the hisses of growlers.

Diego couldn't stop himself; he had to know who had come to his rescue, and slowly eased the hatch open enough to peek outside.

A Unitron robot rolled into view, sending Diego's stomach lurching.

Officer Chip.

The raw terror that had gripped him when death had seemed inevitable now changed into a bewildering tangle of distrust and relief. The robot opened the chute's front panel, revealing a scowling Diego crouched inside. It never failed; the bots would always find him.

Like all Unitron models, this one rolled on three cushioned wheels and had a rounded head with large, friendly optics. But as an Officer Chip unit, it also came equipped with two articulated arms, flashing dome lights, and a gratingly cheerful personality. Worn lettering on its scratched and dented chassis identified it as "CD25."

"Well, would you look at that!" it exclaimed warmly, its screen flickering to display a reassuring smile. "A little boy where he shouldn't be! How about we get you out of there? Can you provide identification, my little friend?"

Diego hesitated, glancing down the now-empty promenade. With no immediate threat in sight, he climbed out and answered. "I don't have any."

Chip tilted, optics whirring. "Oh my! A lost child?"

"I am not!" Diego snapped. "I just... I was hiding from the growlers."

"Were those vagrants bothering you? Now, don't you worry, we'll get this straightened right up, little ranger! First, can you tell me your name and that of your parents or guardian?"

Diego blinked. Why, of all bots, did it have to be an Officer Chip model? He had to tread carefully, or it might report back to Alcalde Carlos.

But then a thought struck him, and his eyes narrowed. If this bot was still operational, that meant others could be, too. So why hadn't they fixed anything? Or dealt with the growlers? And calling them vagrants—what was that about?

The bot reached up and gently patted the top of his head. "Little boy, are you feeling well?"

Diego stiffened. Little? He wasn't little! They were the same height! He rose up on his toes before answering. "If those things were vagrants, what does that make me? Huh? Did they pull you out of the scrap heap? You're just a busted-up clanker!"

But it simply replied with undeterred cheer. "Oh, I'm sorry, did I forget to introduce myself? My name is Officer Chip." It planted metal hands on either side of its chassis. "I'm here to serve and protect. It is my programmed duty to maintain the peace and assist the people of Delta Ring."

Chip shifted, looking Diego over, its optics lingering a moment too long on the empty passkey holder around his wrist. "Now, would you kindly identify yourself?"

Exhausted, angry, and annoyed, Diego's expression darkened. "No."

Chip processed the reply with a series of whirs and clicks. "Very well! For now, I'll call you Vagrant 37A2. Unfortunately, we do have rules, little ranger, and you broke a doozy of one messing with the recycling chute. But how about we handle it with a gentle reminder this time? Just a wee citation for a minor slip-up. We both know you won't do it again, right?"

A buzzing noise emitted from its chest as it printed a ticket, handing it to Diego. "You have thirty days to identify yourself at the Delta Ring Operations Help Desk and pay the fine. Now, I'm sure a smart little Star Ranger like you already knows, but we're under lockdown. You should go to another ring until that status changes, alright?"

"But how?" Diego demanded.

The robot hesitated. "How what?"

Diego clenched his fists, fighting the urge to yell. "I want to leave, but I can't, okay? The Link Pods are shut down. And I don't know where to go. Everyone had to escape Charlie Ring. We all went to Bravo, but... they don't want me there."

Chip paused, humming a pleasant tune as it processed the new information. "You're absolutely right! Thank you for clarifying! Correction: Please proceed to Bravo Ring!"

Diego growled. "But I just said I can't leave!"

Wheeling away, Chip gently chided, "No need to upset the apple cart, Vagrant 37A2. Please move along!"

Diego grabbed his gear and chased after the security bot. "Can't you help me? Where can I stay?"

Chip turned to face him. "Did you misunderstand? You are not allowed to stay in Delta Ring! We have no residents during lockdown. Be a good sport and head to Bravo Ring, young man. You don't want to loiter like those other vagrants, now do you?"

Diego paused, mind reeling. *Does it have a few screws loose?*

But he had no other choice—the robot might lead him to safety and food. He waited until Chip had moved on before quietly following.

After a few meters, Chip stopped, its tone sharpening beneath the ever-present cheer. "Excuse me! Please stop following! You don't want a second citation, now, do you, champ?"

"For following you?" Diego sputtered. He waited until Chip moved on, then continued his pursuit. Robots weren't the only ones who could be annoying.

The pattern repeated, each encounter eroding Chip's perky facade. A small part of Diego found it fascinating—he'd never seen an Officer Chip behave quite like this. Less polished, and somehow more... unpredictable?

After several repetitions, Chip spun sharply. For just a heartbeat, something feral flickered across its face—furrowed brows, a jagged snarl, a flash of too many sharp teeth on its screen—and then it vanished.

Diego lurched back. He hadn't even known they could look upset, let alone furious.

Chip's cheerful smile quickly returned. Its animated eyebrows rotated back to a friendly position, and it let out a long, exaggerated sigh. "Okay, okay! You win, little ranger. If you're set on tagging along, just promise me you'll behave, alright?"

Diego's heart raced. The image of those teeth wouldn't leave his mind. Eyes wide, he gave a quick nod.

The robot led him along the promenade, past the plaza with the Pizzarama, and deeper into a maze of dimly lit back corridors that left his head spinning. Finally, they approached a set of doors labeled "D-ROC."

Chip stopped, pointing at a bright red stripe painted on the floor. "Little Star Rangers are not allowed past this line. Do you understand? Crossing it is a big no-no!"

Diego bristled at Chip's condescending tone. Narrowing his eyes, he glanced at the turret overhead, its raygun silent but ominous.

Reluctantly, he nodded, his worry growing. This Chip seemed to have more than its share of loose screws. The angry look it had flashed earlier was terrifying; its battered chassis was more damaged than any he'd seen on Charlie Ring, and its cheer was dialed up far past normal. Worst of all, it called the growlers vagrants, like they were any other ordinary person. Could it not tell the difference?

He studied the hallway beyond the line. The gleaming floors and spotless walls told a clear story: maintenance was happening, but not where it mattered. A spark of anger lit in his chest. How could it claim to maintain peace while growlers and void terrors prowled the halls freely?

"You guys are useless!" he shouted.

Without a word, Chip rolled into the D-ROC. The doors hissed shut, leaving Diego alone again.

He sagged under the weight of the past few days, rubbing his dry eyes. Suddenly, he couldn't keep them open. With a slow sigh, he sank to the floor. Using his pack as a makeshift pillow, he curled into a tight ball, pulled the travel blanket over himself, and drifted off to sleep.

Sometime later, an urgent biological need dragged him awake, his body sore and aching. The overhead lights had dimmed while he slept, and the corridor remained deserted—save for the watchful gaze of the security turret tracking his every move.

Diego's priority was finding the head; surely, a public restroom still worked. Slinging his pack over his shoulder, he stepped briskly toward the promenade, the uncomfortable pressure making a faster pace unwise. A few wrong turns only added to his misery, but at last, he reached the promenade and spotted a restroom. Better yet—it still worked—one less problem to deal with.

With that settled, Diego made his way back to the plaza where he'd first arrived. He scavenged a few unbroken soda pop bottles from the Quasar Grill and carried them to the drinking fountain. The restroom sinks had also run black sludge before clearing up, so he hoped it was just from disuse and that the water was safe to drink. He let the fountain run until it flowed clear and then filled each bottle.

Food, water, shelter, he reminded himself. *One down, two to go.*

Unfortunately, the other two wouldn't come as easily.

While the bottles filled, his gaze drifted to the darkened, broken sign of the Atomic Pizzarama. Here it was—the real thing.

For a fleeting moment, he could almost hear laughter blending with the strains of a jukebox. Then reality snapped back, leaving him in the quiet, forsaken halls of Delta Ring.

Deciding a quick investigation couldn't hurt, he snapped caps onto the bottles, tucked them into his pack, and crossed the plaza. A rolling gate blocked access to the Pizzarama's inner sanctum. Gripping the cold metal bars, he peered through, scanning the shadowy interior.

The once vibrant colors of the walls and floors had faded, their surfaces marred by cracks and stains. Rows of empty tables and chairs were scattered haphazardly in the main dining area, and one side was filled with dusty arcade machines.

A large, protruding stage divided the room, its dust-hazed curtain framing a crew of animatronic figures. Their oversized mechanical eyes stared into the emptiness, unnervingly keeping watch over the abandoned restaurant.

The lights on the promenade slowly brightened around him. Even with most of the bulbs burned out, Serenity marked a new day. The mellow, brassy tones of a trombone carrying a jazz melody floated softly overhead. Diego strained to catch the tune, but the song warbled and sputtered before finally cutting out.

Just like him, Delta Ring was barely keeping it together.

Reluctantly, Diego stepped away from the Pizzarama, focusing on more pressing matters.

Feeling stiff and sore from the uncomfortable night on the floor, he considered the Starlight Inn nearby. The sign, once carving bright lines of electric light across the facade, had lost most of its letters, leaving only shadows where they had once been. Layers of grime obscured the windows, offering only a murky view inside.

The door began to slide open at his approach, but stopped with a reluctant shudder. He grabbed the edge and dragged it the rest of the way into the wall, the metal grinding in protest the entire way.

Diego's feet stirred up dust in the cramped lobby. A motionless Unibot attendant sat behind a worn chrome counter.

"Hey," he said, waving his hands and expecting it to spring to life. It didn't move.

Furrowing his brow, he climbed onto the counter and nudged the bot's dome with his finger, leaving a mark in the dust.

Still nothing.

Noticing the room rates listed on a nearby sign, a sinking realization settled in Diego's chest. Even if the bot sprang to life, he had no money. The concept was a bit foreign to him. While he'd heard of cash, his entire life on the orbital had revolved around trading goods and services—currency wasn't part of the equation.

He turned his attention to the door leading deeper into the hotel, but it remained stubbornly closed, refusing to budge no matter how hard he tried to open it.

With a sigh, Diego relented and moved on. What he really needed was a cabin in the Living Quarters. But how, without a passkey? He remembered seeing an entrance near the Rocket Ace and decided to check it out.

As he approached the doors, a flicker of hope stirred within him, and he tempered it, bracing for disappointment. Sure enough, they didn't slide open when he stepped closer. Like the inner door at the Starlight Inn, these, too, remained firmly sealed—no amount of pushing or prying made a difference.

Food, water, shelter, Diego thought again, pressing his forehead against the doors as he fought to contain his mounting frustration. Chip's comment about residency came back to him—would his passkey have even worked? Then it hit him: the locked doors could be a blessing in disguise. If he couldn't get in, maybe the growlers couldn't either. Safety might be waiting just beyond the threshold—he just needed to find a way inside.

He grabbed his gear and mentally reached for his gift. The headache didn't strike him this time, but it still faltered, slipping from his control before he could use it to sense dangers nearby. He didn't only hate that his gift made him so weird—he also hated it in moments like this when it refused even to work properly.

With no choice but to move forward with only his mundane senses, Diego tightened his grip on the Top Slugger and pressed on. Having already visited this section of the promenade the day before, he retraced his steps and headed in the opposite direction.

After a plain stretch with nothing notable, he came across a Woolwards Department Store. Inside, the shelves were in disarray, much like the Rocket Ace store—but this place held a treasure trove of items across many departments, from appliances to clothing.

Taking care to keep quiet, he crept forward, climbing over shelves and slipping between racks. Each item he found—shirts, socks, and everything underneath or in between—was added to his growing layers. Piece by piece, he bundled himself up until the biting cold eased.

Passing a trio of mirrors, he froze. A hideous face marred by scars stared back at him. Mottled skin ran in a jagged path along his cheek and down his arm, and his black eye shimmered in violet. No wonder people shied away from him; who wouldn't be afraid? How many nights had he spent wishing this face away? Diego hated everything he saw.

His fingers trembled as they brushed the scars on his cheek. His mom regularly told him how handsome she thought he was, but he knew better. Sure, she might've adored his brown curls, loved his long eyelashes, and said he had his dad's jawline, but none of that mattered next to his growler-like patches of skin.

Everyone knew what growlers looked like. Exposure to void storm energy was deadly, transforming its victims into twisted, grotesque, zombified husks, their skin desiccated and scarred. The same storms also sustained them, fueling the dark, extra-dimensional force that kept them moving. They didn't even age, rot, or starve. Despite this, they attacked anything alive, tearing it apart and feeding— it was like they still remembered hunger but could never satisfy it.

Diego's fingers traced the discolored patches of skin on his face, down his neck, and along his left arm.

This was his reflection, yet he wished it belonged to someone else. It was the face of the boy everyone despised... the boy who was almost a growler... the boy who had summoned the Kraal.

Were they right to banish him below decks? Maybe he hadn't summoned the Kraal, but he belonged down here with the other void terrors.

He wallowed in the bitter thoughts, letting their poison fester, and couldn't help but agree with the crowd's judgment. In that moment, he saw himself as they did—and the sight sickened him. The self-hatred ignited a deep-seated, inner fury. He fed the flames, savoring the burn. He despised what he saw, so how could he blame anyone else for feeling the same?

I'm a monster.

His pulse thundered in his temples, and his chest tightened. The burn erupted in a white-hot storm of hate and anger as he stared at his reflection.

His grip tightened on the Top Slugger. With a raw, feral howl, he swung. The mirror exploded into a thousand glittering shards, the crash reverberating through the store in a violent release that echoed the self-loathing tearing him apart.

He collapsed to his knees, gasping for air, unsure when the tears had started. Each breath came in shuddering bursts as he fought back the sobs threatening to break free. He knew he shouldn't cry. Instead, low moans escaped his lips as the rage faded, leaving a cold hollowness behind. Clenching his jaw, he struggled to pull himself back under control.

That's when he heard the grunts and calls of growlers echoing in from the promenade, and a sharp stab of fear sobered him fast. He'd made a grave mistake allowing himself such a selfish display of emotion.

Scrambling to his feet, he reached for his gift, but it slipped away. Panic surged. He tried again. Nothing.

A crash of a display toppling near the front of the store broke through the still air. Diego didn't hesitate. He bolted for the back, heart pounding, praying this wouldn't turn into a repeat of his failed escape from the Rocket Ace store.

There has to be an exit.

The stockroom was a mess of toppled shelves and scattered boxes. He hurried through the tangle, the growlers' cries sounding louder behind him. Another door finally came into view. Without looking back, he burst through it into a dimly lit back hall, not even slowing as he sprinted down the corridor in a frantic search for a safe place to hide.

Rounding a corner, he came to a halt.

The passage opened into a small cargo room. An airlock filled on one side. Stacks of containers were piled here and there, and two tightly sealed doors were set in the opposite wall. He darted for them.

"No! No, no!" he moaned, struggling to open first one and then the other. They wouldn't budge.

He spun around, heart pounding as the growlers' cries grew closer. He reached for his Top Slugger, only to realize he'd left all his gear behind—he had no way to defend himself. He desperately scanned the room for options. His eyes locked on a vent near the top of a stack of crates, just big enough for him to squeeze through. The cover even rattled in a faint breeze, barely staying in place.

The growlers burst into the room. One howled, "Run!" while another hissed, "Hide!"

Diego lunged for the crates. Halfway up, a growler latched onto his shoe, nearly pulling him down. He kicked hard, twisting and thrashing until his foot slipped free, leaving the shoe behind.

Hauling himself higher, his breath ragged, he grabbed the vent cover and yanked with all his strength. The loose screws shrieked as they gave way.

He wriggled into the narrow opening, his shoulders barely squeezing through. The ductwork pressed against his chest and back, nearly pinning him in place. But not quite. He shimmied deeper, breaths shallow because the tight confines restricted anything more. Thankfully, claustrophobia wasn't an issue for him. Back on Charlie Ring, slipping into tight spaces had been a regular part of his day. It was a skill he'd never realized would one day save his life.

Leaving the growlers behind, he pressed deeper into the duct-work, the light fading with every meter. He could tell there was another vent by the change in airflow. But the room beyond was pitch black, so he continued on until reaching a crossing duct, only to realize that he couldn't make the turn.

At least the growlers hadn't followed him.

He reversed course, inching his way back—feet-first—until he reached the dark vent. With no room to brace himself, he pressed his shoulder against it, but it wouldn't budge. Blindly, he felt along the edges—no screws, no seams, nothing he could loosen even if he had tools. He let his head fall back with a hollow thump.

He waited, straining to hear the occasional groans and hissed words of the growlers. Every so often, he tried to summon his gift, but it remained maddeningly out of reach.

A cold numbness seeped into his heart as he thought back to the heated rage that had driven him to shatter the mirror. He couldn't keep going like this. Running from his problems and throwing tantrums wasn't an option anymore. If he wanted to survive, he had to stop acting like a spoiled child. He couldn't afford to lose control again.

Gradually, an icy calm filled him. He reached for his gift once more, and this time, his special senses flooded back in a rush. He could feel the growlers, their twisted presence lingering, waiting for him. Wasting no time, he nudged them, planting the notion of a sound farther back in the hallway.

They retreated.

Diego slid out of the ductwork and into the cargo room, pausing to take a deep breath. Then another. He might not be claustrophobic, but being able to breathe freely was the best thing he'd felt all day.

Sitting on the edge of the crates, his legs dangling, he scanned the floor for his missing shoe.

As his gaze wandered the room, he considered everything that had happened, and his mind crystallized around an idea. The icy calm threading through his veins drove him back to the Rocket Ace. Sensing no growlers inside, he headed straight to the gear section, grabbed a Z-ball mask, and pulled it over his face.

This would do more than protect him from an enemy's blows—it would hide who he was.

Unchained Melody

In the back office of Woolwards, Diego discovered a break room obscured behind a toppled shelf. Better still, the door locked from the inside. It wasn't much of a defense against wandering void terrors, but it was a refuge and offered a chance to rest.

The light flickered on as Diego stepped inside, adding a faint buzz to the air. The room wasn't much—just a wall of cabinets, a few mismatched chairs gathered around a table, and an ancient coffee machine standing watch over a bowl of dusty sugar cubes.

He picked up a cube and tasted it. Stale, but he didn't care. One by one, he devoured them all, savoring the sweetness that did little to help his hunger.

Turning to the cabinets, he rummaged through the dishes and supplies, uncovering a package of dry crackers, a bag of popcorn kernels, and a box of ketchup packets. It all went into his backpack.

After a fruitless attempt to turn off the light, Diego slumped against the wall, positioning himself between a dusty cigarette vending machine and the cabinets. Pulling a blanket over his head, he shut his eyes and let sleep claim him.

The next day, he cataloged his meager provisions, his stomach rumbling the entire time.

While weighing his options, a memory from science class resurfaced. Serenity's environmental systems—biospheres, recyclers, all of it—operated in a closed loop, and one of their products was Nutrient Polymer Solution: an algae-based fluid most people just called "nutrient sludge."

Auto-food processors used it to generate their bland offerings, but he had no idea where to find one of those, let alone how to make it work without a passkey. But weren't the NPS pipes spread throughout the ring? Could he eat it raw?

Diego grimaced, remembering the slime's awful smell, not to mention it resembled baby poo—both in color and consistency. The thought sent his stomach turning in disgust. There had to be better options.

First, he needed a working flashlight. After prying a functional battery from an emergency exit sign, he used some duct tape and wires, bodgering it to a flashlight from the Rocket Ace.

His gift worked smoothly today, almost as if it had never failed him before. He opted for a new strategy this time, deciding to shadow the growlers as they meandered through the corridors. They were clearly getting into places denied to him, and he needed to figure out how.

After a long wait, his patience paid off when three growlers shuffled toward the Living Quarters. To his frustration, the doors just slid open. It took him a moment to process before realization dawned on him: they must still have passkeys from their former lives.

He berated himself for not figuring it out sooner. But how would he get one of their passkeys? Unconsciously, he tightened his grip on his Top Slugger. The mere thought of confronting them again welded his feet to the deck.

But at least this offered a way inside the Living Quarters. His pulse quickened as he realized he could just stay masked and follow them through the doors. Finally, he'd be inside—his need for shelter was solved.

Keeping his masking in place, he hovered nearby, waiting. But as the minutes ticked by, his excitement faded. He needed to find a place free from growlers. What was the point if he had to follow them inside? Besides, each cabin still required a passkey. No... tailgating a growler wasn't a solution.

Fighting back his mounting frustration, he retreated to the promenade. He had two options to get through a door: find a passkey or break the locks. Recalling a row of televid booths near the Peppermint Club, he wondered if he could use one to look up information on hacking locks.

Approaching the booths, he sensed a gathering of growlers inside the nearby club and hesitated. Were they too close? He just needed to stay sharp and work quietly enough to avoid drawing their attention.

Locating a functioning terminal, he slipped inside the booth, dropped his masking, and pulled the accordion door shut. Its hinges, unused for decades, let out a piercing squeal that echoed across the promenade's vaulted ceiling. He froze, heart hammering. Did any void terrors hear it? Extending his gift, he scanned the area—fortunately, nothing seemed to have noticed, not even the growlers inside the nightclub.

The old Bakelite bench squeaked as Diego settled onto it. He pulled the keyboard close and powered on the terminal, its green glow lighting up his face. The text wavered as the CRT warmed up, prompting him for a password.

Normally, he'd just use his passkey to log in. Fortunately, there was also an option to sign in with a password. He tried his account from Charlie Ring, which was denied. Had he typed his password wrong, or had they already disabled his account?

Deciding he had nothing to lose, he kept trying variations of his password until the system alerted him that his account was now locked out. He shifted tactics, trying to guess the passwords of people he knew, stopping short of locking their accounts. Yet nothing worked —he couldn't get into a single one.

Lost in his efforts, a sudden tapping on the door nearly launched him into orbit. He looked up, and his heart lurched.

Officer Chip stared back at him.

Reluctantly, he pulled the door open.

"Hello, Vagrant 37A2," Chip offered in his typical bubbly manner. "Say, would you happen to be Mr. Diego Alvarez?"

Diego froze. How did Chip know his name? Had he already reached out to La Familia?

Chip's screen flashed a cheerful smile, interpreting Diego's hesitation as confusion. "Not to worry, little man! We've detected some questionable activity on this terminal, which has resulted in someone's account being locked—specifically, one belonging to an adolescent, Mr. Diego Alvarez. If that's you, don't fret! Just visit the Operations Helpdesk with your parent or guardian to sort this out. All you need is your passkey for verification!"

Chip leaned forward. "But, if you are not Mr. Alvarez, are you perhaps engaging in unauthorized behavior? Attempting to access other people's accounts is a big no-no! I'd hate to have to issue a citation. Let's clear this up, shall we?"

Diego's mind scrambled for a plausible explanation. Maybe Chip would believe he had a twin? Then he remembered how the bot acted like growlers were just ordinary people, and an idea sparked.

"Oh!" Diego pointed towards the Peppermint Club. "Some guy said I could use his terminal, and then he went in there; maybe that was him?"

Chip paused, its optics adjusting while considering the Peppermint Club's entrance. "I see! Thank you, law-abiding Vagrant 37A2, for your assistance on this fine day!"

The patrol bot rolled into the club, calling out, "Mr. Diego Alvarez? Hellooo! We need to have a little chat!"

Diego couldn't believe that had actually worked and wisely booked it before Chip shook things up in the nightclub. He didn't even stop running until he passed the Pizzarama plaza and found a safe alcove where he could gather his thoughts.

A heaviness lingered in the back of his mind. His options were dwindling to almost nothing. He leaned against the cool wall, adjusting the Z-ball mask before raking a hand through his unkempt hair.

Food. Water. Shelter. Should be easy, right?

A pile of clothing near his feet caught his attention. Passkeys had to be hidden somewhere in that mess—if not this pile, then another one nearby. Surely, one of those keys could grant him access to a cabin. It seemed glaringly obvious now, and he realized he'd been avoiding the option all along.

His fingers drummed on his thigh. A knot of emotion tightened in his chest. Memories of his parents threatened to surface. He forced himself to focus, shoving the thoughts aside. But that didn't help—he hated the idea of rifling through these untouched graves, even if it was just to find a passkey.

"Nobody will care," he whispered, trying to convince himself. And still, a cold ache lingered in his chest.

In the end, his need for shelter won out. He pushed past the ache, stretched out his hand, and then a memory flickered—a duffle bag tucked away in a locker at the Link Transit Terminal. What if it held a passkey?

Diego straightened. The least he could do was exhaust all his options first, right?

This time, he mentally nudged the void rats before entering the Link Transit Terminal, conjuring the thought of a looming threat coming to eat them. Soon enough, he could feel them phasing through the walls and scurrying away.

He stepped inside, hope ready to ignite. His flashlight beam glanced across the locker. Slightly ajar, just as he remembered. He rummaged through the duffel bag's contents, scattering them across the floor. No passkey. He sifted through everything again, slower this time, but still came up empty.

Grinding his teeth, he swept the flashlight around, stopping at the open doors of the Link Pod. The tangle of debris inside confirmed his suspicion—it was a void rats' nest. A nagging thought stirred, and he shifted his weight, brow furrowing. Rats hoarded all sorts of things. Maybe this group had dragged off a passkey?

His heart pounded as he debated whether to investigate. He could feel them lingering at the edges of his senses, anxious to return. But it wouldn't take long to rifle through their nest and see what turned up... right?

Making up his mind, he approached the open doors, his flash-light pushing back the shadows. The curdling stench twisted his stomach. Two turnstiles flanked the entrance, and as he stepped closer, they flashed red and buzzed—no admittance without a passkey. But he ignored the warning and hopped over the bar.

If he thought it was bad outside, the inside of the Pod was worse. The reek of decay and rot hit him hard. Holding his breath wasn't an option—kind of necessary, breathing—so he settled for short, shallow breaths.

Moving quickly, he used his Top Slugger bat to prod through the debris, not wanting to touch the filth. There—a flash of white plastic. His heart lurched. Among the scattered trinkets, clothes, bones, and remnants of who-knows-what, he spotted a passkey. Carefully, he teased it free and held it under the flashlight. The edges were badly gnawed, and he could hardly make out the name.

He set it aside and kept digging. Another card surfaced, just as damaged. Then, deeper in the nest, he found one in better condition. He wiped his thumb across it to clear away the grime. A name emerged: "John Smith."

Eyes watering from the stench, Diego decided he'd had enough and retreated.

His heart pounded, each beat louder than the last as he approached the Living Quarters doors, anxiety steadily chipping away at his excitement.

Will one of these passkeys actually work?

He hesitated, then held up the cards and stepped forward. The doors slid open, almost as if they'd been waiting for him. A slow sigh escaped his lips, followed by a faint smile. The knot between his shoulders eased, even if only a little.

Diego's elation faded as he surveyed the interior—it was just as neglected as the promenade. But he was in. He started down the maze of corridors that branched off in a sprawling network spanning multiple levels.

At the first cabin, he tested all three keys. Only the one labeled John Smith triggered any response—a flashing red light of denial. It didn't open the door, but it was recognized—one of the keys worked.

Encouraged, he moved on, trying lock after lock. He avoided the wandering growlers by lurking in shadows, masking himself to slip past them, or quietly doubling back when needed.

One hallway stood out from the others. The doors in it were hexagonal, their edges featuring extra corners, and the access pads were set lower than usual. He tried John's passkey on each one. But, like the others, these also flashed red.

Near the end of the corridor, however, a chair held a door open. A noxious stench of decay wafted out. Despite the smell, he stepped inside, sweeping his flashlight around the cabin for anything that might help in his survival.

The low counters and strange decorations made him feel like a giant. Then it clicked—this was an alien Gray cabin.

Diego knew the Grays were common before the Arrival, but he had never seen one in person. None lived on Serenity—at least, not that he was aware of—and none had ever visited with the occasional intergalactic traders who stopped at the station.

From the pictures shown in class, the Grays were shorter than humans, with their namesake gray skin, elongated skulls, and over-sized black eyes. They had gifted humanity with advanced technology —jump ship engines, slipstream drives—and had remained a part of the growing intergalactic civilization.

Finding only a few strange cooking utensils and nothing truly useful, he decided it was time to move on. Slipping back into the hall-way, he made his way toward the human-occupied sections, wondering if John Smith was even human—or just an assumed name for an alien Gray.

Door after door, each failure weighed heavier on him. But it wasn't as if he had anywhere else to go. Sure, he could scavenge for more ketchup packets, but this felt more important. Frustration sim-mered, threatening to boil over, until finally—a soft beep. The light on a lock flashed green. A hiss. The door slid into the wall.

Diego stared, heart hammering in disbelief. A smile broke across his face. Stepping inside, the door sealed shut behind him. His knees buckled, and he dropped to the floor. Eyes closed, he let the tension bleed out, his shoulders sagging as he drew in a shaky breath.

Shelter.

Lights flickered to life, illuminating dust motes drifting through the air. He found the space curiously devoid of the personal touches one might expect in a lived-in home. The layout was the same as the single-resident cabins he'd seen on Charlie Ring. Brittle linoleum crackled underfoot as he moved through the kitchenette, down a short hallway, past a small bathroom, and into a sleeping area.

The sight of the bed brought him to a halt—not for any remarkable reason, but because it reminded him of home. The covers were rumpled and unmade. If not for the dust everywhere, it almost felt like the occupant had simply stepped out earlier that day.

An open suitcase sat on the dresser. Diego searched it first, finding a variety of neatly folded clothes and personal items. Layer by layer, he worked his way to the bottom, where he uncovered a small key and a bundle of letters.

He left the letters on the kitchen table and began searching the cabin for wherever the key might fit. Eventually, he gave up and took a seat at the table.

Hoping to glean something about the man whose home he now occupied, Diego scanned through each letter. To his disappointment, there were no grand revelations, no string of love letters—just mundane bills and correspondence, their faded dot-matrix ink barely visible on the yellowed paper.

Looking over them again, he realized that one letter stood out from the rest—a handwritten note from a woman named Judith addressed to someone named Conner. It spoke of their grandmother's passing. Diego's brow furrowed. Most of the letters were addressed to this "Conner," not John Smith. But wasn't this John's cabin?

Maybe John Smith wasn't his real name? Had Conner inherited the cabin? Or was something more sinister at play? Had Conner stolen John's identity?

Diego set the letters aside. His chair creaked as he leaned back. Whoever John Smith really was—it didn't matter. He had shelter now. Two out of three needs—check.

He turned his attention back to the cabin. Tidying and organizing the scattered belongings gave him a small sense of control over the chaos of the past few days. He even shook out the dusty sheets and actually made the bed—something he rarely did. But for some reason, it mattered now.

When the space felt passably livable, he perched cross-legged on the bed and considered the notebook he'd found. Its mottled black-and-white cover reminded him of his mother's stack of journals. With a sigh, he flipped it open and hesitated a long moment before finally writing:

Donna, it's been rough. But you know that.

His gaze lingered on what he'd written. Why did he address it to Donna? It just felt... right, somehow. He needed someone to talk to—even if they weren't here. His chest tightened, his vision blurring until he wiped his eyes with a frustrated groan.

Pressing the pen to the paper again, he added:

I hope you're okay.

Closing the notebook with a snap, he crawled under the dusty covers, resolving that tomorrow he'd solve his food problem.

Too Many Secrets

The lights in the cabin brightened gradually, simulating dawn. Diego burrowed deeper under the covers, unwilling to surrender their warmth. The room had even adjusted itself to a perfect 21 degrees Celsius. Food was still a question mark, but he had shelter and water—and two out of three felt like a win.

With a reluctant gasp, he rolled to the edge and tumbled onto the floor, pulling the blankets with him. A soft laugh escaped his lips on the way down. He landed in a tangled heap, grinning—until his stomach growled, unwilling to join in the moment.

He unraveled himself from the knot of sheets and stretched, giving out a long yawn. As he shuffled off to get ready, his thoughts turned to the void storms.

During the Arrival, when the Kraal rampaged across every planet, the Union of Stars' military had resorted to nuclear devastation in a desperate attempt to combat the terrors. Not only did the tactic fail, but it also sparked the extra-dimensional void storms.

Diego knew they were bad news on Arcadia's surface, but void storms also struck in space. Nobody fully understood where they came from or how they worked. Were they holes torn into the Kraal's dimension? The reason didn't matter. When a storm came, you quickly found shelter or risked becoming a growler.

And, for spacers, that meant taking refuge in a chapel or relying on a Pounamu talisman. Diego had always found it strange that either one seemed to work, but somehow, they did. He had seen a chapel on the promenade and made a mental note to investigate it before the next storm arrived.

Bundled against the cold, Diego set out to explore. He worked his way through every corridor he could access in Blue Sector—which wasn't as many as he'd hoped—trying John Smith's passkey on door after door. The rhythm wore on his nerves: a swipe, a flicker of hope— then the red light.

At the final door, he ran the card. Once again, the light blinked red.

Diego kicked the door frame, muttering, "Figures."

This passkey seemed limited to the Living Quarters. But his next move was clear: would it let him into the Orbital's information library?

After a quick lunch of ketchup packets and crumbly crackers, he swiped the card at a public televid terminal. The screen immediately flashed an error message:

ACCOUNT SUSPENDED DUE TO INACTIVITY.

LAST LOGIN 9,234 DAYS AGO.

VISIT THE RING OPERATIONS HELP DESK FOR ASSISTANCE.

Slumping into the seat, Diego mulled over this new obstacle. Maybe he could convince the robots he was John Smith, even if he clearly wasn't an old man? But what would they ask? He didn't even know what John Smith looked like, let alone how old he'd be now—just that he'd probably been dead for twenty-five years.

Diego's foot tapped the floor. He chewed a fingernail. With so little personal information, pulling off an impersonation felt risky. Then again, the Officer Chip bot he'd talked to down here seemed to have trouble telling him apart from the growlers. Maybe it could work? Either way, he should learn more about John Smith before trying anything.

His gaze lingered on the passkey, and he wondered where the rats had found it. Had they dragged it into their nest from somewhere else—or was that where John Smith had fallen—in the Link Pod?

Maybe more of his belongings were still there? It would mean disturbing this guy's final resting place, but Diego reassured himself he wouldn't take anything. He'd just look for information.

Besides, the rats had already made a mess of whatever had been there, and he had to find out.

Stopping by the Rocket Ace, he grabbed a pair of bulky welder's gloves—there was no way he was touching that garbage barehanded. Top Slugger in one hand, flashlight in the other, Diego eyed the shadows on the far side of the Transit Terminal. He mentally reached out, pushing at the rats. To his relief, his gift gave him no problem, and they scattered quickly.

Diego wrinkled his nose, again taking shallow breaths. A strip of duct tape fixed the flashlight to the wall inside the Pod, and he pulled on the gloves. Piece by piece, he took the nest apart, tossing debris out to the platform as he sifted through the layers, hoping to uncover something that would help.

The deeper he dug, the more the ammonia burned his nose and eyes, and the more his expectations faded—just trinkets, rotted clothes, and junk. Then, near the bottom, as he pulled out a flattened, soggy fedora, his fingers brushed something solid.

Carefully, he uncovered a battered briefcase. Its leather exterior sloughed off in a damp slab, releasing its inner metal case. His pulse quickened. It wasn't just intact—it was secured with a combination lock, a keylock, and a chain that trailed deeper into the nest.

How curious.

He tugged at the chain, pulling the sleeve of a white shirt out from the debris.

Diego froze.

The chain was a wrist strap—still looped through the sleeve of a shirt someone had worn when the Kraal took them.

John Smith?

He swallowed hard and tried to open the briefcase, but it was locked tight.

Conflicting instincts warred within him. He couldn't stop thinking about the exploits of Victor Shadowstar—comic book hero and intergalactic spy extraordinaire. Who else but a secret agent would carry a briefcase like this?

If this really was John Smith's, whatever was inside might be invaluable—if I'm a spy from twenty-five years ago.

But, he hadn't come to take anything. Just to look. He should put the suitcase back.

And yet... He gave it a shake. Something rattled inside. Mysterious. Tempting. Impossible to ignore.

"Lo siento, señor," he muttered, tugging on the chain until the ragged shirt fell away.

Decision made, he carried the briefcase back to the privacy of John Smith's cabin.

After a few minutes at the kitchen sink, scrubbing away as much grime from the rat's nest as he could, Diego set the briefcase on the laminated table. His fingers skimmed the welded edges—this thing was built like a safe, no doubt about it. He rotated the gummed-up wheels on the combination lock a few times, but it was pointless. Without the key, he wouldn't know if he'd guessed right.

Then he remembered the key from John's suitcase.

His hands trembled as he gently worked the key into the grimy lock. It resisted at first, but with a little pressure, it finally turned.

One part down.

He returned his focus to the combination lock—the last barrier between him and whatever secrets the briefcase held. His gaze flicked to the Top Slugger resting against the wall. He could try to smash the lock off, but what if he broke something inside?

Choosing caution, Diego grabbed a screwdriver and started prying at the edges of the lock.

Victor Shadowstar's adventures played through his mind—stories full of hidden codes, daring escapes, and covert missions against the communist DWA forces.

The lock held firm at first, making him worry if it was too well built. But after some persistent effort, it finally popped off, pieces spilling onto the table. Diego pushed them aside, set the briefcase flat, and turned it toward himself.

For a moment, he hesitated, gripping the lid. "It's probably nothing," he muttered, pulse quickening as he pulled it open. The seal resisted at first, then released with a sticky *schleck* as it broke free.

Inside, a trove of folders greeted him, dry and miraculously undamaged by decades at the bottom of the rat's nest. His heart pounded as he rifled through the contents. Documents stamped TOP SECRET lay nestled among yellowed letters and faded photographs.

One letter, signed by someone named Beverly, caught his eye:

JOHN, REPLY TO YOUR SECNET EMAIL! WE CAN'T SEND
MESSAGES VIA COURIER LIKE THIS. PROJECT ULTRA IS
OFFICIALLY NOW PART OF PROJECT STARGATE. ORDYNE AGENTS
WILL ARRIVE IN A WEEK TO TAKE OVER ADMINISTRATION.
PLEASE PREPARE TO HAND OVER ALL RECORDS.

Project Ultra? Project Stargate? Ordyne? The names only added to the enigma, pulling him deeper into the documents. But the more he peeled back layers of John Smith's activities on Serenity, the more a sense of unease crept over him. A hidden darkness had long lurked deep within the orbital, predating even the Arrival.

Apparently, the entire Echo Ring used to be a secret government lab, complete with a private Link Transit Terminal and a hidden observation area.

Growing up, Diego had heard whispered tales about the horrors lurking in the depths of Delta and Echo Rings—ghosts of those who perished in the cleansing, legions of void spiders skittering through abandoned corridors, and grotesque mutations spawned by the void storms prowling the shadows.

Stories that had kept him awake at night.

Now, they carried a new weight, as if they might hold a kernel of truth somehow linked to Project Ultra's experiments.

So far on Delta Ring, Diego had only run into growlers and void rats. But what if the sealed promenade bulkheads were hiding something far worse? Something born of Project Ultra?

And Echo Ring—was it still home to whatever nightmares the project had left behind?

Among the papers, one stood out: a letter from Serenity Orbital Management granting John Smith elevated access to Echo Ring's mainframe.

Each of Serenity's rings had its own isolated mainframe by design. If one went down, another could take over its operations. But elevated access to one didn't guarantee the same for the others. Still, maybe he could use the Echo Ring's system as a backdoor into Delta's? Then he could turn up the heat, unlock restricted sections, and maybe even try to radio for help.

Not that he expected an answer. There wasn't much left of civilization now. He'd heard rumors that remnants of the old Union of Stars were still around, like The Wardens and The Star Rangers, but he didn't know if that was true or not.

Leaning back in his chair, Diego's thoughts raced through the possibilities. What if Echo Ring wasn't in lockdown? What if it was fine—better food stores, more resources? But how would he even get there? The Link Platform was dead, and the maintenance lifts were locked out, even with John's passkey.

No. Like it or not, getting into the biosphere on Delta Ring seemed more feasible. The documents had sent his imagination running wild, but Delta Ring was his reality, and it came with more than enough challenges. He gathered the papers and stuffed them into a dresser drawer.

His thoughts shifted back to the more immediate problem: convincing the robots he was John Smith.

At the televid booth, Officer Chip hadn't been able to tell the difference between him and a growler—and he'd actually bought the story about someone else letting him use the terminal. Maybe it was worth trying something bolder.

What if he just walked in to "pay his fine" using John's passkey? Would they assume he was John?

Plan set, Diego made his way along the curving promenade toward the Ring Ops Help Desk. After passing the Peppermint Club, the corridor widened into a long, open plaza. Above a double-wide entryway to the left, a sign read: "Delta Ring Operations Center (D-ROC)." It looked the same as Charlie Ring's C-ROC—but more importantly, unlike the rear entrance Chip had taken him to before, this one wasn't guarded by a turret.

He approached, half-expecting the doors to stay shut or present some other challenge like so many others had before. Instead, they parted quietly, revealing a simple waiting area beyond.

Rows of plasti-formed benches and chairs lined the room. Off to the side, a barricaded counter stretched along the wall—but there was no one in sight. Not even a service bot. Diego wove his way through the benches and stepped up to the counter. He tapped a small bell sitting near the edge.

And waited.

Diego pulled the wrinkled citation from his pocket, but it didn't provide any useful instructions. His brow furrowed, and he rang the bell again.

Still no response.

He raised his hand to tap the bell a third time when a door behind the counter cycled open, and in rolled the same exact Officer Chip bot he'd seen multiple times before.

"Good day, Vagrant 37A2!" Chip announced, his voice brimming with enthusiasm. "How may I assist you on this fine day?"

Diego raised an eyebrow. He'd never heard of an Officer Chip model working a desk. Surely there were more robots still operational down here?

"Umm," Diego pulled John Smith's passkey from his wrist and held it up along with the wrinkled citation. "I'm here to identify myself and pay my fine—if that's okay?"

Chip's optics brightened. "Splendid! Let me take care of that for you, sir!" He accepted the card, tapping away at the keyboard for a moment before handing it back. "Thank you for being such a superstar vagrant, Mr. John Smith! Is there anything else I can do to make your day brighter?"

"Well, yeah..." Diego's heart started hammering in his chest, and he blurted out, "My mainframe account was suspended for inactivity. Can you reactivate it?"

"Oh, absolutely! But first, I'll need to ask a few questions to verify your identity. Just a quick little protocol check—easy peasy, lemon squeezy!"

A bead of sweat trickled down Diego's brow. "Sure. But you already know I'm John Smith, right?"

"I do?" Chip blinked, genuinely puzzled.

"Yeah," Diego held up the passkey. "I just paid my fine."

Chip's mechanical eyebrows lifted. "Oh, golly gee, I suppose you did!"

He leaned over the counter and pressed a foil sticker onto the top of Diego's mask.

"There's a gold star for you, little ranger. But rules are rules! As much as I'd love to skip ahead, protocols are here to keep everyone safe and happy. I'm sure you understand."

Diego clenched his teeth, studying Chip. Then a thought rose up: *Was this the last robot left keeping Delta Ring running?*

Grim images surfaced: Chip rolling through empty corridors on patrol. Struggling to change light bulbs just out of reach. Scavenging parts from broken bots in the deep night just to keep himself going.

"Are you working on your own?" Diego asked, a flicker of concern for the stupid thing building—despite himself. "It must be hard without anyone to help."

Chip paused, his posture sagging just a bit. When he spoke, his tone held a note of resigned acceptance. "You have a keen eye, Mr. Smith. But keeping order is crucial, even during strained times."

Diego straightened, remembering his mission. "So, uhh—instead of going through all the protocol stuff, why not skip a few formalities? Then... you can get back to your really important work."

Chip considered the request for a moment. "How about one quick question, and we call it done?"

A knot tightened between Diego's shoulders, but he managed a nod.

"Which room were you assigned during your stay here?"

Diego pinched his lips to hide a grin. "DB215."

"Wonderful!" Chip's optics brightened as he returned to the keyboard. After a few taps, the smile on his screen stretched wide. "All set, Mr. Smith! Your account is good to go! Of course, your official resident status has been revoked due to the lockdown. Rules are rules, after all! Now, is there anything else I can assist you with?"

At the mention of losing residency, Diego's thoughts jumped to the warm bed in John's cabin, and the knot between his shoulders tightened again. Had he just lost access to it? The question burned on the tip of his tongue, but he swallowed it back. Better not push his luck—he could always try to work that out later if needed. Right now, he had other questions.

"Can you let me into the biosphere?"

"Oh my, you don't want to go there! Blue Sector's biosphere is offline during lockdown; there's absolutely nothing to see. While Delta Ring has three biospheres, only Red Sector's is operational."

Diego's eyes narrowed. "So... you're not letting me into the biosphere because of the lockdown, or is it something else? Like, maybe... secret government experiments gone wrong? Is it a Project Ultra thing?"

Chip's smile flickered. "Oh, absolutely not! Our biospheres are *carefully curated ecosystems* designed to maintain perfect harmony among all the creatures within. An unbalanced biosphere would be *quite the fright*, wouldn't it?"

A strained laugh emerged from his speaker—a stilted, mechanical attempt at humor punctuated by awkward pauses. "Ha. Ha. Ha."

Clearly, laughter wasn't the best part of his programming.

"Fine. Then let me into Red Sector and its biosphere."

Chip released a dramatic sigh. "Little ranger, I'm afraid you don't quite understand. Due to the lockdown, all the bulkheads between sectors must remain sealed."

"Not all of them." Diego countered. "The blast door by Woolwards is open between Blue and Gray Sectors. How do you think I got here? It's just the doors to Red and Green that are sealed up."

Chip's enthusiasm dimmed a notch. "My, aren't you the observant one."

Diego pressed harder. "Is there something wrong with the other side? Maybe that's where the government experiments are hiding."

Chip let out an exasperated noise. "Oh, certainly not, Mr. Smith! You have nothing to fear as a vagrant in Delta Ring!" He gave a cheerful thumbs-up. "Everyone's safety is our top priority!"

But it wasn't really an answer, and he didn't offer anything more. Instead, he became inexplicably preoccupied with an invisible smudge on the countertop.

Diego cut his losses. He turned away, headed to the nearest tele-vid booth, and swiped the passkey. The terminal flashed, "Welcome, John Smith," and he felt a little bit lighter.

The screen's green glow illuminated Diego's face as he tapped away at the keyboard. The Orbital's reading library was a resource he knew well from school. Unfortunately, his first query, HOW TO PICK A LOCK, was swiftly met with a warning: RESTRICTED MATERIAL.

Diego froze, fingers hovering over the keys. He knew the system monitored these queries because, in the past, his parents had been no-tified about some questionable searches he'd made. But now, signed in as John Smith, who would it report to?

He entered query after query, searching for a loophole in the system. Each attempt was met with the same denial. His jaw tight-ened. If he kept failing, would Chip show up again, just like last time? He had to be careful. Perhaps if he framed the query differently? He tried a new approach, typing: HOW TO REPAIR A LOCK.

The system hesitated, then spat out a list of documents on maintaining Serenity Orbital's security systems. A grin lit up Diego's face. He pored over the manuals, studying everything from basic me-chanical locks to complex electronic systems. Yet, the one piece of knowledge he craved—how to pick a mechanical lock—remained out of reach. His foot tapped against the floor, patience fraying.

Then he stumbled across something called Galactic Usenet—a resource he'd never seen with his personal access. It claimed to be an intergalactic discussion hub, apparently pre-Arrival, with an endless sprawl of discussion forums organized by topic.

The lack of recent posts wasn't a problem—the archives stretched back decades. One forum quickly caught his eye: "ALT.LOCK-BREAKING." It was packed with detailed posts, and Diego stayed glued to the screen for hours, devouring everything from mechanical lockpick-ing techniques to the inner workings of electronic locks and automated doors.

His excitement dimmed when he realized he needed specialized tools to pick a lock. And, he couldn't just order up a set—he'd have to build them from scratch. That meant trial and error… and a whole lot of frustration. But his options were opening up, and that had to count for something.

Keep a-Knockin'

Diego's efforts to craft lock picks were overshadowed as days turned into weeks with no success. At least Chip hadn't canceled John's cabin assignment. His searches for food yielded less and less with each passing day. The best find so far had been a box of freeze-dried meals tucked away in an emergency shelter—but that only bought him a few weeks.

Adding to his burdens, thoughts of his parents struck at the most unexpected times. One day, he stumbled across a toolkit, much like others he'd seen before—just another box to sift through, and he had already found plenty of tools. But something about the color tugged at his memory, and when his eyes landed on the logo, he froze: *Star Forged Tools.*

Exactly like his father's toolkit.

A lump rose in his throat, and he couldn't look away. His father's calm voice echoed in his mind, bringing back the times they'd spent together fixing things. Strong hands guiding his own. The satisfied hum of approval when Diego did something just right. His mother's smile as she brought them lunch. Her laughter at the grease smudges on his face.

The memories continued, unbidden and unrelenting. His vision blurred with tears, and his heart clenched at the thought of never seeing them again. Anger tightening his jaw, he wiped his eyes with the back of his sleeve, forcing the sobs down. He couldn't afford sentimentality; he had to stay focused on survival.

That evening, he pulled out his notebook and pencil, and the words spilled onto the page in shaky lines.

> *Donna, I found something today that reminded me of my Dad—a toolkit, just like his. I miss him so much. I miss all of you.*
>
> *I hope you're okay. And I hope you have plenty to eat because I think I will run out of food soon. Remember the sludge they taught us about in class? I might actually have to eat it.*

Sure enough, his food supplies finally ran out. Days of fruitless scavenging left him hollow and aching with hunger. The gnawing in his stomach drove his steps until he stood in a back hallway, staring at an access port marked NPS.

Holding his breath, Diego pried the portal open, finding a viscous green-yellow sludge inside. So far, so good.

Then, he had to breathe.

The rank stench hit him hard, curdling his stomach and sending bile up his throat. He stumbled back, gagging.

Once, when the crops had failed in the biosphere farms, his mom had brought home a cultured omelet from the food processor. Knowing it was made from nutrient sludge, Diego had refused even a single bite.

She insisted he just needed to acquire a taste for it—that it only seemed strange because it was new.

He'd thought his reply was clever. "If it's an acquired taste, then why try it at all? I only eat stuff I like."

Of course, she didn't miss a beat. "Everything you've ever eaten since you were born is an acquired taste, rocketboy."

Remembering that name brought an ache to his chest—sharp, at first, but then slowly warming. She'd often called him that—sometimes when he was being difficult, but mostly just to make him smile.

What he wouldn't give to hear it again.

He drew a slow breath, swallowed the lump in his throat, and forced his attention back to the sludge.

So, this is just another acquired taste. Right?

Nauseating as it was, the ache in his belly pulled him forward again. The sight alone was revolting, but he forced himself to scoop up some of the foul mixture and bring it to his lips.

Sour milk and rotten eggs—the taste hit his tongue, his throat clenched, and he reflexively gagged, spitting the first scoop onto the floor. Bracing himself for the second attempt, he clamped his mouth shut against the retching and forced the slimy substance down.

One dreadful handful after another.

When he could stomach no more, he stumbled back to his cabin, curled up in bed, and prayed he'd keep it down.

Miraculously, he did.

Though it was revolting, the gnawing hunger drove him back again, meal after meal. And, as the days passed, his mother's words proved true—the nausea faded with each meal until the sludge went down without triggering his gag reflex. It was still disgusting, and strangely, it left a fuzzy sensation in his mouth, but it kept the hunger at bay.

Food. Water. Shelter—all three needs were now met.

He would survive.

With starvation no longer an immediate crisis, Diego returned to his work on lock picking. What began as a task of necessity quickly turned into an obsession as he struggled to fashion lock picks.

Wanting to understand how it all worked, Diego dismantled one of the cabinet locks in his quarters, spreading its pieces out on the kitchen table. He studied each part, exploring how the picks would shift the pins just like a key.

Days of trial and error followed, filled with strips of bent metal, cut fingers, and muttered curses. It took countless attempts of testing his creations on the locks in his cabin until finally, he had a functional set of crude picks.

The tension bar went into the keyhole first, held under his pinky finger, applying just enough pressure to mimic the subtle turn of a key. The pick came next, held between his index finger and thumb like a pencil.

Inside the lock, a line of pins waited to be pushed into place by a key's unique shape. Diego had to use the pick to carefully feel for each pin, nudging it upward until it reached the shear line—the point where the lock would turn freely.

He soon realized lockpicking was as much about touch and feel as it was about skill. If he pushed too hard, the pins would go past the shear point, and the lock wouldn't budge. He learned to feel the tick on the tension rod when the pressure shifted to the next pin. Once one pin was set, he had to move on to the next until all were in place and he could turn the lock freely.

Eager to test his skill, Diego found himself crouched at a locked door on the promenade. Minutes dragged by, his breath sending puffs into the still, cold air. The initial flutter of excitement he'd started with gave way to a slow burn of frustration.

This lock was much more complex than the one he'd tried in his cabin. Adding to the challenge, the chill made his fingers stiff and clumsy. But he couldn't do this with gloves on. Finally, a subtle shift on the tension bar signaled the third pin clicking into place. Almost there.

Diego was so focused on his work that he didn't hear the faint hum of the floating spybot until it was too late.

"UNAUTHORIZED ACTIVITY DETECTED," the monotone voice blared.

He jumped, heart racing. The lockpicks slipped from his fingers, scattering across the floor. He lurched forward, scrambling after them. After all the time he'd spent making them, the last thing he wanted was to start over.

The spybot hovered closer, its sleek black, wedge-shaped frame nearly a meter across. Its sensor whiskers twitched in every direction. Knowing it had no weapons didn't make it any less menacing—not with that all-seeing camera fixed squarely on him.

On hands and knees, Diego frantically searched for the last pick. The spybot loomed behind him, its presence palpable. Watching. Judging. How long had it been there before it spoke?

"Hey there, little ranger!" Chip's overly cheerful voice boomed along the promenade, sending a new jolt through Diego. The soft hum of his wheels against the deck grew louder as he approached. "Whatcha up to, kiddo?"

"Nothing!" Diego blurted, snatching the last pick and shoving it into his pocket as he sprang to his feet. His eyes darted around, searching for an escape route.

Chip rolled up, giving him a long look. "Exploring with those nifty little tools? Oh, peaceful vagrant, curiosity is great, but tampering with locks is a big ol' no-no. You know that, right?"

The scrutiny made Diego shift from foot to foot, but his bigger concern was Chip's volume. His voice carried far enough that it might draw a wave of growlers.

"I was just... looking!" Diego said, taking a step back and extending his gift to sense danger.

"A little peeky-peek? Or maybe doing something you shouldn't be doing?" Chip's voice pitched up. "Vagrant Smith, you're not getting a gold star today!"

"Oh, hey, look!" Diego blurted, pointing behind Chip. "Somebody's, uh... vandalizing stuff over there! Damaging the... thing!"

Not his best bluff, but he really didn't do well under pressure.

Chip spun around. "Vandalizing?! The thing? Not on my watch!"

Diego bolted, legs stretching as he sprinted down the corridor.

"Hey! No running, superstar!" Chip's perky voice called after him. "That's a safety hazard! I'll have to file a report with the authorities—oh right, that's me!"

Diego didn't wait to hear the rest. He darted through the sliding doors into the Living Quarters, shimmered into invisibility, and wove through a group of growlers. Their fragmented whispers set him on edge, driving his pace even faster. He didn't stop until he reached his cabin and sealed the door behind him.

Bent forward, hands braced on his knees, Diego gasped for breath, sweat dripping from his brow. Half an hour, and he didn't even pick the lock—this was proving much harder than he'd expected.

The failure gnawed at him, but he wasn't about to give up. He threw himself into practice, working again and again on the simple cabinet locks until he could pick them in seconds.

But he had to think about more than just picking a lock.

Chip claimed the local biosphere was shut down, but Diego didn't trust his shifty behavior. He needed to see it for himself. The thought of fruits and vegetables—anything but the sludge—drove him forward each day.

He scoured the back halls and found several large doors that led to the biosphere. But each one was secured with an electronic lock. To get past those, he'd have to pry open the panel and use the manual crank—an effort that felt far more daunting to pull off unnoticed than simply picking a lock.

His hope of getting into the biosphere dwindled until he finally noticed a door he must have passed countless times before. Its chipped and faded lettering read, "Biosphere Maintenance."

This door had a mechanical lock. While it might not lead into the biosphere, it was the first viable lead he'd found. Unfortunately, the lock looked far more complex than anything Diego had encountered before, but he had to try.

Worse, it was in an open hallway near the maintenance lift—fully exposed to any wandering growler or robot, and he didn't want a surprise visitor like before. Even with all of his practice, Diego wasn't confident he could pick it quickly enough to avoid being caught.

The only way to improve his skill was to find a secluded spot to practice on complex locks. Diego set out again, combing every nook and cranny until he found the perfect location: a service door conveniently tucked out of sight in the Link Transit Terminal.

With a little concentration, he used his gift to disperse the void rats that made their home in the terminal, leaving him free to focus on the lock.

His hands cramped as the minutes dragged on. Time and again, he reached the final pin, only to have it slip out of place. Sweat beaded on his brow despite the chill air. He continued until, finally, the last pin gave way with a soft click.

A grin spread across his face as he turned the handle and pushed the door open. Beyond lay vague shapes of shelves holding mysterious items. A switch near the entrance turned on a series of fluorescent lights that sputtered to life.

Old cleaning supplies, boxes of rusted parts, curious equipment, and other odds and ends filled the room. A forgotten desk sat tucked in the middle, almost hidden among the clutter.

Diego knew he should keep practicing on the lock, but the pull of an unexplored room was too strong. He slipped inside and gave the shelves a quick once-over. At the desk, he spotted it—a passkey, nestled in an old wrist strap, just sitting there.

He grabbed it without a second thought, failing to notice the coveralls slumped in the chair—or the worn shoes on the floor.

The card read "Sharon Collins" and looked different from John's, with a red border and the label "MAINTENANCE." A flicker of hope sparked in his chest. Could this give him more access around the station?

He continued to scour the room, discovering a pressurized door tucked around a corner at the back marked "Link Tube Maintenance Access." He paused. Was it possible to navigate the tubes without a Pod? Could he get to another sector of Delta Ring—or even make it to Charlie or Bravo Ring? But what if a Pod arrived while he was inside the tube?

Holding Sharon's passkey between his fingers, Diego hesitated momentarily before swiping it. A green light blinked steadily in response. He cranked the door's wheel until the seals broke free with a pop, then pulled it open.

A frigid blast of air washed over him. Beyond, a yawning darkness loomed. Despite the icy breeze stinging his ears and nose, a grin spread on Diego's face.

Charlie or Echo Ring—wherever he ended up, there would be real food. He never thought he'd yearn for ketchup packets and crackers, but even those were more appealing than nutrient sludge day after day.

A nearly unbearable urge to explore surged through him, but he held back. A journey like this needed preparation. He closed the hatch, the seals hissing as it locked tight, then retreated with a spring in his step.

I Put a Spell on You

Diego tightened the straps of his backpack and gave his gear one last check. For the first time in a long time, he felt a growing excitement, and he couldn't help imagining he was an explorer setting out on a grand expedition. He'd already made a run through Rocket Ace and Woolwards to grab extra supplies—just in case things took longer than expected.

Sure, the icy journey ahead had its share of risk, but it was worth it for the food. And, even if he couldn't get into another sector, maybe he could find a way to Charlie or Echo Ring.

The hatch groaned as he pulled it open, followed by a blast of frigid air. He took a deep breath to steady himself before looking inside. His flashlight beam flickered across the conduits and metal walls of the Link Pod docking chamber. The Pods rested nearby, lined up to the platform doors, with the shadowy mainline tube opening just behind them.

Diego crawled inside, and his stomach immediately lurched as gravity faded.

"Seriously?" he muttered, realizing the Link tubes didn't have gravity plates. It kind of made sense that the plates were built into the Link Pods themselves, since they traveled all over the station, twisting and turning without bothering anyone inside.

Grabbing a handhold, Diego steadied himself. He'd spent plenty of time getting around in zero-g, but that didn't mean he was any good at it. Growing up, everyone played Z-ball. And Raphael? He made floatwork look easy—twisting and darting through the air like a fish in water. But Diego? He flailed and floundered, much to his classmates' amusement.

The memory of those embarrassing times burned his ears.

Ideally, he'd have a spanner before forging ahead—a wrist-mounted device everyone used in zero-g floatwork. It had a magnet-tipped cable on a reel. If you got stranded, you could cast it out by hand, like throwing a line, and then pull yourself in. But he hadn't come across one in any of his searches. Sighing, he pushed off hard, propelling himself into the mainline tube.

Unfortunately, his aim was off, and he missed the tunnel's edge. Frustration growing, he drifted helplessly across the wide tube until bumping against the far side. Scrambling, he managed to grab a handhold, but the effort cost him his flashlight, and now it spun away, its beam tracing the curved walls with each turn.

Tracking the flashlight's rotation, he calculated an intercept course that would also end near another handhold, and kicked off.

Diego's breath created white puffs in the chilled air as he coasted forward, and a thought crept in—what if a Pod came through right now? An image flashed vividly in his mind: A whoosh, then his body slamming against the wall, crushed like a spider underfoot.

"The Pods aren't running down here..." he muttered, his words hanging somewhere between a question and an assertion.

As he closed in on the flashlight, it became clear his trajectory was off. Thinking fast, he shrugged out of his backpack and pushed against it, stretching and kicking with everything he had. His fingers grazed the flashlight, and then his pinky caught a loose wire. He had it.

But the effort had sent him tumbling, and now his backpack drifted away.

The tunnel spun around him in a dizzying blur, and he unleashed a howl of frustration that echoed through the tubes.

He reached for an approaching handhold but missed, hitting the wall with a grunt before tumbling off on a new vector.

Forcing himself to focus, he closed his eyes and thought back to his coach's zero-G advice: *Relax. Find your center. Breathe.*

Before hitting the next wall, he rotated midair and landed feet-first. He even used the rebound to kick off at an angle toward a hand-hold on the far side. This time, he caught it—but the sudden jolt wrenched his wrist as his body swung around and slammed into the wall, sending pain lancing through his shoulder.

"Mierda, mierda, mierda!" he growled, shifting to his other hand and shaking out his arm while hoping he hadn't pulled something.

After a few more awkward maneuvers, Diego managed to recover his backpack, and slowly, his muscles began to remember how to maneuver in zero gravity.

With his gear secured and his confidence growing, he turned his attention to the tube's inner workings. At regular intervals, Pod-sized holes interconnected a cluster of three parallel tubes. Diego figured they must be transfer ports for the Pods to shift between each passage, and the smaller, human-sized tunnel running through the center was for maintenance techs.

He pressed forward, the minutes stretching on as he passed more transfer ports, and a realization dawned on him: he had no idea which direction he was headed: toward Red or Green Sector? All of the earlier tumbling had left him completely disoriented. Did it even matter? Probably not—he just needed to watch out for the next terminal platform, right?

His flashlight swept along the curve of the tube, soon revealing an iris bulkhead door emerging from the shadows. Its spiral seams were rimmed in frost, sealing the tunnel.

Diego's brow furrowed. He hadn't expected to find bulkheads blocking the tubes. But worse—there weren't any controls to open the door. Was this the end of his grand expedition?

No—he refused to stop so soon.

Inside the maintenance tunnel, a small hatch caught his eye. He debated whether he should open it or turn around and see what he could find in the other direction. In the end, he chose to verify if there was another bulkhead first.

Taking a deep breath, he began the slow drift back. The tube's curvature made a straight path impossible, and he bounced from wall to wall like a pinball in an arcade machine. At least it gave him plenty of chances to practice maneuvering in zero gravity.

His journey confirmed it: another irised bulkhead sealed off the tunnel. And just like before, a maintenance hatch waited in the smaller central tunnel.

With images of Vic Shadowstar infiltrating a DWA secret base teasing his thoughts, he forged forward.

The wheel was stiff from disuse, but with some effort, it finally broke free.

Beyond lay a cramped airlock with another hatch on the far side. Blue stripes along the wall shifted to green, which Diego figured meant Green Sector, and he eagerly continued on. The second airlock hatch groaned in protest, releasing a rim of dust that drifted away in an ethereal wisp. He paused, savoring the satisfaction of finally circumventing the promenade blast doors before pulling himself through.

On the other side, the air carried an earthy headiness that reminded him of a biosphere, and the hairs on his neck stood on end.

A thread of unease wove through him—something felt off. Why wasn't it the same as Blue Sector? Had he been right to suspect there was a bigger reason this area was sealed off? Maybe Chip really was hiding something... Diego needed to know.

He reached for his gift to sense what lay ahead, but it slipped away each time. Why now? It had worked so well lately. Should he turn back? Or, had he grown too reliant on it? He hadn't run into anything lurking in the tubes so far, so was it okay to keep going?

Diego surveyed the area. Two Pods waited silently at the iris doors. The quiet felt oppressive in the heavy air. Even the faint hum of machinery seemed more distant, as if the station held its breath, waiting to see what he would do next.

Staring at the Pods, he wondered if anyone was left inside when the Link system shut down. What a horrible way to go, trapped and all alone. Still... at least there weren't any void-tainted creatures in these tunnels. Right?

Curiosity got the better of him, and he pushed off, floating toward the emergency access wheel by the Pod's doors. There wasn't much room to maneuver, but he managed to crank the handle. After a few turns, the doors parted just enough to peek inside—both were empty, which did nothing to settle his unease.

The knot remained between his shoulders, but he decided to continue forward. Spies didn't just stop because they were scared.

He floated on. At first, it was subtle—just a fleeting glimpse here and there as the flashlight's beam caught faint, glistening strands stretched across the tunnel. Minutes ticked by, and the farther he went, the quieter it became. The usual hum of the orbital faded into a stifling silence.

The strands seemed harmless—just delicate threads that brushed against his arms and face. But what were they? Each one added to the unease, and a small voice in the back of his mind hissed: turn back.

Ignoring caution, he drifted past another transfer portal without slowing. His pulse thudded in his temples. He swept the beam of the flashlight ahead, and his heart lurched.

A mass of white filled the tunnel in a soft, ethereal haze.

Finally, it clicked—they were spider webs. His vision came into tight focus, and instinctively, his hand shot out to seize a handhold.

The white haze shuddered, coming alive as thousands of spiders pulsed in their nest ahead.

And they knew he was here.

They began to pour out in a wave that swallowed every surface. There were larger ones, too. Glossy, bloated bodies the size of his head.

And then he saw it.

The big one.

Bigger than him.

Its eyes violet sparks. Its movements slow. Deliberate. Disturbingly unnatural. A void-twisted matriarch.

Her malice hammered on his gift. Blood roared in his ears, and he felt frozen in place.

The horde surged closer, a glistening tide of darkness.

Panicked thoughts filled his mind, each more terrifying than the last: he wouldn't make it back. It was too far. He was too slow.

Without thinking, he reached for his gift, and this time it answered. The air shimmered as his masking took hold, bending perception, twisting focus away from him. But something was wrong. His gift pulled harder than usual, draining more. Too much. Too fast.

And they kept coming.

His pulse quickened. El sentido dotado had always hidden him before. Why not now?

There were too many.

That had to be it. His masking worked by twisting perception, but thousands of tiny, hungry minds were just too much.

His gift broke, slipping away.

The walls pressed in. Fear hollowed out his chest as the swarm pulsed forward. They would be on him soon.

His throat tightened. He couldn't breathe. Every instinct screamed: *Move! Move now, or die!*

He lurched into motion, finally breaking free of his paralysis. His hands scrabbled for purchase on the smooth metal walls, but he struggled—his movements wild and uncoordinated, more flailing than fleeing.

He couldn't move quickly enough. Cold air seared his lungs. They just kept coming, crawling along the walls with ease. No matter how hard Diego pushed himself, they still closed in.

Each heartbeat pounded harder, crushing rational thought.

He couldn't stop imagining hundreds of tiny legs scuttling beneath his clothes, crawling over his skin, followed by the sting of fangs sinking in.

The next handhold drifted close. A wild, frightened voice in his head screamed: Don't touch it! His stomach twisted. His hand trembled. And, the handhold slipped past.

He drifted on—agonizingly slow through the dark.

Behind him, they surged forward. Hisses filled the air, thin and sharp.

He brushed against the tunnel wall. They hadn't reached him yet, but he could feel them—imagine them—a million skittering feet closing in, a storm of whispers scraping at the edges of his sanity.

No escape. No hope.

He was trapped.

Then, with no other choice left, he seized the next handhold, steadied himself, and kicked off.

Ahead, the hatch finally loomed out of shadow.

His hands shook as he wrestled with the wheel. The flashlight slipped from his grip, spinning wildly, its beam illuminating the swarm in brief flashes, followed by moments of horrible darkness.

Abandoning it, he wrenched the hatch open and dove through. As he slammed it shut, he caught one last, terrifying glimpse of countless glittering eyes.

The hatch clanked shut, and the brilliant darkness swallowed him whole.

His senses sharpened to a painful edge. He floated, unable to see anything as he tumbled slowly until his shoulder bumped against the wall. Had he closed the hatch in time? Had any of them slipped through?

His breaths quickened. He blinked into the dark, eyes flicking in every direction, seeing nothing. He couldn't tell left from right, up from down. Shapes appeared in his vision—forming, dissolving, forming again. Things he didn't dare look at too closely.

He wasn't afraid of the dark. He was afraid of what he sometimes saw in it.

"It's just my imagination," Diego whispered to reassure himself, but it came out as a squeak.

He squeezed his eyes tight and drew a long, shuddering breath. Then another. With each exhale, reason slowly clawed its way back.

His fingers swept along the wall until he touched a hatch. He froze. Had he turned himself around? Were there spiders on the other side?

He gripped the wheel that would open the hatch, heart hammering. It was his only anchor to reality as he drifted in the deepening dark.

Fighting to stay calm, he reached for his gift again. It teased him—faint, slippery, just out of reach. Frustration flared. Why did it behave one moment and resist him the next?

After a brief mental struggle, he managed to seize just enough of it to sense the void-tainted spiders' wrongness at his back. He cycled the hatch open to find nothing but absolute black—no spinning flashlight. No spiders.

Adrenaline fell away, leaving him in a cold sweat with tremors he couldn't control. He clenched his fists until they stopped shaking, then sealed the hatch behind him. Bracing his feet, he pushed off—eyes fixed straight ahead, refusing to look at the shapes shifting in the darkness.

All he could do was run his fingertips along the wall, navigating by touch and counting each transfer port he passed. Not that it helped much—he hadn't kept track on the way in, and now he didn't know if he was making progress or just circling the tube's circumference.

At first, he wasn't sure if it was a trick of his eyes or something real. But slowly, a faint green light brightened ahead—an indicator he'd seen before, set beneath the docked Link Pods. The tight knot between his shoulders eased. He'd made it.

He couldn't open the hatch fast enough. Once back in gravity, he sealed it behind him and slumped against the maintenance room wall, arms wrapped tightly around himself. Even now, his imagination summoned the sensation of a million tiny legs skittering across his skin.

Diego muttered, "So. Arachnophobia's a thing."

After this, he doubted he'd ever be able to face a spider again without completely losing it. And of course, he'd have to avoid the spider-like repair bots, too.

As his heartbeat calmed, his thoughts turned inward. The whole experience had been terrifying, but what unsettled him more was how his masking had failed to hide him from the spiders.

His gift had recoiled from his grasp before, but when it worked, it worked. An uncomfortable realization settled in: his sentido dotado had limits, and if he relied on it too much, it might get him killed.

Exhaustion finally dragged him to his feet and back to his cabin, one slow, heavy step at a time.

He made a beeline for the bedroom, leaving a trail of gear along the way, and dove under the covers, yanking them over his head as a shield from the horrors he'd just survived.

All he wanted was to forget—to fall asleep and make the whole expedition disappear. But every time he closed his eyes, his skin crawled.

He rolled onto his back, tossing the blankets aside, suddenly suffocated by their weight.

He had to think about something else.

Taking a deep breath, he stared at the ceiling.

A soft memory surfaced: That time when he, Donna, and Miguel had snuck onto the catwalks, high in Charlie Ring's biosphere. Donna had brought a blanket, and they'd stretched out beneath the latticework, staring at Arcadia in all her bright, stunning, impossibly blue glory.

They'd talked about visiting the surface someday, imagining what it might be like to live planetside. Diego had nodded along, even though he never wanted to leave Serenity.

Eventually, Miguel started snoring, leaving just him and Donna. They'd whispered about nothing. And somehow, that had felt like everything. In that moment, she'd been his entire universe—her bright smile, the way her hair spilled gently across her face—

Diego let out a slow breath, savoring the aching memory as it drifted through him.

How could something feel so warm and hurt so much at the same time?

Big River

Donna,

I don't know where you are right now, but I hope you're back home in Charlie Ring and not stuck with La Familia.

I heard they're something called "pale-igamisses" but I don't know what that means. My dad said it's pretty bad for the girls, because they're forced to marry old men. And the men get lots of wives, too. Hopefully, they don't make you marry one.

I wonder what they do when there's too many guys and not enough girls?

You know that whole "pick the locks" thing I mentioned last time? Well, I did it. I picked one and got into the Link tubes! You would not believe what I found in there. If you were with me, you'd have screamed for sure.

Spiders! Not little ones. Huge. Nightmares. Bigger than people. They moved so fast. I thought I was going to die. I made it out, obviously.

But, I keep thinking... What if I hadn't? Would anyone ever know?

I don't know if you'll ever get to read this, but I hope you do.

That's why I'm writing it, I think. So, if I don't make it, maybe someone will find my journal and tell you what happened. I hope it's me, though. I want to tell you myself.
I miss ~~you guys~~ *YOU.*

*   *   *

Diego stared at the hatch, a cold knot tightening in his chest. A week had passed since his first run through the Link tubes. In all that time, the only food he'd found was a single, unopened bottle of Professor Pep.

Coming back here was the last thing he ever wanted to do. But fear wasn't as strong as the things pulling him forward—like the hope of making it back home to Charlie Ring, the constant worry about Donna, and the desperate craving for anything that wasn't nutrient sludge.

After a final gear check, he tested his two new flashlights to make sure they worked. Satisfied, he pulled a glass bottle from his pack and studied its dark contents. Twenty-five years was a long time, but the seal looked good.

He'd only tasted soda one time before—with his dad—and that was a Pop-a-Cola. His mouth watered just thinking about it.

The cap gave a satisfying hiss when he popped it off, and he took a cautious sip, unsure if it would taste amazing or kill him.

Professor Pep's sweetness hit brighter than Pop-a-Cola, with a tang of berry. He sighed, then chugged the rest in greedy gulps, relishing the sensation of it bubbling down his throat. Holding his breath, he let the pressure build—his dad had insisted this was the most important part of enjoying soda pop.

The swell in his chest grew until he finally let loose a belch so loud it reverberated off the walls. The fizz tickled his nose, and he wrinkled it, grinning like a dope.

For you, Dad.

The smile soon faded. Diego sighed, sparing a glance back at the maintenance room. It was time.

Standing to the side, he pulled the hatch open, half-expecting a swarm of spiders to flood out. Darkness stretched within, and his heart kicked into overdrive. Was something moving in the depths?

"Focus, chavo," Diego muttered, turning on a flashlight. "You'll be fine."

Crawling inside, he launched into zero-g. His movements were steadier than last time, at least.

Before following the mainline tube, he stopped himself on the far wall and scratched an arrow into the surface—pointing away from Green Sector. If he got turned around or ended up upside down, he wanted no doubt about which way to go.

While doing this, he noticed that each transfer port between tubes bore stenciled numbers: DB-5, DB-4, DB-3. The numbers decreased as he continued along the tube. At the irised bulkhead, the sequence ended with DB-1/DK-6.

How did I miss this last time?

Inside the maintenance access airlock, he verified the colored lines changed from blue to gray, not blue to green. That meant he was entering Gray Sector, where Delta Ring connected to Serenity's spine.

Even after all his checks to reassure himself he wasn't walking into the spider's lair, he still hesitated at the hatch, pulse rising. Thankfully, his gift responded without issue. He extended his senses, sweeping ahead to confirm it was clear of void-touched threats. Only then did he push the portal open.

The air felt the same—there wasn't that thick scent from Green Sector's tube. The knot between his shoulders eased, and he clambered through the hatch, sealing it behind him. The numbers decreased until they reached DK-1. He passed through another airlock to find an intersection. Tunnels connected from every direction—up, down, and sideways. He drifted into the open middle of the snarl of tubes, directing his flashlight down each one.

He'd reached Serenity's central spine connecting all the rings.

Checking each direction, a faint red light flickering down one tunnel sent his heart racing. The vivid image of being crushed by a speeding Link Pod flashed through his mind.

But there wasn't a handhold within reach. He flung out one arm, then the other, swiping madly at the air, kicking, twisting—anything to gain momentum. It was useless. And without a spanner, all he could do was wait for his drift to run its course.

Wait to get flattened.

The edge crept closer, but was still agonizingly out of reach. A meter. Centimeters. Diego stretched and strained, clawing frantically until his fingers grazed the metal. Finally, he had a grip, and he pulled hard, hauling himself out of the Pod's oncoming path. He huddled in the maintenance tunnel, heart racing as he waited for the whoosh of the Pod's passing.

Seconds ticked by, each heartbeat louder than the last.

Nothing.

Diego carefully peered out, scanning the tube. The red light still flickered in the distance, exactly where it had been. His cheeks flushed, and he grumbled, "Real sharp, knucklehead. Real sharp."

So, if it wasn't a Pod... then what was it?

The labels on the tube read CK, which probably meant Charlie Ring. Planting his feet, he aimed for the far end and kicked hard, launching himself forward. Fortunately, the spine was straight, not curved, so he didn't have to do the usual pinball routine. The trade-off? A long, featureless, boring drift.

The urge to speed up built inside him. He could pull harder on each handhold, going a little faster each time. But Sir Isaac Newton had a few thoughts about that. He'd have to cancel every bit of force he added now—unless he wanted to take it all at once when he hit the bulkhead. Either he slowed himself before the end, or the wall would do it for him, all at once. Painfully. People broke bones with bad floatwork like that.

"Yay, physics lessons," Diego muttered. "One bruise at a time."

The flickering light sharpened as he drifted closer, resolving into a sign mounted beside a sealed bulkhead:

"DANGER: VACUUM."

A hollow ache wallowed in his chest as the hope of getting home faltered. Was all of Charlie Ring compromised?

His drift hadn't stopped, and the bulkhead suddenly loomed close—too close. Muscle memory kicked in. He rolled, landing feet first, then pushed off at an angle, redirecting his momentum toward the tube's wall, where he caught a handhold.

"Maybe Charlie Ring is fine," he declared, staring at the bulkhead door. "It's just the tubes that are depressurized..."

But even if that were true, he'd need a spacesuit to find out. So, was there another way to get to Charlie Ring?

The maintenance lifts? Inaccessible.

A rocket ship? Unrealistic. He had no way to radio one, and even if he did, they almost always went to Harmony Orbital, not Serenity.

The escape pods? They had no controls, and were just a straight drop to the surface. There was a time when he had considered using one to escape Delta Ring, but the mere thought of being planetside terrified him. Plus, it meant never coming back. Never seeing Donna again.

The bitter truth tightened its grip in his chest: even if Charlie Ring was safe, it was out of reach—for now.

As he drifted back to the intersection, Diego's thoughts turned to Churro—a tiny sugar glider he'd befriended in one of Charlie Ring's biospheres. She was fearless, always darting between vines and stealing food scraps from his hands. But now...?

He didn't want to think about it—Charlie Ring had to be intact. It had to be.

So, should he return to Delta Ring and continue the loop past Gray Sector into Red? Or, had the spiders infested Red Sector, too? He didn't like the idea of finding out, which left two choices: push on to Echo Ring, or try to find a working spacesuit. And just the thought of the second option made his heart race.

Spacesuits. He'd only worn one once, during a training session—some of the most miserable hours of his life. Awkward, clumsy, and terrifying. At least they'd stayed inside the z-ball arena.

It didn't help that he and Miguel had snuck off the night before to watch *Screams in the Silence*—a pre-Arrival horror flick about astronauts stranded outside their ship, trapped in their spacesuits. Spoiler: everyone dies.

No thanks.

So, he either had to slink back to his quarters or press on to Echo Ring. After coming this far, the decision wasn't hard.

The closer he got to Echo Ring, the more a curdling sensation twisted in his gut. It was familiar—an almost primal unease—but try as he might, he didn't know why.

Eventually, he arrived at a junction similar to the last one. He continued into Echo Ring, bouncing along the curved tubes until the familiar shape of a transit terminal came into view.

The maintenance hatch was right where it should be, and Diego crawled through. Gravity returned, but even better—the air was warm, unlike the chill of Delta Ring. Could he actually live down here?

That optimism faltered when he found the door to the terminal jammed tight. Diego yanked and shoved, getting nowhere. Fortunately, he'd packed a small pry bar. He wedged it into the frame and hammered it with the heel of his hand until his palms throbbed.

Finally, the door gave way, peeling back with a series of crackling pops. A wave of humid air rolled in, heavy with an earthy scent, and vines draped over the gap like overgrown curtains.

Pushing them aside, his breath caught in his throat as he took in the scene. The entire Link Transit Terminal—no, the entire promenade—was overrun. Leafy tendrils snaked across every surface, from the floor to the ceilings. Nature had taken over.

His chest tightened as a thought pounded into his mind: were the spiders here, too? Did he just step into a new nightmare? His eyes darted across the overgrown halls, searching for any sign of webbing. Nothing—at least not yet.

Diego extended his gift, straining to sense any void terrors nearby. A few smaller abominations lingered on the fringes of his awareness, but nothing immediate.

He ventured out, stepping through the foliage until a strange, red, fruit-like pod nestled among the vines caught his eye. It almost looked like the biosphere's crisp apples, and his mouth watered.

Tentatively, he reached out and poked the pod with a finger.

It burst, releasing a cloud of spores into Diego's face. He staggered back, hacking and choking as he frantically waved his arms to clear the air.

A numb, mental fog closed in fast. His legs buckled, and he collapsed to the ground, darkness rimming his vision. Gritting his teeth, he struggled to stay conscious. But his thoughts continued to fragment, and his heartbeat thundered in his skull, making it hard to concentrate. Hard to think.

Where am I? The thought came cold and sharp, stabbing through his gut as he suddenly couldn't remember.

Focusing on a vine nearby, he stared at the green tendrils fluttering in an unseen breeze. *How did I get into a biosphere?*

A familiar squeak cut through the air.

"Churro?" he rubbed at the grit in his eyes. *This can't be Charlie Ring.*

Blinking to clear his vision, he focused on the creature nestled in the vines. It seemed like a sugar glider but was larger—about the size of a cat—and its sleek fur radiated a faint, fluorescent light.

"Not Churro," Diego raked his fingers through his hair, struggling to pull his thoughts together. Memories flickered: the Link tubes, Echo Ring, the spore pods...

A sharp crack shattered the stillness, reverberating through the air, followed by a thump. And another. Continuing in a series of ponderous footsteps.

A spike of adrenaline coursed through Diego. He straightened, shimmered into invisibility, and staggered into a nearby alcove while praying his gift would hold steady.

A grotesque, hulking fusion of human and plant lurched from the promenade's shadows, carrying a pall of otherworldly unease that pressed against his senses. Its twisted limbs resembled gnarled, weathered branches.

The footsteps grew louder, resonating with the creak of stressed wood. Clusters of small, honeycomb-like holes perforated the thing's entire form—some oozing a sickly, glowing fluid, others holding something nestled within.

Bile rose in his throat just seeing it. Its presence against his gift was far stronger than any void terror he'd ever faced. He tried to push it, to divert it away like the growlers. But every attempt felt like shoving into a curtain of boiling, pustulent tar. And the more he tried, the harder it became to hold his masking in place.

His gift soured with each attempt, and he gave up, struggling just to keep himself hidden. He held his breath, willing the abomination to pass quickly.

But the creature halted next to him. Slowly, it turned toward him. Its mouth contorted in a silent scream of agony. It had no eyes. Yet it moved as if searching, its head tilting and swaying.

He clenched his fists, nails biting into his palms, heart thudding erratically. Then the thought struck—if it had no eyes, would his masking even work? Doubt surged, and his gift unraveled in a blink.

The creature struck, its arm lashing out.

Instinct took over. Diego twisted sideways, barely dodging the full force of the blow. But pain flared from his neck to shoulder—it had clipped him with its woody claws.

The deep, shuddering sound that came from it was wrong in every way—a warped howl, like the shriek of a violin bow heard through water, somehow too far away and yet unbearably close. Then, the spore pods lodged in its perforated holes erupted, spewing a luminous purple cloud.

Diego held his breath and clenched his eyes shut. He lunged past the spreading cloud, lungs burning as he stumbled blindly over tangled vines. When he couldn't hold it anymore, he gasped, opened his eyes, and ran. Legs stretching, he tore through the overgrowth and bolted into the Link Transit Terminal.

The heavy footsteps followed, creating a dreadful toll echoing in his wake.

Gritting his teeth against the pain in his arm, Diego fumbled with the maintenance hatch, only now realizing his fingers were wet with blood. He put his elbow into the effort, and finally, the hatch gave way. Without even stopping to get a flashlight from his pack, he dove into the Link Tube and yanked the door closed behind him.

Horrible darkness swallowed him whole. He drifted. His breath came in sharp, uneven gasps. For several agonizing minutes, the thudding footsteps continued beyond the walls. But then—at last—they faded away.

"*¿Qué rayos?*" he whispered.

Something from Echo Ring's biosphere had clearly breached its confines.

That's right. I'm in Echo Ring. His memories began to return.

At this point, he just wanted to get back to Delta Ring. Sure, it was dangerous, but it was danger he knew. This place was something else. Too terrifying. He'd come back another time, when he was better prepared.

His wounded arm was numb and tingling. Stabs of pain radiated from his neck as he fumbled for a flashlight. It flared to life, catching crimson droplets glistening as they drifted weightlessly.

His fingers trembled as he unzipped his jacket and pulled back the layers of shirts, gingerly inspecting his wound. He couldn't see much, but at least the cold kept it somewhat numb.

More droplets formed and broke away in the cold air—it was still bleeding. There wasn't time to go back to Delta Ring.

He rolled up the collars of his layered shirts so they pressed tight against his neck, then zipped his jacket as high as it would go. It was a makeshift bandage, but maybe enough.

With that done, he racked his brain for ideas. Were the sections down here sealed off, like in Delta Ring? Or was the overgrown jungle limited to just one sector? Maybe another one had a Link Transit Terminal near a Medbay?

He returned to the mainline tube and pressed on, trying to remember how many sectors Echo Ring had. After a few awkward bounces along the curving tube, he came upon a curious Link station with only a single berth. He stared at it for a moment, then it clicked: Project Ultra's secret lab. They had private Link access, right? Had the jungle claimed the lab too, or had it survived untouched?

Diego drifted into the bay but couldn't spot a maintenance hatch —the only access was through the Pod's docking port doors, and those wouldn't open without a Pod in the cradle.

Blood kept soaking through his clothes, turning them into wet, icy sponges that clung to his clammy skin and sapped the heat from him. Worse—with every heartbeat, a little more of his will to continue drained away. He was already lightheaded and probably wouldn't last much longer. Then, through the fog in his mind, he remembered that the doors should have a manual override.

Sweeping his flashlight around, he spotted a crank mechanism below the dock's collar.

He set the flashlight drifting, angling it just right to keep the space around him lit. Hooking his feet into nearby handholds, he crouched and gripped the crank with his good arm.

The mechanism fought him with every turn, each move sending a fresh stab of fire radiating from his shoulder. Sweat beaded on his brow, and his breath came in tight gasps as he continued working the crank.

When the gap between the doors finally looked wide enough, Diego pulled himself through. But gravity didn't ease in like it did with the maintenance hatches. No—it hit all at once. His stomach lurched as the gravity plates yanked his torso down, even while his legs remained weightless in the tube behind him.

Hissing through the pain, he inched forward on his belly, dragging himself the rest of the way inside. He lay there catching his breath, waiting for the fire in his shoulder to fade before looking around.

Viewports lined the far wall. Starlight cast everything in the chamber into dark, mysterious silhouettes. For a moment, Diego thought he saw movement, and he froze. Was the lab compromised? Or was it just his overactive imagination?

He didn't have time to find out, and he was too lightheaded to even focus on using his gift. Gritting his teeth, he rolled onto his side and forced himself upright.

He had to stop the bleeding.

Into Each Life Some Rain Must Fall

Diego flipped a light switch. Overhead fixtures flickered to life across the room, followed by the buzz and whir of machines waking up. Excitement stirred in his chest, briefly overcoming his pain as he scanned the secret laboratory of Project Ultra. It was far bigger than he'd imagined, sprawling every which way in a chaotic maze of benches, shelves, and chalkboards.

A radio crackled to life somewhere in the clutter, filling the room with the strains of a pre-Arrival tune: Ella Fitzgerald and The Inkspots, "Into Each Life Some Rain Must Fall."

Dust swirled around his canvas high-top sneakers as he made a quick circuit of the room, searching for anything remotely first-aid related. At last, he found a section of the lab cluttered with medical gear —even a medbot tucked into a recessed bay. But, of course, it didn't respond when he waved his hand and called out in an attempt to wake it up.

Scowling, he traced a bundle of cables from the bot's storage bay to a control terminal. That, at least, started up, displaying a few lines of green text:

```
Unistar MedOS™ SYSTEM BOOT - AIOS 5.3.07
© 1962  Unistar Robotics, Inc.
>> SYSTEM CHECK...
>> CORE MEMORY... FAILED. KERNEL IMAGE NOT FOUND
! FATAL ERROR: SYSTEM FUNCTION TERMINATED
AUTOMATED MEMORY WIPE EXECUTED BY SUBROUTINE 09A(TR)
TIME OF EVENT: 14 YEARS, 5 MONTHS, 14 DAYS AGO
>> INSERT Unistar MedOS™ HOLOTAPE TO RESTORE SYSTEM
```

Anger smoldered in his chest. Of course, he'd end up in a med center where the bot had apparently lobotomized itself. Why would it even do that? He didn't know—and right now, it didn't matter.

His eyes landed on an open medkit, its contents scattered across a counter near a sink like someone had meant to return, but never did. He peeled off his layers of jackets and shirts as he approached, leaving a trail of clothing across the floor.

Among the scattered medkit items was a stimpack. Diego stabbed it into his shoulder, and something cold surged through his arm. The room seemed to shift—colors brightened, and sounds became sharper. More importantly, the hot throbbing in his wound dulled. Not gone, but manageable.

He peeled off the last shirt, sticky with blood, and winced as it pulled at the wound. Turning to the mirror, he inspected the ragged gash at the base of his neck, and he froze.

Staring back at him, through the hollow eyes of the Z-ball mask, was his own reflection. He no longer felt the urge to smash the mirror, but the sight still twisted at something deep and ugly inside him.

Jaw clenched, he forced his attention back to the wound. It looked worse than he'd expected—jagged edges, fresh blood still seeping. His chest tightened as he realized just how deep it really was.

Fortunately, there was a wrinkled guide tucked inside the kit— complete with diagrams for treating wounds like this. He gathered what he needed, only to discover that the numbing agent and suturing stapler were missing. The stimpack had dulled the pain, but he doubted it would help much once he started stitching.

Fortunately, the guide offered alternatives that didn't require one.

He took a deep breath and got to work. At the sink, he carefully washed the gash, then, following the guide, poured on the hydrogen peroxide. The sting hit hard, catching him off guard as it foamed in the torn flesh. He gritted his teeth and slammed a fist against the counter. A groan tore from his throat, and he struggled just to stay upright.

After a few shaky breaths, he straightened and kept going. The Mercurochrome stained his skin a vivid red as he dabbed it on, but at least it didn't sting.

Now came the hard part. According to the guide, he was supposed to "trim the wound."

Yeah, no.

Just the thought of cutting bits of himself off sent his stomach churning. And worse: without a stapler, he'd have to stitch the edges together by hand using a needle and thread.

His resolve floundered.

Just cleaning it had been excruciating. The thought of pushing a needle through his skin was far more than Diego could bear.

Desperate for another option, he scanned the lab. There had to be something—this place was packed with all sorts of scientific gear. His gaze landed on a bottle of Wonder Glue, and he remembered how it always stuck his fingers together whenever he tried to use it.

Worth a shot.

To his surprise, the torn skin held. Crude, but effective. He wrapped it with a bandage, red quickly blooming through the gauze. He could only hope he'd done everything right.

He collected his blood-soaked jackets and shirts into a pile, and grimaced at how much blood he'd lost. Worse, there was a faint dusting of spores on everything. A quick glance in the mirror confirmed they were in his hair, too. He dumped the clothes into the sink and filled it with cold water, leaving them to soak.

Wanting to scrub away every trace of the spores, he washed his hair, face, chest, and arms, taking care to avoid the bandage. Afterward, he found a dusty lab coat to keep him warm until he'd cleaned his clothes.

The stimpack left him wide awake and unable to sit still. He scanned the room again—this time with more care, his eyes darting from one strange device to the next.

He approached a chemistry station cluttered with coiled glass tubes, beakers, and vials—most were crusted with the dried remnants of past experiments. Nearby, a circular platform gleamed with an iridescent sheen that could only be of alien Gray origin. Unlike everything else in the lab, there wasn't a speck of dust on it.

As he continued exploring, moving from one strange item to the next, Diego hoped that he might find food that had survived the years. His search paid off when he discovered a closet stacked with crates of something called Soylent Fusion. Each bottle boasted, "Drink a bite to eat!"

He pulled a bottle free, the glass giving a soft *tink* as it bumped against the others. The green liquid inside shimmered with a faint iridescence when the light hit it just right, making him hesitate. *Should it do that?*

His gaze returned to the packaging, noting the Professor Pep logo. *Surely it must have been a trustworthy brand? Or... Was it part of the experiments here?*

He pushed the thought aside. *What do I have to lose? Maybe I'll grow another hand, or it'll make me even more disfigured than I already am.*

Popping the cap off the Soylent Fusion bottle, he brought it to his nose and sniffed cautiously. No stink—just a faint minty scent. Already better than NPS. He tipped the bottle back and took a sip.

The flavor surprised him—a strange milkiness, but not unpleasant. It wasn't as sweet as Professor Pep, but it wasn't terrible either. Most importantly—it wasn't nutrient sludge. That alone felt like a victory.

He finished the bottle.

With the last drops soothing his hunger, Diego turned his gaze back to the lab, ready to continue exploring. But the stimpack's buzz drained away, and the weight of everything he'd faced that day came crashing back—tenfold. His limbs felt leaden, and he blinked hard, struggling to keep his eyes open as he stumbled toward a sofa. The worn plastic cushions creaked as he collapsed onto them, mumbling, "Just a few minutes. Just a few—"

When he awoke, the lab lights remained unchanged, offering no clue how much time had passed. But it had been long enough for his hunger to return. Rubbing at his crusted eyes, he stretched and rolled his shoulder—a mistake. Pain shot through him, sucking his breath away. Groaning, he dragged himself to the sink and inspected the wound, discovering angry red lines snaking outward from the puckered edges.

His fingers tightened on the sink, and a half-forgotten lesson from school surfaced in his mind, warning about infections with red lines like this. Did he fail to clean it well enough? Were some spores from the tree abomination still in there? A heavy pressure built in his chest as he rifled through the medkit again, searching for anything useful. Nothing. No antibiotics. No antivirals. No "anti-void-tainted fungal"—not that such a thing really existed.

He extended his search, scouring through every medical supply cabinet—but still nothing. Just more incomprehensible gear. A refrigerator stood nearby, its shelves lined with vials, but it had long since stopped working. Even if the contents hadn't spoiled, the labels meant nothing to him, and he wasn't about to blindly test mystery formulas in a mad scientist's lab.

"Medbay," he muttered. Every ring had one on the promenade. Even without doctors, there should be a medbot, right? But that meant venturing out into the mutated overgrowth.

A shiver ran up his spine. He wasn't ready for that. Not yet.

"It's fine—I'll be just fine," he said aloud, even though he didn't quite believe it.

He cleaned the wound again, groaning as the hydrogen peroxide fizzed around the glued edges, then wrapped it in a fresh bandage. Unsure what else to do, he turned back to the lab. Time to figure out if he could live down here.

After a breakfast of Soylent Fusion, he hauled his soaked clothes from the sink to an annex off the medical section, the words HYGIENE BAY were worked into the wall with blue tiles set in white. Inside were showers, lockers, toilets, and rows of sinks. Between the mirrors hung faded, rust-pocked metal signs. Each one featured illustrations of smiling faces, paired with slogans like "A Clean Body Makes a Happy Subject" and "Hygiene Means Healing."

He scrubbed his clothes and hung them to dry. Water, check. Shelter, check.

This place had most of what he needed to survive—except a steady food source. There was plenty of Soylent Fusion, but it wouldn't last forever. And, of course, there was the small matter of the terrifying neighbors lurking on the promenade.

To mark the passing hours, he lined up empty Soylent Fusion bottles on the edge of a table while he worked his way through the lab's secrets. Experiment stations, side offices, and storage cabinets all came under scrutiny.

A framed photograph on a desk caught his eye: a large group of people in lab coats smiling at the camera—the scientists who worked here, perhaps? Diego studied their faces, needing to know more, hoping to find something that would explain the purpose of their work in this strange lab.

His gaze lingered on one woman's face—something about her stirred an aching feeling within him, brushing against a part of himself that felt lost.

His brow furrowed, trying to piece together what she had done in the lab. But no answers came. Eventually, he gave up and left the photo face down.

The medical lab was filled with devices labeled for genetic and embryonic procedures. They had apparently collaborated with the Grays on gene manipulation, and he wondered exactly how these experiments had been applied to people. Were they willing subjects?

The logbooks offered tantalizing glimpses into the scientists' work, including experiments splicing plant traits into humans—reminding him of the tree walkers on the promenade. Others described an entire category called "metaphysical research" covering a range of things from the manipulation of dimensional phenomena to *espers*—a new word to him. He skimmed a little deeper, finding details about people with strange abilities like telepathy and telekinesis.

It was all a bit too close to his own gift to ignore. But nothing he read described what he could do. His gift was about sensing void terrors, and those hadn't existed until after the Arrival. The logbooks stopped before then. So, it's not like he was tied to this lab... right?

Still, the journals might hold insights into su sentido dotado, and he made a note to dig in later. He reached for another bottle of Soylent Fusion, muttering "metaphysical" to himself—then paused. Four empties already sat on the table. He should slow down.

He blinked his dry eyes, wondering how long he'd been at this. A whole day?

Glancing around, he realized it would take weeks—maybe longer—to sift through the mountains of information in the lab. He stood, stretched, and wandered over to the viewports.

Arcadia. A stunning blue orb suspended in the black of space. The sight always filled him with awe... and then a flicker of unease. What would it be like to live down there? How did people deal with the unpredictable whims of nature? Why would anyone willingly risk getting caught in a rainstorm—or worse, when it froze into... snow? How did that even work?

Clouds were terrifying.

Up here, you knew when the biosphere sprinklers would turn on. Down there, the clouds could do it whenever they wanted. Without warning. At any time.

Irrational or not, he just couldn't handle the idea. He'd looked it up once, too. They actually had names for this stuff. Fear of clouds? *Nephophobia.* When the clouds went evil? *Lilapsophobia.*

The list went on—*ombrophobia, chionophobia,* and so many others.

Yep, he had them all.

He exhaled slowly, breath fogging the glass, then removed his mask and leaned closer. As more of the world came into view, his heart began to race. Swirling clouds churned over the surface—dark, menacing, and alive with flickers of violet energy.

A void storm was raging on Arcadia.

But that wasn't what spiked his pulse—it was the seething tendrils stretching into space, grasping for the orbital. Serenity was about to fly through the storm's upper sprites.

Diego realized he had no Pounamu. Back on Charlie Ring, if you didn't have one, you had to shelter in the chapel when the storms came. But down here, he had no idea where a chapel even was—only that it'd be buried somewhere in the aberrant jungle of the promenade.

He had to admit that he'd often questioned how necessary those protections really were. With his void-touched abilities, he wasn't sure he needed to worry. While others spoke of the storms with fear, Diego often felt a strange exhilaration when they came. They stirred something inside him, leaving him feeling both energized and unsettled all at once.

The approaching storm made him realize how futile his efforts to survive had been. And with it came the unwanted memories he'd suppressed. The loss of his parents. The torment he'd endured growing up. The trials he'd faced in the months since his exile to Delta Ring.

As he stared into the swirling tempest, an insidious voice crept in, whispering darkness, sowing doubt, telling him he was already lost. So why keep fighting?

It all became a soul-crushing weight pressing harder by the moment. The line blurred between who he was and the monster he feared becoming.

He sagged against the glass, arms hanging limply at each side.

The whispers continued: *Let the void storm come. Let it tear you apart. Become a growler—aren't you already halfway there?*

His gift trembled in response. The deeper he wallowed in despair, the stronger it surged. And he didn't care anymore.

Why was he trying so hard to control it? Wasn't it part of who he was?

With his heart hollowing out for one fleeting moment, he fell to his knees and gave in.

His gift roared to life in a release so powerful—so enervating—it rang through the metaverse. It announced his surrender to the void itself.

And then, without warning, a curdling wave of disorientation crashed over him. His world tilted. Nausea twisted his gut. It was the same dizzying sensation he'd felt during the Kraal attack.

The Kraal was coming.

In a searing burst of violet light, it tore into existence before him, tendrils of unnatural energy snaking from the corners, shuddering, twisting, and writhing. Diego staggered back, bile rising in his throat as he struggled to comprehend the impossible sight.

His very essence felt stretched thin by the Kraal—like every atom in his body was unraveling. Any attempt to focus on it brought flashes of gibbering mouths, horrific tentacles, and shifting shadows looming with menace.

And then with bone-deep certainty, he knew he had only moments left to live.

The fight drained from him, leaving only a heavy stillness. He closed his eyes.

Finally, he could reunite with his parents.

But it didn't take him. Instead, a question hammered into his mind, overwhelming, incomprehensible. A taste of color. A crush of sound. It made no sense, and yet it demanded an answer.

Diego doubled over, clenching his head as a searing pain lanced through his skull.

His breaths came fast and sharp, chest heaving. Instinct took over, and he reached for his gift. It flickered and writhed, teetering just beyond his control. But fear steeled his will. Gritting his teeth, he seized hold of it, eyes squeezing shut as the world around him rippled, and he masked himself.

As swiftly as it had arrived, the wrenching, disorienting nausea faded. Diego opened his eyes. The beeps and hums of the equipment felt strangely amplified in the quiet.

The Kraal had disappeared.

He released his gift and collapsed to the floor, lying on his back and staring up at the ceiling as his thoughts spiraled.

Had it just... gone away?

No. A chill slithered in Diego's gut—he could still sense the Kraal, lurking at the edges of his awareness. It hadn't disappeared, only retreated.

That unease he'd felt since arriving on Echo Ring? It was the Kraal. In all the stories he'd heard about them, they came and went swiftly—they didn't linger.

Which only made the gnawing question more troubling: *Was this the same Kraal that attacked the station? The one that started this whole mess? Had it been here all along? Was it tied to Project Ultra?*

...Maybe I didn't summon it?

Before he could chase the thought further, the void storm arrived. It swept over Serenity Orbital in full force, rattling the floors with its fury.

The storms could rage for hours, sometimes even days. The logical choice was to retreat to Delta Ring, where he knew the location of a chapel. But the mere thought of that long, frigid trek through the depths of the orbital with his injured arm—let alone during a void storm—filled him with crushing exhaustion. The despair that had taken him earlier returned, dragging him deeper.

The void storm's fury intensified, purple light tracing the room's corners like ghostly fingers. Balls of effervescent void energy formed, passing through objects in crackling bursts of painful other-worldly light.

It spread across the orbital, and Diego resigned himself to whatever fate awaited him. It would claim him, or he would survive—either way, it was up to the whims of the universe. He stared at the ceiling, teetering on the edge of surrender. After all, who would miss him? The thought cut deeply, and he pinched his eyes shut against the ache it brought.

But, instead of giving in, he crawled to the wall, activated his masking, and wrapped his arms tightly around his knees. The storm raged on, rattling the station without mercy. All the while, the Kraal lingered at the edges of his awareness. A nauseating weight he couldn't shut out.

Hours passed while the weight of its presence stretched him thin.

It had to be deep in the night by now, if not already morning—but he couldn't fall asleep. The moment he did, his masking would fail.

Robot Walk

Diego woke with fevered chills, his body aching and sore. The wound at the base of his neck throbbed with each pulse of his heart. Sometime during the night, he'd fallen into a restless, uneasy sleep. The void storm had passed. And yet he was still here.

He couldn't decide whether to feel relieved or dismayed.

His injury felt hot and puffy. The shadows seemed to twist and warp as he glanced around, taking on sinister shapes with brightly colored edges.

Maybe it's time to return to Delta Ring's Medbay.

He'd searched it once, but found no food and hadn't returned. Now, with his thoughts unraveling, it seemed like his best option. In his current state, there was no way he could wander out to try and find one down here.

After layering up against the chill of the Link tubes, he gathered his gear and the few items he'd collected—including a working wrist-watch—and stuffed as many Soylent Fusion bottles into his pack as he could carry.

Fever burned in him throughout the journey back to Delta Ring, despite the biting cold. His condition was deteriorating fast. Aches radiated through his body, colored shapes flickered at the edges of his vision, and his breath came in short, shallow bursts.

This is bad. Really bad.

When he finally stepped into gravity on Delta Ring, a wave of dizziness washed over him. The edges of his vision blurred. He staggered forward, barely managing to stay upright, each step feeling heavier than the last.

The sterile glow of the overhead lights in Medbay flickered on as Diego stepped through the doors. The air held a faint scent of antiseptic, lingering even after all these years. Gleaming chrome and cyan enamel surfaces reflected the light in painfully vivid hues.

Diego squinted against the glare, swaying as he scanned the empty room. Four examination beds lined one side, their vinyl cushions cracked and faded from years of use. A sense of helplessness pulled at his will to figure out what to do—he just wanted to lie down on a bed and have somebody care for him.

Shaking his head to clear it, he struggled to think straight. He'd come here for the medbot, right? There, toward the back, a white bipedal robot rested in a charging bay. The sign over its head declared, "For Emergencies."

Approaching, he worried if it'd be just like the one in the lab and wouldn't activate at all. He waved his hand in front of its face. "Hey! Can you hear me? Or are you dead, too?"

No response. Of course not.

Clenching his fists, he glanced around the room, his thoughts flickering through half-remembered medical advice. He just needed antibiotics, right?

Stumbling to the medical cabinets, he found each locked tight. But they were just basic mechanical locks. He retrieved his picks, but with fingers stiff and clumsy, they slipped to the floor with a series of ticking sounds that were far louder than they should be.

Diego dropped to his knees, hands trembling and sweat beading on his forehead as he collected the picks. Gripping the edge of one of the beds, he pulled himself upright, grunting as a fresh wave of pain shot through him. He paused, leaning on the bed.

"I can't do this myself," he hissed through clenched teeth.

His eyes landed on a large button near the medbot. A faded sign above it declared. "Press if Medbay is unattended."

He stumbled forward and stabbed the button.

A low mechanical hum filled the air, joined by clanks and the whir of gears, as the bot came to life. Straightening upright, its eyes flickered to a soft green glow and fixed on Diego.

"What is the nature of the medical emergency?" it inquired in a gentle, feminine voice.

Diego winced as he gingerly peeled off his layers of jackets and shirts, then carefully removed the bandage, revealing the wound beneath. In the sterile light, it looked worse than before—red and puffy, with the lines now thicker, spreading from it like angry lightning bolts.

"Please, have a seat on the examination table," the medbot instructed, leaning forward with a soft hum as she inspected the injury. "How did this happen?"

Diego hesitated, his mouth opening and closing as he struggled to find a reasonable story that didn't involve explaining a giant walking tree trying to crush his skull. Exhausted and unable to come up with anything plausible, he shrugged.

The medbot straightened up. "No matter. I have determined that your condition is not an emergency; please work with the daytime personnel for further aid."

Diego blinked, certain he hadn't heard correctly. "Wait, what? There aren't any! Delta Ring is deserted! I need you to help me!"

"I'm sorry, but my protocol dictates that I can only provide emergency medical aid outside normal business hours. Please speak with the medical personnel for immediate assistance."

Diego growled. "When are normal business hours?"

"The regular staff arrives nine to five each day," she answered calmly as if this were the most obvious thing in the world.

Diego glanced at his wristwatch, then shot back. "It's almost noon, so where are they?"

The medbot paused as she processed his statement. "I am only allowed to provide emergency care outside of business hours. You must return to visit with the medical staff instead."

Her answer only added to his frustration, and he threw his hands in the air. "Nobody is ever coming back. You're it!" He struggled to keep his voice level. "I can't come back to meet the staff if there aren't any, right? Check with the other robots; everything is on lockdown! And what if I die because this is infected, and you didn't help me?"

Her optics flickered rapidly, and for a moment, Diego feared she might shut down again. But then she responded, "Your argument has merit. Very well, I can make an exception based on these extenuating circumstances."

Diego felt the tension in his shoulders ease.

"However," she continued, her tone firm, "as this is not an emergency, payment is required up front."

Diego's relief soured. Clenching his jaw, he waved John Smith's passkey, silently hoping it'd work.

She scanned it, pausing momentarily before adding, "Payment confirmed; thank you for being... patient."

Diego narrowed his eyes, unsure if she was trying to be funny. Frustration lined his voice as he demanded, "Just help me now."

Her tone became soft and reassuring. "Of course. I am Meddi, your emergency medical assistant. I'm here to ensure your well-being." Her servos hummed quietly as she leaned in to examine Diego's wound more closely. A mist sprayed over his skin, making him flinch.

"Please remain still," Meddi instructed. "This is merely a numbing agent." Her cold, mechanical fingers probed his injury. "Interesting," she remarked. "This injury is more serious than the initial scans indicated."

"No way," he muttered softly.

Without warning, she stuck him with a needle, and he lurched. Her hand clamped down on his shoulder, holding him still.

"This will help fight the infection and toxins. Now, please refrain from moving as I clean and dress your wound."

Something she'd given him started to kick in, and the pain began to fade—but at the same time, he felt strange. Detached. Floating.

He stayed silent as she cleaned the wound, followed by slight tugs at the base of his neck as she began stitching. He wanted to watch, but without a mirror, his curiosity went unsatisfied. Besides, every time he moved, her grip tightened.

Once she finished, she applied a healing salve and wrapped the wound in a clean, white bandage. Then she handed Diego a small tube and a bundle of fresh dressings.

"Change it every day. Apply this," she instructed. "It should heal in a few days."

Diego turned the tube over in his fingers. "What is it?"

"Sanan solution," she replied. "The same formula used in stim-packs. It will speed up your healing process."

"Does it expire?" he asked, eyeing the pre-Arrival stamp on the side, "EXP FEB 1965."

Meddi walked back to the cabinet and checked the other tubes. When she returned, her answer was less than reassuring. "I cannot verify its current efficacy. However, while the solution may be aged, it is unlikely to cause harm. There is no need for concern."

Diego let out a sigh. Not like he had another choice.

Meddi's tone shifted as she gave him a slow once-over. "You appear to be underage. Where are your parents or guardians?"

He froze.

So this model can tell ages better than Officer Chip. Great.

He scrambled to think of an answer that wouldn't trigger some crazy robot protocol. What if she decided to keep him here until an adult came for him? That'd be a long wait.

Before she could reach for him with her grabby hands or ask another question, he snatched up his pack and bolted for the door. She called after him, but he didn't stop.

If he ever had to come back, he'd need a story ready.

Volver, Volver

Diego headed through the dim promenade, glad it was free of mutated flora. His steps slowed as he approached an old record store, the hair on the back of his neck standing on end. He extended his gift, conforming that there was a tangle of void rats within.

Unnatural energy always lingered in the air after a void storm, and this time was no different. The storms invigorated the abominations they spawned, infusing them with a dangerous, almost frenzied vitality. But what Diego felt now wasn't just the usual storm-fueled hyperactivity. No, this was more, with an undercurrent of bilious, unsatiated hunger.

His heart hammered as he peered into the dimly lit store. The scent of old vinyl and musty paper mingled with something metallic and pungent that made his stomach clench. *I should go back to my bunk and sleep for a few days. I'm wasted. I don't need to look for trouble.*

But he couldn't ignore the snarl of frenzied darkness at the back of the store—the void rats were feeding. But on what?

Reaching out with his gift, he commanded them to disperse. Although hesitant at first, they scurried away.

The store fell into an eerie stillness, amplifying the soft rustle of Diego's clothes. He crept forward, hands clammy, stomach knotting.

Blood on the floor. Footprints. Streaks. Spatter. He struggled to keep his hands steady.

The beam of his flashlight glanced across the source of the carnage—a body. Facedown. A growler?

Diego felt each dreadful toll of his heart while he inched forward. Something wasn't right. Void creatures didn't attack each other —the rats wouldn't be feeding on a growler.

A part of him howled for him to turn away. It must have known what he'd find—because the body wore a new blue jumpsuit.

He didn't want to look. But he had to know.

His breath quickened as he slowly reached down and turned the body over.

He jerked his hand back.

Miguel.

His knees wobbled. He couldn't breathe. His chest tightened. His heart keened in a mourning wail of disbelief.

When—when did they send him down here? How long had he suffered, fighting off the growlers? But the thought that cut the deepest was: *Why wasn't I here to help him?*

Memories came to him fast and unrelenting. The countless hours they'd spent exploring the forgotten recesses of Charlie Ring together, crawling through maintenance shafts and supply conduits. Visiting Miguel's secret base in an abandoned repair bay—a hideout pieced together from old storage bins, shipping containers, and any spare part he could find.

He'd been so proud of his collection: old crew logs, lost tools, faded maintenance reports, a dog-eared dirty magazine, and a stash of comics they read together by the flickering light of his space ranger lamp. Those moments had been a rare escape, filled with shared stories about the station's history, monster-card trades, and daring adventures inspired by the comics they loved.

But now he was gone.

A cold weight settled in Diego's chest. He had failed his friend.

The brutal truth of how far Carlos would go was inescapable. The full gravity of the situation seeped into his mind, chilling him to the bone. He straightened, wiping away tears.

He didn't know why they sent Miguel down here, but a gnawing worry suggested that this was just the beginning.

Until now, Diego had drifted through each day like it was his personal game of survival, only looking out for himself.

But no more.

He couldn't change what had happened to Miguel, but he could ensure that no one else would suffer the same fate. He'd be ready to help them.

Diego set his pack down and pulled out a small blanket. With reverence, he wrapped Miguel's remains and dragged him to the Recycler. The task was grim, his heart heavy, but leaving his friend for the void rats was unthinkable.

The system locked up, a warning light flashing red. He swiped John's passkey and hit the override. Even then, the light stayed on.

Maybe that was okay. Nothing about this felt right.

But when he checked the next day, the light was off and the chute was empty. For some reason, that hurt. He couldn't explain why —maybe because he had nothing left to remember him by.

He hadn't thought losing someone could ever hurt as much as it had with his parents.

But it did.

Nights were the hardest. In those quiet hours, Diego would press his face into the pillow and pretend the tears soaking the fabric didn't mean anything.

But they did.

He missed Miguel. And the guilt of not saving him cut deeper than he ever expected.

It took a few days before he could bring himself to return to the maintenance lift. By then, the grief had burned through him, transforming into a drive to be ready for when Carlos did this again.

He had a purpose now.

Surveying the area, he weighed his options. It was time to figure out a new home. It would be best to stay near the lift so he'd be ready to rescue anyone sent down. His gaze landed on the Atomic Pizzarama, which had a direct view into the corridor leading to the lift.

He tried the side door marked "Explorers Only!" but there wasn't a lock. Shifting to the main rolling gate, he studied a turn-key switch on the wall, wondering if it might open it up. After several minutes of effort, the last pin finally gave way. He twisted the tension rod, feeling a resistance. The core must be spring-loaded, and it would snap back the moment he let go.

Turning it fully, the gate let out a metallic squeal that echoed across the plaza as it rattled upward. Diego jumped, the pick slipping from his fingers. He moved quickly, catching it midair—a reflexive act that sent a smug satisfaction through him, though it did little to calm his racing heart.

This moment of triumph was short-lived. The lock snapped back into place, and the gate ground to a halt, barely lifting more than a finger's width.

He stared at the small gap, heart drumming, the rattling squeal still ringing in his ears.

Grunts and cries of growlers echoed from around the bend.

Shimmering into invisibility, he pressed himself against the wall, holding still as the growlers rushed into the plaza. They slowed, heads snapping back and forth as they scanned for the source of the noise. Diego prayed they would quickly lose interest. Full invisibility took a lot out of him, so he needed to keep it to short bursts.

He counted each heartbeat, willing them to leave. But it wasn't the same as nudging them when they were dormant. They were prowling now, sniffing the air, pulling at the gate, hunting for the source of the noise, and not so easily diverted.

One stepped within reach.

Its huffing breath washed over him—hot, foul, and rank. He clenched his jaw, swallowing hard to keep the rising bile at bay, refusing to inhale. Time stretched on. Seconds? Minutes? He couldn't tell. His chest burned. Lungs screamed for air. *Why won't it go away?*

The growler lingered, head twitching, searching. Finally, it retreated, and the others followed.

But they didn't go far and clustered near the fountain in the middle of the plaza. Diego's jaw tightened, his teeth grinding. *Just go already!*

His gift strained, pulling from him, pressure building behind his eyes as a headache began to tighten.

He needed to act. The gate was too loud. But he didn't have a choice. So he'd just have to be quick. But he needed some time—he needed them to step away for a bit. What if he distracted them somehow? Would it lift high enough while they ran back?

He crept toward the Quasar Grill, struggling to keep his gift's masking in place. Out of sight, he released it for a moment. After a few breaths, he snatched a plate and shimmered invisible again, slipping back to the Pizzarama's gate.

He worked the picks as quietly as he could while also straining to maintain his gift, until the lock was ready to turn again. He had to hurry up—with every second, he felt his masking slipping away.

Holding the lockpicks in place with his off-hand, he balanced carefully and flung the plate with all his strength. It flew brilliantly, sailing down the corridor before shattering the stillness in a crash that resonated through the air.

The growlers whipped around and bolted toward the sound.

He twisted the lock, and the gate resumed creaking and clattering its way up—but he couldn't hold his gift anymore. In a shimmer, he was visible again.

"Run!" one of the growlers howled as they sprinted in his direction with terrifying speed.

Diego held his ground, pulse hammering, keeping the tension bar firmly in place. And they rushed closer. Every part of him screamed to run—but he needed this to work.

The gate creaked and rattled, rising a centimeter at a time until it was just high enough for him to slip through. He dove under it, rolling into the Atomic Pizzarama as the growlers slammed into the gate behind him. They pulled at the bars, snarling and hissing their chilling words.

He glanced at the gap under the gate, hoping they wouldn't just follow him.

Scrambling to the lock on the inside, Diego pulled out his picks, hands shaking.

The growlers clustered nearby, but he was just out of their reach. He worked quickly—all the while, the gap beneath the gate loomed large in the back of his mind.

One of them pressed its face tight against the bars. Its feet even slipped into the gap under the gate, and Diego struggled to keep focused on picking the lock.

How can they not see it?

The final pin slipped in place, and he turned the core against the spring. The gate descended, bottoming out with a crash.

His heart thundered in his chest as he stepped back. The growlers strained against the bars, eyes tracking Diego's every move, their presence a gut-curdling screech on his senses. Hoping they'd lose interest if they couldn't see him, he gathered tables, chairs, and debris, throwing together a makeshift barricade.

Turning away from the growlers, Diego surveyed the dimly lit interior of the Atomic Pizzarama. An oppressive stillness lingered in the air, thick with the scent of stale, dusty grease.

On the stage, the animatronic figures had not moved from their silent vigil over the room. Diego resisted the urge to inspect them—for now.

He made a quick sweep of the facility, his flashlight glancing over torn arcade tickets and scattered paper plates. Weaving through a maze of dark, dusty arcade machines, he came upon a shattered prize counter. Broken glass blanketed piles of cheap trinkets. After a run through the kitchen and a glance into the restrooms, he finally approached the stage.

He knew each of the characters by name.

At the center stood Rocket Remy, an intrepid astronaut mouse with an electric guitar, frozen in an action pose. Beside him was Cosmic Clara, a sleek, blue-and-white-striped space-traveling cat holding a bass guitar. Rounding out the gang were Galactic Grace, a colorful chameleon at her keyboard; Astro Andy, an astronaut dog on drums; and Jukebox Jack, a saxophone-playing brown bear.

Diego climbed onto the stage, memories of the characters' comic book escapades flickering through his mind. Now, here they were—larger than life.

His gaze lingered on Rocket Remy's guitar. Music had always been a source of comfort for him, tied to countless evenings spent learning to play at his father's side.

He reached for the guitar, only to find it fixed to the animatronic's arms. A prop. He scowled.

Moving on to the storage room behind the stage, he found it crammed with boxes, paper plates, cups, old equipment, and forgotten props. A Rocket Remy costume hung limply from a hook, dust clumping on its fur. Its oversized eyes stared blankly at the floor.

Then, on a shelf behind it, something caught his eye—a glint of polished wood. His heart skipped a beat.

No way...

Nestled between two boxes lay a battered guitar. A real one.

He pulled it free, savoring the familiar weight in his hands. Perched on a nearby crate, he carefully tuned each string. When he was finally satisfied, he strummed a chord. A soft smile touched his lips. He played another, then another. Soon, the music wrapped around him, and he quietly hummed along.

His fingers found the melody of his father's favorite song, and before he realized it, he was singing the chorus:

"Quiero volver, volver—"

He stopped, pressing his palm against the strings to still them.

The lyrics cut a little too close to home: *I want to go back, go back.*

But there was no going back.

A heavy silence filled the room. After a few heartbeats, Diego rose and gently returned the guitar to the shelf.

*   *   *

He lost track of the days as he transformed the Atomic Pizzarama into his new home. The heat couldn't be adjusted like in John Smith's cabin, but keeping watch on the lift mattered more than personal comfort.

His first task was rigging the "Explorers Only" entrance so he could come and go without trouble. After that, regular trips to Echo Ring followed, each time hauling back more bottles of Soylent Fusion. They'd last a while if he could ration them for the times when he couldn't stomach another bite of nutrient sludge.

After weeks of effort, Diego decided the Pizzarama was officially livable. He'd even arranged the arcade machines into a defensive gauntlet leading from the "Explorers Only" entrance.

At the front of the stage, he created a communal space he dubbed *the Den.* He'd hauled in mismatched furniture from lounges and offices along the promenade, building a rough but cozy setup.

He carved out a makeshift bedroom in the corner opposite the arcade, partitioning it off with tables, cabinets, and broken games. His mattress and bedding, scavenged from John Smith's cabin, finished it off. It wasn't great, but it'd do just fine as his personal lair.

Eventually, he gave in to the temptation and retrieved the guitar, spending his evenings quietly strumming its strings while keeping a vigilant eye on the maintenance lift. Music offered a fleeting sense of peace as he played deep into the night, working to remember every song he'd learned, jotting down the lyrics and scores alongside letters to Donna until his eyes grew too heavy to stay open.

*　　*　　*

Months passed uneventfully, marked only by the dwindling supply of Soylent Fusion. Then, one day, returning from a supply run that had included a quick flip through the dusty old magazines and comics in the convenience store, a rattle echoed down the corridor.

The maintenance lift.

A jolt of adrenaline shot through him.

Someone was coming.

He sprinted toward the sound, shimmering into invisibility without thinking. This was it.

The lift slid into view, and his breath caught.

Raphael.

A gut punch of fear and fury hit him, followed by the echoes of Raphael sneering *El Duende* ringing in his mind.

But this wasn't the intimidating nemesis he remembered.

This Raphael cowered in the lift, shivering in the cold, eyes wide and darting about. Each breath escaped his lips in misty puffs, and he clutched a kitchen knife in both hands, trembling as if it were the only thing keeping him alive.

Act 2

Trouble

Diego lurked on the edge of the hall, keeping himself invisible while struggling to summon any sympathy for the trembling boy before him. Did Raphael deserve to receive any help after all the torment he had inflicted?

The terrifying wails of the growlers closed in. Raphael stumbled out of the lift, darting into the plaza, desperately scanning for refuge.

When the first growler rounded the bend in the corridor, Raphael's face drained of color. Gripping the knife, his knuckles white, tears streaked down his face as he sobbed, "No! No! No! I don't want to get eaten!"

Diego's anger faltered. Despite their history, leaving anyone to face such a fate felt wrong, even if it was Raphael. Biting back a growl, Diego released his invisibility and grabbed Raphael's shoulder.

Raphael spun around, falling backward, the whites of his eyes showing at the sight of Diego in his Z-ball mask. He brandished the feeble kitchen knife, pleading, "Don't kill me!"

Diego ripped off his mask and thrust out his arm. "Come on!"

Recognition flickered in Raphael's eyes, and he grabbed Diego's hand, scrambling to his feet. Together, they bolted into the Pizzarama. Diego slammed the explorer's door shut and dropped a heavy bar into place just as the growlers crashed against it.

The pounding came relentlessly, punctuated by low, chilling hisses urging them to flee. The growlers knew they were still there and weren't about to give up. But slowly—agonizingly so—the hammering faded into the faint shuffle of retreating footsteps.

A stillness settled over the room. Raphael's eyes were wide, his chest heaving as he fought to steady himself. For him, the terror of their escape was a raw, brutal awakening. For Diego, it was just another day.

Their eyes locked, and a familiar fear stabbed through him as the past rushed back. Nothing had changed. Raphael still loomed large in his mind—a figure of antagonism and torment. The silence pressed down, laden with old wounds, bitter words, and resentment. Diego felt as if the station itself held its breath, waiting to see what Raphael would do. He braced for the worst.

"How... how are you still here?" Raphael said in a shaky voice.

A storm churned inside Diego—a tangle of fear, anger, and something darker. His throat tightened, and words failed him. So he stayed silent, jaw clenched, stare unflinching.

"Is Miguel here, too?" Raphael asked, nervously glancing around the Pizzarama.

Slowly, deliberately, Diego reached up and pulled his Z-ball mask into place, and the emotions churning within him began to calm.

Raphael gave a strained chuckle. "You scared the hell out of me back there. I thought you were a Deathmark. So... what's with the mask?"

Diego's silence lingered. After a few heartbeats, he managed to get out. "You cried like a baby."

Raphael attempted a laugh, but it fell flat. He waved a dismissive hand. "I bet you did, too, the first time you faced a growler."

Diego's gaze remained steady. Memories of that first harrowing encounter with the growlers flashed through his mind. Where Raphael had lost control of himself and succumbed to tears and panic, Diego had fought to survive.

He had been stronger than Raphael.

With this realization, the knot of dread gripping Diego's chest began to unravel. His perspective shifted, tilting on its axis. The fear of Raphael that had consumed him for years retreated, and in its place, a new feeling emerged: pity.

"It's been a while, amigo." Raphael straightened, studying Diego thoughtfully. "You seem changed somehow."

Diego offered a noncommittal shrug.

Raphael shifted uncomfortably, nervously chuckling before taking a deep breath and changing the conversation.

"So, Carlos decreed that all young men must come down here when they turn fourteen—said it's a 'rite of passage.'" Raphael ran a hand through his hair, visibly shaken by his recent brush with death.

"The psycho calls it God's trial. We either become a man down here... or... we don't, I guess." His voice cracked, taking on a whine as he went on, "First you, then Miguel, and now me. Because it's just my turn, right? And nobody could stop him!"

Diego's brow furrowed, and he finally broke his silence. "But why? Why does everybody go along with it? I suppose I get that they sent me down here because—" he stopped himself, pausing before awkwardly adding, "—but you guys, you know, are not like me."

Raphael swallowed, his eyes taking on a deeper fear. "Everybody is terrified of Carlos and his power. Some people who've opposed him have conveniently disappeared. So now everybody pretends to follow his religious dogma, even if they don't agree. My father didn't say a thing, but my mom tried to argue against it."

His voice went soft, "That's when they took her somewhere and... and they said she would be re-married to one of the Anointed. After that, my father stopped arguing."

It took a moment for Diego to process it all. Carlos was as bad as his parents had feared—if not worse.

"I'm sorry," was all he could think to say.

Raphael shrugged, "It's alright, amigo. So, where is Miguel?"

Diego glanced away. "I... I couldn't save him. I didn't think anyone else was coming down."

Raphael stepped closer, placing a hand on Diego's shoulder. After a moment, he said quietly, "It's not your fault, chavo."

The sincerity in Raphael's words caught Diego off guard. He met Raphael's gaze and reluctantly nodded—though his heart remained wary.

They stood still, the hum of the orbital's systems the only sound around them. In that shared moment, Diego felt his heart soften a little. Could he trust Raphael? Did he have a choice?

Diego broke the silence. "Did any others from Charlie make it to Bravo Ring? Maybe Donna?"

Raphael sighed. "Yeah, some did. But I don't know about Donna. La Familia does things differently. They keep the girls locked away from the boys."

Diego scowled, muttering, "So they are pale-igamisses."

Still, he forced himself to hold onto hope. She could have made it. And even if not, she could still be out there—surviving, just like he had. He desperately needed to believe that.

Raphael raised an eyebrow. "Do you mean polygamists?"

A flush crept up Diego's neck as he realized the word rang true. "Maybe. Yeah."

Raphael shrugged, then gave a dramatic shiver, rubbing his arms through the thin jumpsuit as the cold set in. "You know, it's pinche frío down here."

Diego smiled, watching Raphael's breath forming puffs in the air. "You get used to it."

"And you've survived in this for a year?" Raphael asked with a mix of awe and surprise in his voice.

Diego hesitated. Had it been a year? That meant he'd turned fourteen at some point.

After a long pause, Raphael looked down at his hands. "Diego... I'm sorry. I was an idiot back then. You're cool, I can tell. Can you forgive me?"

Diego studied Raphael, wondering if the remorse was genuine or simply fear-driven. Raphael looked awkward, almost fearful that his apology wouldn't be accepted.

Despite his doubts, Diego finally nodded. "Yeah... sure. It's in the past."

Raphael grinned, scanning the remnants of old arcade machines and toppled tables making up the barricade. "Pretty cool digs you've got here."

"It's secure," Diego offered, trying not to sound prideful as Raphael scanned the room.

"We stick together, right?" Raphael asked, his tone hopeful.

"Of course. And we'll be ready for when others are sent down."

Raphael drew in a deep breath. "Thanks for not leaving me out there."

Diego hesitantly repeated Raphael's assertion, "We're in this... together."

"Good. Because I've got your back," Raphael declared, eyeing Diego's scavenged attire. "Speaking of which, I'm all turtled up down below. It's like everything packed up and left. If I don't warm up soon, I might never see it again. Tell me there are warmer threads somewhere?"

Diego nodded, extending his senses and scanning the promenade with his gift. "There are stores. I'll take you to one. Just stay quiet and do exactly as I say."

He briefed Raphael on what to watch for and how to react, outlining the threats he'd faced—at least those on this level. He was careful to avoid mentioning his journey through the Link tubes—he wanted to keep that a secret for now.

Trailing a few steps behind, Raphael flinched at every creak and rattle as Diego led the way toward Woolwards. Diego used his gift to sense and nudge any threats away. But to keep up appearances, he occasionally pointed out a sudden noise or ominous shadow, and altered their course as though relying purely on instinct and skill.

Raphael's eyes darted about, his grip tightening on his feeble kitchen knife. "How do you slip past everything so smoothly?"

"Lots of practice," Diego offered, hoping he wouldn't ask more. He wasn't ready to divulge his secret.

Raphael nodded thoughtfully. They continued, and he studied Diego, working to mimic each step while straining to detect the same dangers Diego seemed to sense instinctively.

After several more turns, Raphael gestured toward Diego's wrist. "How did you get a passkey?"

"I found one, I guess. They're around... lots of people were lost to the Kraal."

Raphael considered a nearby pile of dusty clothing. Without a word, he knelt and began sifting through it.

"Hold on," Diego said, his objection surfacing when Raphael extracted a pair of lacy undergarments. "Don't go grabbing things."

Raphael stopped, leaving them dangling from his fingers. "Why not?"

Trying to avoid blushing, Diego quickly explained. "I've left the clothes in place. They're kind of like graves."

Raphael lifted an eyebrow. "Then, how did you get your passkey?"

"I found it in some trash."

Raphael looked skeptical. "Since I already started, is it okay with you if I just look for a passkey here? I promise I'll leave the others alone if I find one."

Despite his discomfort, Diego gave a curt nod.

Raphael resumed his search, tossing each article aside as he dug through the pile. His persistence paid off, and he extracted a passkey, straightening up with a triumphant grin. "Found one!"

Diego took a moment returning the garments to a neat pile while Raphael watched quietly, his expression unreadable. They continued, saying nothing more about the piles of clothes, and soon reached Woolwards.

Raphael took the disarray of the department store in stride, scanning the wide variety of merchandise littering the aisles as he followed Diego to the Young Men's section.

Clothes were scattered everywhere—a few still hanging on racks, others in heaps on the floor, with packages torn and strewn about. Raphael needed no prompting and dove into finding something that fit.

"Try this," Diego offered, handing Raphael a pair of dungarees.

Raphael changed out of the blue jumpsuit, tossing it aside before pulling on the rugged pants. Bitterness lined his voice as he started talking again. "Everybody is trying to get on Carlos's good side. We all figure coming down here isn't a trial, despite what Carlos says. It's a death sentence." Raphael flashed a grin, "Or it was."

"Why does he do it? I don't get it."

Raphael shrugged, pulling a sweater over his head. It was too big, but it would keep him warm. "Alcalde Carlos doesn't want competition for all the girls. The big guy has seven wives now."

Diego's eyes widened. "Seven? That's... loco."

"Yeah," Raphael muttered, squeezing his feet into thick-soled boots. "Plus, I've heard the Wardens are also trying to take over Serenity Orbital, but through negotiations or something, not force."

The boys continued searching, adding to the collection of clothes, and Diego found himself comparing his physique to Raphael's. He was keenly aware of his lanky frame, but he had always been taller than Raphael in the past. Now, they stood eye-to-eye. Raphael had also bulked out, his shoulders broadening, and he looked like he might become as athletic as his father.

As they passed the broken mirrors, Raphael asked. "Do you know why they're all smashed up?"

Diego adjusted his Z-ball mask unconsciously. "No."

Raphael studied Diego for a moment before rubbing his arms to get warm. "You're pretty clever. Have you tried asking the robots to turn up the heat?"

"Yeah, I tried. They're not exactly cooperative, especially Chip in Ring Ops."

Raphael's eyebrows shot up. "Officer Chip? There's one down here, too?"

"A standard model," Diego muttered. "I remember seeing a few on Charlie Ring."

Raphael clenched a fist. "Let me talk to 'em. I bet I can convince him."

A twinge of annoyance poked at Diego, and he struggled to suppress his rising irritation. *Why did Raphael think he could succeed where I had failed?*

After the day's events, Diego just wanted to retreat to the safety of the Pizzarama, but he relented and led Raphael to the operations center. They had to duck into a storage closet along the way, keeping silent as a group of growlers prowled by on the promenade, but otherwise made it safely.

A minute or two after they rang the bell, Chip rolled out, offering in an upbeat tone, "Greetings, Vagrant Smith!"

"Uh-huh," Diego started, gesturing to Raphael. "So I guess he's joining me and has some questions."

Chip's optics flickered as he assessed Raphael, and his perky tone gained a strained edge. "At this time, residency isn't permitted in Delta Ring, peaceful vagrant Smith. Will your friend be staying long?"

"He'll be here a while, I think. Same as me."

Chip emitted an exaggerated sigh, directing his attention to Raphael. "Another vagrant, then. How may I assist you today, friendly vagrant B791?"

Raphael squared his shoulders. "Chip, my man. Amigo, we need you to turn up the heat. It's freezing."

"Ah, unfortunately, I cannot help you there. Temperature regulation is dictated by facility protocols, and currently, we are in lockdown," Chip explained.

Raphael's tone grew more insistent. "Can you at least handle the growlers? They're dangerous."

"I'm sorry, peaceful vagrant, I cannot discern between you and these so-called growlers," Chip replied with an upbeat demeanor. "I cannot take any action that might cause any individual harm. And, as long as you don't damage the facility, I cannot restrain you. Besides, the brig isn't large enough to hold everybody!"

Diego watched with mild satisfaction as the conversation unfolded, one frustratingly upbeat but useless answer after another. He counted three times Chip called Raphael a Star Ranger, as if he were some aspiring kid working on a merit badge. Best of all, Chip even gave him a gold star for something utterly meaningless.

Through it all, Raphael's frustration became palpable as he argued and gestured, vainly trying to reason with the robot. Chip remained steadfast, cheerfully offering positive reinforcement with every denial.

"I insist on speaking to somebody in charge," Raphael finally declared, holding up his newly acquired passkey. "I need to file a formal complaint. Get me the manager!"

"I'll note your concerns and relay them, mister..." Chip paused, studying the card, then glanced at Raphael and finished, "Sally Freemont?"

Raphael didn't even hesitate as he beamed, "Yeah, that's me, sir. Sally. Hottest cat around."

"I see," Chip added dryly, "For the record, what is the nature of your complaint?"

"I just told you! Get your screws looked at or something." The fire in Raphael's voice faded before he'd even finished the sentence.

Diego saw it in his eyes—Raphael was finally realizing his efforts were getting him nowhere. He put a hand on Raphael's shoulder. "Come on. Maybe we should go. Leave Chip to his important work."

The fight drained from Raphael. "Yeah, fine."

After they left the ops center, Raphael grumbled, "You do realize that robot is completely loco, right?"

"He certainly has a few screws loose. I think he's stretching his duties a bit, and most of the other robots are out of commission." A grin flashed across Diego's face, and he couldn't help but add, his tone bold, "Miss Sally Freemont."

Raphael straightened, a hint of annoyance flickering in his eyes before he chuckled, turning the passkey over in his hand. "Right. Suppose I set myself up for that one. Should've checked the name first."

Then he glanced at Diego's wrist. "So, tell me, chavo: what name's on *your* passkey?"

"John," Diego replied smugly.

"Of course," Raphael chuckled, draping an arm around Diego's shoulders as they walked.

An unexpected warmth stirred in Diego's chest. Maybe having Raphael around wouldn't be so bad after all.

But, even as he let himself enjoy the moment, a lingering unease twisted in his gut, refusing to be ignored.

That night, as a precaution, Diego sifted through his journal, tearing out anything that might even hint at el sentido dotado. When he reached the first letter to Donna, he froze, the paper pinched between his fingers.

He couldn't risk giving Raphael any ammunition. But... after a long pause, he left it intact, reassuring himself it revealed nothing about his gift. He was willing to take the risk—for her. After all, without any mention of su sentido dotado in his journal, what was the worst Raphael could do?

Surfin' Bird

The next day, after hours spent expanding "the Lair" to make space for Raphael's bunk, they set out for the biosphere's maintenance door. Diego's stomach growled as he paused at a corner.

Raphael grinned, his kitchen knife clenched in cloth-wrapped fingers. "I hope the biosphere's still alive. Can't believe you've been living on nutrient sludge this whole time."

"Not like I had a choice," Diego grumbled. "You get used to it."

He paused mid-step, sensing a group of growlers down the hall to their right. Pointing toward the danger, Diego pressed a finger to his mouth. Without waiting for a response, he darted across the hall in a low crouch, pressing himself against the wall on the other side. Turning back, he motioned for Raphael to follow.

Raphael hesitated, his grip tightening on the knife. For a moment, Diego thought he might freeze. But then Raphael set his jaw and slipped across to join him. The scritch of his feet on the floor seemed impossibly loud to Diego, grating on his nerves.

After a few more turns, they reached the same maintenance door Diego had started to unlock when Raphael first arrived. Diego knelt and pulled out his picks. Raphael hovered close, watching each move, intent on learning how it was done. Minutes ticked by. Time and again Diego had managed to set most of the pins, but the last one kept eluding him. Raphael started pacing, glancing nervously down the hall.

"I thought you said you could do this?" he whispered.

Diego nodded, staying focused on the lock. "I can; it's just a tough one."

Finally, he felt the last pin slip into place, and turned the knob.

"¡Híjole! You did it!" Raphael exclaimed. "Where'd you learn that?"

Diego's mask hid his grin as he eased the door open to find a clean and orderly workshop—a stark contrast to the orbital's general state of disarray. Meticulously organized tools and equipment were neatly arranged on benches and shelves, covered in decades of dust. The faint tang of ozone and oil lingered in the air.

They stepped in and closed the door behind them, scanning the room. On the far side, an automatic door marked "Biosphere Airlock" stood waiting. The steady yellow light of a maglock control panel glowed faintly at its side.

Diego didn't hold out much hope but they both tried their passkeys. As expected, the panel flashed red for each one, denying them entry.

"Maybe we should go find more cards?" Raphael suggested.

Diego considered Sharon's passkey in his pocket. While it hadn't opened any of the main biosphere doors, he had fostered a small hope that, since this was a maintenance room, her access might help him out somehow. But he wasn't ready to reveal Sharon's key just yet. Instead, he had to go for plan B: using the emergency door controls hidden behind the panel. "I think we can get in if we open it manually."

The workshop offered up tools far better than any Diego had found so far. Armed with this unexpected bounty, they dismantled the control panel—only to hit a new problem. Diego stared at the tangle of wires. All he needed to do was disable the alarm, but what he saw didn't match what the Usenet guide had described, and he was pretty sure the system would go off if he got it wrong.

"What's the holdup?"

"I thought there'd be three wires going into the maglock," Diego muttered. "But there are four."

Raphael nodded sagely, eyeing the wires alongside him. "So… we just pull one or something?"

"No!" Diego held up a short wire, "I have to bridge two of the contact terminals, but I don't know which ones."

"¡Ándale, chavo!" Raphael howled, snatching the wire and pressing it on two contacts.

The panel emitted sharp beeps, and Diego's stomach dropped. Lunging for his pack, he prepared to bolt before any security bots arrived.

Raphael laughed. "Chavo! Chill out! Look, it's fine."

The beeping had stopped, and the lights changed to a pulsing blue.

Diego shot him a glare. "Don't ever do that again."

Raphael lifted a hand in surrender, the other still holding the wire in place. "Of course, don't worry. Mi culpa. So can you make this stick?"

Diego returned and fastened the wire to the contacts with a screwdriver, sullenly marveling at Raphael's luck.

The manual crank opened the door slowly, revealing a small airlock chamber beyond.

"Wait a sec," Raphael said. "If we can only open this by hand, how do we close it from inside?"

Diego shut his eyes, realizing the flaw in his plan.

Like any airlock, only one of the two doors could open at a time. That wouldn't be a problem, except the inner chamber had no access panel. Diego's hand hovered near his pocket, feeling Sharon's key, but another idea sparked. "The doors aren't locked from in there—only out here. Maybe you go in first, then I'll crank it shut and reset the maglock. When the light changes, you can open it up and let me in."

Raphael nodded, seeming to understand. Diego put his plan in motion, cranking the door closed with Raphael inside. He stepped back, his eyes fixed on the door, waiting for it to open.

Several heartbeats passed. The door remained sealed. Seconds stretched into minutes, and Diego shifted from foot to foot, a creeping worry building in him. Was Raphael trapped? Diego stepped toward the hand crank, ready to open it manually, when the door hissed and retracted into the wall. Raphael stood inside, his expression sour.

"What happened? I thought it was stuck."

Raphael shook his head, his voice hollow. "Nah, it worked fine. Just—the biosphere's dead."

Diego's emotions flared as he realized Raphael had already looked into the biosphere. He clenched his jaw and slapped the button, sealing them in the small chamber together.

"Why didn't you wait?" Diego snapped.

Raphael shrugged. "Figured I'd just peek. Didn't hurt anybody, right, chavo?"

The inner door slid open, revealing a vast, hauntingly empty chamber covered in shadow. Overhead, the dark expanse of space loomed, separated by a vaulted grid of steel and transparent-alloy panels. A sliver of Arcadia barely glimmered where the canopy met the orbital walls. Stale decay hung in the air, the soil barren, littered with the dead remnants of vegetation, and the chill of Delta Ring remained.

The biospheres were typically part of a circular ecosystem, with lush spaces, cultivated fields, trees, ponds, and wildlife. Here, the emptiness left him with a hollow sense of loss. The chamber's sheer scale was staggering, even greater than a Z-ball arena—easily massive enough to hold two rocket ships end-to-end.

His flashlight flickered over their path as they ventured deeper, passing between support pillars and across the barren terrain. Neither spoke, the grim reality sinking in—there was no food. They'd have to keep eating sludge.

Diego scanned the sterile landscape. He had hoped for a verdant chamber rich with life, but instead, this barren wasteland struck him hard. He kicked at the ground, growling, "Do you think they just killed everything when they shut it down?"

Raphael yawned, his interest clearly waning. "How would I know?"

The thin sliver of Arcadia overhead slipped away, leaving the biosphere cast in starlit shadows.

"We should head out, chavo," Raphael muttered, an edge of unease touching his voice.

They turned back, retracing their steps as Diego swept his flashlight far and wide. He paused when the beam glanced off something in the distance. Approaching, they discovered some agricultural equipment alongside a cylindrical vat, its circular access port sealed tight.

"What's in it?" Raphael asked.

"Probably chemicals or something to help with farming. Doubt it's anything we could eat."

Raphael reached for the wheel on the access portal. "I'll open it."

"I thought you wanted to get out of here?"

"Sure, sure, but you know you want to see inside, too," Raphael said, pulling on the wheel. It protested with a rusty chatter before finally giving way. A wave of rank, earthy odor hit them as he pulled the portal open.

"Algae," Raphael gagged.

Diego hesitated, sensing something wasn't right. The algae felt different, almost like a faint void-touched thing. It wasn't menacing, but something was definitely there. Holding his breath, he glanced inside, shining his flashlight over the vat's contents. A thick mat of algae floated on the water's surface.

He pinched a bit between his fingers, carefully bringing it close to his nose.

"Estellar," Raphael whispered. "Turn off your flashlight!"

Diego complied, and as the darkness wrapped around them, the algae on his fingers shimmered with a soft, ethereal green glow.

Raphael plunged his hand into the vat, pulling it out covered in algae. Soon, the same faint light glistened where it touched his skin.

"Chidísimo," Raphael murmured, wonder coloring his voice. He wiped his hand on his sleeve, only to see the glow gradually fade.

"It lights up when in contact with our skin," Diego observed.

Unable to resist, they continued experimenting with the curious substance. With every handful, a strange euphoria grew inside them. Laughter bubbled up, unbidden and contagious, and a sense of reckless abandon took hold. They painted symbols and playful, if not indecent, messages and drawings across the side of the vat—but those faded quickly.

Raphael traced a skull on his face, and painted glowing lines along his fingers like bones, then pulled off his jacket and shirt to add skeletal ribs. He swung his arms around, oblivious to the cool air. Diego watched in fascination as the light left luminescent trails of green in the darkness.

Curiosity overpowering caution, Diego shrugged off his jacket and rolled up his sleeves. He shoved his arms into the water, past his elbows. When he drew them out, glowing ripples shimmered along his skin. Its touch flooded him with energy. A curious sense of release washed over him, as if the weight of the past year suddenly didn't matter.

Raphael bounded over, his eyes gleaming with wild excitement. "Do I look like a skeleton? Tell me I look like a skeleton!"

Diego grinned, a surge of exhilaration coursing through him. "Straight out of Día de los Muertos!"

"Let me paint a skull on your face, too!" Raphael demanded, dipping his hand back into the vat.

Without hesitation, Diego pulled off his Z-ball mask, a silly grin spreading across his face as Raphael's algae-coated fingers brushed his cheeks. The cold air didn't matter. The glow on their bodies felt electric. Normally, Diego was fiercely private, always careful to cover his mottled skin in front of others. But now, for reasons he couldn't explain, he didn't care.

Their laughter echoed through the chamber, unrestrained and carefree, as they stripped down further, painting one another in elaborate designs and symbols.

One of Arcadia's moons rose in the starscape beyond the canopy, bringing a soft light to the chamber. Raphael threw back his head and howled like a wolf. Diego joined him, and together, they surrendered to the moment. They ran, leaping and hooting across the barren terrain like feral spirits, streaks of light trailing behind them as they moved with pure, reckless abandon.

Diego's vision shifted. Colors sharpened, becoming vividly surreal even in the darkness. A colossal owl materialized ahead, its massive wings stretching wide, halting Diego in his tracks. Raphael's laughter faded into the background, a mere speck compared to the reverent hush that came with the Owl.

Its vast and knowing gaze carried centuries of knowledge compressed into a single moment, pinning Diego in place. He felt an unspoken offer—a silent invitation. Ancient, cosmic secrets flickered in its eyes. Truths so profound they stirred a deep ache in his chest, filling him with an unbearable desire to understand.

"Tell me!" Diego cried, voice trembling.

The Owl stretched its wings in an immense span, reaching beyond the station's walls. It ascended with a few powerful beats, perching in the latticework high above. Diego's heart raced. The need to uncover its secrets drove his steps as he scrambled up a ladder attached to one of the support pillars. Its head tilted as it watched his approach with an inscrutable gaze.

Raphael's laughter rang out far below, calling to him. "You can fly!"

Just as Diego thought he was close enough to receive the Owl's knowledge, it launched into space, disappearing through the glass into the stars beyond. A fierce, irresistible urge to follow surged within him, and suddenly, he felt he could follow it. He stretched his arms wide, and leaped from the ladder.

For a fleeting, exhilarating moment, he felt a sensation far beyond weightlessness—the thrill of freefall. Air whipped around him, and he closed his eyes, convinced his arms had turned into wings— that he wasn't falling but flying.

The impact came hard and fast, knocking the air from his lungs as his body struck the cold, unyielding ground. Darkness closed in, and he thought he heard tree branches snapping—which was odd, because he didn't remember seeing any trees.

Lean on Me

Diego woke with dirt in his mouth and the copper tang of blood on his tongue. Raphael's hoots and hollers echoed around him, oblivious to what had just happened. Diego shifted, and white-hot fire ripped through him.

He didn't feel the pain exactly, but somewhere in the haze, he knew something was wrong. Badly wrong. Maybe a broken leg. Maybe more.

Gasping, he spat the dirt from his mouth and managed to roll onto his back. He took a moment to catch his breath. His gaze drifted to the overwhelming blackness beyond the glasswork canopy, and he couldn't tell if the flickers in his vision were sparks of pain or stars in space.

Mustering his strength, Diego used dirt to scour the algae from his body while feebly calling Raphael for help. He cried out several times until Raphael stepped into his field of vision, exclaiming, "Chavo! You flew! You were amazing. I'm going to go do it too!"

"No!" Diego groaned, feeling his lips going cold. "Med... bay."

"Medbay?" Raphael asked, furrowing his brow.

Diego struggled to speak between gasps, "I'm... really... bad... off."

"You are bad, amigo!" Raphael nodded in admiration, "El chidísimo!"

Diego lifted his arm, groaning, "Help me up."

"Do you want me to help you fly? I can help you fly again!"

Diego blinked, trying to focus as the world swam around him. His breath came in shallow huffs, each inhale a sharp stab to his chest. "Yes," he finally managed to say.

Raphael lifted him from the ground with unexpected strength. Diego held tight, careful to keep his injured leg elevated, relieved to see it didn't hang awkwardly—perhaps the break wasn't too severe.

Shivering from the cold, Diego glanced around, realizing he had no idea where his jacket and shirt had ended up. He stabbed a finger toward the exit. "Medbay."

"What is Medbay? You want to fly there?" Raphael questioned with surprising intensity, his grip on Diego's chest tightening as if ready to lift him higher.

Diego winced, grateful for the algae dulling the pain, but he didn't know how long its effects would last—he needed to get to Medbay before they faded.

Carefully reaching out, he gripped Raphael's chin, locking eyes with him. "Take... me... to... Med... bay."

"A bay?" Raphael's eyes widened, his voice gaining a note of breathless excitement. "Can we find boats there? We can sail on the ocean! Tell me you'll go with me!"

Diego scowled, pointing at the ground. "Clean off the algae with dirt."

Raphael furrowed his brow in confusion. But as he studied Diego's dirt-smeared chest and arms, a wide grin spread on his face. He scooped up a handful of soil and began muttering in a sing-song manner as he used it to scrub away the algae. Diego strained to catch the words, which sounded like an impromptu sea shanty about transforming into a mud-man with his chavo.

Once Raphael finished, Diego leaned on him and they hobbled out of the biosphere. Raphael persisted in his silly chant, urging Diego to sing along so they could be mud men together.

As they entered the corridors, Raphael finally fell silent. Diego hoped this marked a growing realization of his situation.

Diego paused now and then, leveraging his gift to clear their path—each use amplifying the symphony of pain spreading through his body.

At last, they reached Medbay, and Raphael helped him onto the nearest bed. The algae's numbing effect was already fading, and with it, any relief. His nerves blazed with escalating fire. He collapsed back, desperate for unconsciousness to take him.

Raphael's voice came to him, muffled and urgent. Meddi replied, but her words blurred into an incomprehensible buzz.

Diego squeezed his eyes shut, praying for the agony to stop. His gift only made it worse, its unraveling amplifying everything: sound, smell, pain, all blending into a singular chaotic uproar.

Cold fingers startled him as Meddi forced his eyelids open. A light flashed in his left eye, then his right, while she asked questions he couldn't understand. His vision swam. Sounds drowned beneath the thudding in his ears until, mercifully, darkness claimed him.

*　　*　　*

A soft, persistent beeping filled the air, sharp with the scent of antiseptic. Diego's eyes opened to a bleary view of discolored ceiling panels. His tongue stuck to the roof of his mouth, lips dry. Everything felt heavy and sore.

After a moment's effort, he raised his arm, only to have it stop short—something restrained him. Straps? Why was he strapped to a bed? Panic and confusion surged as he struggled to remember where he was and why, and then the memories of their wild antics in the biosphere came flooding back.

Meddi stepped into view. "You are awake," she stated in a no-nonsense tone as she removed the restraints holding him in place.

He turned his head carefully, the muscles in his neck tight. Nearby, Raphael lay slumped in a chair, cocooned tightly in a blanket, eyes closed in sleep, head tilted back, mouth wide open. Dirt and debris marred every visible centimeter of him, and his dark hair was a tangled thicket. Diego figured he didn't look any better, and struggled to understand why they had acted so recklessly.

Meddi moved into his line of sight, and he realized she was repeating a question. "You have had quite the accident. Can you please provide details for the incident report?"

He squinted at her, trying to gather his thoughts through the haze as she fired off questions, probing for details about the accident and any guardians they had who should be notified.

Diego's mind tumbled with disjointed memories. Something about an owl that wanted to talk to him? He couldn't figure out what to say—any story he came up with would sound just as ridiculous as trying to explain the walking trees last time.

"There is no guardian, okay? Nobody. No parents. No one to contact," he rasped, shifting his attention to the cast on his arm. "What did I break?"

"You have fractured your leg, arm, and several ribs, consistent with a high-impact collision. Fortunately, there are no spinal injuries," Meddi said. "I have applied casts to your arm and leg, as well as binding your chest. I do not have the healing solution needed to accelerate your recovery. Therefore, your injuries will take two months to heal, so you should return weekly for a checkup unless you find medical aid elsewhere. I can provide a crutch for mobility, but you will want to move as little as possible for the first week."

She paused before continuing, her tone unwavering, "Naturally, this is information your guardian should be informed of. Whom should I contact?"

"I—uh, I think I'll get back to you on that. I'm feeling… sleepy," Diego mumbled, hoping she'd leave him alone.

Meddi remained nearby, her optics dimming to a soft blue as she silently observed him.

He knew she wouldn't be satisfied with any answer he could give, so he closed his eyes, weighing his options. The irony wasn't lost on him—he had survived on his own for some time, yet now he was being held by a machine that couldn't accept he had no one to look after him. With the casts, he couldn't just run off like last time.

Raphael's soft snores reached Diego, stirring a new churn of worry in his gut as the realization sank in: he'd have to depend on Raphael during his recovery. But what choice did he have?

Taking a deep breath, Diego struggled to sit up with casts on his arm and leg. His head spun as he scanned the room, searching for ideas, until his gaze locked onto the control terminal near Meddi's charging station.

She repeated, "Please provide the contact information for your guardian."

Diego clenched his jaw. Robots were so annoying! He needed to find a way to make her understand—or at least to get her to stop asking about guardians, especially if he had to return each week. "I don't have one," he finally answered, struggling to keep the growl out of his voice.

"That is not an acceptable response," Meddi said, her optics flickering. "You are an unattended minor, Mr. Smith. However, that is not your real name. The actual Mr. Smith is on record at fifty-seven years old, and you are clearly not that age. Orbital security has an individual fitting your description listed as Vagrant 37A2. Until a verified guardian assumes custody, you will remain under observation in this facility."

Diego's heart lurched. Was that why she'd restrained him earlier? Had she already told Chip?

He forced a shrug, weakly waving her off. "Just... go charge or something. I'm sure someone's coming."

Meddi paused, then gave a curt nod before returning to her station. After her optics dimmed, Diego let out a slow, shaky breath, muttering quietly, "Unattended minor? You don't say..."

Should he wake Raphael and run for it before Meddi reactivated? What about his checkup visits? No, he needed a permanent solution. Something that would keep her from strapping him down for "observation" after every visit.

After waiting to be sure she was fully dormant, he carefully slid off the bed. The cold floor shocked his bare feet. He hobbled across the room, steadying himself on nearby cabinets, beds, and scattered medical equipment. Each heartbeat pulsed a fresh ache down his leg.

A hand-worn sign hung across the terminal's front, "Staff Use Only" scrawled in fading marker.

He lifted it—and the brittle tape gave out, leaving the paper in his hand. He set it aside and stared at the dark screen.

Would Meddi wake up if he used the terminal?

Only one way to find out.

With a flick of the switch, the green screen hummed to life. Scanlines flickered as it warmed up, resolving into a login prompt.

Diego knew he wasn't much of a hacker—his ham-fisted attempts to break into the station's library when he'd first arrived had made that clear. And he definitely didn't want Chip showing up again.

Chewing his lip, he racked his brain.

He peeked under the keyboard, hoping someone had written down a password—but no luck. Then he noticed the back of the sign, scribbled in pencil:

> *user: STAFF*
> *pass: SMILE!*

"Wow," he muttered, remembering his teacher warning against writing down passwords—not that he was about to complain. He typed in the credentials—one awkward key at a time. It wasn't easy with one arm in a cast, but he managed.

And he was in.

A grim smile crept across his face as he navigated the menus. Finally, something was going his way. He tabbed through each, searching for anything useful. He had to hurry—he didn't know how long Meddi would stay dormant, or what she'd do if she woke up and caught him digging around.

He started to worry this was a dead end when he found a section labeled "Personalities." He scrolled through a list of choices designed for different scenarios, like "Bubbly Nurse," "Wellness Guru," and "Battlefield Medic." Then, near the bottom, one entry caught his eye: "Configure Personality."

He selected that option and found a wide range of settings, covering everything from "Empathy Index" to "Bedside Manner." One in particular drew his attention: "Hippocratic Compliance." A warning flashed beside it:

> THIS OPTION RELAXES ALL CONSTRAINTS AROUND TREATING
> PATIENTS. USE ONLY UNDER CONTROLLED LABORATORY
> SITUATIONS.

Diego wasn't sure what "Hippocratic" meant, but the option sounded exactly like what he needed. Hoping it would stop Meddi from constantly interrogating them, he enabled it then quickly shut off the terminal and hobbled back to bed.

Some time later, the clank and whir of Meddi reactivating woke him. Raphael stirred on the nearby chair, rubbing his eyes and stretching. Remembering what he'd done, Diego's pulse quickened. Would it work?

Meddi's optics brightened as she approached.

Raphael groaned. "I told you before: we don't have a guardian!"

She ignored him, focusing on Diego with unsettling cheer. "Is the subject experiencing discomfort? I'm here to make it all better," she gently patted his cast. "Just say the word, and I'll remove whatever's causing the problem."

Diego stared at her hand on his cast, wondering what she was trying to say. At least she hadn't brought up guardians this time. "I think I'll be fine. I want to leave now, okay?"

"Of course," she nodded. "Please return if you need additional medical aid. I can assist with any detachments or modifications. On the house!"

Diego blinked. "You can what!?"

But Raphael was already on his feet, quickly bundling up his blanket and hurrying to help Diego. "Don't argue with her, chavo. We need to get out of here before she changes her mind."

Diego didn't need to be told twice. Whatever the setting had changed, he wasn't about to stick around to see how far it went. Raphael helped him off the bed, and together they quickly retreated. Once they were safely away, Diego explained what he'd done.

Raphael grinned. "Stellar!"

As they made their way back, Diego was relieved to find his head didn't hammer when he reached for his gift, allowing him to navigate to the Pizzarama without incident.

Raphael helped him onto the sofa, then waved in the general direction of the biosphere. "Do you think we did all that because of the algae?"

Diego rubbed his temple, pushing against a lingering ache. "I don't know. But I think we were lucky this time," he mumbled, eyes closed. "Maybe we should avoid that stuff in the future."

Raphael hesitated, as if he wanted to say more. When he finally spoke, his voice was surprisingly subdued. "You didn't, uh... jump because I said you could fly, did you?"

Diego managed a faint smile. "No, I'm pretty sure that was all the algae's effects."

Relief washed over Raphael's face.

*   *   *

Diego lay on his bed in the Pizzarama, staring at the ceiling, fingers drumming an erratic rhythm against his thigh. His thoughts spiraled endlessly in his head. Normally, he'd turn to his guitar for refuge, but now it sat nearby, silent and mocking, a cruel reminder of what he couldn't do with his arm trapped in a cast.

After a year on his own, relying on someone else carved a deep well of frustration in him. The memory of past antagonism lingered, and he couldn't shake the worry that Raphael might slip back into his old ways.

But as the days passed, Raphael surprised him. He anticipated Diego's needs without being asked—rearranging the Lair for comfort and keeping food and water within reach.

He also made a point of drawing Diego into conversation, even when he wasn't in the mood to talk. His persistence was disarming, and he had a knack for coaxing out stories. Diego, though selective in what he shared, gradually opened up about the trials he'd faced over the past year. Raphael responded with his own colorful tales—mostly Z-ball-related—which made it feel, strangely, like two old friends just talking.

In the moments when his pain dulled to a manageable ache, Diego began teaching Raphael the survival skills he'd honed, including how to pick locks. Their conversations often circled back to the disgusting monotony of eating nothing but nutrient sludge.

"Ever tried eating the things running around out there?" Raphael asked one day.

"Yeah, but... eating void-rat?" Diego made a gagging sound.

"There's other things, too, right? Like... growlers."

Diego frowned, not quite sure if Raphael was joking. "Growlers used to be people."

Raphael shrugged. "Used to be," he said, as if that made all the difference. "Surely there's something else crawling around?"

Diego thought of the horde of spiders lurking in the link tunnels, but kept that to himself. "Probably, but all I've seen are rodents of unusual size."

"What do they eat? Maybe we could eat that, too."

"They're void terrors; I don't think they need to eat."

"Great. So, let's hunt the rats."

That led to a discussion about the need for better weapons—their current arsenal of a dull kitchen knife and Diego's Top Slugger bat left a lot to be desired.

They returned to the workshop once Diego could manage to hobble around on his crutch for extended periods. Raphael quickly took charge, tapping into skills he'd learned from his metalsmithing father. They scavenged materials from the scrap bins, piecing together crude but functional weapons.

Diego added jagged spikes to his bat, turning it into a terrifying-looking mauler. The two also fashioned a handful of long knives—each crude, but still wickedly sharp. Rafe crafted a pair of swords: simple designs with slotted guards, Bakelite handles pinned in place, and rough pommels welded to the ends. He grumbled the entire time that without a forge, the blades could never be tempered properly, but what choice did they have?

When their work was finally done, Raphael could barely contain his excitement. "Alright, time to put these bad boys to the test," he announced, confidently spinning his swords with a grin that matched his swagger.

Diego shook his head. "I think it's best if you wait so we can go together."

Raphael's eyes narrowed, and he spun on his heel, pacing the workshop. "Come on, chavo. I'm not helpless." He sliced the air with practice jabs. "What's the point of making these if I can't use them?"

Diego held his ground. Raphael didn't know that he'd kept the growlers away with his gift. If they didn't go together, Rafe would be growler food within an hour. But how could Diego explain the danger without revealing el sentido dotado? Should he just tell Rafe about his gift? Or would he see it as a weakness to mock?

No, he couldn't risk the truth. Instead, he racked his brain for another way to channel Raphael's restless energy.

Growing up, Diego had found refuge in books and the hum of comm terminals rather than social interactions. His self-directed study through the orbital's vast library of knowledge had taught him many things, and now an idea surfaced: martial arts.

But could they teach themselves? The idea was almost laughable—didn't learning this stuff take years under the guidance of an expert? However, Diego knew Raphael's enthusiasm for physical challenges far outstripped his interest in academics—perhaps enough that it might keep him occupied.

Weighing his words carefully, Diego met Raphael's gaze. "If you want to live to tell about it, maybe we should train first. Learn some moves before you go charging in. I remember seeing some martial arts guides in Serenity's library."

"Wait—seriously?" Raphael's sulk vanished in an instant. "That's brilliant!"

They spent hours at the public comm terminals, combing through the library and old Usenet groups, digging up every martial arts training guide they could find—many of which came from a distant world called Miratori.

Armed with the information and driven by a need for space to practice, the Pizzarama underwent a new transformation. Raphael cleared an elevated corner of the restaurant, hauling away tables, booths, and debris to create a makeshift sparring arena. They repurposed the animatronic Remy figure, stripping it down to its metal frame and wrapping it in bedding to fashion a crude sparring dummy.

During their first practice session, Diego tapped the sketch he'd drawn from one of the guides. "Maybe lift your arms higher and lean forward more."

"Like this?" Raphael asked, adjusting his stance.

Diego leaned on his crutch, frowning. "Not bad, but straighten your back more. And it said you must focus on your center of gravity—do you know what that means?"

Raphael smirked. "You'd know if you ever bothered to show up to fitness class."

Diego shot him a flat look, his grip tightening on the crutch. The words escaped before he could stop them. "Maybe I would have if someone hadn't made my life so miserable."

The smirk vanished, and Raphael's ears turned pink. "Come on," he muttered. "I said I was sorry. What more do you want?"

Diego drew a sharp breath, biting back the responses burning on his tongue. Neither of them spoke for a few beats. His jaw clenched as he wrestled with what to say. Raphael had apologized, hadn't he?

Shouldn't that be enough?

And yet, it wasn't. Something still lingered—not anger, exactly, but the sense that he couldn't quite trust him.

Raphael cleared his throat, his tone sounding forced. "So, uh... straight back, yeah?"

Diego released a slow breath, recognizing the deliberate shift in topic.

"Yeah." He adjusted Raphael's stance with a nudge of his crutch. "And stop staring at your feet—you look like you're trying to figure out how to tie your shoes."

Raphael snorted. "Nah, I've got that all figured out. I can tie 'em myself, because I'm a big boy!"

A reluctant smile tugged at the corner of Diego's lips. "Shut up and try again."

The session continued, their conversation flowing more naturally as they settled into a rhythm. By the time they finished, Diego wasn't sure if the earlier tension had eased or if they'd just gotten better at ignoring it.

As the weeks passed, they honed their weapons, organized their sanctuary, and refined their martial arts techniques. Slowly, Diego felt the internal walls he'd built against Raphael were beginning to crumble—not all the way, but a little. Something still held him back. He had doubts. Could he ever truly forgive Raphael? Could a single apology erase years of torment?

One evening, after a checkup with Meddi, Diego grabbed a bottle from their dwindling supply of Soylent Drink. He wanted to shake the wariness he still felt around Rafe, but he struggled. For no reason he could name, everything Rafe did that day had just grated on his nerves.

Twisting off the cap, Diego tried to ignore the frustration simmering inside him and took a careful sip, savoring the brief reprieve from nutrient sludge. He hobbled toward the couch, silently counting the days until he could finally shed the casts for good.

Raphael leaned against the table, idly tossing a knife and catching it midair.

Diego stared at the knife, the knot in his chest tightening. But it wasn't the knife that bothered him—it was Rafe.

Irritation flared, creating an edge in his voice. "Do you have to do that?"

"What? It's not like I'm going to drop it." Raphael flashed his usual grin and tossed the knife again—but this time, the throw went wide. His eyes flared as he lunged to catch it, colliding with Diego.

The bottle slipped from Diego's hand and shattered on the floor. He froze, staring at the precious Soylent Drink seeping into the dingy carpet tiles. Something inside him finally broke, and he exploded.

"What the hell, Rafe! Do you ever think about what you're doing?"

"Whoa, chill, amigo—" Raphael raised his hands and stepped back.

"Don't tell me to chill!" Diego's voice shot up. "We're running out of supplies, and you don't seem to care!"

Raphael blinked, his grin evaporating. "It was an accident, alright? I wasn't trying to—"

Diego cut him off. "Yeah? Just like you weren't 'trying' when you made my life hell?"

Years of suppressed anger ripped loose, and he just kept going. "You don't think about anybody but yourself! You never have! You just do whatever you want and don't care what happens to anyone else!"

Raphael opened his mouth, then closed it, his usual bravado faltering. "Hey, that's not fair," he muttered.

"Not fair?" Diego's breath came in sharp bursts as he fought to control the storm raging inside him. "Do you have any idea what it was like? The things you did—the things you said—how much it hurt? You were the worst, Raphael. The absolute worst."

His chest heaved as the rest spilled out in a cold hiss. "I hated you. You made me wish I could disappear. And now—and now you expect me to just forget all that? Like none of it mattered?"

The rattle of the environmentals filled the silence, amplifying the anger hanging in the air. Thick. Heavy. Suffocating.

Diego let out a shaky breath, swiping at his cheeks, furious at himself for showing such vulnerability.

"I—" Raphael started, then stopped. He picked at the broken edge of the table's laminate.

"I deserve that," he said, hesitant. "And... you're right. Back then. The way I acted... to you..."

His jaw tightened. "I've said it before, and I'll keep saying it if that's what it takes. I was a jerk. I was mean. And yeah... I'm sure it must have sucked for you."

Diego blinked, his anger colliding with the remorse in Raphael's voice. His fists tightened, but the heat behind them began to ebb. "It hurt," he admitted quietly. "A lot of people were mean, but you... You were the worst."

Raphael ran a hand through his hair. "I was a stupid kid who didn't know what to do with his own crappy life, so I took it out on you. I hate that I made you feel like that. You didn't deserve any of it."

"Your own crappy life?" Diego's eyes narrowed. "How would that ever justify what you did?"

Raphael's shoulders sagged, and his voice wavered as he spoke. "My parents... they didn't want me around. My mom always told me it was my fault she was stuck on Serenity. That she wished I was never born—"

His voice caught, and he drew in a shaky breath before continuing. "That she didn't want to take care of me. If I stepped out of line, she made sure I felt it. And man, could she hit hard. My dad... he wasn't any better. If I complained, he'd just add a few more kicks. I always wore long sleeves to hide the bruises."

Raphael glanced away, his voice quieter than Diego had ever heard. "The way I treated you... It made me feel bigger, I guess. Like I wasn't the one being kicked around for once." His eyes flickered up to Diego's. "But it was wrong. I know that now."

Diego stared at him, his chest tightening. He had never stopped to consider what was going on in Raphael's life. Everyone on the orbital always seemed so put together, so normal. But now, seeing Raphael like this, a thread of guilt tugged at him, unraveling his anger.

For years, he'd assumed Raphael's actions came from pure malice. He'd never stopped to consider what struggles Rafe might've faced at home. Diego had grown up with loving parents—Rafe clearly had not.

And now, after everything, he'd just blown up at him. Called him horrible. All without a single thought about any troubles Raphael might have.

The silence lingered, heavy with unspoken words. Raphael rubbed his eyes, his voice barely above a whisper. "Can you—can you forgive me?"

Diego didn't know what to say.

After a long moment, Raphael gasped and waved a hand. "Never mind. Forget it. I understand if you hate me," he muttered, turning away.

Diego surprised himself as his hand reached for his Z-ball mask. He pulled it off, drawing a deep breath. "It's okay," he said. A weight began to lift from his shoulders as he continued. "I don't know if I can forget. But maybe... I think I can forgive."

Raphael's eyes welled up, and a relieved smile spread across his face. He stood abruptly, clearing his throat and wiping at his cheeks, muttering something about dust in the air before walking away.

That night, Raphael's energy was palpable.

"We should have a name for the two of us," he said, leaning forward with a grin. "Something to show we're in this together."

Diego raised an eyebrow. "A name?"

"Yeah, like the Renegades—because we're rebels surviving down here. Or maybe Los Sombras? 'Cause we're surviving in the shadows?"

A grin tugged at Diego's lips as he warmed to the idea. "Guerreros? Warriors?"

Raphael considered the suggestion for a moment, then snapped his fingers. "What about the Atomic Wolves? We are in the Atomic Pizzarama, right? Los Lobos Atómicos?"

Diego's gaze drifted over the broken furniture, tangled bedding, and the scattered bits of junk they'd scavenged to survive. The stark reality of their situation suddenly pressed in, making the conversation feel oddly childish.

Not wanting to hurt Raphael's feelings, he chose his words carefully.

"I… don't think we need a name. We're just banished down here. We're not a sports team or heroes. Just… banished."

Raphael's grin widened. "That's it! Los Desterrados! The Banished!"

The name hit a little too close to home for Diego, but he forced a smile and nodded.

"Wait here." Raphael dashed to a stack of boxes. After rummaging for a moment, he returned with a triumphant grin, holding up an old Polaroid camera.

Caught off guard by Raphael's enthusiasm, Diego instinctively reached for his mask. But Raphael put a hand on his arm, his eyes full of a warmth Diego had never seen before. "No mask; I want a picture of us. Together."

Diego hesitated, then relented, offering a tentative smile. Raphael plopped onto the couch, threw an arm over Diego's shoulder, and snapped the photo. Grinning, he snatched the picture as it slid from the camera and darted around the room with boyish energy, shaking it dry.

After rummaging through the prize counter's cabinets, he found a marker and some tape, then fixed the photo to the wall in the center of the Den. Along the bottom border, he scrawled: "Mi Compa."

Diego's chest tightened as he stared at the words, his heart thudding slowly. He blinked to clear his eyes. Raphael was right—there really was a lot of dust in the air.

Mighty Mighty Man

Meddi had removed Diego's casts that morning, and now he and Rafe were gearing up to hunt void rats. Both relief and trepidation twisted in his guts. He was glad to be free—but hunting void rats? He'd never hunted anything before. The defense squads always took care of that.

Diego stretched his arm. It felt wrong—lighter than it should be. His leg, too. It left everything feeling unfamiliar—like he'd been re-assembled incorrectly. He couldn't help thinking about Meddi's frequent offers to make "alterations"—but she hadn't done any. He should know—he'd been there every time.

Still, the sensation left him unsettled, feeding his unease.

This was happening.

He'd wanted more time to stretch out, rebuild his strength, maybe run a few martial forms with Raphael. But the Soylent Drink had run out last week, leaving them with nothing but nutrient sludge.

"Hey, Diego, back before—did any of the girls ever catch your eye?"

Diego ignored Raphael's question. He pulled on a jacket, adjusted his Z-ball mask, and checked the bottles fastened to his belt. A concoction he'd mixed from hazy school-chemistry memories—baking soda, borax, and water, all scavenged from the Pizzarama's kitchen. A viable base solution, he figured.

Void rats spit acid. If they got hit, maybe this would slow the burn. Bases cancel acids... right?

"Come on! There had to be some girl you liked!" Raphael pressed. "It's not like I'll tell anybody. Surely someone caught your eye?"

Memories of Donna surfaced, and a response slipped out before Diego could stop it. "Maybe."

Raphael grinned, leaning forward, his curiosity piqued. "Who?"

Heat flooded Diego's cheeks, and he wanted to change the conversation. But the insistent look in Raphael's eyes made it clear he had no intention of letting this go. Finally, Diego admitted, "Donna."

Raphael chuckled, "Of course, I should have known it'd be Donna. She's definitely one sweet cat."

Diego shrugged, trying not to express too much interest. "Yeah, I guess."

Raphael's eyes sparked. "What would you do if you could be with her right now? Just you two, all alone on a quiet walk in a working biosphere?"

Diego's heart thudded, and an unexpected longing swelled in his chest at the thought. "I...I don't know," he stammered. "Talk to her? Maybe hold her hand... if she'd let me?"

Raphael snorted. "Talk? Hold her hand? Chavo, if I were alone with Donna, I'd be doing a lot more than just that! Can't lie—I've thought about her curves now and then."

Raphael's words lodged in Diego's mind, his back stiffened, and a sharp, unexpected knot of something hot twisted in his chest.

Does Raphael like Donna? Then, what chance do I have? I'm a freak! Why did I tell him I liked her?

Icy fear spun inside him, igniting something he'd never felt before. A rising fire he didn't fully understand. But it burned with the urge to punch Raphael in the face. To throttle him. To wring every thought of Donna from his mind so he'd never think of her again. And at the same time, he felt an overwhelming desire to run and hide.

Beneath it all, he desperately hoped that Donna might feel something for him like he felt for her, and that she didn't ever think of Raphael.

Clenching his jaw against the sudden tornado of unexpected emotions, Diego turned sharply, snatched his Top Slugger, and stormed through the maze of arcade machines to the exit.

Wherever Donna was, he just hoped she was safe.

"Hey!" Raphael called after him, catching up at the door and clapping a hand on Diego's shoulder. "Don't sweat it, chavo. We'll figure something out. You'll get your chance someday."

Diego remained silent, shrugging off Raphael's hand. He focused his gift outwards, scanning the area for void terrors. Sensing no imminent threats, he lifted the security bar and stepped into the plaza.

A delta-shaped monitor bot floated by, its sensor whiskers and cameras sweeping the area.

Raphael fell in step beside him. "That's the second one I've seen this week. Maybe they're fixing things?"

Diego couldn't stop thinking about it. He wanted to demand that Raphael stay clear of Donna. He clenched his jaw, willing himself to calm down, though it still simmered just below the surface. It wasn't like he could claim her—she could make her own choices.

Instead, Diego let out a slow, steadying breath. "I wouldn't bet on the robots fixing anything."

They followed the promenade toward the Link Transit Terminal. During the months of Diego's recovery, Raphael had regularly boasted about his brief stint as a trainee in La Familia's defense squad. "The glory days," he'd called it, regularly regaling Diego with tales of void rat hunts.

"We have to catch 'em off guard," Raphael started into it again. "Hit 'em fast, and they're easy. Just don't let them spit on you—or bite you. They spit acid, and the bite? That's worse than death."

However, Diego wasn't interested in a prolonged hunt to find a lone rat. Wandering aimlessly through the halls while straining his gift to avoid growlers would only leave him exhausted. Fortunately, he had quietly devised a better plan—one born from the techniques he'd experimented with while recovering.

Previously, he would mentally nudge an entire group of void rats as one. But through careful trials with the growlers and void rats that wandered near the Pizzarama, he had learned to nudge them individually. The experiments had given him confidence in this more precise, finesse-driven approach.

He was far less certain about the second technique he'd practiced: holding a void rat in place with his gift. It was a last-resort option, one that unsettled him deeply. The very notion of forcing something to act against its will gnawed at him. His dad had always said denying someone their free agency was the heart of evil. So what did it mean if he wielded his gift that way, even against a void terror? What did it say about who he was if he crossed that line?

Shoving the thoughts aside, Diego focused on the task at hand. With his plan in mind, he led Raphael to the nearby Link Transit Terminal, casually mentioning that he'd seen a rat here before. Of course, he could sense the entire plague of rats inside, but he intended to winnow them down.

The transit station's doors rattled open, mirroring Diego's nerves. Though he'd passed through here countless times, this would be his first time confronting the rats head-on rather than simply driving them away.

He paused just inside, adjusting his grip on the spikier Top Slugger as he worked to steady his jittery nerves. He raised a hand to stop Raphael, tilting his head as if listening while extending his gift again. More than a dozen rats—far too many to confront at once.

Should they head somewhere else? The thought disappeared as quickly as it came. They were already here, and Diego worried that Raphael would just barge in anyway. With sweat beading on his brow, Diego focused his mind, using his gift to separate a couple of the rats while nudging the others individually, encouraging them to phase through the walls and scatter.

"Do you hear something?" Raphael whispered.

Diego nodded, sweat rolling down his brow. He held up a finger in the universal gesture of *shut your pie-hole and wait a minute.*

"There's one or two... I think."

Raphael drew his swords and took the lead, creeping past the lockers and benches. The beam of his flashlight cut through the darkness of the platform, the stench of the rat's nest growing with each step. Diego followed closely behind, Top Slugger clenched in both hands, heart hammering. Four rats remained, and their agitation was growing. They could tell something wasn't right.

Seeing the purple glimmer of their eyes coming from within the Link Pod, Raphael charged forward, swinging at the suitcase-sized void rat coming his way. But it slipped to the side, and Raphael's blow glanced off the floor instead.

Two more rats joined the first, circling Raphael, while the fourth darted past him, heading straight for Diego. Raphael sidestepped their acid spit, but still couldn't land a hit.

As the rat closed in on Diego, he positioned himself to trap it against a locker and swung the bat with all his might. Just before it struck, the rat phased through the door, and his blow hammered into the thin metal, two of the spikes breaking off.

Diego yanked the locker door open, but the rat wasn't inside. He backed away, veering toward Raphael. The rat darted around the bank of lockers, and he swung again.

Once more, it moved faster than he did, leaping inside his blow. Claws slashed at his arm as it spat purple acid in his face. Diego ducked, the Z-ball mask deflecting the corrosive liquid. The rat kicked off his shoulder and ran to join the others circling Raphael.

Bolstered in numbers, the rats hissed and snarled, eyes glowing.

Diego ran forward, using his masking to make himself unseen to the void rat, but still visible to Raphael. He raised his bat and swung hard, finally connecting, but not with any of the remaining spikes. The rat screeched but didn't drop. It turned, eyes locking onto Diego.

In front of him, Raphael swung at one, nearly connecting, but it phased through the floor. He continued his swing, using the momentum to shift his feet and avoid two rats lunging for his open side.

"We're outnumbered!" Raphael yelled, reflecting the same fear rising in Diego.

Diego realized the grave situation he had put them in. Despite his reluctance, he knew he had to resort to plan B, and hoped they could pick them off one at a time. Even then, the idea of using his gift this way weighed heavily on him. But he could see no other alternative, and he masked himself again.

The rat facing him stood upright, sniffing the air in confusion at Diego's disappearance.

Diego clenched his teeth, channeling every fiber of his ability while silently praying it would work. His temples pulsed with the effort, and his skin prickled with waves of needles. But it worked—the creature remained frozen in place, unmoving.

Raphael whirled, spotting the rat. With a howl, he brought a blade down, slicing into its leg.

The creature shrieked, writhing on the ground, but still alive.

At that same instant, a hammer of fire slammed through Diego's skull. He let out a clipped yell and staggered back against the locker. His face drained of color, and he doubled over, losing his breakfast.

This wasn't the usual side effect of overusing his gift. He struggled to make sense of it. Did it have to do with the connection he'd forged to hold the rat in place while Raphael struck?

It left him sick to his core.

Still clutching the locker, Diego fell to his knees, coughing and spitting. His gift shuddered inside him, slipping from his grasp.

Putrid, gut-clenching waves radiated through him, echoing the wounded rat's screams.

"Are you okay?" Raphael called out, maneuvering toward him, keeping the other three rats at bay with broad, defensive swings.

Diego straightened, feet unsteady, giving a faint nod as he wiped his mouth. His heart pounded, and he gripped his Top Slugger with both hands—they had bigger problems.

Eerie purple eyes glowed as the rest of the rats returned, phasing through walls and floors, drawn by their wounded mate's cries.

"¡Caray!" Raphael growled, his voice lined with panic. "I thought you said there were only a couple here?"

"About that—" Diego gritted through clenched teeth as the growing horde closed in, sealing off their escape route. Their hissing filled the air. Acid dripped from their gaping mouths, sizzling as it hit the floor.

The rats' eyes glowed brighter, searching for an opening. Diego and Raphael moved back to back, turning slowly, their weapons swinging in a defensive rhythm. An uneasy balance developed between them and the rats. But it wouldn't last. The rats knew they had the advantage of numbers—they just needed the right opportunity.

The acrid smell of burning rat saliva overpowered even the stench of their lair, making Diego's stomach twist in knots. His body trembled from using his gift as he had, and he loathed himself for even trying. With his gift flailing on the edge of control, he couldn't have hated it more—why had he thought trying something new was worth the risk?

"We need a plan," Raphael growled.

Diego didn't know what to offer. He could mask himself and Raphael, even make them invisible, but it wouldn't work while the rats watched.

"The maintenance room!" Diego shouted.

Raphael followed Diego's lead, matching his steps as they retreated. Diego kept his Top Slugger raised, his other hand feeling behind him as they edged along the wall until he found the doorknob. They lurched inside, slamming the door shut.

He knew this was only a temporary reprieve. His eyes darted towards the Link Tube maintenance hatch just past a clutter of shelves to the right. The weight of Sharon's passkey sat heavy in his pocket. Would the rats pursue them through the zero-gravity tubes? His gift still surged in his mind, thrashing against his control.

The rats' anger pressed on his senses, boiling and building. They would soon arrive.

Raphael leaned against the door, gasping to catch his breath.

Diego backed away, voice low. "Did you forget that void rats can phase through walls?"

Raphael's eyes widened, and he darted to Diego's side.

A purple snout pushed through the wall, forcing Diego's hand.

"Turn off your flashlight," he hissed.

Despite a growing panic over his thrashing gift, Diego reached for it anyway. And he didn't do it gently—he seized it.

A breath escaped his lips as it steadied in his mind. Relief bloomed, tainted by nausea and the relentless pounding in his skull.

But he had it.

Grateful for the darkness, he masked himself and Raphael.

Rafe, unaware of the change, kept his focus on the rats closing in. They both took measured breaths, moving as little as possible. More rats phased through the walls, their glowing eyes a malevolent light as they snuffled around, searching for their prey.

Every muscle in Diego's body tensed as he fought to maintain the invisibility, mentally nudging away any rat that ventured too close. He prayed Raphael wouldn't notice the subtle muffling effect of the masking. At least the darkness concealed the shimmering vision.

Each heartbeat stretched longer than the last, but the rats finally began to lose interest. One by one, their hissing faded as they slipped back through the walls.

Diego let out a long, shaky breath, releasing his gift. He slumped against the wall, his entire body trembling.

Rafe flicked on his flashlight and turned to Diego, a grin of pure relief spreading across his face. "Can you believe our luck? I thought we were done for!"

Diego nodded, bile lingering on his tongue.

Rafe's expression fell, and he sighed heavily. "Mierda, Mierda, Mierda. I really thought we could do it. But, didn't I say we should only take them one at a time?"

"They're tough," Diego murmured. He glanced at Raphael, then lurched upright—acid burns smoldered on his clothes.

"Take your jacket off!" Diego commanded, pulling a bottle from his belt. He quickly poured the base solution over each spot. "Is it on your skin anywhere?"

They checked each other, using the last of the solution where needed.

Wringing out his damp shirt, Rafe pulled it back on, shivering against the cold. "Didn't you say water doesn't stop acid?" he asked, nudging the tattered jacket with his boot. "So how come this water does?"

Diego slumped into a chair. His gift was still thrashing, and he wasn't in the mood to explain the science of acids and bases again—but he did anyway.

Raphael shrugged, examining a burned patch on his shirt. "If you say so, chemistry's not my thing."

Then he glanced at Diego, brow furrowing. "Chavo! You're paler than a corpse. You get bit?"

Diego shook his head, waving Raphael off as he wrestled against the urge to wretch. "I just need a moment."

Raphael chewed on his lip as he studied Diego, then waved a hand toward the platform. "Strange, wasn't it? Why did that one just stand there all frozen?"

Diego didn't know how to answer the question. Was it time to explain his gift to Raphael? Things were better between them now, weren't they? Even so, with exhaustion weighing on him, he didn't want to face the inevitable questions and merely offered a shrug.

Raphael grinned. "Must have been distracted by you tossing your cookies."

They eventually decided to wait a bit longer before venturing out—which suited Diego just fine. Still battling nausea, he sat on the floor, head between his knees.

Raphael found an office chair by the desk and spun in it slowly. After a moment, he asked quietly. "Think I'll ever go back home?"

Diego didn't look up. "Not as long as Carlos is in charge."

Raphael kicked at a stray bolt, sending it clattering across the room. They both froze, listening for the rats to return. The silence was almost more unsettling than the noise.

"Really, Rafe?" Diego hissed after a few seconds passed with no sign of danger.

"I know, I know!" Raphael groaned. "But there has to be something I can do! I want to go home."

Diego turned to him, disbelief etched on his face. "The two of us taking on Carlos and the entire defense squad who have rayguns?" He waved at his Top Slugger leaning against a shelf. "Two scared little boys with handmade swords and a big stick? We'd be quite the threat, I'm sure."

Raphael's eyes thinned. "I'm not a little boy, you know. I matter."

Diego glared back, saying nothing.

Raphael growled. "So you want me to live like a rat down here for the rest of my life? All alone? Just us guys? I need a *chica* to keep me warm, you know?"

Diego hadn't considered his future much beyond survival. He lowered his head back between his knees, his shoulders rising and falling with each unsteady breath.

After a long, thoughtful pause, he muttered, "Maybe something will change. Just keep quiet for a minute; I need to let my stomach settle."

But it was really his gift that he needed to get settled. Would he draw the attention of the Kraal if he couldn't bring it under control?

Closing his eyes, he carefully stretched his senses, wondering, *Is it still down there?*

An icy chill lanced through him.

It was.

You Rascal You

Raphael waited while Diego sat curled up on the floor like a baby. Said his tummy hurt. *Seriously? A few rats and some blood was enough to break him? How did somebody that soft survive down here for a whole year?*

Diego finally stood, still looking shaky. For a heartbeat, his eyes went distant, staring at nothing, then he muttered, "We can go out now."

Raphael had seen that faraway look before—usually right before Diego said they needed to take a different route, and his suspicions were growing. How did he always manage to steer clear of danger? It was uncanny. Unnatural.

They stepped out of the maintenance room onto the station platform. The rat he'd hit was still there, trying to crawl away, leaving a trail of blood smeared behind it. Weak.

Diego whispered, "Put it out of its misery."

Rafe smiled, crouching beside the thing, watching it struggle— looks like he'd have to take care of the scary monster for Diego. He ran a finger along its back, feeling the sticky warmth of its blood. It wheezed, eyes dim.

"So pathetic," he spoke softly. "Void tainted freaks of nature don't deserve to live."

Diego stood behind him. Didn't help. Just urged, "Hurry up and finish it."

Rafe stood slowly, his irritation building. "Don't be weak, amigo. This thing would eat us alive if we didn't fight back."

Deciding to do this his own way, he didn't draw a sword. Instead, he turned to face Diego, and pressed the heel of his boot to the rat's head. Slowly. Deliberately. Watching as Diego's eyes flinched behind that creepy mask.

The rat squealed, a thin, high sound, until it ended with a satisfying crunch.

Raphael drew in a slow, shuddering breath, surprised at how good it felt to show the thing who really had the power. Then he snatched his prize by the tail and held it up. "We feast tonight!"

There was more than just a pizza oven in the Pizzarama's kitchen. It had prep areas and even a working stove. Rafe tossed the rat onto the cutting board and grinned. "You ever cut up an animal before?"

Diego shook his head.

Rafe dove in, eagerly hacking and slicing away. Slippery bones, strange organs—none of it fazed him. If anything, it was fascinating to see its insides. He even found something that he hoped was its acid sac and sliced it open. Purple slime oozed out, sizzling and smoking on the cutting board.

"Check it out!" he grinned.

Diego swore and grabbed a rag.

Eventually, they had a pile of meat.

Diego filled a pot with water and set it on the stove.

Rafe frowned, "You want to boil it?"

He grabbed an empty pot, and set it on the burner next to Diego's, then cranked the heat to high. "You don't boil meat, chavo, you cook it over a flame. Or fry it. That's what the traders said."

"Do you know how to fry it?" Diego glared.

"Do you know how to boil it?" Raphael shot back.

They locked eyes.

Raphael grabbed a handful of meat and dropped it into his pot. The sizzle was glorious, filling the air with a rich, greasy smell they'd never known before. Real meat had always been for the elite.

They both fell silent, listening to the crackle, breathing in the scent.

But it didn't last long. The meat stuck to the bottom of the pot. When Raphael tried to turn it with a spoon, it tore apart, leaving blackening bits welded to the bottom. Wisps of smoke curled up, quickly swelling into a cloud that reeked of burnt meat.

"Get it off the stove!" Diego shoved the pot from the burner.

As the haze thinned, Raphael could see that look in Diego's eyes. He wanted to say something, but at least the guy kept his mouth shut.

Picking through the blackened bits, Raphael tasted a piece, and Diego quickly followed. Without a word, they stuffed their faces, not sparing even the charred bits.

"It's better than the sludge." Rafe wiped greasy hands on his pants.

Later, they sparred until their muscles burned and sweat poured off both of them—a welcome relief in the chilly air. When they finally finished, they collapsed into worn chairs.

Diego always took his mask off when they exercised. Rafe couldn't decide if he liked it better when he wore it or not—neither was a pleasant sight.

Studying Diego's dark and purple eye, Raphael's suspicion grew. There was more going on here than he was saying. Every time he got that look, he then knew exactly where to go. And today, the rat... Maybe it was time to just ask.

"So, mi chavo," he finally said, "I can't stop thinking about how the rat acted, you know? It just froze like a statue. Wasn't normal, right? There has to be some reason..."

Diego looked away, wiping his brow too slowly. Too deliberately.

Raphael pressed. "That was you, yeah? You've really got void powers? That'd be *muy estellar*, chavo."

There was a pause. A long one.

"Not void powers," Diego finally muttered. "Mom called it *mi sentido dotado*. It's nothing, really. I can tell where they are, even through walls. And... I can sort of make them not notice me. Push them away, too. And... yeah, I tried something new. held it in place."

Rafe's eyes lit up. "So that's why it froze like that!"

Diego nodded, a faint smile flickering across his face. "Yeah."

"That's loco! *Muy chingón!*" Rafe exclaimed, but the excitement in his voice didn't match the sour twist in his gut. *So everybody was right. El Duende. But, there has to be more. What else is he hiding?*

Diego shrugged. "It's not that big a deal. And it takes a toll. Headaches. Sickness. I can't do it all the time."

Rafe asked more questions, playing it cool while he mulled over the angles. Something like this could be useful. Dangerous, too.

"Look, I don't like talking about this," Diego eventually said. "And I don't want others to know. So if more guys get exiled down here, can you keep it quiet?"

Raphael forced a warm smile. "Anything for you, mi compa. You can trust me." He grabbed a towel, wiping his face. "So what's next? Want to try it again?"

Diego's answer came too fast. "No. That went very badly."

Raphael nodded slowly. *So that's how it is—open the door for me but then just slam it shut. We'll come back to it later. Maybe it's time he heard me out... time to push him out of his comfort zone.*

Raphael kept his tone loose, like he was just thinking aloud. "Well, then. What if I cut a hole in that blast door? We've got the plasma cutter in the workshop... could get us into Red or Green sector, you know?"

Diego's eyes bugged out under his messy hair. "You want to cut a hole in a blast door? The one that keeps us breathing if there's a de-pressurization event on the other side?"

Rafe lifted his hands in mock surrender. "Whoa, you're the one who said the biosphere worked over there. And if it's between some 'maybe-danger' in the future or choking down sludge every day right now? Easy choice for me."

Diego leaned forward, head in his hands. Long enough that Rafe had to resist saying something. Didn't hurt to be nice, afterall. And, he needed him. Best give the guy space, and maybe he'd come around.

Eventually, Diego sighed. "I don't know... I don't think we should. But the rats—maybe we could lure them out, one at a time. I just don't know what they're attracted to."

Raphael leaned back, jaw tight. *Fine—blow me off again.*

But he could play along. "Jonah said they like the reactor waste, and that's why the reactors are all sealed up with shields and things."

Diego's voice shifted into that know-it-all tone. "Reactors are sealed up to shield everything else from radiation, not to keep the rats out."

"That too," Rafe had to take a long swig from his bottle, tempering his response. "But Jonah wasn't just telling a story. He said the reactors do something with salt, and burn radioactive waste, turning it into other stuff. Trust me, I didn't believe him at first, 'cause he said it made gold, but then Mr. Orlando backed him up—"

Raphael couldn't let it end there. "And Mr. Orlando *also* said it kept rats out, you know. So they do want into them. And why else but to eat the stuff inside the reactor?"

Of course, Diego had to one-up him with an explanation. "They're single-atom molten salt reactors. Molten! That means the salt and metal at its core are so hot they've melted. It's so hot the rats couldn't get close enough, even if they wanted to."

Diego paused, thinking it through. "But your point does tell us one thing."

"It does?"

"There might be a way to stop them from phasing through things. If something about the reactor lining keeps the rats away, can we figure out what that is and use it in a trap? I wonder if that lining is anywhere else on the orbital?"

Rafe paused, a thought teasing his thoughts. "You know... when I went back for our stuff in the biosphere, there were void-rat prints all around the algae vat. And it looked like they'd been into it, 'cause we left the door open. All the tracks were fresh, too—they'd not done this before. So, maybe that vat has the same lining?"

Diego grinned. "Could be, but you just figured out what we can do."

Raphael blinked. "I did?"

"What if the rats love the algae? That can be our lure. And then we could leave the vat intact."

A few days later, they were finally ready to test the algae-lure idea. And about time, too—Rafe was sick of Diego's slow, overthinking ways and wanted to show him what it meant to take action—the way a real leader would.

They dripped a trail of algae from the Link Transit Terminal, along the promenade, and into a travel agency. Crouched behind an overturned table, they waited. Rafe had made a new sword just for this, with a wide, flaring tip—perfect for punching through void-rat armor.

Scratching claws reached his ears, and his grin spread. A shadow slid forward, emerging through the doorway as a void rat. It paused, nose twitching. Could it smell them? *Mierda!* What if it could sense him the way Diego sensed void terrors?

Rafe's grip tightened on the sword.

The rat shimmered, darting forward.

Rafe lunged, swinging with both hands. The blow hit true—took the thing's head clean off, and left the blade buried in the linoleum.

Now that's how it's done.

That evening, after they'd finished cooking the rat, Rafe sprawled on the battered couch, one arm dangling lazily over the side. Diego, towel slung over his shoulder, announced he was heading off to clean up at the Starlight Lounge. Rafe was only too pleased about that, and had to work to feign indifference.

When the sound of his footsteps finally faded, a smile touched his lips.

Time to dig through Diego's things.

He moved quickly, heading straight for their Lair. Diego's bed was buried under crumpled blankets, clothes, and assorted junk—no cleaner than his own corner. But he wasn't here to dig through dirty laundry. He was looking for something more.

Diego was an oddball, always shifty and secretive. The guy couldn't even change his clothes without slipping off somewhere private.

"What's he so scared of?" Rafe muttered. "Worried I'll see his little pop gun?"

He snorted—probably for the best. Nobody wanted to see more of Diego's scarred-up, creepy skin than they had to.

Raphael lifted blankets and nudged aside random junk, hunting for something useful. He knew that Diego had to have something hidden away—something he could use to his advantage.

Circling the bed, his eyes locked on a storage container wedged among some boxes. He pulled it free and rifled through the contents, considering each item—like a well-worn notebook.

He flipped it open, tracing the jagged edges of missing pages. Curiosity gnawed at him. What had Diego thought was so important that he had to tear it out? Who else would even see it?

He skimmed ahead, rolling his eyes at the juvenile scrawls addressed to Donna. "Chavito's sure flipped for that cat—not that she'd ever go for him. Now, me? She'd melt like butter in my arms."

At the bottom, neatly folded, was a woman's scarf. He picked it up. The careful way it was stored told him it mattered—though why, he didn't know yet.

He unfolded it slowly, bringing the center to his nose and drawing in a slow, deep breath, wondering who had worn it.

Donna?

His fist clenched the fabric.

No way she'd go for him. Not a chance.

He gave the rest of the items a cursory glance before re-folding the scarf and putting everything back in place. Diego had hidden parts of himself here—private, tender pieces Raphael hadn't figured out yet.

But he would.

Let the Good Times Roll

As the weeks passed, the boys settled into a routine that almost felt normal—sparring in the mornings to warm up, tinkering in the workshop afterward, hunting void rats when they needed a break from the sludge, and scavenging for supplies in between. They pulled lock cores while out exploring, piling them on the Den's table where they could practice lock-picking without risking being caught.

Competitions inevitably sprang up, with their sparring matches and speed-picking challenges feeding into each other. While Rafe usually had the upper hand in the arena, Diego left him in the dust on the locks. Sometimes he had to force himself to slow down, because if Rafe lost too often, he'd demand a rematch in the arena.

They were getting along, and the walls Diego had built around himself lowered a little more each day, making him wonder if they might actually become friends. That didn't mean everything was rosy, of course—too much time together and even friends grated on each other's nerves. When it did, he'd slip off to a quiet corner of the Pizzarama to play melodies from his past.

Rafe found his own outlet. Using scavenged brushes and paint, he covered the walls in murals that weren't half bad. His subjects ranged from mutant rat gladiators and exploding toilets in space, to comic-book panels of their misadventures, and—of course—a pin-up girl with proportions that defied all reason, which Rafe spent way too much time trying to get "just right."

Up to now, he'd been content to follow Diego's lead, but Diego worried how long that would last. So when Rafe wanted to go scavenging on his own, Diego didn't argue. However, the moment Rafe was out of sight, Diego masked himself and followed at a distance.

Rafe crept through the shadows, heading straight for the piles of clothes fallen from victims of the Kraal's attack. The careless way he rifled through them grated on Diego, but he held back—he didn't want to risk the fragile peace forming between them. Was it time to stop being sentimental about the clothes and just let Rafe do his thing?

When Rafe approached another pile, Diego turned away.

Later, when he returned to the Pizzarama, Diego asked casually, "Find anything interesting?"

"Nothing much," Rafe muttered, clutching his pack as he slipped past the arcade-game wall into their Lair.

His solo ventures continued, and every so often, he'd add something useful to their stash of tools, supplies, and gear. He always made a point of saying where he'd found each item—and it was never from a pile of fallen clothes. Diego chose not to press him on it.

After one trip, Rafe chucked a hand-knit beanie at him. "You said you wanted a good hat. So… here. And don't make it weird."

Despite its scratchy texture, Diego wore it when they scavenged together. It did help keep his ears warm, and Raphael seemed to appreciate seeing him wear it.

One of Rafe's prized finds was a navy-blue law enforcement jacket from before the Arrival, reinforced with armor plates and embroidered with the letters "SEO." He decided the "S" didn't stand for Serenity anymore, and with a wolfish grin informed Diego it meant "Sex Enforcement Officer." He kept repeating this until Diego finally acknowledged him with a flat, "Yeah. Clever."

The jacket soon became a staple of his wardrobe, alongside his treasured Starblaze superhero T-shirts.

Diego sat on the sofa in their Den late one evening, strumming his guitar as his thoughts circled back to Raphael's desire to explore another sector. He wanted that too. But cutting a hole through the bulkhead? Not happening.

So should he tell Raphael about Sharon's maintenance passkey? They could take the Link tubes into Red Sector... but even thinking about it knotted his shoulders. No—something still held him back. He wasn't sure if it was the way Raphael lied about where he found things, or the uneasy sense that maybe their budding friendship wasn't real.

Either way, Diego knew the maintenance passkey wouldn't unlock the blast door—he'd already tried.

Raphael's voice broke into his thoughts. "Julian must have gotten in good with Carlos, or he would've been sent down by now."

Diego silenced the strings of his guitar. The mention of Julian brought a surge of memories he thought he'd gotten past.

Chest tightening, he struggled with how he should answer, and finally asked, "When was his birthday?"

"Only two months after mine, but that was a while ago."

The longing that radiated from him left Diego feeling hollow, followed by a simmering unease. If Julian did come down, would Raphael revert to his old ways? Diego needed to change the subject.

Setting down his guitar, he declared, "I think we should do it."

Rafe looked up, confusion evident. "Do what?"

"Cut our way into Red Sector."

A grin spread across Rafe's face. "Now you're talking!"

Diego was already working through the logistics in his head. "First, we have to find a way to keep our work hidden. We can scout it out and locate any cameras, then identify if other security measures are in place. My biggest concern is what happens if there's a vacuum on the other side?"

Raphael waved his hand. "Cutting takes time. We can punch a hole first and see if there's a vacuum. If so, we can patch it up right away."

They debated the possibility of finding a manual override crank for the bulkhead door, but quickly discarded the idea: not only would it be incredibly laborious, but any passing robot would have no problem seeing it was open. A small hole would be easier to hide.

Still, even cutting through the blast door would take time, and they'd have to pull it off without raising an alarm. To do that, they needed to disable the station's cameras nearby—and in a way that it wasn't easy to figure out who did it. Chip knew them well enough that he'd stop by the Pizzarama from time to time, so he'd have no problem tracking them down.

Diego's brow furrowed. "If we can't disable the cameras without getting caught, what if we make it look like an accident?"

"An accident? How does a camera high on the wall get 'accidentally' broken?"

Diego snapped his fingers. "Chip said he couldn't tell us apart from growlers, right? Maybe we dress up like growlers and run around smashing cameras."

But where? They couldn't cut through the smaller side-corridor doors because they were too exposed. That left the promenade, where debris and kiosks at least offered something to hide what they'd done.

Rafe wanted to hit the blast door into Green Sector—it was closer, and not right next to Ring Ops. Diego had no intention of setting foot in Green Sector again, but he couldn't come up with an argument that satisfied Rafe. In the end, he simply insisted: they'd break into Red Sector, not Green, and as a consolation, he conceded Rafe could play the growler.

Their strategy revolved around the men's and women's restrooms on opposite sides of the promenade. Rafe would have to pass in front of Ring Ops to reach the blast door, but they offered good cover.

If all went to plan, after breaking the cameras, Rafe would retreat to the men's room, ditch the costume, and grab his gear. A ventilation duct in the ceiling was his way out. After a short, claustrophobic squeeze, he'd drop through a second vent into the back hallway and slip away undetected.

They stashed Rafe's swords and combat gear in the men's room, and he pulled a ragged suit over his clothes while Diego helped smear just enough grunge on his face and hair to pass as a growler.

Once ready, Diego slipped across the promenade and into the women's room. Even with Delta Ring vacated, his cheeks flushed as he stepped inside. He'd only peeked in here once—it wasn't for guys, after all—but now it was part of the plan. From here, he could watch over Rafe without drawing attention to his escape route. And unlike the men's room, this one had a walled-in stall at the back where he could hole up if things went south.

Doing his best to imitate a growler, Rafe moaned dramatically and shambled toward the first camera, eyes vacant, movements jerky. A loosely held metal bar dragged behind him. After a quick glance to be sure no bots were in sight, he gripped it in both hands and swung hard, smashing the camera in a crash of glass and electronics.

An alarm blared, and Rafe flinched, dropping the pipe. His gaze swept the corridor in a panic before locking on Diego, half-hidden behind the women's restroom door. Ignoring Diego's frantic hand signals to go the other way, Rafe bolted inside, yanked off the tattered suit, and crouched beside him.

"Wasn't expecting that!" he gasped.

Diego shot him a pointed look. "Yeah, here's a question, brainiac: where's your swords?"

Rafe froze, his gaze flicking to the men's room across the promenade.

"The alarm will attract the growlers. We should go—" Diego started.

The rumble of a maintenance door cycling open cut him off. Chip emerged, flanked by a fierce-looking security bot Diego had never seen before. Its heavy metal strides reverberated through the deck. In its wake scuttled a six-legged—

Spider!

Fear spiked through him before reason caught up. It was just another repair bot, but knowing that didn't stop the rush in his veins. His throat tightened, and he adjusted his Z-ball mask just to keep his hands busy.

Rafe hadn't even noticed; he was too busy scowling at the bots heading to the damaged camera. The alarm cut out, and the repair bot skittered up the wall.

The looming security bot's burning red eyes scanned the area for trouble. Chip began rolling back and forth in a patrol pattern, his polite announcements echoing through the empty promenade, cautioning peaceful residents against disrupting Delta Ring operations.

Then they both heard it—the cries and groans of growlers echoing through the halls, drawn by the alarm. Diego stepped back, but Rafe grabbed his sleeve. "Hold on, let's wait and see how this plays out. I've never seen that big fella before. Just look at that plasma cannon. He should mow down those growlers in no time."

But the large robot did not use its plasma cannon. Instead, it joined Chip in delivering electric shocks that proved remarkably effective in scattering the growlers.

Chip maintained his upbeat tone and apologized with each jolt he administered. He even called out the names of recognized assailants, "Ahh, is that you, Miss Evenstein? So sorry for this." Zap! "You should disperse peacefully. And I'm sorry to inform you, but you now have yet another fine added to your account for civil unrest. Please refrain from such actions in the future!"

The boys watched, slightly bemused, as growlers scattered in all directions amidst the chaos—until one bolted straight for the bathroom door they hid behind. They scrambled back—Diego making for the walled stall, while Raphael planted his feet. A grim smile curled his lips as he snapped into a *Jeet Kune Do* stance and declared, "We can handle one measly growler!"

Before Diego could argue, the growler crashed through the door. Once a young woman, her features were now twisted and scarred. She wore a tattered sweater and skirt, with plaid stockings torn to ribbons. Her hands curled into claws, with stained fingers ending in jagged nails.

She turned and froze, gaze locking on Diego. Her stare was intense—too focused for a growler—and fixed not on his face, but on his head. A hiss slipped from her lips. "Mike?"

Diego pulled off his beanie, wondering if that was what caught her attention, and tossed it aside. Her gaze tracked the hat, leaving him unnerved. Growlers didn't act like this—usually, their mindless hisses made no sense.

He tugged at Rafe's sleeve. "Come on, while it's confused."

Her face hardened in rage, and she lunged. "You bastard, Mike!"

Diego swung his Top Slugger at her head, but she shifted, catching the blow on her forearm. The spikes sank deep, but she didn't even flinch—instead, she turned, and he lost his grip, leaving the bat buried in her arm. But this barely registered when she hammered a punch into his chest with the force of a battering ram. He staggered back and dropped to his knees, gasping. She ripped the bat free and tossed it aside.

Rafe darted in, hammering a flurry of punches into her side.

Then, faster than they could follow, she spun and kicked, sending him flying across the room. He hit a partition hard enough that it collapsed in a twist of metal and plastic wreckage, and he lay still in the debris.

Diego spotted the bat near Rafe and darted forward, hoping to slip past her. But she seized his collar and clamped her hands around his neck, hoisting up and slamming him into the mirror.

Glass shattered and rained around him. His feet kicked at the air, and he clawed at her hands, desperate to breathe. Sparks swam in his eyes. Through the haze of pain, he saw the wound on her arm knitting shut, and realized with start clarity: *We're were going to die.*

"You left me, Mike!" she howled.

Rafe groaned, coughed, and pushed himself up from the wreckage. He spotted the Top Slugger and grabbed it with a gasp. With one arm hanging limp, he clenched his teeth and forced himself upright with the help of the bat.

Diego's vision dimmed, and he barely heard her shout as she shook him, "I waited for you!"

Raphael limped up behind her, clenching the bat in one hand. Mustering all his strength, he swung and planted it into the back of her head with a sickening crunch.

She released Diego and staggered back a few steps before falling to the ground.

Diego slumped against the wall, holding his throat and wheezing as color returned to his vision.

Raphael added a few more blows to ensure she stayed down, still favoring one arm, before sinking to the ground.

"That," he winced, "hurt."

"Yeah," Diego tried to say, but it only came out as a whisper.

Raphael forced a weak chuckle. "So, chavo, did I hear that right? You have a girlfriend and didn't tell me?"

The growler's words left Diego chilled, but he didn't have time to dwell on them—there were more pressing matters at hand. Raphael's face had no color, and a pool of blood spread at his side.

"You don't look so good," Diego rasped.

Rafe could only manage a weak nod before closing his eyes.

Diego found a metal shard buried in Raphael's side, along with several gashes, and his arm lay at an odd angle—probably broken. Should he pull the shard out or wait until Medbay? He couldn't remember any of his first-aid training.

Fumbling through his gear, he retrieved a stimpack and jabbed it into Rafe's thigh. Eyes still closed, Rafe gave a soft sigh as the medication's numbing agents and stimulants took effect.

Diego pulled the shard free because he couldn't bandage Rafe with it still there. Rafe didn't even flinch, but blood welled faster. Diego tore off his shirt, pressed it to Rafe's side, and wrapped his jacket around him as a makeshift binding.

Rafe's eyes fluttered open, and he groaned.

"Hold this tight," Diego said, guiding Rafe's hand to the bandage. "Now maybe you can understand why I never wanted to hunt the growlers?"

Raphael managed a weak grin and gave him a thumbs-up.

Peeking outside the restroom, Diego realized the robots hadn't even noticed their brush with death. He helped scatter the growlers with his gift, expecting they'd have to wait for the robots to finish repairs. But, to his surprise, they retreated into Ring Ops.

He didn't question the opportunity. With the path clear, Diego guided Rafe to Medbay and activated Meddi, unsure what to expect— ever since he'd reprogrammed her, she'd been... odd. They hadn't had any major emergencies since she'd wrapped him from head to toe in casts, but some of the things she'd said on his follow-up visits had left him unsettled.

"Welcome to Medbay, my trouble-prone test subjects!" she announced with just a little too much cheer. "Looks as if you'd had another crisis? As you know, there is no staff available. But have no fear, I'm here to save the day... and your life, if I must. All in the name of science, am I right?"

"Sure," Diego growled, helping Rafe onto a bed.

She wasted no time, peeling away the blood-soaked jacket and shirt, muttering under her breath, "You two obviously need adult supervision. But who am I to complain? More work for me."

After examining Rafe's wounds, she let out an almost theatrical sigh and planted her fists on her hips. "Unfortunately, it seems no major organs were affected. Such a missed opportunity."

Moving to his arm, she continued her diagnosis. "Not broken. Possibly a torn tendon or ligament. But I have wonderful news! This is a great opportunity to test an amputation technique. And today's your lucky day—it's on the house!"

Raphael's eyes locked onto Diego, the whites showing. "The hell you do to her, chavo?"

"Can you... help him without amputating?" Diego asked, slowly edging toward her control terminal.

"There are options, of course," she said in a deflated tone. "Though they are fairly routine. Some stitches, clean bandages, and a sling should suffice."

"Do that!" they said at the same time.

She made a noise of disapproval but started working.

Diego eyed the Velcro restraints on the table. His visits since breaking half his bones had been short—mostly to avoid tempting her to strap him down again. This was their first true emergency since his "adjustments" to her programming, and he still wasn't sure if she'd insist on keeping Rafe for observation until a guardian arrived.

"So, maybe we can go now?" Diego ventured once she finished giving Rafe his recovery instructions.

"Of course," she said, stepping back to her charging station, "Do come back when you are ready for some experimental procedures. Judging by your track record, I expect to see one of you again very soon!"

A few days passed, and aside from Raphael's occasional jab about Diego's "girlfriend," neither of them mentioned the growler's strange behavior. But her actions weighed on his mind. He'd never seen one behave like that before. Had she really recognized the knit beanie? The possibility sparked questions he couldn't answer.

Everyone knew the person a growler had once been was lost; what was left was just a lifeless monster. But this one seemed to retain memories of her past life. It left Diego questioning everything he knew about them.

Soon enough, Raphael's restless energy boiled over. Declaring himself fit for action, he insisted they resume a full training routine. Even with his arm in a sling and bandages wrapped around his chest, he pushed through every exercise without complaint.

When not sparring, he prowled the Pizzarama, checking and rechecking weapons and gear. His movements were almost frantic—as if staying still might let something catch up to him.

After his third circuit one evening, he declared. "We should do a growler hunt."

Diego blinked. "Are you serious? That last one tossed you around like a rag doll—and if you haven't noticed, you're still all wrapped up."

"I don't mean right now!" Raphael snapped. "When this is gone, and we're ready."

He shifted his grip on the sword in his free hand, and muttered. "Besides, I didn't have my swords then. Would've gone differently if I did."

His gaze drifted, and his voice took on a distant note. "When I finally took her down, it was… amazing."

Diego hesitated. What, exactly, did he find amazing? Almost dying? The fight? The kill? But he held his tongue, saying only. "I don't think it's a good idea. It's reckless."

Raphael's jaw tightened, and he shot back, "Agree to disagree," before striding away.

Come On-A My House

After an awkward morning avoiding Raphael, Diego decided he needed time alone to clear his head. His fifteenth birthday had passed a few days ago. He'd thought about saying something, but the tension with Raphael had left no room for that. Claiming he wanted to do some solo scouting, he was surprised when Raphael nodded and said, "I'll hold down the fort." It was the first words they'd exchanged all morning.

An idea had been simmering in Diego's mind, sparked by an issue of Victor Shadowstar's comics, where Vic had used fake photos to fool the security cameras. They wouldn't have to destroy them, if that would work.

Once the idea took root, Diego couldn't let it go. But he wanted to map out the camera placement before mentioning it to Raphael. Plus, he needed time alone to work through his thoughts, especially now that he didn't dare write in his journal.

He stood near the bulkhead leading into Red Sector, surveying the area but not really seeing it. His mind was elsewhere, running in circles. With a sigh, he raked a hand through his long, dark curls. He had to admit, things between him and Raphael were starting to feel… strange.

Unable to focus on figuring out the cameras, Diego meandered through the desolate corridors, poking around the shops he hadn't visited recently—he didn't expect to find anything new, but the distraction was welcome.

Raphael's behavior gnawed at him. It wasn't just confusing; it was unsettling. Was it simply the bleakness of their situation that had changed him, or was there something deeper, something darker, lurking beneath the surface?

Stopping at his favorite convenience store, Diego rifled through a familiar stack of faded magazines. The brittle pages featured articles brimming with optimism for the future. He half-hoped to uncover something he might have missed, but really he knew he was here just to skim that one periodical—the one that always lingered in the back of his mind.

One cover featured a smiling family in matching jumpsuits stepping out of a sleek, chrome spaceship, the tagline declaring, "Colonial Expansion Is Great!"

Diego set it aside, his movements suddenly furtive. He needed to find it, he realized—the magazine he secretly found pleasure in looking through—although admitting it, even to himself, felt embarrassing.

He knew it was indulgent, but it stirred something deep inside him as he lingered over its tantalizing photos. It left him feeling a flicker of shame and was a secret he'd carefully kept from Raphael. But he was alone now, so what harm would it do?

When he finally found it, his pulse sped up, and he glanced around before opening its glossy, full-color pages.

His fingers almost shook as *Fusion-Powered Cooking* unfolded like a forbidden treasure. Photos of food he'd never even heard of taunted him—roast turkeys with glistening skins, pies with lattice-work crusts, and towering ice-cream sundaes dripping with sugary syrup.

Given his endless diet of sludge, flipping through the pages was almost painful, with each picture leaving his mouth watering and his stomach twisting with longing.

Finally, he reluctantly slid it back into its hiding spot at the rear of the rack and moved onto a stack of *Starburst Chronicles,* featuring a superhero wielding a raygun on its cover. The subtitle read, "Starblaze returns to battle the Cyberplasm Lords!"

He'd seen it before—the only reason it was still here was that Raphael had already taken a copy, and six more were on the rack.

Diego sighed, his mind drifting back to the camaraderie he'd shared with Raphael before things started to get odd. For someone who'd struggled to have friends, the bond had felt amazing.

But now, doubts festered. Why did Raphael suddenly want to hunt growlers? Was this his bloodthirsty side emerging? Or... was he right? In their situation, was it such a bad idea to hunt them?

Even the thought left Diego deeply unsettled. He shook his head, trying to ignore the churn in his gut. Maybe he could get Raphael to talk through things and clear the air.

Diego paused at a copy of *Cosmic Quarterly.* Bold predictions leaped off the pages: personal robots, a revolutionary fusion fuel to combat the communist threat, and more. But the relentless optimism rang hollow, and Diego shoved the magazine back into the rack with a scowl.

Unease about Raphael refused to leave his thoughts. With a frustrated sigh, he turned away from the magazine rack. Shoving his hands into his jacket pockets, he headed toward the Atomic Pizzarama, extending his senses like he always did, and his steps faltered.

Growlers were in an excited frenzy ahead.

A spike of cold stabbed through him. Had Raphael gone looking for trouble?

Diego broke into a run, abandoning caution as worst-case scenarios churned in his mind. The sounds of conflict echoed from a side corridor, and he veered in that direction.

What if the growlers were too frenzied for him to use his gift on them? Clutching his Top Slugger, Diego masked himself just before rounding the corner, and came to an abrupt halt.

The growlers swarmed ahead, their focus fixed on something— or someone. Raphael flashed into view for a heartbeat, then disappeared, and a heavy clunk echoed through the hall. The growlers clawed and scrabbled at a circular maintenance hatch.

The overwhelming stank that filled the hall left no doubt—Raphael's bolt hole was a port into the sewage system. Diego unmasked himself, howling and banging on the walls to draw the growler's attention. Their heads snapped toward him, one snarling, "No! Go!"

Diego bolted away, zigzagging through the corridors with the growlers only steps behind. A stitch flared in his side, cutting his breaths short. He rounded a corner and pressed into a narrow gap between support girders, shimmering into invisibility. The growlers thundered past, their snarls and footsteps fading as they charged on.

After catching his breath, Diego made it back to the maintenance hatch just as Raphael crawled out, dripping with the treatment-plant's finest sauce. Two other boys followed and immediately started shaking in the chill air.

That's when Diego pieced things together—the lift must have arrived while he was away, bringing two more exiles.

Raphael wiped a filthy hand across his eyes and struggled to his feet. "Diego, thank God," he gasped.

The smell was revolting.

"Skyway Lounge," Diego gasped, trying not to breathe.

A few months back, they'd pried open the lounge's rear access and rigged it so they could barricade the door. More importantly, it had warm showers—something these guys seriously needed.

One of the other boys pointed toward the lift. "Luca! He ran the other way!"

It took Diego a moment to recognize Julian and another beat before the words sank in. He blinked. "There were three of you?"

The other boy, darker and taller than Julian, shivered uncontrollably but nodded.

Diego's mind raced. "Raphael, take them to the Lounge. Check the lockers for clothes. Stay there!"

Raphael drew a dripping, goopy sword with his good arm, keeping the other close to his chest. Diego turned and sprinted down the corridor. Raphael would protect the other two, but Luca was alone, somewhere in the depths of Delta Ring.

The haunting memories of his friend, Miguel, bubbled up—how he wasn't there to save him. Fear and guilt churned in his mind. He shouldn't have left the Pizzarama. He and Raphael had become too lax, and now these three had to face the consequences.

He bolted past the maintenance lift, his eyes scanning every shadow, slowing at a crossing corridor. Signs of recent conflict were evident—a scrap of fabric, a shoe kicked to the side, and blood-smeared footprints continuing onward. Hope sparked within Diego— the guy had survived one encounter, and he might have a chance if he could catch up before it was too late.

Diego raced down the corridor, breaths coming short, his steps echoing off the walls. His pace slowed when he sensed a knot of growlers ahead. Their cries and hisses came from the Rocket Ace hardware store. Diego's eyes tightened at the irony—Luca had stumbled into the same place where he had been cornered when he was first exiled.

A pressure wave hit him. His ears popped, and the floor trembled with a slight rumble. White smoke billowed out from the entrance of the hardware store, and an alarm started wailing.

Diego used his gift to become invisible and cautiously entered the store. Growlers stumbled around, disoriented and confused by the white fire retardant cascading from the ceiling. He scanned the store, struggling to see through the lingering smoke and drifting foam.

His gaze finally landed on a figure clinging to a light fixture on the ceiling as it swung precariously back and forth. While Diego didn't know Luca personally, the torn blue jumpsuit and missing shoe confirmed it had to be him.

The fire retardant stopped falling, yet the alarm continued its wail. Chip would arrive soon, and with this scene, he might even bring that bruiser of a security bot along. Diego used his gift to mentally push as hard as possible, taking advantage of the growlers' disorientation, and was relieved when they quickly scattered.

Diego released his invisibility and called out. "Luca? Come on! We gotta go!"

Luca froze, his eyes widening as they locked onto Diego's mask, but he didn't falter. Unwinding his legs from the light fixture, he dangled by his hands for a heartbeat before dropping to the ground with a solid thud—but his feet slipped out from under him and he sprawled face-first, disappearing beneath the foam.

Diego lunged forward, grabbing Luca's arm and pulling him upright. They darted through the cluttered aisles and ran for the hidden back door—something Diego had discovered behind a shelf, a month after his first visit.

They barreled into the back halls just as Chip's cheerful arrival echoed through the store.

Diego and Luca sprinted down the dimly lit corridor. Luca's bare foot slapped the cold floor with each step. Diego slowed down as they rounded a corner, glancing back to ensure they weren't being followed. "Are you okay?"

Luca nodded, though he was clearly shaken. Diego continued to a secured maintenance door and punched in a code—one of the many things he'd discovered since his exile started. The door hissed open, and they entered a new service tunnel leading to the Atomic Pizzarama.

As they proceeded at a slower pace, Diego asked. "That was loco. What did you do back there?"

Luca beamed. "Oxygen tank, steel wool, battery."

Diego's voice was a mixture of surprise and disbelief. "You blew up an oxygen tank on a space station?"

"Would you rather I got eaten?" Luca shot back. "Besides, I didn't blow it up. I just opened the valve. It was a flash fire. Took a while, too, since all the batteries were nearly dead."

Diego studied him, noticing his singed hair. "You sure you don't need Medbay?"

"I'm fine," Luca muttered.

"Good, 'cause I'd rather stay away from Meddi."

"I thought you were a void terror for a second," Luca admitted. "Scared the tar out of me. You never really know, y'know?" He gave a forced laugh, then kept talking, his voice quick and shaky. "My aunt turned. After a void storm. It was... bad. We had to, uhh—you know. My dad said it was mercy. You have to act fast if anyone's void-touched. You can't trust 'em anymore. They'll go full growler just like that." He snapped his fingers.

Diego didn't answer. The words twisted inside him—familiar and unwelcome. Just more proof he shouldn't tell anyone about his gift.

Back at the Pizzarama, Diego explained how to set the security bar once he left, and tossed Luca some clothes he dug up from his Lair, hoping they were at least somewhat clean. He found Raphael and the others huddled in the Skyway Lounge, its dusty marble floors now smeared with mucky footprints. The three had cleaned up, at least— even if still damp, shivering, and bundled in ill-fitting clothes.

"Chip and the growlers are having a party over at the Red Rocket, which should keep them distracted. So, if you hurry, you three should be able to make it to the Pizzarama without me. I'll swing by Woolwards and grab some warmer things that fit."

Relief flashed in their eyes, and Raphael shot Diego a quick nod.

He returned to the Pizzarama with armfuls of clothes. The new arrivals eagerly picked through them, layering up as they settled into the worn chairs and sofas of the Den.

Diego recognized Julian, but the other two were new to him.

Arturo, with lanky arms, dark brown skin, and wooly hair tucked under a sailor's cap, had claimed a seat on the sofa, drawing a blanket around himself. The whites visible in his wide eyes betrayed the fear he tried to hide as he quietly took in everything around him.

Luca sat hunched in a chair with his knees tucked up, white canvas high-tops peeking out from under the blanket he'd wrapped around himself. Thanks to his earlier exploits, the olive-toned skin of his face was taut and shiny, his hair singed, and his eyebrows missing.

"I still can't believe you started a fire!" Julian declared, tugging on a second argyle sweater—the price he paid for declaring blankets were for babies.

Luca growled. "Stuff it. At least I didn't do the brownwater backstroke."

Julian's eyes flared. Diego had stayed quiet so far, letting everyone settle in, but now he had to step in before things spiraled. Straightening his Z-ball mask to steady his hands, he stepped forward.

"Okay," he began. "First off, I'm glad everybody made it. I know this isn't exactly a great home, but it works. We stick together, we survive."

"You're Desterrados now," Raphael cut in with a grin. "So, which one of you's top dog? Arturo looks the oldest."

Julian snorted. "What, you want us to line up by age like we're in school?"

Arturo grinned. "I'm not even fourteen yet. I just sprouted early."

"Not even fourteen? How long till you are?"

"Four months."

"You're a year younger than me, and still taller?" Julian threw up his hands, "I keep hearing about this growth spurt thing, but I'm not sure where to find it."

A few thin smiles flickered, but no one could bring themselves to laugh.

After a moment, Diego asked, "What about you, Luca?"

He hunched down and muttered, "Couple months behind Julian, I guess."

Raphael kept things going with light questions about themselves and their families. The talk was quiet, but Diego watched everyone relax with each answer, and realized Rafe was smart to give them a chance to open up first.

When it felt right, Diego shifted back to survival. He walked them through the Pizzarama, from the Lair to the kitchen and restrooms, noting there were showers in the Skyway Lounge, and finished at the barricaded front gate. "But remember," he emphasized, "until you've proven you can handle it, do not leave the Pizzarama without Rafe or me escorting you."

Julian furrowed his brow and asked, "Yeah, sure, but reel it back for a minute. How are you guys still alive? And what do we eat?"

Diego's features clouded. "It wasn't easy at first..." He told the story of their survival, including living on nutrient sludge and void rats for every meal. Julian looked queasy at the thought, but Diego knew any resistance would fade once hunger set in.

"You'll toughen up," Raphael added, pointing to their sparring arena.

Luca and Julian reluctantly nodded, and Arturo repeated Diego's earlier statement, "We stick together, we survive, right?"

The conversation continued with a few more questions bouncing back and forth until Raphael asked, "Why did they send all of you at once?"

Julian crossed his arms. "My father said it was about control. The Wardens wanted more access to the orbital, and some of the Anointed thought it was a good idea. That's when Carlos got all riled up. He declared it was time to send more of us down. Something about people's wavering faith needing to be tested."

Diego didn't know much about the Wardens—just a few tidbits from school. After the Kraal arrived and the Union of Stars collapsed, the military rebranded themselves as the Wardens. They still claimed to be the last legitimate remnants of the UOS, although his teacher had speculated the new name was just a way to hide the fact they'd been the ones dropping bombs everywhere.

The Star Rangers, once the Union's exploratory branch, had taken a different path. Now they wandered from system to system, trying to keep the peace and bring hope to a universe that had mostly forgotten what hope felt like.

Julian's tone picked up a petulant edge as he stabbed a finger at Luca. "But really, it's his fault I'm here. My father had worked it all out with Carlos so I didn't have to come down, but then *his* parents had to go and start talking about how wrong it was." He glared at Luca. "Well, the Anointed straightened that all out, didn't they?"

Luca's expression darkened at Julian's jab, and his reply started with fire. "Stuff it! They didn't do anything wrong. They're okay— they're—" His lower lip began to tremble, and he halted as his voice wavered, emotion bubbling close to the surface.

Raphael stepped forward, crouching to bring himself eye level with Luca, "Hey, amigo, it's okay. Julian didn't mean anything by it. You don't have to say a thing if you don't want to. We're all the Desterrados now—exiled together."

Arturo cleared his throat, his voice surprisingly deep. "Carlos had Luca's parents taken away. Nobody's seen them since they protested. That shut everybody up—even my folks."

A heavy silence settled over the boys until Raphael finally exhaled, breaking the tension. "Luca, I'm sure they're fine."

Diego glanced at Luca, not so sure he could make the same claim.

The uneasy quiet returned until Luca spoke softly. "What he said about the Wardens... it's true. I heard some of the Anointed arguing on the concourse. Carlos was furious, saying he could handle 'things' and get it all cleaned up without the Warden's help."

"Cleaned up?" Arturo's brow furrowed.

Luca shrugged. "Right after that, the defense squads made a big push, rounding up all the growlers they could find, loading them into the maintenance lifts, and sending them down..."

He didn't need to say more. His words hung heavy in the air until Julian moaned, "Down... here?"

Raphael clapped his hands. "Enough! Time for exercise."

"Right now?" Julian moaned, pulling the blanket he'd covertly claimed a little tighter. "But it's cold."

"Exactly." Raphael's grin took on a feral look. "That's how you stay warm down here."

Julian's gaze shifted between Raphael and Diego. "So, Rafe... who's in charge?"

A few heartbeats passed. Raphael hesitated, casting a glance at Diego. They had never talked about it before. Diego opened his mouth, scrambling for words to explain that they didn't need someone in charge, that it was better if they just all worked things out together.

But Raphael spoke first. "Diego is."

Surprised, Diego studied Raphael, trying to understand his intentions. Rather than reassure, the statement left him feeling more uncertain than ever.

Yakety Yak

Before Diego realized it, a month had slipped by. The Pizzarama grew louder, messier, and more alive as the newcomers settled into life on Delta Ring. He and Raphael took turns guiding each boy through the derelict corridors of Blue Sector, teaching them how to move quietly, what dangers to avoid, and useful bolt-holes to duck into if the growlers closed in—one of which Arturo and Julian were already familiar with.

Raphael started sporting a thin mustache to complement his SEO security jacket. He claimed it made him look authoritative, but to Diego, the whole package—paired with his ever-present Starblaze superhero T-shirt—had the opposite effect, making him look like a teenager desperate for validation.

Luca revealed a knack for gadgets. He rigged a tripwire at the main entrance from scavenged arcade game parts that would unleash a cacophony of video game noises loud enough to wake the dead.

Somewhere between the sweat, the failures, and the small wins, a brotherhood began to take root. And with it came a mantra, repeated whenever tempers frayed or hope wavered: "We stick together, we survive."

But there were unexpected changes, too. The "Mi Compa" selfie Raphael had taken with Diego vanished from the Den, and his behavior shifted—especially around Julian. The two reconnected almost instantly. Soon Raphael favored him on training runs, leaving Diego with Arturo and Luca.

Diego didn't resent their friendship—but he couldn't stop feeling kicked aside. He tried to take it in stride. Julian had his moments, usually with a well-timed joke, but mostly he was just surly, and Diego was happy to keep his distance.

What set him on edge the most, though, was how Raphael wouldn't let up about hunting growlers.

"What if they get into the Pizzarama and we're cornered? We should thin the horde."

Every time, Diego would shut him down, which only added to the growing tension between them.

Not that he was wrong about the risk. But there was more than one way to solve a problem. Direct conflict wasn't the answer. So Diego cleared the back corridor leading to the Skyway Lounge, then called everyone together to go over the plan.

Arturo nodded. "Right. If growlers come, we slip out the back and head to the Lounge."

Raphael hung back, face dark, and muttered, "We should hold our ground."

Diego snapped. "Why is everything about fighting with you?"

Raphael's face darkened, and he stormed off.

Arturo winced. "Ouch."

Only then did Diego notice how tight his chest had become. Maybe he wasn't cut out to be a leader—he hated the spotlight.

Now that there were enough boys for a proper rotation, someone always stayed behind to watch the maintenance lift. This time, Diego was glad it was his turn. Comfortable silence settled in after the others left for the workshop, and his thoughts shifted back to Raphael.

No matter what Diego tried, every interaction they had ended up crackling with unspoken words. It left him wondering if Raphael was shifting back into his old ways. As he mulled over this, an idea began to form: What if they broke into Red Sector together—just the two of them? Would that help clear the static between them? The last attempt to deal with the cameras had ended poorly, but he could share his plan about tricking them with a photograph.

All he needed was the old Polaroid camera.

After an hour digging through almost every corner of the Pizzarama, Diego came up empty. Raphael had been the last to use the camera, which left only one place to check: his things in the Lair. Diego had avoided them so far, but maybe it was time.

He picked through the clothes, cabinets, and gear around Raphael's bed, trying to avoid disturbing too much. Finally, he found the camera in a buried bin—but what stopped him cold were the stacks of passkeys crammed alongside it. At least a hundred, by his quick count.

A flame sparked in him—why did Raphael need so many passkeys? He stewed for a moment, then quickly returned everything to where he'd found it.

Later, when the others had split off to their own devices, Diego caught up to Raphael in the Den. "Hey, uh... after you're all healed up, maybe we could give Red Sector another shot? Just us two."

Raphael studied him for a beat. "Sure. But how?"

"Remember The Crimson Directive? When Victor Shadowstar snuck into the commie base and used photos to fool the cameras? What if we tried that? Might buy us enough time to cut through the door. Only... I can't find the old camera."

Raphael grinned. "That could work! Like Vic himself directing our mission!" He hurried off to the Lair and came back a moment later with the camera.

Diego reached for it, but Raphael didn't let go.

"You know," he said softly, "it's a shame you can't use your powers to hide us from people and cameras, like you do with void terrors. Then we wouldn't even need this, right?"

Diego's pulse spiked. He hadn't told Raphael about his masking... or had he? Stepping closer, he kept his voice low. "Doesn't work on cameras. Just void terrors, and—uh, things like growlers and rats."

Raphael arched an eyebrow. "Which are void terrors."

Diego gave a quick nod.

"Come on, you must've tried using it on people?"

"Using what?" Diego's voice came out thin.

"Your void powers, chavo."

Diego's stomach knotted. Did Raphael actually know more than he'd told him, or was he just guessing? Diego had never been able to lie without his face giving it away, and Raphael knew it.

He stammered, "Sure, but, uhh... nothing. Just works on terrors."

"Weird. Seems like it should."

Diego forced a shrug, willing his voice steady. Time to change the subject. "So—I had another idea. Maybe we should gather all the passkeys we can? Chip said the robots can access different sectors. If we find the right key, maybe we can get into another one. Or... you already have some?"

"Sure," Raphael said after a moment. "I've got a couple. Want me to gather more?"

"Oh, it's not a big deal; we can split the work," Diego tried to keep his tone casual.

But Raphael was already on his feet. "Nah, don't worry about it. Gives me something to do. I'll get on it right away."

Diego had half-hoped Raphael would just admit to the horde of passkeys under his bed. Instead, he came back later with maybe seven, like that was all he had. "Here. I'll find more tomorrow."

When everyone gathered for lunch, Diego put the keys on the table and told them to pick one for themselves. They eagerly sorted through the cards, arguing over which name to claim.

Of course, Raphael had to slip in a barb, pushing a passkey into Luca's hands. "You'd make a cute Sally, chavo."

Luca scowled and shoved it aside. Diego's jaw tightened at the old Raphael bleeding through.

Soon enough, everyone wanted to try their new keys at the public televid booths.

An idea had been percolating in Diego's mind, and he was eager to dig deeper. He claimed one of the two functioning terminals for himself, leaving the others to negotiate turns on the remaining one.

Julian argued outside the booth, his words stretching higher. "Why can't I just send a message to Mother?"

Raphael's voice held an edge. "I already told you. We can't risk Carlos finding out we're alive."

"But he said we could return if we survived."

"Did he give you a way to report back?" Raphael snorted. "This was always a one-way ticket, chavo. Keeping our survival quiet is the only card we've got. Best to keep it to ourselves for now. I'm working on how we can use it to our advantage."

"You have a plan?" Arturo asked.

"I'm working on one," Raphael boasted.

"News to me," Diego muttered.

The terminal's green glow flickered across his face as he combed the Usenet hacking forums. Everything would change if he could get control of the mainframe. No more arguing with Chip, he could just turn up the heat. Unlock the maintenance lift. Maybe even meddle with Bravo Ring to help them get back. The possibilities felt endless. Having control of the mainframe could open doors—literally.

But how did you even hack a computer?

He dug through scraps of information until he hit a wall: the public terminals were locked down tight. If he wanted to pull this off, he'd need a console with better network access.

So far, nothing in Blue Sector fit the bill. Every terminal outside the public booths was either dead or broken. There was the one in Echo Ring, but he wasn't ready to tell the others about the lab. Not yet. For now, he'd just have to keep an eye out in Red Sector.

Shifting gears, he searched the station's library for COMTRAN programming manuals. The forums had made one thing clear: to get anywhere in the mainframe, he had to learn to code. The manuals were dense, stuffed with references to books he couldn't even find, but he stuck with it until the others were ready to go.

The next evening, Raphael dumped a mountain of passkeys onto the table. "Feast your eyes on my haul!"

Arturo asked, "Do we need that many?"

Raphael grinned. "Diego thought one of the lost passkeys might get us into the other sectors. So, I gathered this lot to test his theory."

That lit everyone up. The new boys practically shoved Diego and Raphael toward the exit, insisting they bring back something tasty. Diego barely managed to grab his Top Slugger before he and Raphael were hustled out of the Pizzarama.

They knew the halls well enough to find their way without trouble, and soon they were in a narrow service passage facing a blast door blocking their way into Red Sector.

Diego kept watch, glancing between the shadows and the cameras, certain it was only a matter of time before Chip rolled up. Raphael swiped card after card, adding groans and exaggerated sighs with each failure. Diego was sure he'd already tested them, and decided to see if he could catch Rafe in a lie.

"Where'd you say you found that jacket? Any passkeys with it?"

Raphael froze mid-swipe, a flicker crossing his face. "Uh… a closet, I think. But no passkeys."

"Where exactly? Maybe we should double-check?"

Raphael's shoulders tightened. "Living Quarters. But I'm telling you, chavo, there wasn't a passkey anywhere. Don't you trust me?"

"Too bad. A cop's passkey might've opened this right up."

As expected, none of the cards worked. That left them with their original plan: cutting a hole through the promenade blast door, and they returned to give the bad news. However, they were met with a bizarre sight when they stepped into the Atomic Pizzarama: Cosmic Clara, the animatronic explorer cat, now sat front and center on the stage, posed regally in a battered armchair.

"Welcome back!" Arturo's deep voice carried across the room. Julian stood beside him, arms crossed, nodding in satisfaction.

With her shimmering blue-and-white striped fur, wide teal eyes, and makeshift crown, Clara looked almost regal, like some ancient cat-goddess overseeing her subjects.

Almost.

Except now she was dressed in a set of frilly girls' underwear.

"You guys… did all this?" Diego asked. His face burned, not only because he couldn't stop staring at the scanty outfit, but also because he saw the look Raphael shared with Julian. The new boys wouldn't have gone to Bobby Soxers alone. No, Raphael had planned it all.

Julian flashed a hungry grin. "We figured the Desterrados needed a mascot. Cosmic Clara seemed perfect—she has curves!"

Raphael clapped Julian on the back. "A sexy mascot! I approve!"

Diego wasn't mad they'd made a mascot, or even about her outfit. What got him was Raphael pretending this was all spontaneous, when it clearly wasn't. That, and he still wasn't sure how he felt about having a robotic overseer watching them all the time.

"You guys don't think it's… a little creepy?"

Arturo's grin stretched wider. "It's for morale. She's… inspiring."

Luca edged forward, pointing at the bag of passkeys. "Any of them work?"

"Any what?" Raphael asked, still admiring Clara.

"None of the passkeys opened the door," Diego replied. He caught a flicker in Luca's expression, something that struck a chord in him that he didn't quite understand. The others were too busy joking about Clara to notice Luca slip away. But Diego did

That evening, he found Luca hunched over a table, tinkering with a pile of salvaged electronics. Diego shuffled his feet, feeling out of his element. After a few hesitant starts, he managed, "You're good with things. Gadgets, and stuff…"

Luca looked up, blinking. "Thanks," he muttered, his gaze dropping back to the parts in his hands. "My dad taught me a lot. Before…" He trailed off.

Diego waited, a knot rising in his throat as thoughts of his own parents surfaced. "Do you think about him a lot?"

Luca swallowed, fingers teasing at a wire. "Every day," he whispered.

"When they took my parents for standing up to Carlos, I thought maybe… maybe it'd just be for a day or two. But then the Anointed sent me, Julian, and Arturo down here… and yeah. I know we can't go back. But…" His chin wobbled, and for just a moment his face teetered on the edge of tears. His voice broke as he forced the words out. "I just want—I just want to know if they're okay."

Struggling for something to do, some way to offer comfort, Diego gave Luca's shoulder a light bump. "I'm sure they are," he said. But even as the words left his mouth, they sounded hollow.

Luca nodded, eyes locked on the electronics in his hands.

Diego wished he knew what else to say. How to help. But nothing came. After a long moment, he muttered, "Well… yeah," and stepped away, leaving Luca to his thoughts.

Itsy Bitsy Spider

Once free from his arm sling, Raphael's first move was to head out on a solo scouting trip. With all the new chavos around, he needed some "me" time.

To avoid any nosy bots, he went out of his way to find a back corridor where the lights had all failed. Flashlight in one hand, passkey spinning idly in the other, he approached the bulkhead separating Blue and Green Sectors.

"Lou Bancroft" had been the former owner of his SEO jacket, and apparently, the good officer had enjoyed access to more areas than Diego ever had.

A flicker of satisfaction curled Raphael's lips—Diego was clueless. And Raphael was about to step where Diego never had: Green Sector.

That is, if the blast door actually opened. His pulse quickened as he tapped the passkey against the scanner. The light blinked green. A clank, a hiss, then the door rattled open.

Beyond lay a corridor filled with an ethereal white sheen. He brushed his fingers against a few sticky strands, and it took a moment to register: they were webs. Layer after layer, spun into an eerie, silky cloud that filled the corridor. A shiver crawled up his spine, equal parts horror and fascination.

Swinging his flashlight through the haze, Raphael froze. Eight massive eyes, each the size of his fist, glared back at him.

His hand darted to the door control, then stopped. The "face" didn't move. He exhaled a shaky breath, a faint chuckle escaping as he stepped closer. "It's just an exoskeleton husk. Some spider shell. Big, but not alive."

He had to have it. Flashlight clenched between his teeth, he drew his knife. Sticky strands clung to the blade, fighting him with every stroke, but he hacked away enough to pry the headpiece loose.

Setting it down, he tugged at a mandible, already planning how he'd present his "find" to Diego without raising suspicions.

Then a shadow stirred deeper in the web.

"¡Mierda!" He yanked the mandible free and slapped the door control, stumbling back. The door crawled shut, agonizingly slow, until it sealed with a hiss.

Only then did he breathe again.

A shudder rippled through him, and he couldn't shake the sensation of tiny legs crawling across his skin. He let out an embarrassingly girlish yowl while hopping from foot to foot and furiously rubbing his arms. After pulling himself together, he straightened his collar and cast a quick glance around. Good. No witnesses.

All Shook Up

They spent several days preparing to break into Red Sector, and the speculation of what they would find only grew wilder—ranging from enough food to last a year to Deathmark hordes just waiting for their arrival.

The real challenge, however, was the plan itself. Diego felt the kiosks and debris on the promenade gave them the best chance to conceal their work, but the others insisted on scouting the back corridors again, just in case they'd missed something.

After rehashing it far too many times, they finally agreed that the promenade's blast door was their way in. It took some work, but they managed to wedge the plasma cutter inside a Cosmo Creamery kiosk.

The pastel paint was chipped and faded, and it had a goofy cow in a spacesuit on its side, but it suited their needs and offered decent cover. Once Luca oiled the wheels, the cart even rolled without screeching. Arturo added his own twist, painting over the "ce" everywhere with a bloody-red "S" to become "I Scream."

Ideally, they would look like nothing more than a vendor moving into place. Not that they had any ice cream. Or customers. But Chip wasn't exactly the sharpest bot around.

The story of Diego and Raphael's last run might have colored their decision, but Luca, Arturo, and Julian all chose to stay behind—not that they'd admit to being afraid, of course. It was just "better logistically," right?

Diego's sweaty palms slipped on the handles as he and Rafe pushed the rattling cart. He kept glancing at the Delta Ring Ops maintenance door, half-expecting the bruiser bot to storm out.

"Relax," Raphael muttered. "Just act natural."

Diego swallowed hard and forced a nod, though his heart still hammered in his chest.

Raphael sauntered into Ring Ops, launching into a list of safety complaints to keep Chip distracted while Diego rolled the kiosk past the entrance. At the blast door, Diego extended the ladder and climbed up to the first security camera. He took a moment to line up his Polaroid, then snapped a picture.

The camera made a soft *grrrr* as it spat out the film. Diego shook it lightly, watching as the image faded into being. Once sure it would work, he taped the photo to the end of a stick and eased it in front of the lens.

He slid down the ladder and hurried past Ring Ops, ducking into the men's restroom. The women's was still a wreck from their last attempt, with twisted partitions and broken glass everywhere—a memory neither of them cared to stir up.

Raphael soon arrived, and they waited quietly, watching the corridor for any sign of trouble.

"Looks like it worked," Rafe whispered after a few minutes.

"Yeah," Diego agreed. They slipped back to the kiosk, and Rafe started reassembling the plasma cutter while Diego repeated the process with the remaining cameras.

Rafe fiddled with the cutter, muttering so low it was almost lost. "I still think we should just do Green Sector instead."

The words struck a chord and Diego straightened from rearranging the cover. He had shut down this option a dozen times already, never offering an explanation. He just couldn't consider it. There were still nights when he woke drenched in sweat, haunted by the thoughts of a million spiders crawling all over him.

"I'm not having this argument again," he said flatly.

Rafe stretched, forcing a yawn. "Hey, if you say so, *el capitán*. I won't question why you're so spooked by Green Sector. Me? I think we'll be just fine in Red."

Diego studied him a few beats longer. The sharp, metallic tang of heated steel bit at his nostrils as Rafe started the cut.

So far, everything had gone smoothly—too smoothly.

"Got through," Raphael muttered, shutting off the plasma cutter.

A small, blackened hole at knee height trailed faint wisps of smoke that curled gently in the air. No howling vacuum sucked the air into space.

Grinning, Rafe resumed his work, extending the cut into a meter-wide circle. He tacked short bars along the edges as makeshift handles. Diego gripped them as Rafe neared the end, steadying the plate so it wouldn't fall and ring loudly against the floor.

The heavy disk shifted slightly when Rafe finished the cut, and together they worked it free. Beyond the breach lay a scene much like the promenade on their side, with flickering signs, broken kiosks, and debris scattered across the floor. Yet somehow it was also different. Untouched. Waiting to be explored.

The knot between Diego's shoulders loosened, giving way to a flicker of excitement as he took it in.

While Raphael stowed the plasma cutter, Diego poked his head through the hole, scanning for surveillance cameras. He repeated the trick with the Polaroid photos on the other side. Then they grabbed their gear and ventured into Red Sector.

Moving down the promenade, Diego kept his senses sharp, mentally nudging any growlers away from their path. There were more of them here, making him wonder how many had lingered since the Arrival, and why there weren't this many in Blue Sector. Then it hit him: the lift by Pizzarama was connected to the main plaza of La Familia's ring. When they sent growlers down, they used the other lifts—the ones that led to Green and Red Sectors.

The two boys advanced at a cautious pace through the back halls until they reached a food court. Diego had never seen one before.

They scoured ruined counters and storage rooms, finding little more than decomposed food and rancid soda-fountain syrup. Then, tucked away in a vending supply closet, they uncovered two unopened cases of Atomic Cakes.

The sweet, fluffy treats had endured decades, waiting for them. They tore cellophane wrappers open and stuffed the spongy, neon-yellow cakes into their mouths. For a moment, they simply ate, making the occasional quiet sound of satisfaction. It was a feast to their senses, food that felt alive. Without a word, they devoured two more before Diego reluctantly closed the box.

"We should save some."

The strain of using his gift to keep their movements hidden from the growlers had worn on Diego, but the sugar buzzing in his veins pushed him onward. Leaving the food court, the promenade opened into the Community Center. Faded murals of athletes in Serenity Orbital's exercise uniforms stretched across a series of doors, each marked for a different activity.

Raphael slowed, and eagerness lit his voice. "Z-ball! We gotta look. Come on!"

But Diego barely heard him. His eyes had locked on the Stellar Adventure Park sign. Some letters had fallen, the lights were dead, but a giant cartoon fox still held an information board. A grin spread across Diego's face as he pointed at a line: "Explore and play in the trees of the biosphere."

Rafe's eyes lit up, and he hurried to follow him through the doors that rattled open. They found a souvenir shop inside, with empty shelves, and the scraps of old inventory scattered across the floor. Behind the ticket counter, a robot's head popped briefly into view before it ducked back down, muttering about dangerous patrons.

Rafe approached slowly, raising his hands to show they meant no harm. "Easy tin can. We're not growlers."

The robot's rectangular head cautiously peered over the counter, its cartoonishly large eyes flickering as it scanned them. The scratches and dents across its chassis told the story of its rough survival. After a moment, its red optics softened to a welcoming blue.

"Apologies, visitors," its voice warbled with a nervous edge as if it was ready to bolt at the first hint of trouble.

Raphael leaned on the counter. "We need to get into the Adventure Park."

A pleased hum came from the robot as it straightened up with newfound confidence. "Ah, yes," it replied, its tone steadying. "Now, will that be two full-day child adventure passes?"

"Adult," Raphael scowled, straightening his back a little.

"Of course," the robot chirped, taking Diego's passkey for payment. "Thank you for complying as paying customers, unlike the unruly sorts who frequent here without proper tickets."

A printer whirred inside the counter, spitting out two blank tickets. "Please accept my apologies; I assure you these are valid. There is no more ink, you see. We have not received a supply shipment for some time. I've filed complaints with corporate, but haven't received a response."

"You don't say." Diego managed a smile, half amused, half sorry for the bolt-brain that had kept at its post all these years.

The robot gestured toward a pathway leading to a gateway at the back of the souvenir store, cheerfully announcing, "Follow the lighted pawprints to your right, heed all of Stella Fox's cautionary signs, and enjoy your visit to the Adventure Park!"

"Thanks!" Diego offered before chasing after Rafe. He still didn't like bots, but keeping them happy cost him nothing.

Only a few lights embedded in the floor flickered to life. Others blinked on and off, as if unsure whether to guide them forward or warn them back.

They passed through a decorated gate into a cylindrical airlock chamber. The entrance slowly rotated around the room until it revealed the biosphere. Warm, humid air thick with the scent of earth and decay embraced them. Both boys grinned. It was life. Not the bone-chilling cold of the ring's corridors.

Raphael bumped Diego's fist and they stepped onto an overgrown path.

Diego had forgotten to scan ahead with his gift, and the moment he did, a cold knot tightened in his chest. A different kind of void terror was somewhere in the biosphere. Something he didn't recognize.

He dropped into a crouch, pulled Raphael down with him, and put a finger to his lips.

The biosphere's sounds pressed in. Water trickled somewhere deeper. Leaves rustled in an artificial breeze. An occasional animal cry echoed, but it was too hard to tell if it was a bird, a beast, or something worse.

Diego shut his eyes, stretching his senses, trying to figure out what he had felt. It wasn't the usual growlers or void rats. This was stronger. Greater than growlers, but also different from the Kraal.

"This place is swimming with void terrors," Diego finally whispered.

"That's why you're here, right? So we can wander without them bothering us?"

Diego's shoulders tightened. The words landed wrong, like Raphael kept him around simply for what he could do. But surely he was overthinking it? He exhaled slowly, letting it slide. "I need more time to study things. I think it's too dangerous."

Raphael's eyes narrowed. "We need to explore. We can't go back to the boys empty-handed."

"We won't. We've got the Atomic Cakes."

"Yeah, but that's hardly anything." Raphael waved him on. "Come on. Just a little farther."

Diego glanced ahead. The path split—one stairway climbing into a tangle of vines, the other winding around the base of a massive artificial tree trunk. At the junction stood a crooked, kid-sized cutout of Stella the Fox. Her cartoon grin and oversized eyes still showed through the water-streaked, peeling paint. In her paws, she held arrows, one pointing to the "Adventure Zone," the other to the "Learning Zone."

He hesitated, then looked back the way they'd come. His instincts to retreat tripped over his deeply seated need to spend just a few more minutes in this living, breathing ecosystem.

"Fine," he sighed. "But at the first sign of trouble, we go."

Because the stairway was overrun with tangled vines, they followed the path around the tree trunk to an archway marked "Learning Zone." Inside, moisture beaded on the walls and gathered in pools across the floor. Torn, moldy signs had once explained how the biosphere worked.

Raphael drifted toward a placard on hydroponics while Diego spotted clusters of raspberries in an overgrown plant display. He plucked them carefully, alternating between stuffing his mouth and filling his pockets. Juice ran down his chin as he reached for another—then froze.

The biosphere had gone still.

No rustling leaves. No distant calls. Nothing.

A deep, rattling howl tore through the silence, triggering a primal instinct in Diego's bones: run or be eaten. His heart hammered as he sensed void terrors closing in.

He dove into the overgrown display, Rafe following close behind. Thorns snagged their sleeves, but they pushed deeper. Diego masked their presence just as a group of growlers thundered through the room without slowing—almost as if fleeing something. One hissed words as it passed: "Let it eat us!"

A static pressure followed, gnawing at his gift and twisting his stomach. The walls trembled as a hulking terror contorted through the entrance, flailing its arms as it clawed for the growlers.

What might once have been human was now warped beyond recognition. Spiny ridges tore along its back, jutting out from beneath mottled skin, and its eyes burned with an eldritch glow in an unnatural flickering light—eyes that looked nowhere and everywhere all at once. It walked on two legs, though its twisted posture hinted at a creature forced to move against its nature. Too many limbs extended from its misshapen torso, each moving with insect-like precision, each hand tipped with unnaturally long fingers.

The very sight of it sent a shudder through Diego. Its mouth stretched impossibly wide, filled with gnarled, disordered teeth. The howl that erupted shook the air, spittle flying as it broke free of the doorway and lurched after the growlers.

And then it froze in place. Nostrils flared. Its horrible eyes swept the room.

Diego held his breath. Every heartbeat hammered in his chest while the beast prowled, twitching with dreadful, pent-up energy. His lungs burned desperately for air, but he had to hold still.

Finally, the terror retreated. Its howls echoed through the air of the biosphere as it lumbered away. Diego's body trembled as the tension drained from his muscles.

Rafe, pale and wide-eyed, whispered, "What was that?"

"Deathmark, I think," Diego said in a shaky voice.

"I'm ready to go now," Rafe squeaked.

After waiting to be sure it had truly moved on, they slipped from cover and retreated through the corridors of Red Sector, pausing only long enough to grab the boxes of Atomic Cakes. Their steps carried an urgent restraint, driven by a primitive need to distance themselves from the Deathmark in the biosphere.

At the blast door, Raphael reattached the cut metal panel with a few spot welds. "We can figure out hinges and a bolt later… a really big bolt."

With the makeshift repair finished, they slid down to the floor, their backs against the cold wall, finally relaxing.

Raphael pulled the welding mask off and wiped the sweat from his brow. "That was… something else."

Diego took several deep breaths, then reached into his pocket, pulling out a handful of slightly mashed raspberries. He inspected them, lifted his z-ball mask and popped one into his mouth. His eyes closed and he sighed in pure relief as the bright sweetness flooded his senses.

He held out his hand, offering some to Raphael, who popped a few into his mouth and moaned, *"Néctar de los dioses."*

Diego nodded, and they silently enjoyed the berries, letting the lingering terror fade and their rational minds settle back into place.

"I think we should keep the story simple and not mention the Deathmark," Diego eventually said. "Maybe just tell them the biosphere works, but is dangerous."

"Yeah. Those chavitos already wet themselves thinking of growlers outside the Pizzarama. No need to give 'em nightmares."

They sat in the quiet for a few more minutes. Despite the danger, they both knew they'd be back. As they walked back to their home, Diego's mind lingered on the growlers they'd seen. One had been a young woman with long, dark hair, and for a fleeting moment, she had reminded him of Donna. His stomach twisted.

She's safe up in Bravo Ring. She has to be.

They returned to find Julian, Arturo, and Luca waiting anxiously. A celebration erupted at the sight of the Atomic Cakes. They devoured the entire box, and the sugar quickly hit their systems. Soon, boasts, dares, and laughter filled the air, and everyone's pent-up fears were released in a flurry of frantic, impromptu activity.

The jukebox spun up, filling the air with the bright, bouncy rhythm of Elvis Presley's "All Shook Up."

Growlers hammered at the Pizzarama's gate, but they ignored them—even if it seemed odd. Diego just figured they were attracted by the noise, and they all trusted in the strength of their fortifications.

Games were invented on the spot, dares and challenges sprang up, and laughter filled the room. For a while, they forgot about their exile—they were simply boys being boys, taking comfort in each other's company.

As the night wore on and the sugar highs faded, the conversations softened into low murmurs, and the room that had once buzzed with energy finally settled into a hushed calm.

Yet Diego only felt more alive. A warm current hummed in his veins, and he let it wash through him. His eyelids grew heavy as he sank deeper into it, reveling in the way it made him feel.

For the first time in months, he wasn't afraid or hungry or angry. He just felt... good.

Too good.

And then it clicked. That soft, electric flutter pulsing through him—he knew what it was. His stomach lurched, and shame cut through him. He had wallowed in it. Basked in it. Loved every second. Loved what made him like the void terrors.

Because feeling that way could mean only one thing.

A void storm was coming.

I'm So Lonesome I Could Cry

Diego sprinted to the gate—not that he needed the violet flicker in the air to know a void storm was coming. He seized his gift. The gift he hated. Hated that it proved he was like the growlers. Clenching his teeth, he shoved against them with all his strength to clear their exit.

Arturo was right behind him, shouting, "Void storm! Where's the chapel? I don't know where the chapel is!"

Diego forced his voice steady. "You know the routine! Follow me!"

They spilled onto the promenade—Luca still wrestling with his pants, Rafe half-hopping as he jammed on his boots.

Every step came at a cost. Diego's skull pounded as he fought to hold the void terrors back; with the coming storm, they were more active than ever.

At last, the chapel's heavy wooden doors curved into view—they'd make it. Diego almost believed it—until the wall beyond bled painful light, and a pulsating ball of void energy pushed through.

Julian stumbled. Diego yanked him upright without breaking stride.

The sphere slid toward them, crackling, hissing. Tendrils lashed the walls, snapping in its wake.

The chapel doors came nearer with every stride. Not fast enough. The sphere would reach them first. And there was nothing Diego could do.

The deck answered with a shimmer, and void rats phased upward in a seething mass behind the sphere. It halted, shuddering, its colors swirling as though some unfathomable mind wrestled with indecision.

The hesitation was all they needed. They bolted through the chapel doors, slamming them shut with a boom that sealed off the chaos outside. A heartbeat of stillness, then ragged gasps as they fought to catch their breath. Diego counted heads—everyone made it.

Arturo doubled over, hands on his knees. "¡Madre mía!" He gasped. "I didn't think we'd make it."

Luca knelt at the altar, bowing his head. The others exchanged glances, saying nothing. Usually, at this time, the mothers and brethren gathered there, rolling their beads and muttering prayers to any saint they could name, while the children sat wide-eyed on the benches, too scared to speak. But Luca gave no such display.

The boys spread out across the benches. The floors shuddered, and the orbital groaned as the storm raged on, leaving each of them alone with their thoughts.

Diego drew in a long, slow breath, trying to find a place of calm. Every part of him buzzed—and the fact it felt good sickened him. He should have sensed it sooner. Should have warned them. Instead, he'd reveled in it, and that had nearly cost the others their lives.

He hated it. Hated himself for it. But it wasn't like he could get rid of it. Raphael's off-handed comment from Red Sector surged back —that he was only useful when he used his gift.

Maybe I am just a tool. A cursed blade they can't throw away.

Closing his eyes, he let the bilious thoughts simmer. But the longer he lingered on them, the worse he felt. The darkness spiraled until it was like the last time in Echo Ring's lab—when he'd thought about just being done. Because even if he couldn't cut his gift out, he could just... he could just... a knot formed in his chest as he struggled to finish the bleak thought.

And then—almost like a whisper—he felt his mom. The way she would wrap her arms around him when things were too heavy. He swiped at his cheeks, hoping no one saw his sudden tears. But her memory steadied him; her voice telling him to think happy thoughts. She was right. He had to think of something else—anything else, or he'd sink too far.

Luca straightened, shuffled back, and slid onto a bench in the front. His gaze never left the floor. The boys remained silent as the storm's rattling filled the chapel with restless energy.

Diego's mind wandered to the nature of the growlers. The words they spoke made no sense... unless they actually weren't mindless undead at all. What if they were just sick people? And if that was true, what did it mean when someone killed a growler? The thought lingered, cold and unsettling.

Julian groaned, asking a question to no one in particular. "I don't know what to think about all this. How can Carlos be a prophet?"

Luca spoke without looking up. "You need to separate God and the good book from what Carlos preaches. They aren't the same thing."

Arturo shifted uneasily. "My family was never really into religion—" He caught himself, reflexively adding, "Except now we believe in Carlos's teachings." A sheepish look crossed his face. "I mean... I guess I don't have to say that anymore, right? No one's going to report me here."

The others gave a mix of nods and shrugs, and Arturo continued. "Did you guys hear that visiting trader a few months back? The one talking about people worshiping the Kraal, thinking it'll keep them safe?"

"Cults," Luca growled, his voice filled with disgust.

Raphael stretched out on the bench. "Yeah. But it seems weird, you know? Seriously, why would anyone worship the Kraal?"

Luca turned, his expression hard. "Because they're cowards. Desperate people will bow to anything if it means surviving. But void-touched things are evil. We should hate them, not worship them."

The words cut deep. Diego blinked hard, forcing himself not to flinch, not to let anyone see how much they stung. If Luca hated the void-touched this much, what would he think of el sentido dotado? The thought lodged in him, making him certain he had to keep it secret.

"I guess I can understand that," Arturo muttered, his gaze lingering on the chapel's broken stained glass panels. The lights that once lit them from behind had long since failed. "Then what is it that protects us here? The room itself? Or prayers?"

The chapel listened, but no answer came.

At last, Julian spoke, "What about those spacer talismans? Pounamu, right? They work like chapels, somehow? A trader tried to sell one to my mom. Said they had some kind of ancient power, which is why spacers don't need chapels. She said it was heresy, of course."

Arturo's eyes widened. "So, it's not just holy places?"

Luca exhaled loudly.

"Come now, tell us what you really think," Julian drawled.

Luca hesitated a moment before speaking. "Sacred places have always been a refuge—even before the Kraal, before the storms. I heard about the Pounamu too. So... maybe there's something to them beyond just being holy. Something about faith itself?"

No one replied. The storm rattled the orbital.

"Oh no!" Julian bolted upright. "Please tell me somebody grabbed food?"

A scatter of shrugs and reluctant head shakes.

Julian groaned and flopped back down. "Great. Let's hope this is a short storm and not one that lasts for days."

Arturo rubbed his arms. "Man, I thought the nights down here were bad enough with all the things lurking around, but this...."

Julian chuckled. "You could cozy up with your sniffles and a soggy pillow each night, like Luca."

Luca just stared ahead, jaw tight.

"Enough," Raphael snapped.

Julian sucked in a breath, his gaze darting between Diego and Raphael. Then he slouched back on the bench. "Yeah, fine. Whatever."

Diego stared at Raphael. The defense was unexpected, but it didn't leave him comforted.

The hours ticked by, stretching deep into the night, and still, sleep eluded them all. Every time someone started to drift off, they were jolted awake by the thunderous rattling of the orbital or the wails and clamor of excited void terrors outside.

"Gaaaah," Raphael groaned eventually, breaking the silence. "Let's talk about something. What does anyone know about Death-marks?"

Julian rubbed his eyes, stretching with a tired yawn. "They're worse than growlers. They don't just eat you—they tear your soul apart. If a Deathmark gets you, there's nothing left. Not even for the next life."

Raphael's voice went quiet, his eyes distant. "I think that... might be right..."

Diego wished Raphael hadn't brought up the topic. The urge to share their own terrifying encounter with the Deathmark tugged at him, but a glance around at pale faces and wide eyes changed his mind. Some things were better left unspoken.

The storm raged on, and Diego stretched his gift out, testing the limits of how far he could sense the void terrors. Then, something else stirred—a familiar resonance pulling at him from Echo Ring.

The Kraal.

The realization slammed into him. He pulled back instantly, praying it hadn't noticed.

Frustration knotted. He despised his gift, but it wasn't going away. He wanted to understand it. Even master it. But any attempt to test it was met with horrifying danger. And he wasn't just playing with fire; whenever he pushed his gift, it seemed to tease at the frayed edges of the universe.

He just couldn't win.

More time passed, and gradually, the orbital no longer rattled and groaned. In the storm's wake, a nervous quiet settled over the chapel. They gathered their gear and ventured out. The sounds of innervated void terrors echoed through the corridors, keeping them on edge as they made their way back to the Pizzarama.

Once they'd secured their gate, Diego checked his watch and groaned. "Five-thirty in the morning! No way I'm getting to sleep."

"Speak for yourself," Luca grumbled, trudging toward his bunk.

Julian leaned back on the sofa, grinning. "Nothing like a good bedtime cry to help you sleep, eh, Luca?"

"Quit being an ass!" Diego snapped.

Julian raised his hands in mock surrender, but the grin lingered. Diego ignored him and started after Luca, who didn't even bother pulling off his high-tops. He just collapsed onto his bunk, turned to the wall, and pulled the blanket over his head.

Diego hesitated. He wanted to say something. But what? Promise he'd make Julian stop? This had to be about more than that.

Who am I kidding? I'm not some wise old mentor. Luca's not even a year younger than me. Why would he care what I have to say?

The thought soured in his chest. After a minute, he withdrew and joined the others sprawled across the couches and chairs in the Den.

The days passed, and Diego noticed Luca pulling back. It worried him. He'd seemed resilient at first. But had that only been a facade? Diego completely understood Luca's desire for solitude. The constant presence of everyone was wearing on him, too. Still, he didn't stop trying to reach out, but each attempt was met with a terse, "We're not buddies or anything. Just leave me alone."

Diego got it—he really did. But the brush-offs still stung.

*   *   *

A couple months had passed since Arturo, Luca, and Julian arrived, and scavenging runs had shifted from protecting and teaching, to them holding their own. Despite that, they didn't want to venture out alone—the rule to pair up had become an expectation.

One afternoon, Raphael announced, "I've come up with a way to prove you're ready to go solo."

Diego raised an eyebrow—this was the first he'd heard of it.

"Follow me," Raphael led them through the back corridors until he stopped at a junction and pointed to a line on the floor.

"It's a Challenge Course. There are obstacles designed to test your agility, stealth, and quick thinking."

He pulled a green crystalline energy cell from a pocket—oblong and a little larger than the bouncy balls Arturo loved to ricochet around the Pizzarama.

"Each of you will run this course with one of these," he explained, pulling out two more and setting them on a ledge. "They're fragile, so take care. Bring it back in one piece, and you pass."

Julian squinted at it, smirking. "'bout the size of my left nut."

Arturo snorted. "*Yours*, maybe." His grin stretched wide. "Mine are king-sized."

Raphael tossed the crystal cell from hand to hand. "Nuts. Marbles. Family Jewels. Doesn't matter—growlers will tear'em off just the same."

Watching it play out, Diego's irritation mounted—Raphael really should've run this by him before now.

"Julian, you're up first," Raphael declared, holding up an energy cell. Julian carefully took it in hand and stepped to the line.

"Follow the flags," Raphael instructed, pointing to a piece of red cloth tied further up the hall. "It's not about speed—just be careful, and you'll be fine."

Arturo clapped Julian on the shoulder with a grin. "Make it back with your manhood intact, my man."

Julian nodded and set off at a slow jog.

"You guys stay here," Raphael said after Julian turned the corner. "I'll keep track of things."

Diego extended his senses, focusing on keeping the void terrors at bay. Frustration at how fast this was unfolding gnawed at him. The orbital's usual creaks and groans marked the passing time.

Finally, Julian sprinted toward them from a different hall, holding the crystal aloft. Its green glow was unblemished, but his eyes showed a hint of fear. Arturo pressed him about what to expect, but he just shook his head, refusing to say a word.

Arturo took the next crystal cell, setting off on the course.

The silence stretched thin. At one point, a distant yelp echoed through the corridors—Arturo.

Luca nervously shifted his weight from foot to foot.

Moments later, Arturo emerged holding the crystal aloft. His teeth flashed in a triumphant grin. "Piece of cake," he declared, although the tightness in his eyes told a different story.

Luca hesitated before reaching for the last cell, his fingers trembling slightly. He cast a wary glance down the dim hall, clearly reluctant.

"Maybe we should call that your virginity," Julian chuckled. "No risk of you losing that."

Luca's face darkened, jaw tightening. Without a word, he gripped the crystal and started down the hall.

Sweat trickled down Diego's temple as he split his focus between watching the halls and using his gift to keep the void terrors at bay. He knew Raphael had something planned—the guy never could resist taking things up a notch. And Luca—quiet, wide-eyed, jittery—would be his ideal target.

Minutes dragged by until a scream of pure terror shattered the stillness. Luca careened around the corner, his eyes wide, a gash bleeding on his cheek. Behind him came a wild, flailing figure with a massive spider's head.

Diego's gut clenched, and he flashed to his brush with the spiders—until he recognized this was just Raphael in the ratty old Remy costume, now modified with a grotesque new head. Luca, however, hadn't made the connection. The sight of the spider's head—nearly half a meter wide with eight glittering eyes—had sent him into full-blown terror.

Raphael lunged, tackling Luca to the ground. Luca howled, thrashing frantically as he struggled to break free. The green crystal flew from his hand, shattering against the wall.

They wrestled on the floor, Raphael gripping Luca's back pocket, trying to pin him down. Luca caught a flash of glittering eyes inches from his face, and terror consumed him whole. A broken scream ripped out.

He kicked and clawed, thrashing wildly as Rafe held on. In a final, desperate surge, Luca scrambled free, leaving his pants in Rafe's grip. He bolted down the corridor half-naked, his ragged howls echoing through the station.

Diego had wanted to step in, but a new problem demanded his attention—the noise had drawn void terrors. He clenched his teeth, pulse heavy as he stretched his gift to its limits, straining to steer the growlers away—even at the edges of his reach. His control frayed, and he didn't know how long he could keep it up. If Rafe had just shown him how far the course went, he wouldn't have to push so hard.

Raphael stood up, pulled off the spider headpiece, and planted his boot on Luca's pants. He smirked, ugly and triumphant. "Got you good."

Luca slowed, breath hitching as he realized he wasn't about to die. His face burned red, shoulders hunched, fists pulled up in his sleeves. He wiped at his eyes, smearing quiet tears into the blood on his cheek.

Julian smirked, pointing at Luca's bare legs. "Those briefs don't look so white anymore, chavito."

"Shhhh!" Diego snapped, struggling to concentrate. He couldn't hold them back anymore. His chest tightened as he counted the growlers closing in: seven, ten... twenty.

The laughter died as their guttural cries echoed through the halls.

"Time to go!" Diego yelled.

They grabbed their belongings, adrenaline surging. Luca glanced at his pants crumpled in the hallway—just as the growlers rounded the corner. Choosing safety over dignity, he bolted with the others.

The growlers' hisses and cries echoed off the walls as they picked up speed. The Pizzarama's entrance came into view, but Diego knew they needed more time. "Keep going!" he shouted, falling back.

He threw his arms wide and yelled to draw the growlers' attention. The mob lurched, some staggering in confusion, others veering toward him.

Pounding footsteps and ragged cries closed in as he darted into a side corridor. Precious seconds lost, but hopefully it bought enough time for the others.

Fingers seemed to snatch at his clothes. Every instinct screamed to look back, to see how close they were. He needed somewhere to hide. Then—one of their bolt-holes: a trick wall panel.

He wriggled into it. Outside, the growlers thundered past.

Wedged between conduits and wire, his body trembled with anger over the crap Raphael had just pulled. When he sensed they were far enough away, he slipped out and headed for the Pizzarama.

The familiar murmur of voices reached him as he approached, buzzing with nervous energy. They'd made it back.

He stepped through the barricade. Faces turned, worried and pale, but his glare silenced all conversation. Diego's eyes locked onto Raphael, who, for once, didn't look so sure of himself.

Trouble in Mind

The evening sank into a nervous quiet, each boy wrapped in his own thoughts. Raphael had withdrawn to the kitchen, which suited Diego just fine—he wasn't ready to face him yet.

He wanted to talk to Luca, but after his previous failed attempts to connect, an invisible wall seemed to have grown between them. Frustration simmering, he pulled out his guitar, hoping the familiar chords might calm him, but he couldn't find the right tune.

As the night wore on, Diego watched Luca withdraw even further, pulling a blanket over his head as he curled up on the couch. Diego knew all too well what it felt like to be humiliated, angry, and alone. Watching Luca suffer in silence left a cold ache in his chest.

When Luca finally tossed the blanket aside, Diego noticed the telltale red eyes and puffy cheeks; he'd been crying. Diego called out, fumbling for the right words. "Hey, can—"

Luca shot him a glare that made it clear he didn't want to talk, and retreated to the Lair.

Diego set his guitar down. Memories of Raphael's torment flickering through his mind as he wrestled to figure out what words would make a difference. Later, when Luca peeked around the makeshift barricade into the Den, Diego pretended to be focused on his guitar while watching from the corner of his eye.

He darted toward the back room, and nobody else seemed to notice.

Diego waited a beat, then quietly followed.

As he approached the door, he heard a low moan, then a whisper that stabbed an icy shard through him.

"I'm worthless."

Diego pushed the door open, only to see the back exit closing—Luca had left, not even bothering to gear up. What was he thinking? Diego shimmered into invisibility and slipped into the back corridor.

Luca shuffled through the promenade, paying no heed to caution. His shoes scraped against the floor, arms hung limply at his side, and an occasional sniffle echoed through the quiet.

Diego's heart thudded in time with each of Luca's pensive footsteps. He recognized the weight of despair but had no idea what to do. Everything he tried always failed.

Extending his gift, Diego pushed any void terrors away, keeping Luca protected and hoping to give him a moment on his own. He waited for the right moment to approach, mentally debating what to say while trailing him turn after turn.

Finally, Luca groaned in frustration and collapsed to his knees, his shoulders trembling with silent sobs that shook his frame. Each shudder echoed painfully in Diego. He yearned to reach out, to say something—but that would reveal his gift. And Luca would hate him.

He hesitated, considering slipping around a corner to drop his invisibility. As he took a step back, a cold realization struck—Luca's aimless, careless walk hadn't been random. He wanted to find a growler. But he didn't even have a weapon.

Tears streamed down Luca's cheeks, and a heart-wrenching look crossed his face. He moved before Diego could react, drawing a small knife and pressing the blade against his wrist in a violent motion.

Diego shimmered into view and dropped beside Luca, wrenching the knife away. Clinging to Luca's wrist, he tore off his mask, facing him directly. His voice broke somewhere between a command and a plea: "No!"

Luca stared at him, eyes wide with pain and shock. He struggled to push Diego away, his wrist slick with blood, but Diego only tightened his grip.

"Why not?" Luca's voice cracked. "You guys don't care. And it's because of me that mom and dad were taken—" he shuddered. A raw, desperate, keen escaped his lips. His whole body trembled under the weight of the words.

The amount of blood coming from Luca's wrist was frightening. "You're hurt," Diego said, working to keep his voice steady despite his racing heart. "Come on. You need help right now."

Luca's resistance crumbled, and he went limp, allowing Diego to pull him to his feet. He shrugged out of his jacket and wrapped its sleeve around Luca's wrist before guiding him to Medbay. Once there, Diego inspected the wound, relieved to see Luca hadn't cut too deeply.

Deciding he didn't need to activate Meddi, Diego slipped out his lockpicks and opened the cabinets, searching for the right supplies.

Luca stared into space, eyes unfocused, as if even blinking took too much effort.

Diego's chest ached. He knew that emptiness—he'd lived with it for years, angry and lonely. They were more alike than Luca knew. So why couldn't he reach him? Why couldn't he find the words?

He bandaged Luca's wrist, then sat beside him on the exam bed.

Luca spoke quietly. "Where did you come from?"

Diego's stomach dropped. He couldn't tell him about el sendito dotado. A dozen explanations flickered through his mind, none of them good. No matter what he thought of, he came up short. The right words just wouldn't come.

Luca huffed, taking his silence the wrong way. "Doesn't matter. I'll just try again. Nobody cares."

"Of course we care," Diego said too quickly. "You're one of us. You're a Desterrado."

Luca turned toward him, eyes flat.

Diego swallowed the lump in his throat. Luca didn't need platitudes. So he just said what was true. "I followed you, didn't I?"

Luca's lip trembled.

Heat welled in Diego, pushing the words out—awkward, but true. Softly, he stumbled through them. "I... I care. So you're wrong."

Luca's eyes shone. His chest heaved—then he broke, burying his face in his hands as sobs wracked his body.

Diego moved without thinking, wrapping an arm around his shoulders. When Luca didn't pull away, Diego held on tighter. Luca leaned into him, his whole form shaking from the release. They stayed that way until the storm of tears ebbed.

At last, Luca wiped his face on his sleeve, sniffling. "Look at me. A crybaby."

"There's nothing wrong with that," Diego said. "It's hard out here... I get it. I've... I've had my moments, too." The words came roughly, but maybe Luca needed to know he wasn't the only one lost in the dark.

Luca scoffed. "Yeah, whatever. Stubbed your toe—big deal. It's not the same thing. I can't do anything you can, and I always want to cry. But boys aren't supposed to cry."

Diego breathed slowly. "I'm more like you than you think. I keep things bottled up, and there've been times I wanted to give up."

Luca's eyes narrowed. "So then, why didn't you?"

The memory flashed: his night alone in Echo Lab, waiting for the void storm to take him. "I... don't know..." he blinked, vision blurring. "Whatever. Doesn't matter. I just couldn't, okay? I'm here for you now, right?"

Luca's reply was barely audible over the hum of the orbital. "But... I'm not tough like you guys. I can't even help out with things. I have nothing to offer."

"Are you kidding?" Diego's voice lifted in surprise. "When you arrived, those other two weaklings had Raphael to help them out. You were alone, and you still did better than I did when I was sent down here. Do you know what I did? I hid. I hid and cried."

Luca's brow furrowed. "Did not."

"Did too. And *you* not only stood your ground, you blew up some growlers while you were at it." Diego chuckled. "If that's not clever, I don't know what is. You're a genius with gadgets."

Sparks of color lit Luca's cheeks. He looked away, staring down at his hands. The white bandage stood out against his warm olive skin.

Diego remembered something his mother had once told him. "I know... as guys, we're expected to be tough. Machismo and all that. But I don't think being tough means hiding our feelings away." He paused, a knot forming in his throat, and then continued softly, "I think... It's okay to feel things. Happy. Scared. Sad. Boys have feelings, too! Being tough means accepting that truth—not hiding from it. And... and asking for help if we need it. Talking to somebody."

Luca stared at him, meeting Diego's gaze. The fear and hopelessness were still there, but so was a glimmer of understanding. Slowly, hesitantly, he nodded.

They sat in silence for a while until Diego asked. "Are you going to be okay?"

Luca hesitated, the weight of his darkness still in his voice. "I don't know."

"Okay, I understand. But I will ask you again tomorrow—because I care. And again the next day. Every day, if I have to, got it?"

Luca glanced down, pinching his lips to hide the smile teasing at the corners of his mouth.

"I'm serious," Diego said. "If you ever feel that way again, come find me. And... if I need someone to talk to, I'll come to you. Deal?"

Diego raised his fist, and Luca hesitated only a heartbeat before bumping it with his own.

Needing to steer away from the heavy, mushy stuff, Diego slipped off the bed and grabbed a bandage strip for the cut on Luca's cheek. "You'll probably have a scar. But that's good, right? Chicas love scars."

Luca's eyes clouded. "Doesn't matter. No girls are coming down here."

Diego winced. Wrong move. He fumbled for something Luca might actually want to talk about. "Here's what I can't figure out," he said, dabbing at the scabbed cut. "How can Carlos be a prophet when he does things like sending us down here?"

Luca's brow furrowed. "Unrighteous dominion. That's what my dad called it. When someone uses religious authority to do bad things, hiding behind righteousness so people don't see the truth."

"Sounds like your dad's a smart guy."

"Yeah," Luca said quietly.

*   *   *

The next morning, everyone gathered on the worn sofas and chairs in the Den. Luca kept his hands tucked into his sleeves, but the bandage on his cheek remained a clear reminder of yesterday's events. Arturo fiddled with the locks on the table while Raphael and Julian spoke in low, guarded tones.

Diego stood, his expression serious. "A few things are going to change," he announced, meeting each of their gazes. "I think it's time we establish some rules."

"Rules?" A storm brewed in Raphael's eyes.

Diego ignored him. "First, we're all in this together. Acting against the group or causing harm to any one of us violates this rule."

Raphael sighed loudly.

"The second rule," Diego hesitated. "Actually... no—we should come up with the rest of the rules together. Like sharing food... and things like that."

"Things like that?" Raphael gasped. "Cut the farce and say it. You're just mad about my challenge course."

Before Diego could reply, Julian interjected, "And what if someone breaks a rule? You gonna put us in timeout?"

Diego's gaze shifted between Raphael and Julian. "There will be a punishment," he said, uncertainty threading his voice. He hadn't thought that far ahead, and rushed to add, "But we'll decide what it is —together."

The room fell quiet. Finally, Arturo broke the ice. "I think it's a fine idea. We stick together; we survive, right? This isn't about Rafe— it's about all of us. Like, we should share food. No hoarding."

Raphael and Julian exchanged hesitant glances, but Luca nodded in agreement. A tentative conversation began, gradually gaining momentum as they debated their new code of conduct.

After several suggestions, Raphael finally suggested a rule: "Everyone trains daily." When nobody disagreed, his shoulders relaxed a little.

Luca's suggestion caught the other guys off guard. "Everybody bathes once a week—or more if someone says you stink."

Julian and Raphael groaned in unison, and Julian muttered, "Okay, mom."

Luca scowled. "Y'all stink, okay? It's nasty!"

Julian straightened. "I don't stink—"

"Your feet are the worst!" Arturo interrupted with a grin, earning a few chuckles and nods from the others.

Raphael leaned forward, sending a dark look at Diego. "I have another idea. We should check each other weekly for signs of becoming a growler. You never know when it might happen."

The room fell still, unease growing. Glances darted around the circle.

"What do the signs even look like?" Arturo asked.

"Scars?" Luca suggested.

"Diego has scars," Julian declared. His gaze locked onto Diego as he continued, a note of challenge in his voice. "Does that mean he's becoming a growler?"

Diego fought the urge to adjust his mask. "I've had these scars my whole life. They don't mean a thing."

Silence stretched, heavier this time.

Finally, Arturo spoke. "Since we don't really know how… maybe we shouldn't do it."

Raphael leaned back with a casual shrug. "Fair enough," he said. "It was just an idea."

The conversation shifted as they deliberated over punishments, agreeing on a range of consequences scaled to the severity of the offense. For minor missteps—like skipping chores or taking more than one's share of rations—penalties included losing bedding for a night or taking on extra duties.

More serious offenses—like reckless actions that jeopardized everyone's safety or arguments that disrupted group unity—would result in an overnight stint alone on the promenade. The harshest punishment, however, was reserved for the gravest offenses: intentional sabotage or actions that endangered them all. These would result in extended isolation, possibly even a whole day exiled in Red Sector.

At the mention of Red Sector, an uneasy silence fell over the group. Diego clarified. "Only if there's no other choice. I think if someone's actions endanger us all, there has to be consequences."

Raphael's voice carried a defensive edge. "So, if we agree to these rules, does that mean you'll then punish me?" His gaze shifted toward Luca.

Diego studied Raphael. "Do you think we should?"

Raphael shifted in his seat, his jaw tightening. "Mierda, I don't know," he muttered, his gaze dropping briefly before meeting Luca's eyes. "I'm sorry, amigo. I went too far."

Luca held his gaze, his expression thoughtful. After a pause, he replied. "I think the rules should apply to the future, not the past."

As the tension eased, Diego summarized what they had agreed upon, then looked around the circle, meeting each gaze in turn. "Are we all in agreement? One hundred percent?"

One by one, they nodded, raising their fists in unity.

"Los Desterrados," Diego declared.

"We stick together; we survive," the others said in chorus.

Paint It Black

Despite the danger, Diego and Rafe continued expanding their reach in Red Sector. They blocked off corridors, found bolt-holes, and pieced together anything they could find into barricades that created a safe route to the biosphere. But all the 'together time' didn't actually help their relationship any.

So Diego turned to his guitar, finding himself in a quiet corner of the Pizzarama one night. The idle melodies carried no real tune, but they helped calm his restless mind. The spider head from Raphael's costume still weighed on him, nagging at the edges of his thoughts. It bothered him—not enough to confront Raphael, but enough to leave him wondering.

Spiders that size were only in Green Sector... weren't they? Had one wandered into Blue? Or worse, could more get in? Surely Raphael didn't have a way into Green Sector? Diego shook his head and focused on the steady rhythm of his playing, trying to push the useless speculation aside.

The music was gradually settling his nerves—until Raphael dropped into the seat beside him. "I want to talk."

Diego stopped strumming.

"I've got an idea, and I think it'll bring everyone together."

Diego raised an eyebrow.

"A ritual," Raphael went on, his eyes bright. "With the algae. A way to bond us as a brotherhood, you know?"

"I'm not sure we should touch that stuff again," Diego's brow furrowed.

"No, it'll be fine," Raphael said quickly. "We dunked ourselves last time, so we'll use way less. Don't you remember how good it felt? It'll lift everyone's spirits, I know it."

He laid out the plan, point by point. Diego remained skeptical, but Raphael's energy was hard to resist. Against his better judgment, he found himself warming to the idea.

"Alright," he finally caved. "I guess we can try it—but only if we go easy on the algae."

That evening, they stepped into the desolate biosphere. The soft scratch of their footsteps echoed through the chamber. Diego trailed behind, following the others to the squat, cylindrical tank.

Julian's impatience broke the silence. "Okay, Rafe, why'd you drag us all the way out here?"

Raphael wrenched open the tank's service port, releasing a sour, wet stench strong enough to make a few of them gag.

Arturo wrinkled his nose in disgust. "Snap, amigo! That cochinada's gonna kill us."

"Turn off the lights," Diego said quietly. One by one, their flashlights flicked off.

Darkness settled in, broken only by faint starlight filtering through the latticework above. Raphael dipped a finger into the slime and held it up. A slow glow blossomed. "It does this where it touches you."

Despite the smell, Julian, Luca, and Arturo leaned in, curiosity pushing out their disgust. Diego lifted a hand, stopping them.

"Not yet."

Raphael's tone shifted. "We are the Desterrados. Cast out, we forge our own family—a brotherhood of equals." He stripped off his jacket and shirt. Goosebumps rose on his skin, visible even in the dim starlight. "We turn anger and pain into strength as brothers. This is our solstice ritual. Solsticio."

Diego dipped a brush into the algae and began tracing stripes, swirls, and circles on Raphael. Honoring his request, he shaped a feathered serpent winding from his brow down his shoulders, arms, and chest.

An air charged with unspoken energy fell over the boys as each stroke bloomed in light.

When he was finished, Raphael looked otherworldly—a figure straight out of legend.

Diego intoned. "We stick together; we survive."

Raphael echoed the words, his voice carrying ritual weight. Then, reverently, he added, "This is my nagual. My guiding spirit form. It represents me. Defines me."

Diego had already considered the natures of Arturo, Luca, and Julian, weighing which spirit forms suited them best. He approached each in turn, his strokes shifting from tentative to sure as the glowing marks brought their naguales to life.

Arturo tugged off his headband, letting his dreadlocks spill free. Grinning, he stood still while Diego painted broad arcs along his arms and ribs, expanded discs of light around his eyes, and finished with glowing racing stripes down his back.

Julian huffed. "Nice. Tallest one of us gets stuck with a sugar glider. They're pocket-sized!"

Arturo just laughed, stretching his arms wide. "Guess that makes me fast. You'll never catch me."

Luca pulled off his layers of flannel, baring his lean frame. Diego painted fur-like tufts around his eyes, then jagged strokes along his jaw to suggest a wolf's muzzle, with marks along his fingers like claws. As a finishing touch, he traced circuit patterns up his arms and across his back to reflect his tech skills.

Rafe lifted his chin. "A wolf?" His tone hovered between approval and doubt.

Luca curled his fingers, studying the glowing claws. His voice came quietly, but his eyes held firm as he met Rafe's gaze. "Yeah. Wolf."

Diego gave his shoulder a squeeze and turned to Julian.

Julian scowled. "Better not make me a pig." He crossed his arms, barely suppressing a shiver as Diego began.

This was the one Diego had wrestled with the most. He painted sweeping spirals around his eyes, then ran a streak down the bridge of his nose to suggest a beak. From his temples, he flared feathered shapes into a crest. Comets curled along his arms and feathers fanned out down his back, each tipped with a glowing eye.

Julian twisted, trying to see what he'd drawn, but couldn't.

Arturo grinned. "Cosmic peacock, my man."

Rafe grinned, giving Julian a friendly shove. "Fitting! You're the only one of us who cares if his shirt matches or his hair's combed."

Julian straightened, lips parting like he wanted to object—but then he closed them, eyes narrowing.

Diego's heart started pounding. Now, it was his turn.

He had always kept his scars hidden beneath sleeves and bandages, going so far as to change in private to avoid long stares and awkward questions. No one but his parents had ever seen him so exposed—until the last time he and Rafe had been here. And only then because the algae had made it feel easier not to care.

He swallowed hard, suddenly wishing he'd just dunked his arms in it from the start.

The others were watching, their forms glowing in the dark. Did he really want Rafe so close? Touching him, even?

Before they'd left the Pizzarama, Diego had slipped into the grungy restroom and unwrapped the bandages around his arms and hands, where his clothes couldn't hide. It had been an act of resolve. He would see this through. He had agreed to it, after all.

Drawing a deep breath, he pulled off his mask and reluctantly pulled his shirt over his head, exposing his chest and arms to the others for the first time.

Raphael dipped his fingers into the algae and stepped closer. For reasons Diego couldn't quite name, he wanted to step back—but forced himself to stay still as Raphael traced along his jawline.

The strokes started slowly. Raphael carefully outlined Diego's eye sockets, but he froze when his fingers brushed the scars on his cheek.

Diego tensed, resisting the urge to flinch. Raphael's scrutiny was too close. Too much.

For a moment, Raphael's jaw tightened, his expression unreadable, then he continued. Unease flickered through Diego as his touch turned deliberate, painting over the scars as if trying to erase them, moving down his neck and arms.

Diego shifted his feet. After a moment, he stepped back. "That's enough."

Raphael offered a half-grin, his tone light but his eyes sharp. "Just finishing the perfect *Calavera*, chavo."

A skull. From Día de los Muertos.

Diego let out a relieved breath. A grin slowly spread across his face, helped along by the algae's growing euphoria. *Rafe wasn't acting odd; I'm just overthinking it, right?*

The boys all glowed with an ethereal light. The markings pulsed faintly, awakening a primeval connection within each of them. Anticipation danced in their eyes. The dim chamber took on a surreal, dreamlike quality. The weight on their shoulders lifted—just a little—and the future didn't seem quite so bleak.

Raphael struck a drum, drawing their attention.

To Diego's surprise, Raphael handed everyone a Z-ball mask—a deviation from his outlined ritual. He finished by offering Diego's mask back to him.

Unease coiled in Diego's gut, cutting through the algae's intoxicating haze.

What now?

Raphael pointed at Diego's mask. "That's more than a decoration. It's a map of everything Diego has faced. Every mark tells the story of a battle he's fought, a challenge he's overcome. It's a testament to your strength, compa."

He turned to the others. "Our masks will tell our stories, too. They will be maps of our personal journeys of strength, and a sign of our brotherhood."

He painted a crystal shape on each mask. "This is a mark of valor. It represents your triumph over the Challenge Course. Each of you has shown your strength," he paused at Luca for a heartbeat, then added the same crystal mark. "You too, Luca."

With the masks finished and in place, Raphael struck the drum. Its deep rumble reverberated through the chamber. He took a deliberate step. Another beat. Another step. Julian joined the procession, followed by Arturo, Luca, and finally Diego.

Trails of light followed the boys as they mirrored Raphael's movements. Fueled by the algae's intoxicating energy and the beat of the drum, they surrendered to the primal rhythms with wild abandon. Their steps gained momentum. Their pace escalated into a whirlwind of hoots, leaps, and primal howls that echoed through the chamber.

For a brief time, they shed the weight of exile and embraced the euphoria of simply belonging.

And then the drumbeat stilled.

Raphael held his arms high in a silent signal. Gradually, the boys slowed. With the algae's glow fading, they faced one another, their masked faces creating a sense of unity.

Diego broke the quiet. "We stick together; we survive."

The others repeated the words.

Raphael added, "Forged in the dark, we leave our mark."

Everyone but Diego echoed the new line. He studied Raphael, uneasy with this second deviation from the plan.

Raphael slowly removed his mask. In silence, they gathered their things and began the walk back to the Pizzarama.

*   *   *

The next morning began with a chorus of groans. The boys blinked against the dull ache behind their eyes, heads heavy, thoughts fuzzy. Grumbles echoed around the room—that it was too bright. Too loud.

"Why does it feel like my brain's melting out my ears?" Arturo muttered, cradling his head.

Eventually, they dragged themselves through a quiet breakfast of Nutrient Sludge. Afterward, without explanation, Raphael fetched his mask and began shaping it to resemble a feathered serpent's head. Luca joined him, working gray fur and Astro Andy's fangs into his mask to give it a wolf's features.

Soon, the others joined in. Gemstones, scales, and scraps of color were added to bring their masks to life. The scent of glue and paint filled the air, punctuated by bursts of laughter as they lost themselves in the simple, creative outlet.

Diego worked in silence, hollowing out the eyes of his white mask with black paint and tracing a skull's grinning teeth in careful lines. He finished it with colorful swirls and dots, making it into the likeness of a Calavera-painted face.

As he worked, the question that had nagged at him since the Solsticio wouldn't leave him alone. Did Raphael pick it as an insult? What was he trying to say? His suspicion finally surfaced, and he glanced at Raphael.

"Why a Calavera? Kind of grim, isn't it? Since it's about death."

Raphael paused, brush hovering mid-stroke. Something flickered across his face before he answered. "The Calavera isn't just death, chavo—it's about crossing between worlds. You've been through stuff that should've ended you, but here you are. You watch over us, keep us alive. That's strength, even if nobody else gets it."

Diego's chest tightened. The recognition felt good, but there was something sour in the way Raphael spoke. His ability with words was uncanny. He could quickly deliver a thoughtful compliment as effortlessly as a cutting insult.

But even if Diego hated to admit it, Raphael was right. The Solsticio had helped to unite the Desterrados.

The room settled into a quiet rhythm as they worked.

Luca eventually broke the silence, dropping his brush with a sigh. "Is this it? Are we just stuck here forever?"

Julian spoke up. "What if we found a way back home? They'd let us back, right? Or maybe we could just fight them?"

Frustration pricked at Diego. He'd gone over this with Raphael more times than he could count, and it seemed he'd have to keep repeating it for everyone. "Do you really think we could take on La Familia? They've got rayguns. They control everything."

Julian's voice went thin. "But I don't want to stay here forever."

Luca muttered, "Well, we can't just hop on a rocket ship and leave."

Arturo's voice came softly. "I... I always wanted to be a pilot."

Wanted.

His dream was dead, and the air in the room deflated beneath its weight.

Raphael slapped his hands on the table. "Maybe we can't take La Familia head-on, but we'll figure out something. We just need a plan."

"Carefully," Diego cautioned. "I think we need to be smart. Spend time understanding Serenity better. Learn her weaknesses. Maybe then we can figure out a way."

Nobody had any more ideas. Silence settled again, heavier than before.

"Quiet as a funeral in here," Julian muttered.

Arturo pushed to his feet. "Enough of all that. We'll figure something out eventually. But we've got bigger problems right now. Why doesn't anybody ever want to talk about the next void storm?"

Raphael blinked. "What exactly do you want to talk about?"

Arturo strode toward Clara. "So, I can't stop thinking about chapels and things. And—hear me out—what if we made our own pounamu, or something? If it's just a sacred space we need..." He swept his arm around the Pizzarama. "Then why not here? What is a chapel, after all? We already call this place home, and Clara's watching over us, too."

The others exchanged uncertain looks.

"Another void storm'll come," Arturo pressed.

Diego frowned. "What exactly are you proposing?"

"I was hoping you guys could figure that out," Arturo admitted with a grin. "I don't even know what a pounamu's supposed to look like. Maybe we give one to Clara? How do we make this a sacred space?"

Julian drummed his fingers, then grabbed a pen and paper, sketching as he spoke. "It was green, and carved like a teardrop."

Perhaps it was the paint fumes in the air, or just how strung out they were from the night before, but the idea didn't seem half bad. It wouldn't get them back home—but it could help them survive.

"Yeah," Raphael said slowly. "Why not?"

So they set to work. Arturo, Julian, and Raphael focused on crafting the pounamu, while Diego and Luca transformed Clara, swapping her scanty attire for something more dignified. They hung the pounamu around her neck, and finished it all by hanging their newly adorned masks on the ragged velvet curtain behind her—all except Diego, who hesitated before pulling his back on.

That night, Diego's thoughts were haunted by what the future might hold for them on Serenity Orbital. The camaraderie they'd built was real, but it wasn't enough. They needed more than masks, rituals, and some primitive goddess they'd made up; they needed a plan for what came next.

Like it or not, it was time to open up—at least about Echo Ring.

He rose from his seat and stepped in front of Clara.

"I think I need to tell you something," he began. The others looked up, eyes curious.

"I've kept a secret," he admitted. "Before any of you arrived… I went down to Echo Ring."

Their eyes went wide, and the air might as well have been sucked out with how still the room became.

"I found a lab there." Diego continued nervously. "It has supplies we could use. Maybe even things we could leverage against La Familia."

"Hold on." Arturo cut in, eyes blinking. "How? How did you get there?"

Raphael ignored him, giving Diego a hard stare. "Why haven't you told me—us—about this before?"

"Because it's dangerous," Diego answered Raphael, not Arturo. "And we had a lot of other things going on. But now... now I think it might be worth the risk."

"How—did—you—get—there!" Arturo growled. "The lifts won't move. Link's busted. So how?"

A sly smile played on Diego's face. "What do the Link Pods travel through?"

Looks of understanding spread across the others as they connected the dots.

"You went into the tubes?" Julian asked. "Isn't that, like, dangerous?"

"The Link is offline down here. I've never seen a Pod moving," Diego answered. "We'll need to prepare. It's below freezing in some of the tubes. And... I've encountered things before. But we can avoid them."

"Things?" Julian asked.

Diego hesitated, realizing that even speaking of it gave him the heebies. "Spiders," he finally managed.

"Spiders?" Arturo raised an eyebrow.

"Void spiders," Diego clarified, spreading his hands wide.

"Oh! Is that where Rafe got the spider skull from?" Arturo asked.

"Carapace," Julian grumbled, crossing his arms. "Spiders don't have skulls. Technically, he has a cephalothorax—the part of the carapace with the head and thorax. They shed it when they grow."

"Whaaaaat?" Arturo grinned, leaning closer. "Julian, you're a spider nerd?"

Julian scowled.

"Why is it," Luca said quietly, "nobody seems alarmed by the idea of monstrous, gigantic spiders?"

Raphael grinned, leaning back. "Void terrors come in all shapes and sizes, right?"

Diego cleared his throat. "Somebody needs to stay here to monitor the lift. And it's probably best if we take a few days' supplies, just in case."

The boys fell quiet again, exchanging glances. Nobody wanted to be left behind, but they all recognized the importance of having a sentinel in case another exile arrived while they were away.

"We don't need to decide right now," Diego said. "We need to get things ready first."

They spent the next week preparing. Diego briefed them on what they would encounter, from the freezing cold to the overgrown promenade and mutated plants. He led them to the maintenance hatch inside the Link Transit Terminal, where they took turns refreshing their floatwork skills in zero gravity.

As the day of departure loomed, the question of who would stay behind resurfaced.

To everybody's surprise, Raphael stepped forward. "I'll do it. Someone has to make sure everything goes smoothly here. I can go another time."

Relief and respect flickered across the boys' faces—all except Diego. He'd never known Raphael to be that altruistic, and he wondered what the angle was.

The Hunter

Raphael waited until the others were well on their way before gearing up and heading out. He prowled the corridors with purpose, avoiding growler hordes, skirting void-rat nests, and keeping clear of cameras that might draw out the robots.

Now and then, a whisper leaked out: "Carlos, I don't belong down here. I matter."

His path carried him deeper into Blue Sector until, at last, he found a lone growler. Dressed in bloodied medical scrubs, it had once been a middle-aged man. The mouth was pulled tight, showing blackened teeth. It swayed in the corner, rocking from side to side, breaths coming in quick, shallow huffs. Diego called this behavior "dormant."

Raphael drew his sword and crept closer. When he was near enough, he struck fast, putting all his force into an overhead swing that planted the blade deep into the back of the thing's skull. A gurgling hiss slipped from its lips as it staggered and collapsed.

Raphael's eyes were elsewhere, a shadow crossed his face, and he spoke softly. "I'm not a freak like you."

Crouching beside the body, he gently straightened the limbs, wiped the grime from its face, and combed its hair to hide the damage.

The effort made him look almost human again.

Raphael leaned close to his ear. "Hey, freak. What do you think of me now?"

A long sigh shuddered out of him. He closed his eyes. "I matter."

Then he stood and dragged the body to the recycler as if hauling a bag of trash. The hollow clang of the door rang down the corridor.

Task complete, he pulled his knife and carved another notch into his belt.

"I matter," he said again.

Blue Moon

Their journey through the Lift Tubes was cold and uneventful, filled with frigid silence and the occasional creak of metal, and the boys were too focused on potential dangers to engage in any small talk.

Once they reached the tubes of Echo Ring, Diego had to confront something he'd been avoiding: he could sense the Kraal more distinctly again, lurking at the fringes of his awareness. Why was it still here? He'd have to keep his gift as muted as possible.

Diego showed everyone how to open the lab's private Link door. The comforting pull of gravity and escape from the biting cold were welcome reliefs.

After shedding their layers, everyone paused, marveling at the sight before them. Relief welled up in Diego—the room was just as he'd left it: strange equipment, blinking lights, and shelves stacked with dusty volumes of research.

He made a beeline for the bookshelf he remembered. His fingers skimmed a row of COMTRAN manuals, coming away coated in dust. There had to be more here than what he was able to find in Serenity's digital library.

"Wow," Julian whispered, eyes wide as he took in the breadth of the room.

"This place is incredible," Arturo murmured, already drifting toward a nearby keyboard and terminal.

"Don't touch anything until we know what it is," Luca urged. "Let's take inventory first."

Diego realized the wisdom in that idea—he should have done that on his earlier visits.

They spread out under Luca's guidance, moving between workstations and shelves, cataloging items, offering up the occasional theory for what something did, and trying to make sense of all the forgotten science.

Diego paused at a cluttered desk. There it was, just as he'd left it so long ago. A chill prickled his skin, and he hesitated, his fingers hovering over the picture frame nestled under a stack of papers. Of all the things in this lab, why did this one picture have such a hold on him?

He drew a deep breath, pulled it free, and turned it over.

The faces of the scientists stared back at him, their smiles frozen in a moment long gone. His eyes locked on the woman who had first caught his attention.

The soft ache stirred in his chest again, teasing at something out of reach. Was she a relative? His grandmother, perhaps?

He realized how little he knew about his parents' past. How did they end up on Serenity? Were their families residents long before The Arrival?

Now, staring at this woman's face, he couldn't shake the sense that there was more to his family's past than he knew.

"Check this out, guys!" Arturo's voice broke Diego's reverie. He blinked, putting the photo back on the desk.

Arturo stood across the lab, holding up a brace of syringes. The liquid inside glowed faintly even after all these years.

"Crazy, right?"

"Put it down," Luca warned. "We don't know if it's toxic."

They continued, but the urge to explore soon overcame interest in Luca's careful approach. When he was distracted by a curious device with cooling fins, Arturo and Julian took it as their cue. They exchanged a glance and wandered off.

Diego had his own plans. Breaking away from the others, he approached the side office where he'd seen the working terminal. John's passkey unlocked the door. He pulled the chair out from the desk, pulse quickening as he scanned the red sticker fixed on the terminal's edge: "TOP SECRET: AUTHORIZED PERSONNEL ONLY."

Perfect.

The terminal hummed faintly after he pressed the power button. To his delight, John's passkey unlocked it without a hitch. Menus filled the screen.

He paused, cracking his knuckles. The revelation was exhilarating, but he had to be careful. One wrong move, and he could trigger a lockout—or worse, summon the security robots.

The menus seemed endless, each leading into systems dense with jargon that might as well have been written in the language of the alien Grays. His growing confusion left a deepening sense of inadequacy in his chest. How could he ever learn this without an instructor?

But if he wanted any hope of pulling this off, let alone doing it without triggering its defenses, he had to learn.

He retrieved a dusty COMTRAN manual from the bookshelf and settled in for another attempt to learn programming. The yellowed pages were as confusing as the manuals he'd found in Serenity's library. But these pages had examples.

This was where it started. He stopped at the first one and typed:

```
PRINT "Hello, World!"
```

The terminal beeped, and the text appeared:

```
Hello, World!
```

He clapped a hand over his mouth, and his feet drummed out his excitement on the floor. It might not have been much, but he had just made the computer do a thing!

Encouraged by his success, he kept reading. Data, he learned, was just stuff—like the words in emails or the numbers in a list. Programs were like hands inside the computer, reshaping data, pushing it around a network, and showing it to people when they needed it.

The more he explored, the less intimidating it became. Like a spoken language, COMTRAN had its own syntax and structure. The deeper he got, the more he realized he'd wildly misunderstood programming. He'd always thought it was about lots of math and scary algorithms. Computer "science," right? But no, it felt closer to art and music.

The rhythm of coding started to make sense. It was poetry of logic. Commands were words, grouped into "statements" that told the computer what to do. He thought of those as verses. When the verses were put together into "routines," they became complete poems or songs. There was even a similar elegance to the way they were crafted.

Taking a break, Diego stretched and wandered around the lab. He spotted Luca tinkering with a spacesuit.

"Planning on taking a spacewalk?" Diego asked.

Luca jumped, cheeks flushing. "No! I just needed a part. And—well, it's odd, isn't it? Having a spacesuit here?"

Diego pointed toward the outer bulkhead. "There's a private airlock—probably so they could dock directly to the lab."

Luca nodded, his gaze drifting back to the suit. Sensing that Luca wanted to keep at his work without disruption, Diego moved on.

He found Arturo and Julian in the dimly lit promenade observation room. They looked both fascinated and horrified as they considered the greenery overtaking the orbital's corridors. The vegetation seemed to pulse with energy—a mass of swaying vines and creeping plants, broken only by the occasional flash of color from strange, alien flowers.

Diego joined them, his reflection merging with the wild scene on the other side. "Did you see any sugar gliders?"

"They're all over," Arturo said quietly. "But how did this happen? Did it come from the biosphere?"

Diego shrugged. "I only went out there once, and... that was more than enough for me. I'm just glad this lab's sealed off from it all."

Arturo's brow furrowed. "So you don't know if there's any supplies out there? Gears, tech—anything we could use against La Familia?"

"Maybe, I just don't know. Although… I saw a repair bay on a map, but it's not close. Could still have a rocket ship in it."

Arturo's eyes lit up. "A rocket ship?"

"Sure." Diego smiled. "You suddenly know how to fly one?"

Arturo opened his mouth—then closed it again.

"What about food?" Julian asked, licking his dry lips.

"There's fruit," Diego said. "Grows on the vines. Looks juicy. Could be the best thing you've ever tasted… or filled with mutagenic void acid. You're welcome to step out and try one."

Julian looked thoughtful for a moment, then asked, "You said you saw a walking tree?"

"Not really?" Diego rubbed his eyes. "No booming voices or mossy beards like those talking trees in that fantasy book about rings. Just… tall. Fast. No eyes, but it still knew exactly where I was. I think it might've been a Deathmark. I heard they can take any shape."

Julian backed away from the window, and Arturo blurted, "You've encountered a Deathmark?!"

Diego blinked. He wanted to mention the one on Red Sector, but held back, shrugging instead. "Yeah… I guess so."

Without moving any closer, they leaned in to peer out the window. Diego grinned and left them to their nervous observations—he had work to do.

The next chapter was about control systems, and control of the mainframe was exactly what he wanted. As he read on, though, he realized it focused on program logic—the instructions. So it wasn't exactly what he had expected, but still interesting.

```
FOR X IN (1, 2, 3, 4, 5) DO
  PRINT X
END
```

The code essentially told the computer: "For each number from one to five, print that number."

Diego spent hours working through the basics—testing snippets of code, adding complexity little by little, working through each error one line at a time. Piece by piece, the puzzle slipped into place, and he realized programs were more than poetry or song.

Where art was about expression—emotion, meaning, or the experience itself—programming added utility. It was about instructions that made things happen—the difference between experiencing a great song and using that song to make gears turn.

Or better yet, it was a recipe. His dad wasn't much of a cook, but when he tried, he followed recipes to get something on the table—even if the results weren't always great.

A program told the computer what to do, the way a recipe told someone how to cook a meal. It was the same challenge: finding the right words to explain what you needed. All he had to do was figure out the syntax of this foreign language so he could convince the computer to do what he wanted.

"Okay, kiddos, playtime's over!" Julian called out. "Time to put your toys away. The big boys want to go home."

A playful groan drifted in from Luca. "Aww, do I have to?"

Diego smiled. It was good seeing Luca fit in. He stretched his stiff muscles, slid a few COMTRAN manuals into his backpack, and they headed out. Only a few grumbles were made about the biting cold on their float back. When the door hissed open, Delta Ring's chill air came as a strange relief.

*　　*　　*

The others drifted in and out of Echo Lab over the next week, but most of the time it was just Diego and Luca—like today.

"Check this out!" Luca's shout echoed from the lab, pulling Diego away from the terminal. He found him fiddling with two contraptions that once were portable heaters, but now bristled with added coils and electronics, duct-taped and zip-tied together.

Diego smiled. "Heaters? That would be amazing! But... will they really warm up the whole Pizzarama?"

"No. Too small. And they're not heaters anymore."

Diego frowned. "Then what are they?"

A sly grin spread across Luca's face. "You'll see. It's a surprise."

They packed the devices and made the long float back, Luca offering no hints the entire way. The hatch had barely sealed behind them in Delta Ring before he was already off, carrying one of the machines. "Hurry, and bring that one."

Diego did as instructed, hustling to catch up. "You're just not going to tell me, are you?"

Luca's grin remained, and his eyes narrowed mischievously, but he kept silent. He led Diego along the promenade to a "Restricted Access" door—which, apparently, his passkey could open. Inside the cramped utility room, Luca pushed wires aside and fixed the gadget over a sensor block.

Soon after he switched the device on, frost gathered on its coils.

"Okay, what exactly is this?" Diego asked, his curiosity piqued as he watched the white rime spread.

A flash of pride lit Luca's eyes. "If we can't adjust the temperature setting, we can trick the sensors into thinking it's colder than it actually is. The system should compensate by raising the heat."

Diego let out a short laugh. "Clever! You're freezing the sensors to make it warmer inside."

"Exactly. If it works, we should feel it soon."

They placed the second device, and by the time they returned to the Pizzarama, the difference was noticeable—a growing warmth replaced the air's crisp edge. The boys shed their hats and jackets, slapping Luca on the back and hailing him as their savior.

*　　*　　*

Things were finally looking up. The bots hadn't dismantled Luca's devices, and the heat remained steady. Their trips to the lab became routine—Luca even claimed a workbench for himself, where he would push half-broken junk just a little too far, often with spectacular results.

Best of all, Diego's mom would've been proud. Vegetables were an occasional high note in their sludge-and-rat diet. Sure, it was a need for variety in their meals that made it happen; avoiding all the terrors in the biosphere was no light task. But the result was the same: vegetables.

One evening, they found themselves admitting that life wasn't looking so bad.

"It's been seven months since you guys showed up." Raphael pointed out. "You know what this deserves? A Solsticio."

The others lit up at the idea of celebrating their small victories. That night, they gathered in the derelict biosphere. One of Arcadia's moons, Aetheron, filled the lattice overhead and cast the chamber in ethereal light.

They helped each other where needed, using the glowing algae to trace out their naguales—a sugar glider, wolf, peacock, feathered serpent, and Diego's calavera, complete with ribs and arm bones. Diego was cautious with how much he used, but the others embraced it fully, relishing how it sharpened their senses, as if they were tapping into something ancient and primal.

When they were ready, Raphael went to his drum but didn't pick it up. Facing the others, he said, "There's one more thing."

From a bag, he drew a freshly killed void rat, sliced its neck, and caught the blood. The chamber stilled as he traced it across their masks and arms, filling the spaces between patches of algae. Diego's chest knotted. He wanted to stop Raphael but couldn't quite grasp what he was doing—or why.

Finally, Raphael took up the drum, and Solsticio began in earnest. The boys bounded around the biosphere, their wild cries and howls weaving in the air with the drumbeat. A feral connection to the universe surged through Diego—raw energy both thrilling and unsettling.

He surrendered to the rhythm, joining the transcendent, wordless bond with the others. But beneath the frenzy, the blood-mark soured in his mind, leaving a shadow beneath each of his steps.

I'll Fly Away

"Growlers!"

Julian's shout ripped Diego from his dream—Donna beside him, warm and pressed close as they soared through the sky. His skin tingled with electric anticipation that left him breathless.

Then it was gone. The real world crashed in: growler snarls and cries echoing through the Pizzarama.

Panic jolted him upright. He reached for his gift, but the dream's heat still clung to him, now tumbling with fear and dread. His emotions raged, and el sendito dotado slipped away.

Their Lair erupted. Boys tumbled from their bunks. Blankets, comic books, and elbows flew as they crashed together in the dark, hopping into their gear. Diego fumbled for his boots, heart hammering, reaching again for his gift. Smoke would've been easier to grab.

"Hit 'em hard, drive 'em out the front gate!" Rafe barked, already swinging his blades as he shoved past the others. "Desterrados don't back down!"

A growler lurched into view, clawing at Diego. He dropped his boots, rolled across his bed to snatch his Top Slugger, and yelled, "Not the front! Out back—like we planned!"

The growlers were everywhere—scrambling over arcade machines, shoving between tables. The boys struggled to stay together, fighting their way back, only to find more pushing in from the storage room.

"We're trapped!" Arturo shouted.

Rafe shot Diego a look—part anger, part question. Diego knew what he wanted: for him to fix this with his gift. But he had nothing. He shook his head.

For a heartbeat, neither wanted to back down. Neither knew what to do.

Julian screamed—a raw, horribly animal sound—and then it cut out. A growler's fingers clamped around his skull, dragging him backward.

Rafe leaped forward, blades slashing, forcing the thing to drop Julian in a heap before it turned on him.

Diego dodged a swipe and stumbled to Julian. Blood, hair, flashes of bone. No time to look closer. He hauled Julian's limp form up, grunting, struggling to keep his footing in threadbare socks.

If only he could use his gift. He had to try again, but he couldn't swing the bat, hold Julian, and focus all at once.

"There!" he snapped, pointing to a sheltered corner.

Rafe's fury carved space around them as they fought step by step forward.

Diego set Julian down, hand at his neck—but it was all too mangled to find a pulse. He was breathing, at least.

Barely.

Meddi could save him—but they had to be quick.

Diego fought to steady himself, focusing on his gift. A flicker came—enough to sense the growlers. They had a clear path.

"We can make it out the front!" he gasped.

Rafe wrestled Julian onto his shoulder, staggering as they pushed for the gate. Diego followed, forcing ragged bursts of his gift against the growlers—anything to get some space—while Luca and Arturo brought up the rear—bloodied, battered, swinging wild.

A growler lunged. Clawed fingers raked Arturo's leg. He howled —stumbled—and Luca caught his arm, bracing him as they hobbled on.

They spilled into the plaza. Arturo and Luca cut toward the Skyway Lounge—their rally point.

"No—this way!" Diego shouted.

But Rafe barked over him, "Medbay! We've got to reach Medbay!"

Arturo and Luca froze, eyes darting from one escape route to another.

"That's what I said!" Diego snapped, shoving under Julian's other shoulder to help Rafe move faster.

Arturo and Luca staggered back in line, circling alongside as they pressed forward. Diego strained to keep pushing at the growlers with his gift—but he couldn't do everything at once, and it failed him.

The growlers burst from the Pizzarama, guttural cries tearing through the air. And then, from the side corridors: answering calls.

The boys half-sprinted, half-stumbled along the promenade—Luca helping Arturo; Rafe and Diego hauling Julian's slack weight. The freezing deck bit through the holes in Diego's socks. Muscles burned, breath ragged, and finally, Medbay came into view.

The glass doors slid open, and they stumbled through. Rafe and Diego lowered Julian onto a triage bed. His face was ashen where not covered in blood, and under Medbay's stark lights, the full extent of his wound became clear. Arturo limped in with Luca's help, his bleeding leg leaving dark red spatter beside Julian's heavier trail.

"Got it!" Luca shouted, finding a security bolt for the doors and slipping it in place just as the growlers arrived. Fists pounded against the glass.

Arturo hopped away from the doors. "They're going to break through!"

Diego sprinted to Meddi, slamming his hand on the "emergency medical assistance" button. She whirred to life, her sensors focusing on him.

"No time for questions. We have a real emergency," Diego barked, pointing to Julian. His voice dropped to an urgent hiss. "This is life and death."

Meddi moved quickly to Julian's side, extending her surgical and diagnostic arms, but her usual sardonic demeanor was absent.

The growlers hammered at the door. A crack spread through the reinforced glass. Diego had to act before they broke through.

He sank into a chair and closed his eyes, catching the slippery thread of his gift. If he couldn't drive the growlers away, he'd have to make the others invisible—everyone would notice—but he'd do it anyway and face the consequences later. He pushed against the growlers.

There's nothing here. Empty room. What's that sound up the hall?

The pounding on the door began to ease. One by one, the growlers stumbled off, their snarls and groans fading into the distance.

Diego's hands trembled, knuckles aching in clenched fists. He stared at them a moment before slowly uncurling his fingers.

Luca and Arturo exchanged bewildered glances, unable to grasp why the growlers had suddenly broken off. But they were safe—for now. All eyes went to Meddi and Julian.

A nurse bot descended from the ceiling, flooding the table in harsh light—half of which flickered and died. Unbothered, the bot cut Julian's clothes away to bare his chest, pressing sensors onto his body, ignoring the ones that wouldn't stick.

Meddi's arms blurred as she scanned and assessed, announcing each action as she worked. The boys hovered close, hope and fear etching their faces, the medical jargon lost on them.

"Severe cranial injury detected," Meddi announced. "Multiple fractures, extensive intracranial hemorrhage."

A suction device was deployed as she worked on the head wound, while a third arm lifted away fragments of his skull.

The heart monitor flatlined, sounding an atonal alarm.

"Initiating cardiopulmonary resuscitation," she continued. Her arms hammered Julian's chest in perfect rhythm as the nurse bot inserted an airway tube.

Diego couldn't tell if anyone else was even breathing, but in that moment, he wanted nothing more than for her to save Julian.

"Administering epinephrine," she said.

A needle-arm extended toward Julian's chest—then froze.

"Error: medication unavailable. Continuing cardiopulmonary resuscitation."

She resumed hammering his chest.

Diego's heart thumped slow and heavy. He remembered the way Julian's scream had cut out—and he knew. That was when…

When…

He couldn't face it. Meddi could still do this.

She continued working, but the heart monitor held flat, its shrill tone unchanging.

And then, she stopped.

"Ceasing resuscitation efforts."

Raphael's face went hard, his eyes cold, and he stepped back without a word.

"Try again!" Arturo blurted, his voice cracking. "You can still help him. We're… we're going to Woolwards tomorrow. He wants new socks—the—the Royal Heather wool ones."

He swallowed hard, then added quietly, "Said I should try some too…"

"I'm sorry," Meddi said. "If I could have saved him, I would have. Earlier intervention might have improved outcomes."

No one spoke. No one moved. No one even breathed. It was just too much.

After a pause, Meddi added, "However, I do have an experimental procedure—"

Diego hissed, hand snapping up. "Unless your next words are about bringing him back—the way he was—don't say another word."

She hesitated, optics flickering, then stepped back.

The boys stood in stunned silence, their faces etched with a mix of grief and disbelief. A stillness settled over the Medbay. Once a place of healing, it now felt like a tomb.

Meddi gently pulled a sheet over Julian's body. His form lay still beneath the white fabric.

They had spent months training for combat, confident in their skills. Now, they stood frozen, struggling to process the swift, brutal reality of death.

Luca's eyes were red-rimmed, his voice barely above a whisper. "What—what do we do now?"

Johnny I Hardly Knew Ye

The overturned arcade games, smashed chairs, and scattered belongings in the Pizzarama were a brutal reminder of what had happened. Luca and Arturo moved slowly, straightening what they could. Sweeping glass. Righting a table. Gathering clothes, comics, and games. Keeping busy. Trying to put things back in order—as if that would help make sense of it all.

Raphael had other priorities. He dragged Diego into the kitchen, eyes wild and burning. Before Diego could react, Raphael seized his collar and yanked him close.

"It's your fault he's dead. I'll never forgive you for that."

The venom in his voice hit harder than any punch Diego had ever taken. His chest tightened. The room tilted.

"I—I did everything I could," he stammered. "The growlers... they were everywhere. I tried to get us out. I did..."

Raphael leaned in, knuckles white.

"Trying wasn't enough," he spat. "My best friend is dead because of you. Because you wouldn't use your void powers. Because you slowed us down when he needed help. Meddi said it—she could've saved him if you hadn't screwed it all up."

"I'm sorry," Diego said numbly.

Raphael's eyes narrowed. He shoved Diego back. "Sorry won't bring him back."

Diego stood frozen as Raphael stormed away. He knew that nothing he said would change Rafe's mind, so he said nothing.

The kitchen was eerily quiet. Diego put his back to the wall and let out a shuddering breath as he slid to the floor.

Julian's scream seemed to linger between heartbeats.

Diego didn't hate Julian. Sure, he could be a real dick sometimes, and they'd certainly had their differences. But he could also crack them up when they needed it most. Dinner wouldn't be the same without his overblown French accent describing a five-star cuisine in a way that left them all drooling. Stupid, but somehow it helped to choke down the nutrient sludge.

And his quick wit. Once, when the lights had suddenly cut out, Julian didn't even miss a beat. He just clicked his tongue: "Pschht— this is your co-pilot speaking. Please remain calm. We'll have everything back in order as soon as the pilot stops fooling around with the stewardess and I can find the light switch."

Most importantly, Julian was a Desterrado. One of them.

He breathed deeply, chest tightening.

Rafe's right. If I could control my gift, I could have helped everyone sooner. I could have done more.

Diego buried his head in his hands and cried.

*   *   *

The Atomic Pizzarama was heavy with silence that was interrupted only by an occasional cough, the *vrrp* of a chair sliding back, or the whisper of broken glass being swept up.

Then Arturo's voice came from the back room. "What the— chavos! Get in here."

Diego arrived with the others, and Arturo pointed at the rear door, which hung open. The locking bar leaned untouched against the wall. Not bent. Not broken. Just never set. The growlers didn't break in; they'd just walked in.

The boys exchanged nervous glances, the air thick with blame.

Raphael kicked the back door shut. "Come on! Who was it?" His glare swept over them. "We need to find out who it was, so he can answer for it. We have rules for a reason, right?"

Arturo cleared his throat. "Ummm… Diego, didn't you use it last?"

Diego scowled. "Not a chance. I always lock it."

"Hold on," Luca raised his hands. "We can't just start accusing each other."

"Are you saying that because you did it?" Raphael snapped, his eyes narrowing at Luca.

Diego spoke quietly, choosing his words carefully. "Maybe it was an accident. We're all tired. Somebody probably just… forgot. For all we know, it was Julian."

After a few heartbeats passed without comment, Raphael stabbed a finger at Diego.

"No. This was because of *your* 'run away from danger' plan! Julian's blood is on you."

Diego clenched his jaw. "We need a second way out, Rafe. What if we had been trapped and couldn't get out the front?"

"Well, we weren't trapped, were we?" Raphael's face flushed. "Your desire to run away and hide is what got Julian killed. We could have fought them off. The growlers aren't invincible, Diego. We just need to be smart about it."

Luca and Arturo exchanged uneasy glances, torn between stepping in or letting the fight take its course.

Diego boiled inside. Arguments lined up in his head, ready to launch, but he bit them back. The weight of Julian's death made any defense feel hollow.

Raphael's voice tightened. "We should be fighting the growlers, not running from them."

Their eyes locked. Seconds passed without a word until Diego finally sighed, "Fine. Let's try it."

The thought turned his stomach. But he was too drained to argue anymore.

Raphael's eyes gleamed. "About time."

Diego nodded, but he couldn't shake the image of Julian's body lying under the white sheet—who would be next?

That night, they held a Solsticio in his memory. Unlike the others that were lusty and full of life, this one was subdued and haunted by his absence.

It took a few days to prepare for Raphael's hunt, but finally they geared up around the battered table in the Den, eager to test the latest refinements on their weapons.

Arturo swung his sledgehammer, grinning at Luca. "Come on, everyone names their weapon. This is Mauler!"

Luca checked the battery pack of his modified sword, flicking it on to create a low electric hum. "I... haven't named mine yet," he admitted, glancing around. "Has everyone else?"

Arturo pointed a thumb at Diego. "His is 'Top Slugger.'"

"That's its brand name," Luca corrected. "He didn't name it that."

Raphael stood on the stage, a bright green Starblaze T-shirt vivid beneath his SEO security jacket. He cleared his throat. When all eyes were on him, he lifted Julian's mask from the curtain and hung it on the front of the stage beneath Clara's throne.

"So we don't ever forget him."

Then he handed the other masks out. "These aren't just for protection," he said quietly. "They're part of your nagual, your identity as you face the dangers ahead. Wear them on every hunt as a reminder of who you are."

Diego crouched, fingers tightening the worn laces of his black canvas high-tops. Rafe's ceremony was too much, and every minute closer to leaving knotted his stomach tighter. Were the growlers as afraid of them as they were of the growlers? And, if there was any trace of humanity still in them, wasn't hunting them the same as hunting people?

Diego pulled the knot tight, and the shoelace snapped. He stared at it.

Arturo said. "But Diego said there could be hundreds—maybe thousands in all three sectors. Can we really take them all?"

Diego clenched his teeth, straightened, and flicked the broken lace aside. "We just need to be smart about it."

Luca grinned, eyes bright. "We can handle them like void rats. Set traps and pick them off one by one. We don't need to face them all at once."

"Exactly." Raphael's eyes became distant for a moment. "They're easy to take down one at a time."

Easy was far from how Diego would describe their last encounter.

Arturo fiddled with his mask. "But how do we lure one out?"

"Maybe luck will favor us," Raphael said, casting a knowing glance at Diego, "and we'll find one isolated, right?"

When Diego finally gave him a nod, Raphael turned towards the exit, raising a fist. "Let's move out, Desterrados!"

Diego led them through Blue Sector's back corridors, searching for a target that wouldn't overwhelm them. He stretched his gift, sensing, searching, pushing himself—until, at last, he felt one, alone and away from the others.

He stopped, pressing his ear against a door, making a show of listening for any hint of danger. Raphael raised a single finger in silent inquiry. Diego nodded.

With a tap on the control panel, the door slid open, revealing a solitary growler shuffling aimlessly inside. It wore a ragged orange maintenance jumpsuit. A rusted hammer swung from its belt with each step it took.

But something about the way he cradled the object in his hands —gentle, almost careful—set him apart. His eyes were fixed on it, unblinking, as he muttered in a low, broken voice: "Safe. Safe. Safe."

Raphael gestured silently, directing everyone to spread out. They moved through the dimly lit room, careful to avoid alerting it as they wove around toppled shelves and scattered debris.

The growler's head snapped up. Diego locked eyes with it. For a brief, harrowing moment, he saw past the grotesque decay, catching a glint of something deep within. Its eyes flared, and it moaned, "She's safe?"

The others attacked, but Diego hesitated, troubled by its actions. It lashed out with alarming speed and strength, and the melee unraveled, just as it had when the growlers swarmed the Pizzarama. Alone, their training held; together, they just got in each other's way.

With every move, every swing, every lunge, it edged closer to a killing blow. Cuts and bruises piled on as it beat them down—a glancing slash here, a brutal kick there. They were slowing with each one, and still hadn't landed a clean hit.

Raphael finally barked, "Distract it! I'll take it down myself!"

Diego and the others shifted to defensive tactics, darting in only to draw the growler's attention.

The moment it exposed its back, Raphael lunged, his sword carving a wide arc that crunched into its skull. The growler spasmed, staggered forward a few steps, and collapsed to the floor.

They gathered around its form, breaths ragged, bodies still trembling with adrenaline.

"Just have to get its head right away," Raphael gasped, shaking blood and other bits from his blade.

Arturo lurched to the side and heaved.

"Let it all out, chavo," Rafe muttered.

The wet sounds continued, and Luca paled, hand clamping over his mouth—looking very much like he might be the next link in an unpleasant chain. But he shut his eyes, drew a slow breath, and held his ground.

Once Arturo returned, Raphael knelt at its side, dipping his fingers into the spreading pool of its blood. Rising slowly, he approached Luca. "With this kill, you have become more than you were before."

In his deliberate, solemn way, Raphael marked Luca's mask with the blood. Luca straightened, giving a single, firm nod. He moved to Arturo, repeating the mark.

But Raphael hesitated when he turned to Diego. Something in Diego's eyes made him lower his hand. A heartbeat later, he moved on, marking his own mask.

The others started talking, but Diego tuned them out—his focus was on the fallen figure. Not a monster, he reminded himself, but a person—someone who had once been alive, with a name and a life, maybe even a family.

Remembering it had flung something during their fight, he stepped away and scanned the room. There, near the wall: a once-pink ribbon, now dull with grime, hair clip still attached.

His pulse slowed, and a cold ache clenched tight in his chest. The stitched lettering, threadbare from being worked again and again, spelled out a name—

Katy.

And he remembered its words.

She's safe.

The End of the World

That evening, the hunt's electricity had burned off, leaving the Pizzarama in a restless, damp quiet. They were sprawled around the Den, Luca and Diego at the table, locks scattered between them, untouched.

Luca dropped a pick. It clicked against the surface. His voice stayed low, meant only for Diego. "—I know. I just can't let it go. I don't even know if they're alive."

Diego met his eyes. "I'd like to think they are. "

"Maybe it doesn't matter." Luca leaned back, chair squeaking. His next words came loud enough to carry. "We're all gonna die down here anyway."

Arturo looked over and nodded slowly, like he'd been waiting for someone to say it out loud.

"No way, chavo," Rafe said, catching his knife from the air. "We've got plans. Plans in plans."

Arturo frowned. "You say that—but, like, what?"

Rafe grinned, nodding toward Diego. "All his keyboard time has a purpose, right? Keeping secrets like a true boss. Must be cooking up something big."

Heat crept up Diego's neck. "I'm... working on something. Just not ready. I've got a lot to learn."

"Something?" Rafe huffed, throwing the knife with a flick of his wrist. It sliced past Diego, thunking into the arcade cabinet across the Den.

Diego glanced at the knife. "I hope I can hack into the main-frame. Fix things. Maybe we can use it against La Familia."

Arturo whistled low. "That's a big plan. Getting close?"

"Well—" Diego chewed his lip. "I haven't gotten far. It might not even work out."

Luca studied Raphael. "So what about *your* plans, Rafe?"

The smile faded from Raphael's face. "I have something in the works."

"And you're not going to share," Arturo said flatly.

Rafe leaned back, hands laced behind his head, eyes thinning. "Eventually. You'll see."

The talk meandered on with what-ifs and half-formed ideas stumbling around, but nothing stuck. By the time it sputtered out, the air felt heavier, and a weight settled on Diego's shoulders. Now he had to make a plan, because he didn't think Raphael had one.

*   *   *

Diego was back in Echo Ring's lab, sorting through boxes of holotapes. A dusty machine the size of two refrigerators filled the center of the room. A minicomputer—and apparently, in this case, "mini" just meant "smaller than a mainframe." But Diego wasn't in the lab's computer room for some dead relic. He was here for the shelves of holotapes.

He'd spent the last hour stacking the tapes by type and use, searching for a copy of MedOS so he could reload the bricked medbot. Why it had formatted itself, of all things, still left him scratching his head. But a working medbot down here could prove useful.

The lights flickered, and a loud zap snapped through the air, making Diego jump. His elbow clipped one of the stacks, and they all went down like dominoes—one pile into the next, until the whole lot spilled across the floor. Muttering under his breath, he poked his head out of the computer room door.

Luca stood dazed, hair on end, a faint wisp of smoke curling upward. Diego was relieved he looked no worse off—at least not compared to the *other* times his experiments had gone wrong.

"You okay?" Diego wandered out. The scent of ozone and burnt plastic lingered in the air.

"Yeah. I think I overloaded the capacitor," Luca admitted, raking fingers through his hair in a crackle of static.

"I think you might be right," Diego said as he perched on a nearby stool. "Need any help?"

"No," Luca's voice flattened. "I'm good."

Something in his tone made Diego pause. After a minute, it was clear he wanted to be left alone, so Diego retreated to John Smith's old office instead of the computer room—he just couldn't bring himself to start over with the tapes again right now.

He glanced at the lab notes stashed beneath the COMTRAN manuals on the desk—a fraction of Project Ultra's research into esper powers.

There were a lot in them—overwhelmingly so. But he'd occasionally find an intriguing tidbit that helped him understand a little more about su sentido dotado. He'd kept his interest in the metaphysical experiments hidden from Luca—he didn't want to raise any suspicions. He wanted to tell Luca about his gift—he'd almost done it more than once. But each time, he remembered the fear and disgust in Luca's voice when he talked about void-tainted things, and he was too afraid of losing him as a friend.

Diego hated his gift; so why would Luca feel any different?

Every week, the truth became harder to admit. As much as he wanted to open up, silence felt easier. Safer.

But the unspoken secret had thickened into a wall between them—real or imagined—and Diego found himself pulling away without even meaning to.

And he hated that. Luca already carried enough. His moods still swung between bursts of restless energy and periods of brooding, quiet darkness. But at least he didn't seem to sink as deep as that one time

—and his quiet periods were less frequent. Except, now Diego wondered if he wasn't slipping into one again.

That night, they crashed in their usual spots—Diego on the cot and Luca on the couch. Starlight filtered in through the portals, casting everything in a faint glow. The smell of dust, oil, and old chemicals kept Diego awake longer than he wanted.

He heard it an hour later.

A soft rustle. The shift of fabric. A quiet sniffle. The sound of someone trying very hard not to make a sound.

Diego rolled over. Luca was curled up tight on the couch, knees drawn in, blanket pulled over his head.

The sound came again—small, shaky. Muffled crying.

Diego's chest tightened. He should have noticed Luca's dark cloud sooner. So, should he say something? Do something? Or... maybe Luca just needed space?

The soft sounds didn't stop. If anything, they grew worse.

Diego knew the dark thoughts that must be spiraling through Luca's mind. Before he could talk himself out of it, he grabbed his blanket and padded across the floor. His steps slowed as he neared the couch, still not sure what to say.

Luca froze. A shuddering huff came from under the blanket. "Sorry," he mumbled thickly. "You can go back. I'm fine."

Diego didn't answer. He squeezed onto the couch and curled up back-to-back with him. Close, but not touching. There wasn't enough space, and his feet dangled off the edge. He didn't care.

"I'm right here... if you—y'know... umm... for anything." He couldn't get it quite right, but felt Luca needed to know he wasn't alone. After a heartbeat, he repeated what mattered: "I'm right here."

The simple words hung for a moment, carrying a strength he hadn't expected. He almost blurted something more to explain he didn't mean to be mushy or anything—and then stopped. Maybe it was fine as it was.

Luca sniffled. The cushions shifted. But he didn't tell him to go away.

They stayed like that. Quiet. Still.

Diego could feel Luca's warmth at his back.

Luca kept fidgeting, but the sniffling stopped.

And then—soft, even breathing.

*   *   *

Rafe's grief had curdled into a need for order and control, and his "plans" started with a list of demands for change. He called everyone to the Den, standing at the base of the stage with Clara framed behind him. Once everyone took a seat, he began.

"From now on, nobody leaves the Pizzarama alone. We'll always have an escort. At all times. Right, Diego?"

Diego frowned. *This is already what we try to do. So what's he playing at?* He could sense Rafe cooking up something, but didn't know what it was. Luca and Arturo were watching, waiting. Diego gave a nod, playing along with the script—for now.

Raphael paced. "We'll eat at the same time every day. And everyone must bring back hunted food on time. No exceptions."

Arturo raised his hand. "But what if something goes wrong?"

Raphael's eyes narrowed. "Make sure it doesn't. Efficiency and predictability are how we stay alive. Right, Diego?"

Diego's foot drummed against the floor. Eating at the same time every day wasn't the worst idea. He and Raphael had fought a lot lately, so maybe a little leeway was worth the peace? He nodded again.

But Raphael had more. "We're implementing security checks, too. Every morning, you'll give a passcode to prove you're not a growler."

"A passcode?" Luca frowned. "What kind of passcode?"

"Something simple—a phrase we all know and can repeat. It ensures none of us are compromised. We'll change it every week."

The rules kept stacking. Curfews. Rigid watch rotations. Stricter punishments. Raphael laid it all out like a dictator drafting laws.

Diego's shoulders knotted tighter with each decree. He'd worked hard to build trust, to make this a group effort. Now Raphael was grinding it into dust, replacing collaboration with mandates. Diego's foot tapped faster against the floor, until finally—

"Rafe, this is a bit much. We don't need half these rules."

Raphael's tone softened. "Oh—sorry, maybe I misunderstood. I thought we were in alignment. We already talked about this, and you nodded just now. So why the flip-flop? We simply want stability, compa. You said you wanted us safe... or don't you?"

Diego's mind lurched. How could Raphael so easily twist everything like that?

Words jammed in his throat. The edges of his vision sharpened. Heat flashed across his face. And then—his gift flailed. Sensing it slipping away, Diego clamped down hard, forcing it under control.

Raphael's voice shifted, gaining a warm note. "Hey, you feeling all right, compa? We can wait if you need a minute. That rat stew can sometimes hit like rocket fuel. Full-on blow-out-the-toilets kind of deal."

Arturo snorted. Luca shook his head with a slight grin. The ripple of humor left Diego standing alone.

Raphael didn't wait. "Now, I'm not trying to boss anyone around. We just want to stay alive. Is that so bad? It's like the Hunts—you gave us the green light, and now we're safer for it. We all thank you for that. This is more of the same. We can always scale back later, once things settle."

"We all know you're still in charge, Diego. I thought you wanted this too—just like you wanted the Hunts. Of course, it's your call." He turned to Luca and Arturo, hands open. "But we just want to feel safe. Right, guys?"

Arturo nodded quickly. Luca shifted his weight, glancing at both of them, but said nothing.

Diego drew in a long, slow breath. *It's fine. A little thing, like he said. We'll get back to normal soon enough. Just his way of working through the grief. And if I argue with him now... it won't end well.* The knot in his shoulders didn't ease, but he finally said, "Yeah, sure. Just for a little while."

In the days that followed, his frustration only grew, and it became crystal clear that Raphael's grief had hardened him. It showed in every interaction: the tight set of his jaw when someone hesitated during a security check, the clipped tone he used when the schedule wasn't followed to the minute.

The rigidity began to take its toll.

The easy camaraderie they had once enjoyed faded, replaced by an underlying static. Conversations thinned to quiet exchanges. Meals, once lively with jokes and shared stories, became silent affairs.

Diego wanted to talk through the changes. To work out a plan for dialing things back. But part of him worried how Raphael might react—he had become too unpredictable. Diego never knew which version he'd get: the compassionate friend, the clever manipulator, or the bloodthirsty tyrant. Over time, it felt easier just to nod along and not risk setting him off, and the right moment never came.

The weeks blurred together, and a fragile sense of order took hold. Soon enough, Raphael's strict regimen of mealtimes, patrols, security checks, and training drills became routine.

Solsticios happened more often and were slowly reshaping under Raphael's influence. A lock of their hair burned as a sacrifice. A prick of their finger. A token taken from one of the growlers they'd killed. A chant whispered to the beat until it became habit.

Arturo and Luca eagerly embraced it all, and Diego didn't know what to do.

*   *   *

Nature's call dragged Diego from sleep. He blinked hard, struggling to come out of the lingering fog. Padding out of the Lair, the cold tile of the Pizzarama slapped his bare feet, and he remembered the restroom floors. Sticky. Rarely cleaned. But the urgent pressure that had pulled him awake continued its wail. He squared his shoulders. No turning back now.

When he passed the watchtower, something caught his eye. Raphael—the one on watch—sat slumped in the chair, unmoving.

Had he fallen asleep? Diego hesitated. A few steps closer, he saw it for what it was: a crude dummy dressed in Raphael's clothes, not Raphael himself. Anger flared through him. Raphael had made the rule months ago: *no one abandons their post.* So where was he? Did he think the rules didn't apply to him?

254

Diego scanned the room. The soft sounds of sleep drifted in the still air, but he knew that was only Arturo and Luca. Had Raphael slipped outside? He had to find out.

Priorities first—he was about to burst. A quick stop averted that crisis.

He grabbed a jacket, shoved his feet into his hightops, and quietly stepped onto the promenade. The orbital lights had dimmed for the night, leaving the corridors shrouded in flickering twilight. Diego stalked the derelict halls, his form shimmering and barely visible, senses on high alert.

Ahead, the faint green glow of a CRT terminal spilled out from a public televid booth. Diego moved closer, his mind racing. Raphael sat on the edge of his sea, the clack of his keystrokes echoing in the stillness.

The unease that had simmered in Diego's gut for weeks twisted and churned. This was a blatant violation of their rules. So why?

Diego needed to see what Raphael was up to, but the booths were made for privacy and fit only one person.

Suspicion gnawed at him. What could Raphael possibly be doing in there? He could do research in the day when others took their turns at the televid terminals. A game on the terminal? But why now? Email? That would be another violation—no contact.

The tapping of keys cut off, and Diego froze. Raphael's head poked out, scanning the corridor.

Diego held perfectly still, hoping he wouldn't notice the shimmer of his masking. A heartbeat stretched until it hurt. Then Raphael flicked the terminal's switch and retreated down a side hall.

Diego waited for his pulse to calm before returning to the Pizzarama. He rolled back into bed, mind tumbling with worries and questions that plagued him into a restless sleep.

Act 3

Ac-Cent-Tchu-Ate The Positive

Diego used Echo Ring's lab to get away from Raphael's changes. His strict rules were only the start. With each hunt, he blurred the boundary between survival and savagery. Blood rituals. Chants. It gave Diego the chills. He'd seen the religious fervor of La Familia—but this was different. Raphael's way was darker, more dangerous, and it seemed to pull the others in.

So Diego stayed in the lab for weeks at a time. Some days he buried himself in the metaphysical project journals; other days he hunted for cracks in the mainframe, poring over lines of code, configurations, and commands until his eyes burned dry. Raphael and Arturo would drop in now and then, but only for a few hours. Luca stayed longer.

Diego blinked, trying to focus on the words glowing back at him. The ceiling light flickered overhead. A ponderous thumping carried through the floor—there was a walker nearby on the promenade. He held still, counting the steps until it passed, wondering if Luca had even noticed.

It faded, leaving only the quiet hum of the station. Diego exhaled and resumed his work, scanning the endless lines of code until a detail on the screen brought him up short.

The date.

His sixteenth birthday.

The realization kicked hard, hollowing out an ache in his chest. Years had passed since his exile, and the weight of this time bore down on him. Memories of past birthdays flickered through his mind —laughter, cake, presents, the warmth of his parents' love.

Not anymore. Just the harsh reality of another year trapped in the lower rings. A year since Arturo, Luca, and Julian had arrived.

Looking back, he realized there had been signs of the time slipping by. How often had he picked through Woolwards because his clothes no longer fit? At least now, the hoodie that once swallowed him whole finally sat right on his shoulders.

He stood, stretching—suddenly aware of how much he'd grown. Then he wandered out to where Luca was working. The guitar strains of Johnny Cash drifted from the radio. Diego dropped into a seat, leaned back, and let the music wash over him. His fingers picked out the chords in the air. When the song ended, stillness settled in, occasionally interrupted by the rattle of Luca's tools.

After a while, Diego sighed. "Do you ever think about the future? I mean, really think about it?"

Luca paused, looking up from his work. The weight in Diego's eyes seemed to catch him off guard. "I suppose," he said, setting aside a vacuum tube. "Why? You okay?"

Diego deflected the concern with a soft smile. "Yeah, I'm fine. Just... learning Astrix and COMTRAN is harder than I thought. I don't know if I can really make this work. We need to figure out other plans, I guess."

"You did hack my parents' account so I could see their messages," Luca offered as encouragement.

Diego tapped his finger on the workbench. "Wasn't really a hack. You just guessed your mom's password. Sure, I'll keep trying to figure out how we can hack the mainframe. But... what if nothing we try works out? Then what?"

Luca thought about it for a moment. "We can't stay locked up forever. But..." he glanced away. "I do like what we've got going on down here. Do we really need to go back?"

"So, You have no problem with Carlos doing whatever he wants in Bravo Ring? You don't think he'll come after us eventually? And what about your folks?"

"I saw the messages. I know they're fine." Luca's jaw tightened. "If anything, I'm worried going back might cause them more trouble. So, as long as Carlos leaves us alone, yeah, I think I'm good with all this. I don't need to be a hero or change the world, Diego... I just want a place where we can live without anyone messing with us. What we really need is just a little more balan—" He cut himself off, a flush creeping up his cheeks.

Diego lifted an eyebrow. "Balan?"

"Ohh, never mind," Luca mumbled, turning away to hide the color in his face.

Diego couldn't let it go. "Come on, spill it. What is 'balan'?"

Luca cleared his throat, then gave a shrug. "Balance, you know... More girls. What we've got now isn't so bad, but it's missing, uhh, well, yeah."

Diego burst out laughing, "Balance!" He could relate, he'd often longed for Donna's company.

A cheeky grin lit up Luca's face. "Yeah."

Diego nodded, his laughter fading. "You're not wrong. We could definitely use a little more balance."

*   *   *

Diego stared at the code on the screen, reviewing it one more time. He'd been at this for a while, but maybe this time it would work. He blinked hard, squinted, then hit enter.

For a moment, nothing. He counted the seconds, ready for another failure. Except this time, lines of telemetry began scrolling on the screen.

"Luca... Luca..." His voice started as a whisper. He slapped the table, trying to get his attention, then broke into a shout. "Luca! Get in here!"

Luca came in fast, catching himself on the doorframe before yanking off his goggles. His hair sprang up in wild tufts.

"I did it!" Diego jabbed his finger against the glass screen. "That's Echo Ring's antenna feed!"

For a heartbeat, they just stared, stunned.

Diego lurched forward, hunching over the keyboard. A few more keystrokes, and static crackled from the speaker. Another command, and it cycled through the frequencies until, very faintly, they caught a voice through the noise:

"—ontrol, this is Skybolt Queen on approach to Harmony."

A long hiss of static, and then. "Copy. Adjusting heading as requested. ETA one hour. Skybolt Queen, out."

"Harmony?" Luca breathed.

"Harmony Orbital!" Diego grinned.

Luca's eyes widened. "Of course, we're only getting half the conversation. They're on the other side of the world."

Their excitement quickly sharpened into purpose.

"We have to send a message!" Diego yanked the keyboard closer, diving through menus until a flashing error filled the screen: "49.14.A: check failed."

He tried again. And again. Even after a reset, the same error glared back. He pulled up the code reference manual, scanning the pages until he groaned, "It's the antenna. Something in the transmit array is dead. We can't send."

Luca gave a crooked smile. "We can listen. That's huge!"

They listened for a while, finding a lot of static and a very few signals. Most were encrypted, but a few slipped through—garbled conversations from distant ships, even faint bursts from Arcadia's surface.

All the while they debated options, reluctantly agreeing that fixing Echo Ring's central antennas was far too dangerous—for now. The station's robotic security would cut them down before they got anywhere near it.

"So we build our own," Luca suggested. "We've got an airlock. We can push it out from there."

Diego flung up his hands. "Why did it take us this long to think of that?"

Luca grimaced. "Parts?"

"But if we can send a message…" Diego straightened. "What if we tried contacting the Wardens or the Star Rangers? Think they'd help if they heard about what Carlos is doing?"

Luca looked uneasy. "I've heard nothing good about the Wardens. Bringing them in might just mean trading one evil for another."

"What about the Star Rangers? Think they'd even care?"

Luca nodded slowly. "I heard they go around as judges or something. Doesn't hurt to try, I suppose."

They cleared a chalkboard in the lab and started outlining the things they'd have to do to make an antenna. It would take research and plenty of scavenging runs. Signal boosters, power couplings—who knew what else. But it felt possible.

Diego glanced at the rack of spacesuits, already dreading the thought. Maybe he could talk Luca into handling the spacewalk part.

*   *   *

The antenna's telemetry had been a high point, but since then, Diego's progress had stalled. He still hadn't cracked the layers of security protecting Serenity's mainframes. His only lifeline was a phrase he'd seen countless times on ALT.HACKERS: "Once you were in a system, you could gain any level of access, given enough time."

Time, he had. Progress, he didn't. Each month dropped another stone in his pockets, making every step harder.

Diego woke early in Echo Ring's lab with a dark cloud needling his thoughts. A shower in the Hygiene Bay didn't wash it away, so he loaded a string of songs into the radio and cranked the volume—perhaps the music would shake it loose.

"What's wrong with you!" Luca groaned, burrowing deeper into the couch.

Diego grinned and took a seat at the keyboard, but the smile faded quickly.

Everyone expected him to have a plan, and they wanted to know the details. But he wasn't ready to open up yet. Even his new ideas stayed locked away—like using John Smith's card to call the maintenance lift from Echo Ring. He didn't dare tell the others about that, though. They'd only want to rush back to Bravo Ring. But with La Familia still in control, what was the point? No—the lift was just one part of a larger plan.

First, they needed leverage—there had to be a way to unseat Carlos so it would be safe to return. At least, that's what Diego kept telling himself. But he still had nothing.

Raphael was cooking up something too. Diego hadn't caught him sneaking away to the televid booths at night since the last time, but he knew that was only the start. Whatever it was, Raphael kept it close.

The more he thought about their whole situation, the more his drive faltered.

Bing Crosby came on and the volume went up, followed by Luca joining in with the chorus, "—we better... Ac-ceeeent-tchu-ate the positive."

Diego stared past the terminal's screen, eyes distant. Good advice, sure—but so hard to follow.

A crash shook the walls. Then another. They followed the noise to the observation room, where a walker hammered the one-way glass. Its grotesque form loomed against the slithering vegetation outside, which seemed to pulse in response to each blow.

Luca whispered, face pale. "It can't see us, can it?"

Diego's voice was just as quiet. "I'm more worried about how long the glass will last."

He wanted to push at it with his gift, but what if Luca noticed? Didn't matter. He balled his fists and shoved—only to plow into that same, sickening tar-like presence he remembered from last time. It curdled his gift so fast he gagged.

"The radio!" Luca blurted, already bolting from the room.

The music died, and Luca returned. They held their breath, praying the walker would lose interest.

But the blows continued, each reverberating through the walls. Diego braced himself, preparing to try again.

"We need to distract it," Luca said. "One of us could go out there and lure it away..."

"Don't even think about it!" Diego snapped. "Look, I–I'm going to…" He started, wanting to warn Luca in case the next attempt flattened him.

But Luca cut him off. "My device! I haven't tested it, and there's a power problem, but—" He bolted before Diego could finish.

Diego watched the glass shudder under each blow. His stomach churned just being so near the thing.

Luca flew back in, clutching an orb trailing thick cords. He dropped it on a chair and flicked a switch.

Pulses of energy flashed from the device, each stabbing into Diego's skull. His gift howled in response. He doubled over, tearing his mask free as bile rose in his throat.

The walker's grotesque form froze. One arm hung high for another strike, then it shuddered backwards into the vegetation.

The orb glowed an ominous white-orange, and smoke curled up. Luca lurched and pulled the power. "It worked," he coughed, examining the blackened housing. "But I think it's fried."

Diego slumped into a chair, rubbing his forehead. Luca poked at the device, muttering to himself. After a moment, Diego managed a bitter smile. "Well, you did say you needed to test it…"

Luca looked up, a scowl forming. "Yeah, but now I have to start over! Why couldn't that thing have waited just a little longer so I could get a good power source?"

He picked up the orb and hauled it back to the lab, leaving Diego alone with his thoughts.

Whatever the device was, it didn't seem to bother Luca at all. He hadn't even seen me nearly hurl. Hadn't seen me at all.

It was a harsh reminder that, no matter how hard he tried to fit in, he wasn't really one of them. Thanks to his gift.

God Only Knows

Diego closed the maintenance hatch behind Luca. The metallic clang echoed through the cramped storage room, and the seal hissed into place. He flexed his fingers and rubbed his cheeks to shake off the Link tubes's biting chill.

They'd been gone a week while Luca rebuilt his device, and now he was eager to show the others—though Diego's excitement was layered with trepidation. Not just from the pain it caused him, but he'd become increasingly convinced that the growlers retained some spark of humanity, and this left him reluctant to join in their growler hunts.

They approached the Pizzarama, but something felt off, and Diego froze.

"What is it?" Luca asked.

Diego shook his head, his ears straining to pick up any sound beyond the hum of machinery and the murmur of conversation. And then it hit him—a new voice came from the Pizzarama.

"Another exile," he said.

Stepping inside, they found not one, but two fresh-faced boys sitting on the sofa, looking bewildered and scared.

Arturo's dark eyes met Diego's. "While you were away, Nico and Kenji were exiled. I was on watch and got them in safely."

Raphael leaned back in his chair, arms crossed, a smug expression teasing at his lips.

Diego turned to the new arrivals. "Are you two okay?"

One of them nodded hesitantly. "Yeah, I guess. It's just… I don't know what to feel. Oh, and I'm Kenji."

The other boy—Nico—sat quietly. The tag still dangled from the cuff of his purple AstroTec hoodie. His wary expression almost made him look even smaller. His eyes widened when Diego turned towards him, but he remained silent.

Kenji sported a tropical button-up shirt a few sizes too big for his lean frame. His broad cheekbones, flat features, and cropped black hair sharply contrasted with Nico's rounded, swarthy face.

Kenji continued. "We knew it might happen, but I guess we hoped it wouldn't. Then, one day, the Anointed came for us."

Nico gave a faint nod.

"I thought we were done for!" Kenji added, his voice lifting with a touch of nervous energy. "Nobody knows you guys are still alive down here!"

Raphael stood, giving a casual stretch. "Well, these chavos are part of the group now. And I've already taken care of their initiation."

"Initiation?" Diego snapped to look at Raphael.

Arturo's face darkened. "We ran them through the Challenge Course, and we did an impromptu Solsticio—gave them masks and everything."

Diego's eyes flashed with disbelief and anger. "You what?"

Raphael shrugged. The casual gesture was at odds with the fire in his eyes. "It had to be done. They need to know the rules. They need to understand how things work down here."

Diego clenched his fists as he fought to keep his composure. "Rafe, we should have discussed this first."

Raphael stepped forward, closing the space between them, his expression hardening in defiance. "Someone had to. We dealt with what was really important while you were off playing with your toys in the lab."

The room stilled.

Diego glanced at Nico and Kenji, then at the curtain where their masks hung. Dried blood stained the edges of the two new additions. The sight made Diego's stomach churn. This wasn't right. He couldn't let Raphael's methods define their way of life. He had to figure out something to do to rein Raphael in.

Luca stepped forward. "Shouldn't they have at least been trained first?"

"Nah, I adjusted the challenges to account for their inexperience," Raphael shot back. "And they both made it through just fine." His last words came with a pointed look at Luca.

Nico and Kenji turned a shade paler, unease written on their faces. They didn't look like they agreed with Raphael's assessment. Diego wrestled with how to respond, frustration simmering. Why was Raphael doing this? They needed unity, not fear.

Diego knew that pushing the confrontation with Raphael in front of everyone would only escalate things. He studied Nico and Kenji. They looked so young, so small—faces a map of bewildered uncertainty—round, innocent, and utterly unprepared for the harsh reality they were tossed into.

He wondered if he'd looked just as lost when he first arrived. The thought hardened into conviction: he would protect them—even from Raphael.

But first, he needed to find common ground—something to diffuse Raphael. He had to pull him back from the edge before he dragged the new boys into his darkness.

"We'll start fresh tomorrow," Diego announced. "We'll go over the rules, routines, training—all of it. Together."

Diego turned to Nico and Kenji. "Welcome to the Desterrados."

Their eyes lingered on the mask Diego wore, drawn to the faint violet glimmer in his left eye. They quickly looked away, nodding in unison.

Arturo changed the subject. "Luca, did you bring back another gadget?"

Luca glanced between Raphael and Diego before nodding, and he proudly held up his device—a bodgered amalgam of alien technology, pulsing lights, and coiled wires a little bigger than a fist.

"This," he began, "uses some alien Gray tech I found in the lab from their esper experiments. Think of it like a raygun—but it sends out pulses that drive the growlers away."

Arturo eyed the device. "How do you know it works?"

"We tested it on the void-tainted things in Echo Ring."

"How does it work?"

"The energy cell only lasts five minutes," Luca warned, flicking the switch. A low hum filled the room, resonating deep in their bones. Diego winced as the sharp pain shot through his skull, and he rubbed his temples. No one else seemed to notice his discomfort—their attention was riveted on the device as they exchanged excited glances.

Raphael hopped onto the stage with cat-like grace, grabbed his mask, and shouted, "I think it's time for a hunt!"

They left Nico and Kenji to hold down the Pizzarama and moved out. Their flashlights cast shaky beams over shattered glass and peeling paint as they navigated Red Sector's less-explored corridors. Every creak and rattle of the aging Serenity heightened their senses, and adrenaline surged through their veins.

The eerie cries of a growler horde echoed through the air from a plaza ahead. When they stepped into view, the growlers immediately lunged.

Luca activated the device, and it pulsed. The growlers recoiled, some letting out guttural howls before they scattered.

After several more of Luca's tests in the lab, Diego was ready for it, so while it hit him hard and painfully, he was able to deal with it.

"We have five minutes!" Luca yelled.

The boys took off after the retreating abominations. The chase was a chaotic departure from their usual process of carefully selecting a target. At each turn, the growlers split in different directions, and the boys pursued the dwindling group.

During the frenetic chase, a growler turned to face Diego. Time seemed to hold its breath. His steps faltered. He felt like all the oxygen had been ripped from the room. There was no doubt—he recognized her instantly.

Donna.

Her beautiful face stared back at him, now twisted and grotesque. Her eyes were tainted with otherworldly violet threads.

Donna.

His heart wrenched as he stared at the girl who had captured it —now reduced to a monstrous shell of herself.

"Donna," he whispered. Despite her monstrous transformation, he couldn't look away.

Her once-silky dark hair hung in tangled, matted clumps around a gaunt, scarred face. The tattered remnants of her old clothing clung to her emaciated frame. She still wore the outfit from that day in the plaza on Charlie Ring, so long ago.

And none of that mattered. It was still Donna.

For a fleeting moment, recognition seemed to flicker in her eyes. But it vanished—if it had ever been there—replaced by the vacant, feral stare of what she had become.

Grief and anger surged, tightening around his chest. The thought of harming her—even like this—was unthinkable.

"Keep moving!" Raphael's shout jolted him back to the moment.

Diego forced himself to swallow the shock, hiding his turmoil from the others. Donna darted down a side corridor, disappearing into the shadows. Diego pointed toward a group running in the opposite direction, and everyone followed without question.

To his relief, no one seemed to have recognized her.

His steps slowed, and he fell to the back. *Does she remember me?*

The question pulled on him, but he had no time to dwell on it as he chased after the others. He hadn't summoned his gift yet—the device made using it even more painful. Fortunately, he didn't have to.

Soon they had one cornered. Diego stood back and let the others finish it. Cheers and laughter erupted, echoing through the corridors.

Raphael knelt at the thing's side, preparing for one of his rituals.

Diego grabbed his hand. His voice came out quiet, but harder than he expected. "NO."

Raphael paused, leaning back ever so slightly. A flicker crossed his eyes. He almost looked… confused? Surprised? Scared?

Diego had never been this firm with him before, and... Raphael didn't fight back—just scowled and stood. Nobody noticed the exchange.

"This changes everything!" Arturo shouted, pumping his fist.

The group made their way back to the Pizzarama, Diego trailing behind, a shadow of himself. Someone started the jukebox.

Diego stood apart from the group, his eyes unfocused. His thoughts roiled. A Beach Boys song drifted through the air, and the chorus, "God only knows what I'd be without you," hit hard. The sight of Donna—twisted, grotesque, yet still somehow Donna—burned in his mind.

The line between friend and foe, which he'd tried to maintain yet couldn't stop thinking about, had blurred into nothing. The cost of their survival weighed heavily on him. They had to fight back, did they not? It was kill or be killed, right?

Raphael clapped him on the back. "We finally have a way to take control of things."

Diego managed a weak smile, nodding in agreement. "Yeah, we do."

The device had given them a powerful advantage—but he no longer wanted to hunt the growlers. But it was more than that. The way the device clawed at his mind. He felt it, just like the growlers. So what did that say about him? Was everyone right all along? Was he part growler?

And if they were right about that... then maybe they were right about him summoning the Kraal. His gut clenched, and he struggled to push the thought away.

It wasn't my fault.

The image of Donna's face twisted and deformed as a growler haunted him, and he retreated to a quiet corner to be with his thoughts. What if they caught her in one of their hunts? He couldn't just leave her out there alone—he couldn't abandon her to be another victim.

But how could he possibly save her?

His thoughts reached back to the lab's research. There had to be a hint somewhere in the records that could help her. Maybe she could be healed. A seed of hope took root that he could save her, even as another part of him whispered she was already lost.

Diego had to try, but the first step was making her safe—even if it meant breaking Raphael's rule about never going out alone. He couldn't live with himself if he didn't take the chance.

He prepared everything in advance, carefully placing her scarf, his gear, and supplies where they wouldn't draw attention.

The next night, once everyone was deep in sleep, he slipped from his bed, activated his gift, and shimmered into invisibility. The guys lay sprawled nearby, faces softened in sleep, oblivious. Diego crept past them, heart pounding, each step careful.

He retrieved his gear and reached the rear exit, heart hammering as he silently prayed Luca wouldn't hear the door from his watch post. Then he was out.

He returned to the Red Sector, mind churning through his plan. Growlers didn't need normal sustenance, and Diego hoped he could lock Donna away somewhere safe until he figured out what to do.

But doubts plagued him as he prowled in search of a place to keep her safe and hidden from their hunts. Was there even a way to recover from being a growler? Was she really still there, deep inside, or was she lost forever?

He scoured supply rooms, stores, offices, and shops, but each came up short—until he remembered a restaurant in the food court with a broken walk-in freezer. They'd searched it a few times before and never found anything of value, so it was unlikely anybody would go back there.

Diego moved through the tables and chairs and past signs advertising the daily specials. He found the freezer as he'd expected, cluttered with disarrayed shelves and empty boxes labeled with names of products he didn't even recognize, like "fries" and "patties."

He straightened the room and bodgered the handle so it couldn't open from the inside.

Now, he had to find her.

Venturing back out, he extended his senses. Inspired by what he'd read of the esper powers, Diego had learned to identify the unique presence of individual growlers. Considering his familiarity with Donna, he hoped to distinguish her from the others.

He reached out, hoping to find the brightness he remembered feeling when near her years before. A bubbly happiness mixed with fierce determination. Would she still feel that way? Even if not, he believed he could still recognize her.

There—a familiar flicker at the edge of his reach. He focused. The sensation sharpened. It felt familiar.

Diego followed the trail, heart racing, navigating through the twisted hallways past broken storefronts and debris-strewn floors. The closer he got, the stronger the connection felt. His surroundings blurred as he concentrated on what he felt must be Donna.

He rounded a corner in the upper levels and there she was, standing amidst several other growlers, each rocking dormantly.

Diego's heart ached. He'd longed to be with her for years. To talk to her. To listen to her. To be with her.

Around her wrist hung her favorite bracelet—a chain of tiny stars and planets. But her once-bright eyes were clouded, her skin pale and gnarled. And still unmistakably Donna.

He stepped closer, each heartbeat heavier than the last. He had found her. But the real challenge was just starting. He had to get her to the freezer, hide her from the hunts, and somehow figure out how to cure whatever it was that made her a growler.

His gift stirred inside him, feeding on his worry. He hated it— hated that it meant he was like them. And now Donna was one of them. But he wasn't a growler. Couldn't be! Yet every time he used his gift, the doubt needled him: what if he was?

Not that he had a choice. He had to help her. Had to use it. Shaking his head, he focused, keeping his masking in place for the others, but easing it a little bit with Donna. Then, as lightly as he could, he let a breath of his gift touch her mind, offering calm. Safety. Warmth.

"Donna," he spoke softly. "It's me. Diego. I'm here to help you."

For a moment, her eyes seemed to clear, and he thought he saw a flash of who she once was.

A growler nearby muttered. "Don't look back."

Donna's lips moved as if she were speaking, but no sound came out. Diego leaned closer until he caught the faintest whisper: "Save me. Save me. Save me."

His heart lurched. "Come on," he said. "I have a place where you'll be safe."

Diego took her by the arm. She jerked, her head snapping around, searching for what had touched her—but with his masking up, she couldn't see him. He brushed his gift against the bilious darkness coiled around her mind. It wasn't the same as the nudges he'd used on other growlers—those were quick flashes, like passing a hand through flame. You felt the heat, but it didn't burn.

This was different. He had to hold on. The darkness clung to his gift, sticky and foul, staining him. He strained to keep his calming note steady, imagining it as the blanket she'd once brought when they lay looking at the stars. He wove into it the warmth and joy he'd felt then, and wrapped it around her mind. Keeping her safe. So she would come with him.

He hated himself for it. Forcing her to follow him felt wrong. Taking away someone's free agency was the very nature of evil. Was he doing that now? Or was this somehow different? He didn't know what else to do.

"Donna, please," he whispered, pulling gently on her arm. His voice shook as he struggled to keep it calm. "I need you to come with me."

She hesitated, then took a step forward.

Diego's chest surged with hope.

Each shuffling step came as a painful reminder of what she'd become. But she followed him.

It took longer than he wanted, but at last, they reached the freezer. Diego ushered her inside, closing the door behind them. She turned, a low huff slipping from her lips.

Donna.

He'd grown taller than her. She looked frozen in time—a twisted reflection of the girl he remembered.

Guilt washed over him. Locking someone up felt wrong. Least of all, a girl he was fond of. It read like a horror story. But this was different. He was doing it for her. For her. The thought almost steadied him—until he remembered: isn't that the same thing the psychos in the stories always said?

His guts curdled. Then he pictured Raphael finding her as a growler. No—he couldn't let that happen. He had to keep her safe.

"Stay here," he whispered, his voice breaking. From his pocket, he pulled the scarf and looped it around her neck. "I'll come back for you. I promise."

He closed the door, the lock clicking into place. Leaning his back against its cold metal surface, he slid down to the floor. Exhaustion and relief washed over him. He had done what he could.

But the sight of her, trapped in that small, dark room, tore at him. He knew it was the right choice, so why did it feel like a betrayal? He shook his head, forcing himself to focus on the bigger picture.

As he returned to the Pizzarama, he checked the time—only a few minutes until the guard rotated. Worry gnawed at him; if Raphael found out he had left, there would be hell to pay. But Donna was worth the risk. He would do anything for her.

Resetting the back door lock and alarm took longer than expected. He hurried through the dark, finding his bed in the Lair. Each second seemed to chase his steps. Heart racing, he dove under the covers, gear and shoes still on, and dismissed his invisibility.

Movement caught his eye.

Across the room, Raphael sat upright in his bed. The darkness hid his features. Diego's chest lurched. But Raphael said nothing. He stared at Diego for far too long before finally rolling over.

*   *   *

The words "ASTRIX SYSTEM LOCKOUT" flashed on the screen, and Diego's stomach plunged into a personal black hole.

ECMS04: the dusty minicomputer in the room off the lab. A dead relic, until Luca coaxed it back to life, and it became Diego's playground. His sandbox to test riskier hacking programs. If he messed it up, he'd just wipe and reload Astrix. And since ECMS04 wasn't on Serenity's network, he could hack away without fear of repercussions.

That should have been his buffer. His safety net. He'd used it plenty of times—just not this time.

He'd been alone in the lab for days, working on his latest hack. His confidence had swelled—until he tried it.

Now, staring at the terminal, the kept flashing: "ASTRIX SYSTEM LOCKOUT"

He was cut off from the mainframe. His one back door slammed shut. Without it, he had nothing left to work from. No launch point to attack the other mainframes. No way forward.

A part of him wanted to hammer at the keyboard, to try every trick he knew to reset the lockout. But that sort of reckless behavior was exactly what had triggered it in the first place.

Diego raked a hand through his sweaty hair, his pulse racing. Why hadn't he just tested this last program on ECMS04 first? Everything else had been fine. So the *one time* he skipped that step was when he needed it. Groaning, he lurched upright and paced the lab, thoughts spiraling.

There had to be a way to fix this. There had to be. But he couldn't stop fixating on the worst-case scenarios. Was the lockout permanent? If it didn't automatically reset, then what? Would he have to trek through the overgrown jungle of Echo Ring to find its Operations Center? Did Echo Ring even have functional maintenance bots left to handle an account reset? And would they believe he was John Smith, like Chip had?

The notion of venturing into the mutated wilderness outside the lab sent his anxiety into freefall.

His fingers itched to try something—anything.

He hated waiting. Each tick of the clock seemed slower than the last. The minute hand crept along at a snail's pace, while the hour hand might as well have been glued in place.

He scanned the lab, reluctantly searching for gear that might help if he had to venture onto Echo Ring's overgrown promenade. But he couldn't get his heart into it.

Everything was unraveling, all because of one stupid move. The others wouldn't accept stalling much longer—they wanted results, proof of what he could do.

But he'd been focused elsewhere, lost in Project Ultra's endless volumes of metaphysical research and medical experiments. Most of it made no sense to him, but he was desperate to find something that could help Donna. And in the process, he'd ignored the mainframe. So yeah, maybe he'd rushed through this last attempt.

Worst-case scenarios piled up in his mind. If all the bots were offline, he'd have to break into the data center, navigating a gauntlet of magnetically locked doors, alarms, and armed turrets—not to mention the tree walkers and growlers.

Had he just destroyed his best—and possibly only—chance of pulling off his plan to hack La Familia's mainframe? Why hadn't he just tested his code first? Or, better yet, set up backup accounts while he still had access to John's super admin user?

Unable to sit still, Diego bundled up and started into the Link tubes. It was time to trek back to the Pizzarama... perhaps the lockout would reset later.

But he didn't even reach the junction with Serenity's spine. The gnawing worry and fear of failure dragged him back to the lab.

Two hours passed.

Three.

Finally, the terminal screen flickered and cleared, and the familiar Astrix login prompt scrolled into place.

Diego tried John's credentials, pulse thundering.

The system let him back in.

A ragged groan escaped him as he slumped back in the chair. He stared at the ceiling, exhaustion weighing him down. A glance confirmed: two in the morning. The soft pillow of his bed called, but he couldn't stop now. He had to make sure this wouldn't happen again. Blinking hard to stay awake, he pulled the keyboard close.

Man of Constant Sorrow

"See?" Kenji set a bowl of mashed potatoes on the table. "Told you all we had to do was boil and mash 'em. Don't know why you guys thought it'd be hard."

They eyed the gray heap with open skepticism.

"Not like Mom's," Nico muttered.

Arturo snagged a fork and dropped into a seat. "I don't know what y'all are waiting for, but I haven't had mashed potatoes in forever!"

A debate broke out over how to divide the portions, peppered with a few jokes and playful jabs. But Diego could tell it was forced—the tightness in a smile, the weak edge in a voice. The frustration never really left them.

They had no future and complained more and more about the lack of any concrete plan to get home. Raphael, of course, insisted he had something in the works but never offered details. All the while, he berated Diego and Luca for not sharing their progress in the lab.

Diego pulled off his mask, letting his long curls fall to cover the scars on the left side of his face. He hesitated before starting in, fork in hand, lost in thought.

After months of practice, Kenji and Nico had truly become Desterrados—hardened and ready to face even the growlers. In that same time, Diego had found nothing to help Donna.

Why had he ever believed he could heal her? He wasn't some genius from Project Ultra—he was just a kid with a grade-school education and a knack for staying alive.

But he couldn't set her free—that would leave her vulnerable to the hunts. So when he was around, he still joined them, just to steer the others away from her.

Frustration knotted his gut, and he clenched the fork tighter. He needed to refocus and channel his energy into something productive, like the antenna project. Luca had said he needed help finding parts. With it working, perhaps he could summon a real scientist—

A hot, wet slap struck the back of Diego's head. He blinked, fingers finding mashed potatoes in his hair. Slowly, he turned. Raphael sat grinning, spoon still in its firing position.

"What the hell, Rafe?" Diego growled, brushing at the mess. He usually tried not to react to Raphael's stunts, but this was so infantile, he suddenly didn't care.

Raphael smirked. "Just thought I'd bring you back to the party, Diego. You're barely with us anymore, even when you are."

Diego had let it roll off him for too long, bottling up the frustration instead of confronting Raphael. Locking it away. Burying it deep. Letting him do what he wanted—because that was better than a fight, right?

Then it struck him—their dynamic had slipped back to what it had been years ago. The old fear suddenly clawed its way up, but he shoved it down hard. He wasn't that boy anymore.

And still, that glint in Raphael's eye. Diego clenched his fists to stop his hands from trembling. Something inside him creaked—a beam stressed nearly too far. But he had to stay calm. Don't fight in front of the guys. Not here.

He tried to keep it steady, but his voice came out thinner than he wanted, pitching up. "You think this is funny? Grow up, Raphael."

That should have been the end of it. But Raphael's eyes lit, and the old cocky smile spread across his face. Absent for years, it was back.

Nobody else could tell how much Raphael was goading him. To them, it looked like Rafe being Rafe. And that almost made it worse.

Fire stoked in Diego's chest. His forehead pulsed with each heartbeat. Even his gift howled in righteous fury.

Raphael leaned forward. "Aww, come on, look at you clenching your teeth. You know I'm just kidding. Be the big leader—man up. Tell us about your plans already. You've been in Echo Ring's lab for so long, and still have nothing to show us. So, what's really going on down there with you two? Getting to be... special friends?"

A few snickers rippled around the table. Luca's cheeks flushed, his mouth starting to open. Diego caught his eye, giving a quick shake of his head. Not worth it.

Raphael let his voice drop, suddenly speaking to Diego alone. "Do you have something to share? Another... secret?"

The way he said it twisted Diego's stomach. This wasn't childish innuendo. He was threatening to expose his gift. Let everyone know he was void touched. And he'd brought Luca into it too. That wasn't an accident—it was calculated, a warning of how easily Diego could lose his closest friend.

Diego's vision sharpened. Fire surged in his chest. His ears pounded. He thought that Raphael had changed. That they had built something better. But no.

For far too long, he'd buried it, doing everything he could to avoid confrontation because ignoring Raphael was easier than starting a fight. Now it all snapped loose at once.

The room tunneled to Raphael's smirk. Before Diego knew it, he was on his feet, fist half-raised—ready to end it once and for all—but he caught himself at the last second.

Raphael's grin widened.

He'd won.

He kicked his chair back and dropped into a fighting stance. "Bring it on, *chavito*. It's been a while since we went head-to-head. Let's see if you've actually improved any."

The others quickly circled, cheering and egging them on, blind to the fact that this was more than roughhousing. But Luca stayed back, silent, brow furrowed.

Diego squared his shoulders and clenched his fists. Raphael was stronger, but he still had the edge when it came to agility and speed.

Their first exchanges were cautious, testing each other. Raphael jabbed a punch, but Diego deflected, his Jeet Kune Do training guiding his movements. Raphael unleashed a flurry of punches, each one faster and harder than the last, but Diego blocked and dodged every one.

The others' shouts blended into the background.

Raphael aimed a punch at Diego's ribs. Diego twisted, narrowly avoiding the blow, and retaliated with a quick jab to Raphael's side. Raphael barely flinched, grinning, then delivered a powerful kick to Diego's stomach. The impact forced the air from Diego's lungs, and he stumbled back, gasping.

Raphael laughed, a grating sound that set Diego's teeth on edge. "Had enough yet? Or do you think you're better than the rest of us and can do your own thing whenever you want? Wandering off whenever you want..."

Diego straightened and unleashed a flurry of kicks to keep Raphael on the defensive. Raphael deflected most of them, but one landed. He grunted—more annoyed than hurt—and lunged forward with renewed fury.

The room seemed to shrink as the fight intensified. Where Raphael seemed to relish the chance to knock Diego down a notch, Diego knew he had to wait until the right moment to strike.

Then it came.

Raphael overextended on a punch, throwing off his balance. Diego saw his opening and made a sweeping kick that knocked Raphael to the ground.

Diego stood over him, chest heaving. "Stay down, Raphael."

But Raphael wasn't finished and sprang back to his feet in a single hop, a wild look in his eyes.

"No chance," he growled, barreling into Diego. They hit the floor, grappling in a feral knot of arms and legs. Whatever martial arts training they'd had was gone; it was now a wild scramble—until Raphael pinned him.

His breath burned hot against Diego's ear as he leaned in close, hissing words meant only for him. "I'm not like you. I matter. You're just a mistake of nature."

The room fell quiet. The others hadn't caught the words, but they felt the shift.

Leaning in had left Raphael off-balance. Diego bucked hard, twisting under his weight, and they rolled. He tore free, scrambling to his feet.

Raphael wiped sweat from his brow as they paced each other. His grin twisted into a sneer. "Come on, Diego. Tell us your secret!"

Diego leaped without even thinking, fists flying. But Raphael's taunts were just made to break Diego from his groove. Diego's charge left him open.

Raphael moved fast, driving a solid punch into the side of Diego's head. It felt like an iron beam slamming into him. He reeled, then crashed to the ground.

But Raphael didn't stop there. He leaped on Diego, kicking him again and again, his eyes blazing. Diego curled into a ball, trying to shield himself, but the kicks kept coming.

Luca darted in, grabbing Raphael's arm. "Enough, Rafe! Back off!"

Raphael shook free, eyes lit with fury as he wound up for another kick, spittle flying from his mouth. "He needs—he needs to—"

Everyone piled on, hauling the struggling Raphael away with all their strength.

"That's enough, man!" Kenji shouted. "You won—let it go already."

Luca helped Diego upright. "You okay?"

Diego wiped blood from his lip, eyes locked on Raphael. "I'm fine."

The air in the room stretched tight, silence underlining the significance of what had just happened.

Nico's soft voice came a moment later. "Loco."

After that, nobody said much. Diego and Raphael kept their distance. The others tried too hard to pretend everything was normal, tossing out scraps of small talk that fell flat.

Diego grew restless. They couldn't keep on like this. He stepped in front of Clara and cleared his throat, "Umm." He stopped, unsure how to even start. Everyone's eyes fell on him. "So, maybe we're bottling up too much. All of us, I mean—me too." He sighed. "We've got plenty to be mad about, but we never really talk about it. Not what we feel. Just what we want to do. Right? All our big plans. Maybe we should do that, though." He almost sat down, then added quickly. "Talk about how we feel, I mean, if that's okay."

Silence settled. Eyes darted around, nobody willing to go first. Raphael crossed his arms.

Kenji spoke quietly. "Yeah... you two aren't really mad at each other. You're mad 'cause you've been down here too long."

Diego and Raphael exchanged a glance but said nothing. Diego was willing to let them believe that, if it helped.

Kenji shifted. "I'm—uh. Right. Talking about how I feel. So... I'm afraid of becoming a growler."

Nico sighed, eyes fixed on the floor. He looked like he might actually say something. Kenji nudged him gently. "Just spit it out."

His voice came out barely above a whisper: "My folks... know I'm alive?"

Diego's chest tightened. He didn't have an answer. Kenji opened his mouth. Shut it. The silence stretched.

Arturo finally broke. "Okay, fine! We're stuck down here with no future. It's a prison, and it pisses me off!" He gestured wildly around the Pizzarama. "I'm sick of this place!"

"We could move to the Living Quarters," Luca said, though his tone lacked conviction. "Maybe it wouldn't be so bad if we each had our own cabin?"

"But the Living Quarters don't have Clara or Pounamu," Diego countered. "And we can't watch the lift for new arrivals."

Silence again. Longer this time.

Arturo groaned. "So what? We just become a monastery of celibate monks until we die of old age?"

Raphael leaned forward, eyes burning, emboldened by his victory. "Talking about our feelings won't get us home, Diego. We've talked about plans long enough. It's time for action. Confront Carlos. Take him out. We've got the device—we can threaten to unleash the growlers on the upper decks. Put me—" he caught himself. "I mean, put one of us in charge, and we can run things!"

Diego's stomach churned, and his tone hardened. "Using the growlers as weapons? Just let them loose on everyone? Do you even hear yourself? Your families? That's insane!"

Raphael snapped back. "Well your ideas aren't going anywhere. Besides, it's not like we'd actually do it. We'd just make them *think* we could."

Diego's voice rose. "Carlos won't believe that without proof. *Then* what, Rafe? You'll send growlers up anyway? Has *this* been your big plan the whole time? No." He rubbed his temples. "We need to be smart about this. There are other options. Maybe we contact the Star Rangers or the Wardens—"

Raphael cut him off. "They'd ignore us. Or worse, conscript us. We can take control of Serenity. Stop being such a coward."

"Why does it have to be all or nothing with you, Raphael? Surely there's a middle ground—something that doesn't get everyone killed."

Raphael crossed his arms. "What exactly do you suggest, Diego? Are you really working on a plan? Or should we just sit here praying for a miracle?"

"Of course not. I mean, I do have a plan. I'm getting control over the mainframes. I just need to figure out how to use it to our advantage."

"You've said that how many times now?" Raphael growled.

Kenji raised an eyebrow, leaning forward with interest. "Wait— do you have control of La Familia's mainframe?"

"Well, no... but I do have root access on Echo. I can control comms, surveillance, locks—things like that."

Kenji frowned. "And how does that help us?"

Diego swallowed back a growl. "I'm working on getting the same access on Delta next, as a test. Then the others. But it takes time. I just think if we can get full control of all Serenity's mainframes, it'll be what we need."

He scanned the group. Their faces were tired, expressions flat, eyes heavy with doubt. Too much had happened today, and they looked more skeptical than ever. He had to give them hope.

"I—" he started, and then the words tumbled out before he could stop himself, "Maybe I can make the maintenance lifts work."

The room went still.

Raphael's grin came slowly—a glint of triumph in his eyes. "Now we're talking. So we *can* send the growlers up top."

"No!" Diego barked. "I already said it: we're not using the growlers as weapons! We need to be smart about this."

Raphael leaned forward, eyebrow arched. "What should we do then, el capitàn? This isn't something we can out-think! We need action, not analysis. Or—" He paused, eyes narrowing. A silver edge crept into his voice. "Or maybe you like us being stuck down here. Maybe you enjoy ruling your little kingdom. How long have you had access to the lifts? Why didn't you tell us right away?"

Then he circled back to the jab from before, trying to goad him. "What other... *secrets*... are you keeping from us?"

Diego clenched his jaw, mind racing. How did Raphael do it so easily? He'd already played him once tonight, and here he was spun up again. Raphael twisted words without effort, flipping everything upside down, yanking his strings like a puppeteer.

It was maddening. The harder Diego pushed back, the more Raphael made it sound like he was the problem—like he was the villain, not the other way around.

His instincts screamed to deny it, to argue, to tell everyone he didn't want to keep them here. Insist he had no secrets—but he did.

And that was the trap. He couldn't speak from truth. Anything he said would be hollow. He'd sound like a petulant child whining, *nuh-uhh!*

Exactly as Raphael wanted.

So Diego swallowed his anger and forced himself to stay silent, refusing to give Rafe the satisfaction.

The quiet thickened until Luca finally spoke, his voice light as he tried to help. "Honestly? I'm fine staying here. We've got things working. I like my independence. We just need a little more… balance in the genders, you know? No offense to the current company, of course."

The room exhaled, and the boys seized on it—almost too quickly.

Arturo chuckled. "Luca, I like where your head's at. Balance! But… how? We've got no leverage."

Ideas started flying, tossed back and forth.

Diego took a moment to steady himself, pulling his frayed emotions back into place so he could think. He had to find a way to convince them there were better options than Raphael's reckless plan.

But the itch in the back of his mind wouldn't quit. What if… Raphael wasn't wrong?

Could I use my gift to leash the growlers, rein them in, and safely use them as a weapon?

No! Absolutely not. The mere thought curdled his stomach. He shoved it down, disgusted with himself. Why would he even let his brain go there?

He was so deep in thought, he didn't notice Raphael slip close until a venomous whisper came at his ear. "You can't think of anything else, can you? Just admit it—confronting Carlos is the only real solution. We can use you—your… well, you know. With your powers, you still have some value."

Diego snapped around. "Using the growlers is insane!"

Every eye turned in their direction.

"Maybe you're just afraid," Raphael said. "Afraid to take real action. Afraid to make the hard choices. Afraid to be a bold leader."

Diego's fingers flexed open and shut, but he held himself in check. "This isn't about fear. It's about not becoming the monsters we're fighting against. So let me make this clear—" His eyes locked on each of them in turn. "We're not sending growlers up top. I will figure something out."

Raphael turned away with a dismissive scoff. "Whatever. Run back to your lab, Diego. Hide behind your terminals and lab notes."

The room fell silent. Diego scanned the others' faces, searching for a flicker of support. But all he found were averted eyes—except for Luca. Luca met his gaze with a faint shrug, his furrowed brow an apologetic plea, as if to say, "I tried, but I can't risk it."

Diego's chest tightened. "I just need time," he said softly, his voice steady despite the knot in his throat. "Time to get control of their mainframe."

The quiet in the room deepened. Diego gathered his gear and walked to the front gate. He paused, glanced back, and locked eyes with Raphael. "Don't do anything stupid." He didn't wait for an answer.

Outside, he pressed his forehead against the cool wall, pulling in slow breaths to steady himself.

Muffled laughter drifted through the gate—Kenji cracking a joke. Already, the tension was fading, like his absence made it easier for them to move on.

A cold hurt coiled inside him, tightening his chest until his breaths came shallow. It felt like he'd lost more than just a fight with Raphael.

Diego exhaled hard and forced his shoulders straight. He turned toward the Link Transit Terminal. If they wouldn't trust him, he'd do it alone. He would find a way to save them all. But he had to move fast —before Raphael did something rash.

The Great Pretender

Raphael moved quickly, his mind churning through his plans. It was hard to get a time when Luca and Diego weren't in the lab. But Luca was on watch, and Diego was snoring with everyone else back in the Pizzarama, leaving him the whole night to set things up.

Soon enough, those two would realize they weren't the only ones capable of reading Usenet and making things.

He clambered out of zero gravity into the lab on Echo Ring, not bothering to close the door behind him. Scanning the shelves and bins, he quickly located what he needed—tubes, tanks, valves, and all the right pieces. He worked carefully, assembling each component and disguising the setup so those two wouldn't notice anything had changed.

Once finished, he checked his watch—he'd make it back just in time for the call. Sparing a last glance around the lab, he grinned, savoring the thought of the mayhem that would soon unfold.

Raphael pulled himself through the long float back to Delta as fast as he could. He searched for the right televid booth—one with a working terminal and a broken camera. A glance confirmed the promenade was empty, and he stepped inside.

Satisfied, he rechecked his watch, muttering, "David always had a soft spot. Always wanted to help. He'll do it."

Raphael knew it was a gamble, but it was worth the risk. Winning required multiple strategies, and he didn't plan on losing. But would Carlos answer the call? And what if they ignored his instructions and Luca's father was there?

The seconds ticked down to the appointed time. Raphael took a deep breath to suppress his jittery nerves, then punched in the connection code. The line buzzed, the small cathode-ray screen showing gray static before snapping into focus. Carlos's face appeared in black and white, occasionally distorted by scanlines. His gruff voice echoed through the receiver, demanding, "Are you there? I can't see you."

Raphael grinned—Carlose was alone. Adopting a higher-pitched tone he thought might resemble Luca's, Raphael replied with bravado, "Alcalde Carlos! It's Luca. Glad we could talk."

"So it's true." Carlos continued, his tone flat and insincere. "Luca, my boy, I can't tell you how glad I am to hear you've survived. Now, why's your video not working?"

"Camera's fried, amigo. Tech issues down here. Growlers have, uhh, eaten all sorts of things. Nothing works like it should."

Carlos grunted. "I thought you could repair anything. Why would a broken video camera stop you?"

Raphael's pulse quickened. "Uhh—right, Yeah. I've just been so busy building things, you know?" His mind raced to add depth to the lie. "Like yeah, did you know I made a new robot? Clara, we call her. She's the only thing to keep me and the boys company—"

Carlos's eyebrows furrowed, and he snapped, "The boys? How many of you have survived?"

Raphael grinned. "Not your concern. But we're doing just fine. In fact, I'm having fun rebuilding all Clara's friends at the Atomic Pizzarama down here."

Carlos waved his hand impatiently at the screen. "Get to it, Luca. Why the call? You know you can't come back up."

"Yeah, yeah, I kind of assumed you wouldn't honor that request, old man, but you know what? I figured out a way to control the growlers. That's how I've survived. But the boys are getting restless. We need something to keep them satisfied," Raphael studied Carlos's face, searching to see how he'd react.

The man was as unflappable as a wall. "Growlers? Sure you can." His voice dripped with skepticism. "And Kraal, too, right?"

"Carlos, listen up. I'll just lay it out clearly. This isn't a joke. Do you want me to send some up top to prove it? Me and the boys; we've hacked the systems. We can mess with elevators, security doors, you name it. So tell me, what would happen if growlers suddenly started roaming around inside your compound?"

A pause filled the air, and this time, a crack appeared in the man's facade. "You couldn't. You wouldn't do that. Your parents—"

Raphael's calculated laughter echoed through the connection. "Of course, I wouldn't do that. But those growlers are gonna start roaming. And me and the boys, we're not so sure it's worth keeping them in check, you know?"

Another pause hung between them, and Carlos's eyes thinned. "What do you want?"

Raphael could hardly believe it was actually working. "Carlos, we need some balance in our lives. We want to see some girls coming down to match the boys, keep us company, you know? Equal numbers, balance the scales, and we keep the growlers under control. And if not, well... it won't be pretty."

Carlos's tone flattened. "Girls? What's this nonsense, Luca? You know it was the will of God for you to be sent down there. Your survival alone shows His hand in your selection."

Raphael stifled a growl at Carlos's argument. His words sounded hollow and manipulative. Forcing himself to maintain composure, he pushed back, "It's not a request, Carlos. We're holding the line down here but need something in return. Do it, or the growlers will roam."

Carlos grumbled. "You're playing a dangerous game, Luca. You don't want to poke this bear."

"You worry about your growler problem, Carlos. We got our ways down here. Just do this before you send another chavo, and we'll be fine. Call it a truce."

Raphael slammed the receiver down before Carlos could ask anything else. His heart hammered with the thrill of his audacity. A grin spread across his face, blinding him to the danger he'd stirred up. He didn't care—he'd just done what Diego could not: finally gained the upper hand on Carlos.

Stand By Me

A month had passed since his fight with Raphael, and the rift between them had only widened. Diego mostly kept to the lab, with the occasional visit to the Pizzarama to make sure Raphael hadn't dragged them off the deep end. The silence was heavy when Raphael was around, less so when he wasn't. But that didn't stop Diego. Nothing about the Desterrados leadership had been settled, and he wasn't about to let Raphael just do whatever he wanted.

Aside from Raphael's drama, Diego had plenty to keep him busy. He'd hacked into Delta Ring's mainframe, using a vulnerability in a humidity controller. From there, he'd opened a backdoor, giving him remote access from Echo Ring.

Access to Delta wasn't his biggest win, though. Luca still dropped by the lab, and together they finished building a new antenna.

"Ready to go?" Diego asked, tugging at the butt of the snug spacesuit underclothes. It just wouldn't quit riding up, and he wondered if he should've picked a larger size.

Neither he nor Luca had wanted to do the spacewalk, but someone had to go out and set up the antenna. A game of rock-paper-scissors had decided it, and Diego lost.

He was terrified, though he'd never admit it to Luca. The memory of his first spacesuit training still clung to him. At least that had been in the safety of the Z-ball arena, not the unforgiving emptiness of open space.

Luca finished checking the antenna's connections, then nodded. "Everything's good. Let's do this."

Diego took a deep breath, heart pounding. He returned to the airlock and finished wrangling into the spacesuit. Luca had said he should just skip all the extra things—who needed the personal plumbing when it was just a short ten-minute walk? But Diego did it anyway —doing it right helped calm his nerves, even if only a little.

His hands trembled as he adjusted the gloves, then initiated the sequence to open the airlock. The suit expanded, tightening as the air disappeared around him.

The external door slid open, revealing the star-speckled abyss beyond. Diego swallowed hard. His pulse thundered in his ears. He tugged at his tether one more time. Slowly, he eased out of the hatch— then froze.

Arcadia loomed beneath him, stretching far, surrounded by deepened black that never ended.

His fingers clenched on the handhold. He couldn't move, couldn't look away. So far down. So open. His breath quickened. Shallow gasps. His throat squeezed tight. Every part of him screamed to retreat, to claw back into the safety of the station.

"Say something, chavo. All I can hear is you breathing," Luca's voice crackled over the radio.

Diego forced himself to take slow, steady breaths and managed a shaky reply. "Just trying to get my bearings."

"Hah! Told you it'd be scarier than training in the Z-ball arena. Come on, admit you're scared—it's fine. I'd be pissing myself out there. So I guess it is good you hooked up the plumbing, in case you spring a leak."

It wasn't very funny, but Luca's banter chipped at the ice in Diego's chest, and he forced himself to play along. "Yeah, yeah. But it might be best that I'm the one doing this—I didn't see any little-boy waste connectors for you, chavito."

Diego triple-checked that his tether was secure, then focused on his hand—still clamped on the handhold—and willed his fingers to loosen.

"Really?" Luca shot back. "So what you're saying is they were too big for you." Then, his friendly teasing stopped, and his voice softened. "But, seriously, you okay?"

"Yeah." Diego took in a deep breath, forcing himself to release the handhold. Slowly, he maneuvered the antenna into position. "Just about to deploy it now."

He located the interface port on the orbital's hull and used duct tape to fix the wires in place, letting the antenna drift free. As long as he focused on the work and didn't look past Serenity's hull, he had no problem.

"All done," he said, quickly pulling on his tether to draw himself back into the airlock.

"Testing the link…" Luca replied.

Diego pressed the button to seal the door. Gravity slowly came online, pulling him toward the deck, and the spacesuit relaxed. He removed his helmet. The door leading back into the lab slid open.

"It's online—" Luca started.

A shrill alarm cut him off as the system announced, "Hazardous atmospheric contaminant detected."

Luca's head snapped up. They glanced around wild-eyed, breaths shallow. Then a faint hiss whispered through the air, almost lost beneath the announcement.

Before they could take another step, a flash lit the room—then a deafening explosion. The shockwave hurled Diego into a workbench, twisting him painfully wrong. Everything spun. Diego floated, struggling to get his bearings. The gravity had cut out.

A high-pitched ringing filled his ears. Darkness edged his vision. And, a new sound—the howl of air ripping out through a hull breach.

"Luca!" Diego shouted, scanning across the room. There—he drifted, arms and legs limp.

The lights flashed red. Air was running out. Even if Echo lab wasn't sealed off from the rest of the Ring, the breach would have triggered the emergency bulkheads. Diego had to act—and fast.

Dodging debris tumbling toward the rupture, he grabbed a cable and hauled himself to his helmet. After snapping it in place, the suit began to puff and tighten—not from its oxygen feed, but from the lab's air bleeding out.

He wanted to check on Luca, but sealing the breach came first. Diego ripped a repair kit from the wall and kicked off toward the damage.

Escaping air howled through the clumped wreckage, twisting into snapping, vaporous cords. He had to clear it before applying the patch. One piece at a time, he wrestled the tools, charts, microscopes, and other debris free, until a fissure the length of his hand showed. But it wasn't clear yet; a large containment cylinder was pinned in place by the pressure.

Straining for leverage while weightless, Diego braced against a cabinet bolted to the deck and shoved until it gave way. More shards tumbled in. He batted them aside and used his back as a shield while he worked.

His suit kept tightening as the pressure dropped—the lab's oxygen was almost gone.

He popped the seal on the repair kit. It scissored open, and he yanked out a plate coated in expanding foam, slapping it over the fissure. The plate shifted, foam slipping through the cracks—outside the viewport, thin threads streamed into space. He pushed hard, holding it in place until it finally set.

The warning lights shifted from red to orange—air pressure stabilizing. Diego's suit relaxed as the lab began to repressurize.

Snagging an emergency oxygen mask and first-aid kit, he launched himself toward Luca, who still floated motionless across the room.

As he closed the distance, Diego tore off his helmet and shouted, "Luca!" His voice came out muted in the thin air.

Luca didn't stir. Blood pooled around a gash on his head, trailing away in a string of red beads.

Diego reached him at last and tugged the oxygen mask over his face. It hissed to life as he pressed it in place. Turning to the cut, Diego was relieved to see it wasn't deep, and he wrapped Luca's head in quick, clumsy bandages.

Luca's eyes fluttered open as Diego finished. His hand shot up, pushing at the mask, brow furrowing.

Diego held it in place. "Easy, Luca. Just breathe deeply."

Luca focused on Diego, recognition dawning. His breath condensed in the mask, and he mumbled. "What happened?"

"Explosion. Hull breach," Diego said, glancing around the lab, which was still cluttered with drifting debris. "I fixed it. Are you okay?"

Luca nodded weakly. "Yeah, I think so."

Pale and bandaged, he joined Diego as they drifted around, trying to figure out why gravity hadn't returned. The culprit ended up being a blown gravitic plate. They patched around it, and slowly, everything was pulled back down to the deck.

Only later, while cleaning up and checking for further damage, did they discover the new antenna was missing. Outside the viewport, the only trace left was a scrap of duct tape. The explosion had torn it away.

Months of work—gone.

*　　　*　　　*

Nobody showed more concern over their well-being after the "accident" than Raphael. But Diego didn't believe it for even a second. Hydrogen peroxide tanks didn't just move themselves across the lab. But he had no proof, and he worried if he said anything, it'd just sound like a weak attempt to counter Raphael's growing influence.

Diego went with them to that week's Solsticio, but kept to the sidelines. It felt hollow now—no longer a way to connect with each other in their isolation. Too many rituals and too much symbolism. All the algae, chanting, howling—it just set his nerves on edge.

Raphael orchestrated it like a pro—keeping the excitement going, basking in their devotion. Luca had even joined them. Diego's chest tightened as he watched all five of them bound around the biosphere, bodies glowing, masks bloodied, losing themselves in the ritual.

Breaking away from the others, Raphael strutted toward him. "Too bad you won't join us, Diego. A true *capitán* of the Desterrados would be out there, leading the Solsticios."

The challenge was clear. Raphael leaned close, eyes gleaming behind his mask, but his voice was soft. "These rituals make us strong. Unite us. If you're not part of that, what does it make you?"

Diego's eyes tightened. "Strength isn't found in masks, rituals, or any of this. You're losing your humanity."

Raphael smiled, circling him. "This is about power. Control. Something you just don't understand. Humanity is a luxury we can't afford. We're dealing with monsters out there, and every growler we kill keeps us alive another day."

"Have you ever thought that the growlers aren't just monsters?" Diego shot back. "That there's still a person inside—that maybe they could be healed?"

For a heartbeat, Raphael faltered. Then he laughed—a deep, mocking sound that echoed loudly. "You're loco, Diego—a weak, loco chavito. Leaders have to get their hands dirty. Just the way it is."

"And that's the heart of it," Diego hissed. "You don't mind getting your hands dirty. Frankly, I'm surprised you could even figure out how to make a bomb."

Raphael's eyes narrowed. "Prove it. Tell them. See who they believe. But it won't be you. They'll believe what I tell them to believe."

Diego turned and left the biosphere before he lost control. Using his gift, he masked himself and wandered the halls. His feet carried him to Red Sector, almost of their own accord, to where he'd sequestered Donna.

He pressed his forehead to the freezer's window, watching her. Her chest rose and fell, fingers twitching. Here she was, still locked away months later. His heart sat heavy, knowing he wasn't sure he could actually save her.

Diego closed his eyes, Raphael's words rattling around in his head. The rituals, the scheming, the violence—was it all just to seize control? Diego didn't even want to be in charge.

Only the Lonely

Raphael knew it was risky, but he had to find out if Diego and Luca had uncovered anything that could tie him to the bomb. On a day Diego was in Echo Ring, Raphael caught Luca coming back from the Skyway Lounge; a bag of laundry in one hand, a damp towel draped over his shoulder. Raphael gestured down the promenade. "Let's take a walk."

Luca glanced at the Pizzarama, his expression contemplative, before letting out a resigned sigh and falling into step beside Raphael. No words, just their footsteps echoed through the curving corridor as they meandered. Satisfied they were far enough away, Raphael steered them into the Bobby Soxers clothing store. Thanks to Arturo during one of his scavenging runs, the mannequins in the windows were posed suggestively.

"I know why you want to talk," Luca finally spoke. "And I don't want to hear it."

With a friendly smile, Raphael turned to face him. "Luca, my friend, there's no need for hostility. I just want to understand your true desires. To give you a chance to speak openly."

Luca lifted an eyebrow, "Really? Okay, then. Did you set the bomb in the lab?"

Raphael's pulse quickened, but he masked it with concern and just the right amount of indignation. "What? Of course not! I thought it was an accident. Or did you find out something else? Was it the Anointed?"

Luca paused, and Raphael knew he'd planted a new possibility into Luca's mind.

"Why would the Anointed even be down there?" Luca asked, confusion lining his face. "I thought they didn't know we were still alive?"

Carefully adding a touch of desperation to his voice, Raphael pressed on. "I don't know. Maybe they found out about us? I'm really worried about it, too. That's why we have to act quickly! We need to stop La Familia, or some day they could come after us!"

He continued, his warm tone masking the strategic edge in his words, "Diego's plan is admirable—reaching out to the Star Rangers for help. But let's be honest, Luca, do we really want strangers poking their noses into our business? We've got a good thing going here, don't we?"

The look on Luca's face said he wasn't convinced, but he did concede. "I mean, yeah, things are going good—but your grand plan to unseat Carlos has some real problems. Even if you take him out, what about the other Anointed? They won't just roll over and let a bunch of teenage guys be in charge."

Excitement lit Raphael's eyes. Just getting Luca to talk was the first step; whether he agreed or not didn't matter—he was on the hook now. Raphael didn't even miss a beat.

"That's where you underestimate my vision. Carlos is only a figurehead. Remove him, and doors open. Leadership isn't about authority; it's about vision. And I have one, Luca. A future without La Familia, where everyone can be safe on Serenity Orbital."

Luca lifted an eyebrow. "Think a little much of yourself?"

Raphael's laughter echoed through the empty store as he casually leaned against a dusty clothing rack. "Maybe! But don't you trust me? Have I ever steered the guys wrong?"

"Uh. Right." Luca didn't sound convinced, but then asked. "Seriously though... how would that even happen?"

"That's where your plan comes in. Staying down here, maintaining our way of life, setting our own rules—imagine if we could have both. I lead up there; you guys take care of things down here—with a more agreeable mix of the girls, of course," he added with a grin. "Together, we keep the balance. A harmonious coexistence, chavo."

Luca shook his head. "I don't know why I'm even talking to you, and I'm still not sure it wasn't you who set the bomb."

Raphael sighed, wrapped an arm around Luca's shoulder, and looked him straight in the eyes. "It hurts that you even suspect me. You know I trust you with my life. Don't you trust me? Of course, I wouldn't do anything to hurt any of the Desterrados."

Luca held the gaze, and Raphael could see him considering the words, weighing each. Then Luca pushed Raphael's arm away and growled, "Right—because you're everyone's best friend down here."

But Raphael had seen, even if for a moment, that glint of interest in Luca's eyes, and he knew he had planted the seeds. He could be patient.

"That's the beauty of collaboration, chavo," Raphael said. "Together, we're stronger. Just don't forget the possibilities—you stay down here with your special girl, doing what you want, no one to bother you." He gave Luca's shoulders a friendly squeeze. "But you're right, now isn't the time. Let's head back before anyone thinks the growlers ate us."

Somebody Nobody Wants

Diego sat on the threadbare couch of the Pizzarama, teasing out a few chords from his battered guitar.

Luca groaned, waving a hand at Kenji's feet propped on the table. "Seriously, do you ever wash those things?"

Kenji grinned, staring at the toe poking through a hole. "My feet are naturally aromatic. You just have a delicate nose."

Luca lifted an eyebrow, mouth opening for a response, when arcade sounds wailed to life.

"The Anointed!" Arturo shouted from his lookout post. He leaped down and scrambled away in a panic. "They just threw—"

An explosion swallowed the rest. The barricade blew apart, spraying the room with splinters of arcade panels, tables, and chairs. Soldiers in tactical gear stepped through the smoke, kicking aside the wreckage, rayguns raised, scanning the room.

Everyone scrambled, ears ringing as they dove for cover. Raygun beams lit the air in bright flashes. The guys kept their cool, crawling to their gear and snatching up weapons.

Diego grabbed his Top Slugger bat and turned toward the rear exit, bellowing, "Plan 3!"

Raphael's voice countermanded. "Not this time! Hold your ground, Desterrados!"

The gunfire shifted, from bright flares to concentrated bolts that blasted through their sanctuary, smashing arcade games, decorations, and personal belongings.

Furious they were doing this again, Diego snapped, "The plan is to retreat!"

Raphael hissed. "Do you want them to destroy everything we have?" His words sparked a flurry of stubborn looks. "We've spent years fighting growlers, while those guys just hid. This won't be like last time, we've drilled group tactics. They have no idea how fierce we can be!"

Diego saw the fire burning in everyone's eyes. Maybe Raphael was right. Any one of them alone had more combat experience than their attackers combined.

The plasma tracing Raphael's blades lit his face—the latest addition to his weapons. "What do you do when fighting guns with swords? You bring the fight to them. Dodging a few raygun bolts is nothing compared to a growler's punch. Who's with me?"

Anger smouldered in their eyes. Even Diego felt it. This was their home.

A collective nod rippled through the group. Luca shot Diego a reluctant look, then shrugged. Diego answered with a nod. "Fine, let's do it."

Raphael howled like a wolf, and the others joined in, voices echoing across the chamber: *We're not afraid of you. We're coming.*

They moved with a grace that defied the gunfire, darting from cover to cover, closing the distance fast. Nico took a hit to the shoulder and dropped with a cry. Diego tossed him a stimpack as he passed, hoping he'd be okay.

Then the boys were on them, blazing swords and spiked clubs swinging. The soldiers staggered back, forced into close-quarters combat, using their guns like clubs.

Diego slammed his bat into a soldier's unarmored shin. It landed with a sickening crunch. The man howled and collapsed.

The clash of blades and battle cries filled the air as the boys fought for their home. Their independence. Their right to survive.

Surprised by the ferocity, the invaders' confidence crumbled. With two men down, they dragged their wounded in a hasty retreat.

"Don't let them get away!" Raphael shouted. "We can use 'em as hostages!"

The guys gave chase, hooting and howling as they cut off and encircled the retreating soldiers in the middle of the plaza. A smile formed on Raphael's face as he gave his burning swords a casual spin.

"Back off, or we shoot!" A soldier barked, raising his rifle and standing protectively over their wounded.

Raphael chuckled, pacing with dramatic flair. He opened his mouth to reply—then it happened.

A cry echoed from deep within the station. Low. Feral—a chilling warning rolling through the corridors.

The growlers were coming.

Raphael's casual demeanor disappeared as he snapped into a combat-ready stance. He shot a sharp, pointed look at Diego—a question Diego understood instantly.

Still charged from the standoff, he stretched his senses toward the approaching horde. His pulse spiked. There were too many. The fight must have reverberated through the halls, calling to them like blood in water.

Diego clawed through his options, desperate for something—anything—that might work. Then it came back. That disgusting thought. Both horrifying... and thrilling. The struggle tore through him in a blink, though it felt endless.

Could I steer them? Just at the soldiers. They attacked us first...

The idea twisted in his gut. Wrong. Of course, it was wrong. Fighting the growlers was one thing. But turning them on people? Using them as weapons?

His fury countered. They'd exiled us down here, and *now* they send soldiers to finish the job? The notion of how powerful the growlers might be as a force teased at him. Why shouldn't he—?

No! He couldn't. Wouldn't.

Diego glared at the soldiers, then shook his head hard before he changed his mind. "Too many," he hissed, angry he'd even considered the idea.

Raphael held his gaze for a beat, then quickly motioned for everyone to fall back. The Anointed dragged their wounded into the lift just as the growlers loped into view.

The Desterrados retreated into the Pizzarama, Nico joining them to hastily shove tables and chairs into a makeshift barricade.

"Hold tight!" Raphael barked as the barrier shuddered under the assault.

Diego strained with the others to keep it in place, but his mind lurched back to that dark thought.

How is it wrong? Because I'm forcing them against their will? Do they even have free agency in their state? What if I steer them just a little... just a small nudge? If it keeps us alive, isn't that worth it? And if they go after the soldiers... that's their choice. Right?

The rationalizations slipped around inside him, oily, convincing, sickening. The growlers were so close, so many, their presence bore down on him. He wanted to push them away with his gift—but not now. Not in the shadow of these thoughts.

What am I turning into?

His pulse hammered. Control of his power frayed. Even though he stood shoulder to shoulder with the others, the shouting and chaos seemed far away.

Was this darkness always inside me? Why would I even think about turning growlers on people? Is it because Rafe suggested it, or am I really the villain everyone thinks I am?

Self-loathing surged, raw and furious, dragging up his deepest fear: *Maybe I really did summon the Kraal all those years ago.*

His heart thudded. Cold. Hollow.

The past hammered him—that day, that moment. The screams.

And a bitter thought surged, hot as a live wire: *I am a monster.*

His gift thrashed in answer. He was slipping. Losing control. Again.

"Stay back!" he gasped, not even meaning to say it.

A warning. To the growlers? His friends? Himself?

He clenched his eyes tight, breath shuddering. The storm inside him raged, fueled by the growlers' nauseating presence. And somewhere deep down, a small, weary part of him wanted to let go. Just let it happen.

But then, the pounding on the barricade began to ease. Slowly—mercifully—one by one, the growlers shambled away. Their stink faded from his thoughts, and Diego pieced himself back together, horrified at himself.

In the hush that followed, the boy's shoulders dropped. Once again, the Pizzarama was wrecked. No one spoke. They drifted apart, quietly picking through the mess.

Raygun burns blackened the walls. The stink of melted plastic hung thick in the air. Their stuff was everywhere, scattered among the wreckage of toppled arcade machines, splintered tables, and broken chairs.

Clara had taken a direct hit. Half the synthetic fur on her face was melted, exposing the bare mechanics beneath. One eye hung dark; the other flickered weakly. Sparks crackled from her depths. She slouched on her throne, one paw raised in a frozen mockery of a wave.

Diego moved through the room. The damage was a hard reminder of how exposed they really were. Doubts tightened around him, coiling into a singular thought: *Maybe Rafe's right. Maybe fighting is the only way.*

He stopped at a cabinet that had taken a direct hit, its contents strewn across the floor. Raphael's things.

Something caught his eye. He knelt, pulling a photo from beneath scorched clothes and twisted metal. The two of them, with "Mi Compa" scrawled in Raphael's messy handwriting.

He stared at it, his chest tightening.

Of course, he'd noticed when the photo disappeared—shortly after Julian arrived. And now, here it was, hidden in Raphael's things.

Diego drew in a bitter, jagged breath. He'd wanted to believe they were friends—even if only for a while. Wanted to believe the photo had vanished for some other reason. He clenched the photo, the edges biting into his palm.

Framed

A week had passed since the attack, and they were all still on edge. Diego hadn't even bothered visiting Echo Ring. No one could explain how La Familia knew they were alive, and that unanswered question left everyone on edge, waiting for the next invasion.

One evening, as the day wound down, the rumble of the maintenance lift broke the stillness. From his post on watch, Luca hollered, "Someone's coming!"

They scrambled into action, ready to get the jump on the Anointed. In moments, they had grabbed weapons, geared up, and darted for cover in the debris-strewn plaza in front of the Pizzarama. They fanned out, masks in place, glancing down the corridor into the open lift.

But there was no squad of soldiers—only a boy curled on the floor, tied up and stripped of the usual jumpsuit. He looked far too young to be sent down. Lying on his side, he twisted, straining to see past the shadows.

The Desterrados exchanged glances, wariness giving way to confusion.

Raphael stepped forward. "It's just a kid," he muttered, sword loose in his hand but ready all the same. The others followed, wondering if this was a trap.

"Small," Nico said quietly.

The kid's eyes widened as they closed in. He thrashed against the ropes, wriggling deeper into the corner of the lift. Diego crouched at his side and sliced the bindings. He flinched but stayed silent, sitting up and curling forward, hugging his knees, trembling.

Diego took his mask off, asking softly, "What's your name?"

The boy looked up, his blond hair falling across his round face. "Sammy. And you're all the—all the boys sent down? Still alive!"

One by one, masks came off, the others relaxing as it became clear this wasn't a trap.

"Hey little guy, how old are you?" Arturo asked.

Sammy scrambled to his feet and lifted his chin, defiance flickering in his blue eyes. "I just turned twelve, and I'm not little."

"You're younger than anyone else sent down here," Luca said, studying him. "All bound up and stripped like that—it doesn't make sense."

Sammy hugged his bare chest against the cold. "I wasn't exiled. Carlos sent me down without telling anyone. He even took my jumpsuit. Told David to mess it up like a growler got me." His lower lip quivered, "Said I was too much trouble to keep around."

The boys fell silent. Carlos's cruelty seemed to know no bounds. Remembering the fear and abandonment he felt when he was exiled, Diego put a reassuring hand on Sammy's shoulder. "You're safe with us now. We'll take care of you. Come on, let's get you some warm clothes."

They led Sammy to the Pizzarama, eyes wide as he took in their sanctuary—still being repaired, but one hundred percent theirs.

Everyone pitched in to get Sammy settled: finding clothes that would fit, showing him around, and making him feel welcome. When the flurry of activity calmed, Sammy sat on a sofa in the Den studying Clara.

Raphael had waited long enough. "Okay, kid, out with it. You said you were too much trouble. So, what did you do?"

Sammy shrugged, trying to look brave, but his face fell.

Diego offered him a rare Atomic Cake. "Why were you tied up?"

Sammy eyed the treat, then tore into it, speaking between bites. "I heard Carlos talking to David about you guys. He said nobody could know you were down here. Then he saw me listening and got real mad. I tried to run, but they caught me, took all my stuff, and dumped me in the lift." He licked the crumbs from his fingers, then looked up, grin flashing. "So... los Desterrados. You guys are loco!"

Diego froze—Carlos shouldn't know that name. A murmur ran through the group. Diego shared a glance with the others, then turned back to Sammy. "Los Desterrados? Did Carlos say that? Tell me everything."

Sammy leaned forward, excitement showing as he rushed his words. "Oh yeah. Carlos said he was talking to somebody in the Desterrados who told him everything about you guys. I couldn't hear it all, but he seemed mad that some attack didn't work."

"Who?" Raphael's voice cut through the buzz that had kicked up at the revelation. His gaze briefly flickered to Luca. "Who was he in contact with? Did he give a name?"

The room fell silent. Sammy looked around and shifted, looking pleased to be the one with the answer. "Luca?"

Shock rippled through them, every eye turning to Luca. He went pale, trembled, then blurted, "No! I would never! You know I wouldn't!"

A cold knot twisted in Diego's chest.

"Luca," Raphael said, his voice steady, almost commanding, "tell us the truth."

Luca's eyes flared wide. "I am telling the truth! I've never spoken to Carlos. Why would I?"

Raphael's stare hardened. "How do we know you're not lying? Just tell us why you contacted Carlos."

Sammy leaned forward and piped up. "Oh, yeah—Carlos also said Luca wanted him to send girls down. That had him hoppin' mad for sure."

The words were electrifying. Where some had wavered, their looks now turned dark.

Luca's voice cracked; he raised his hands and stumbled back. "I didn't do it!"

"You sure look nervous for an innocent man," Raphael grumbled.

Finally reading the room, Sammy shrank into the sofa, eyes darting between the older boys. They shouted over one another, voices clashing, each trying to force his view. Through it all, Raphael's voice carried above the rest—calm, confident, feeding the flames of mistrust and aiming them at Luca.

Diego took a deep breath. Nobody was listening. His chest churned with confusion. Sammy had no reason to lie, but it made no sense. He raised his voice. "Quiet! I think we need to stay calm and get to the bottom of this without losing our heads. Maybe Luca didn't actually do it?"

Raphael crossed his arms. "Then how do you explain what Sammy heard?"

Diego glanced between Sammy and Luca. Sammy looked earnest, wide-eyed. Luca looked desperate, nervous. Diego swallowed. "A misunderstanding. Maybe Carlos wanted to frame you, Luca. We can't jump to conclusions without proof."

Luca nodded, his shoulders easing.

Raphael shot back. "There is no other way, Diego. Carlos would only know we are called the Desterrados if somebody here told him. And the only one of us who wants to have Carlos send down girls so he can stay here is Luca. Everybody knows that's his plan. That's clear proof."

Diego struggled to make sense of the storm swirling around him. Luca was his closest friend—he didn't want to believe it. But what Sammy said was pretty spot-on for Luca.

"We have rules!" Raphael shouted, eyes blazing. "If Luca betrayed us, he has to be punished!"

Luca's face paled. "You have to believe me. You know I wouldn't do that!"

Diego shook his head, torn apart inside. He wanted to believe Luca. Somehow, Raphael must have done something, but what? He had nothing to go on. Looking around at the other boys and their growing anger, he realized that if he didn't do something, the group would do it anyway.

Luca's voice came weakly now, barely heard. "It had to be... Raphael did something. I don't know what. But it has to be."

Raphael didn't even flinch. He let out a sharp laugh, shaking his head. "Classic. The liar always points at someone else when the walls close in. Just look at him. Shouldn't he be more confident of his innocence, if he really was?"

Diego's thoughts snagged on an old memory—Raphael hunched at a terminal in the dark. For a heartbeat, he thought he saw it clearly: this was all Raphael.

But Raphael was right... Luca's pale face, his frantic denials—it struck a chord. For a moment, he saw himself standing in the plaza years ago, facing a mob that had already decided his fate. He'd sworn he was innocent, too. And yet... a cold weight pressed against his chest. He just wasn't so sure anymore. And... maybe Luca was in the same position?

This sliver of doubt seeped into his thoughts. The parallel was hard to ignore. And his own memories of what had happened during the attack so long ago were all a blur.

I don't want to believe it, but... Luca's always talking about balance.

"He said you asked for girls," Diego's voice came as barely a whisper, stretched with frustration, disbelief, and reluctance. "That's what you've wanted this whole time, isn't it? So we can be comfortable down here, away from Carlos?"

The look of betrayal in Luca's eyes cut deeply. Diego's stomach turned. No—he wanted to believe Luca. Raphael's handprints were all over this.

The group erupted into shouts and arguments. They began to chant, their voices merging into a single, relentless demand. "Punish him! Punish him!"

Diego's chest tightened as he struggled to focus, his emotions spinning through anger, hurt, and frustration. He wanted to howl, to make everyone shut up so they could find the truth. All he knew was that the friend he had trusted now stood accused, and he wasn't sure of his innocence. This left him torn between the rising fury of his friends and the desperate, pleading look in Luca's eyes.

Raphael seized the moment, raising his voice above the din, wielding Diego's words as a knife. "We have rules, isn't that what keeps us civil? Here we stand, with Clara as our witness. Judgment must be made." He put his hand on Diego's shoulder, his voice low. "Remind me, what's the punishment for deadly betrayal of the brotherhood's trust?"

Diego's mind raced to catch up. Why was Raphael already talking about punishment? No judgement had even been made!

Luca fell to his knees, his voice breaking. "Please, Diego! I didn't do it!"

Diego wanted to side with Luca, but the weight of the group's anger was too much. "I... I don't know what to believe."

Raphael stepped forward, his voice cold and commanding. "Diego, you're the leader here, are you not? You need to make a decision. Do we follow the rules and punish him? Or do the rules change depending on how you feel?"

The room fell silent, all eyes on Diego. He felt a crushing weight pressing down on him. If he didn't punish Luca, it would undermine everything he had built—he'd tear the group apart and hand it all over to Raphael, and they'd become feral monsters no worse than the growlers they hunted. But if he did, what would that mean for Luca? He needed to support Luca.

"I think we shouldn't act too quickly; we should take time, think about it, and not act in the heat of the moment—" Diego started again.

Raphael pressed, "We have rules, and there are no exceptions if you break them."

A chorus of nods.

"The most severe punishment we have is exile to Red Sector," Raphael continued. "I think this is warranted, considering some of us could have died in that attack. How long will it be, Diego? A month? A week? Forever?"

He didn't want to send Luca away at all. He needed time. Time to figure this out, but the anger in everybody's eyes made it clear that he had to act now or—or—who knows what. He was afraid of what would happen then, and his confidence that Luca was telling the truth wasn't absolute.

Diego met Luca's gaze, the desperate plea in his friend's eyes cutting deeply.

"One day," Just saying the words hurt. "Luca will spend one day alone in Red Sector."

Luca slumped, staring at the ground.

"One night? Not much of an exile," argued Raphael.

Diego snapped his head toward Raphael, glaring. The faint purple flecks in his left eye flared.

Raphael took an instinctive step back but quickly recovered, his smirk twisting. "Well, he can't take his gear then."

"He can," declared Diego.

Raphael flung his hand out, his voice rising. "Look at what the Anointed did here! What if somebody had died?"

Arturo growled, "Yeah, send him away in nothing but his skivvies!"

Diego shook his head. "One day. And he can take his gear."

Raphael hesitated, considering Luca with a calculating glint in his eye. "Fine. One day. But he leaves the growler device here."

Luca's eyes widened, tears welling at the edges as his breath quickened. "Diego, don't—" His words faltered, voice trembling with disbelief and hurt.

Diego's chest tightened, his heart pounding painfully. He wanted to take it all back, to say something that would make this easier, but he couldn't back down. Not now. Not in front of Raphael. "Luca, leave the device. You can take your gear."

A smile crept across Raphael's lips, his satisfaction practically radiating.

Luca's gaze locked on Diego for a long, heavy moment. The betrayal in his eyes was unmistakable.

"I—" Diego started, desperately searching for the right words—but nothing came. The silence stretched, more painful than any argument.

Luca turned away, his movements stiff and robotic as he gathered his gear. He layered up against the cold of Red Sector, his jaw set hard. He didn't look at Diego—not once.

Quietly, he walked along the promenade, the lights dimming into evening mode. The others followed at a distance, reflecting a mix of worry, anger, and, for Raphael, a hint of smug amusement.

Diego quickened his pace, catching up to Luca. "Wait," he said, reaching out to grab Luca's arm.

Luca yanked it free and spun around to face him. His eyes were distant and hollow, with an edge of ice. But he said nothing.

Diego's hand lingered in the air before dropping to his side. He swallowed hard, then spoke softly. "Stay hidden. Stay safe."

Luca shot him a cold, piercing look, his voice raw and broken. "Yeah, whatever."

He turned and climbed through the bulkhead leading to Red Sector. Raphael stepped forward, sliding the metal panel into place and bolting it shut, sealing Luca inside.

The others drifted back in silence, the mood somber. Diego trailed behind, his thoughts racing. He remembered the dark place Luca had gone to when he'd first arrived. What if he went back to that now? What if he just gave up?

Diego's mind churned with plans to slip away and follow Luca, to keep watch over him from the shadows and make sure he stayed safe. But Raphael hovered close, almost as if he knew what Diego was thinking.

The night stretched on, awkward, quiet. Nobody wanted to talk, and the tension in the air was almost suffocating. One by one, they all drifted off. Kenji helped Sammy set up a makeshift bed on the couch, reassuring him they'd figure out a proper spot in the Lair after Luca returned.

Diego barely heard Raphael muttering under his breath. "Who knows, maybe we'll have a spare bed tomorrow."

Diego wasn't about to let that happen. Once everyone had fallen asleep, he shimmered into invisibility and slipped out of the Pizzarama. He searched Red Sector high and low until he came across Luca sprinting away from two growlers. Diego maintained his invisibility while he focused his mind and nudged the growlers in a different direction.

Luca stumbled to a stop, gasping for breath, his hand pressed against a bleeding gash on his arm. He took a moment to wrap it with a strip of cloth, one-handed, before pushing onward. Diego followed close behind, his senses extended, straining to hold everything at bay.

Eventually, Luca reached an upper hallway with a row of round windows offering a view out to space. He slid down the wall, his eyes fixed on the stars beyond. Diego took a position farther down the corridor, masked and invisible, keeping watch while focusing his energy on holding the void terrors at bay. The effort of doing this for the entire night stretched his limits—but he had no choice.

You've Got To Be Carefully Taught

Every clang of metal, hiss of steam, and rattling groan from the aging Serenity Orbital scraped at Diego's senses. Holding his invisibility for hours had stretched him thin. He closed his eyes, fighting the dull ache in his head as he struggled to stay awake.

Luca had stirred once in the morning, then slumped back against the wall, staring vacantly at the stars. Diego's chest burned with the need to explain. He wanted to step out of the shadows, to tell Luca he was sorry for not believing him. But he stayed hidden. Right or wrong, the punishment stood. Changing it now would erode all the work he'd done to keep everybody civil, and hand control of the Desterrados to Raphael.

Diego's past left him terrified of being seen as a freak. He dreaded letting Luca learn the dark truth about his gift. Could Luca set aside his prejudice? He was Diego's closest ally. His friend. Or was that bond now severed? A leaden weight wallowed in his gut.

Luca shifted, a shiver coming over him in the lonely hallway. The orbital's lights dimmed—another day ending. Luca had to notice. Had to realize he could return.

Diego checked his watch, the minutes ticking by with maddening slowness. After an hour, it was clear Luca didn't plan on going back. Diego crept around a corner, dropped his invisibility, and stepped into view. "Come on. You can come back now."

Luca turned his head. His gaze met Diego's, expression hardening. The betrayal in his eyes pierced him to the core. He didn't move. Didn't say anything. With each unspoken heartbeat, the knife twisted deeper. At last, he stood and brushed past Diego.

"Luca, wait," Diego called. "I'm sorry. I had to do it. The others —they wouldn't have understood if I didn't do it."

But Luca didn't even slow. Diego watched him go, afraid something had shifted between them—something that might never heal.

He hurried to catch up, trailing a few steps behind as they approached the portal to Red Sector. The others were waiting, each face clouded with disapproval.

"I just went in to get him," Diego offered, the excuse sounding weak even to his own ears.

"You okay, Luca?" Nico asked quietly, fingers worrying the frayed edge of his AstroTec hoodie.

"I'm fine," Luca answered flatly. "Hardly saw anything the whole day."

Raphael caught Diego's eye, muttering just loud enough for him to hear. "How lucky for you."

Luca pushed past the others, heading down the promenade. Only then did Diego notice Sammy wasn't among them.

Raphael's scowl vanished, and he turned to catch up with Luca, his voice suddenly warm. "Hey, chavo!" He held out a worn leather bomber jacket, "All's forgiven. Welcome back to the Desterrados. Take this as a symbol of our acceptance. You're a new man now."

Luca hesitated, studying the jacket. After a moment, he took it, his expression unreadable. They returned in silence, no one willing to break the tension of unspoken questions.

When they stepped into the Pizzarama, Diego's gaze snapped to the couch. Sammy sat huddled there, knees drawn tight to his chest. His hair was shaved in jagged patches, raw red lines, and scabs marking where the razor had cut too close.

Diego went straight to him, jaw clenched. Forcing his voice steady, he asked, "Hey, you okay?"

Sammy's eyes were puffy and red. He nodded, sniffled, and wiped his nose on his sleeve.

"What happened?" Diego pressed.

Raphael cut in. "Just ran him through the challenge course. He'll be fine."

Arturo laughed. "He almost pissed himself. Then, when he realized it was just Rafe in a costume, he kicked him in the family jewels. Didn't know our chavo could hit such high notes."

"He failed," Raphael growled, his face darkening.

"I thought we weren't doing any more challenges," Diego shot back. "And, he's just a kid!"

Sensing the brewing conflict, the others decided they had better places to be and slipped away one at a time.

"It's part of being a Desterrado; get over it," Raphael declared. "Everybody else did it, so why not the newbie? No one else had a problem with it."

"I think Sammy did. So why shave his head?"

Raphael crossed his arms. "He shouldn't have kicked me. I had to teach him some respect. It's part of the initiation now."

"Respect?" Diego's voice rose, trembling with suppressed fire. "This was about humiliating him. About showing your dominance."

Raphael's eyes narrowed. "He needs to toughen up, fast. We can't have a little kid causing problems. It's a harsh world down here, Diego. He has to learn that."

Diego took a deep breath, trying to rein in his anger. "No, Raphael. We don't need to be cruel to survive. We can be better than this."

Raphael's lip curled. "Better? You're a naive idiot, Diego. You always have been."

His tone carried the same edge he'd used when they were in school, snapping Diego straight back to feeling small, weak, cornered. His response came thin. "—I'm not naive."

Raphael stepped forward, eyes blazing. "You're weak. And your weakness will get us all killed."

The words snagged his thoughts and tumbled his emotions. He wasn't that little boy anymore—yet somehow Raphael could send him right back there. Diego growled, his voice breaking. "I'm not weak! I'm trying to save us. You want to turn us into monsters."

Raphael leaned in close, his breath hot. "Then perhaps you should've left Luca to stand his punishment alone. A real leader would have. Otherwise, what kind of exile is it? And sneaking out on your own? Breaking the rules isn't much of a leader's example."

Diego's face flushed. A part of him knew Raphael was baiting him, goading him to lose his cool. But the fire boiled over. "So you take it out on Sammy?" he hissed. "That's leadership to you? And you're one to talk—I've seen you sneaking off on your own solo excursions."

Raphael's eyes narrowed, and he stepped closer, their faces inches apart. "You know that thing you want kept a secret? Your little edge that none of us have. How you're such a freak?" His voice dropped lower, darker. "Keep that in mind before you say anything else. Whatever you think you know about me, you can't prove it. And thanks to your absence today, no one trusts you. So much for rules. You should've heard what the boys had to say about you."

Diego clenched his teeth, fear and fury colliding. Old memories surged, bringing with them the scorn, the isolation, the loneliness he'd once felt. For a time, the Desterrados had replaced that with a connection he'd never known before. But that was gone. Raphael's corrosive influence had changed everything, leaving him feeling like an outsider again.

Raphael sneered. "So tell me, how did it feel being the big leader, making the tough calls? You should've seen your face when you walked in and saw Sammy. Priceless."

Diego's thoughts blurred, everything narrowing into a haze of helplessness over failing to protect Sammy. His emotions stormed, breaking loose. Raphael had pushed his buttons until he tipped over the edge. His gift responded in kind—unraveling, slipping, surging.

Diego gripped the table for balance, eyes clamped shut, clinging fiercely to the fragile control he had left. The nausea and pain nearly doubled him over, but he was getting better at reining in his gift before it tore completely free.

"Yeah. What I figured. A coward," Raphael whispered.

The words sliced through him. He wanted to fight back, but the risk was too great. The fear he'd call to the Kraal if he lost control hung over him. He held his tongue, standing still, breath ragged, until Raphael's footsteps faded.

Minutes ticked by as he fought to restrain his gift. At last, his emotions calmed, and with them his gift. He opened his eyes—and there was Sammy, on the couch, eyes wide, silently watching him.

"Mierda," Diego groaned, collapsing into a chair. He tore off his mask and cradled his head in his hands, long hair falling around his face. His temples pulsed with each heartbeat. The lights were too sharp, every sound too bright.

He exhaled slowly, trying to center himself. The fight with Raphael had left him drained. He hated how easily Rafe could pull his strings.

The scrape of a chair made him lift his head. Sammy had pulled close.

"I won't tell," Sammy whispered.

"Tell what?" Diego asked quietly.

"What he said. Is it really true? Can you talk to growlers?"

Diego huffed. "What gave you that idea?"

Sammy leaned closer, his voice barely audible. "I figured it out. Earlier today, Arturo asked why you looked like a growler. Then Kenji wondered if it meant you could talk to them. Rafe told them to shut up —said they were wrong. But then just now, he said—"

Diego raised a hand to stop him, studying the boy a moment. Sammy fidgeted with a pendant at his neck. Diego sighed. "You sure do hear a lot—and notice things the others don't."

Sammy beamed. "I have a good memory, too."

Diego managed a faint smile. "And you're humble. But be careful with that, okay? You've got a way of hearing things you shouldn't, and isn't that what landed you here in the first place? Hearing the wrong things can be dangerous. Maybe give it a rest?"

Sammy's brow furrowed as he considered the advice.

"Hey, what's that you've got?" Diego asked, nodding at the pendant.

Sammy clenched it tightly. He hesitated, then slowly opened his hand to reveal a small circular disk. "It's Saint Michael. I was born on Michaelmas. My mom gave it to me for protection."

It showed an angel lifting a sword high, the surface bright from constant handling. "Your mom's smart. You should always keep it with you."

Sammy tucked it back into his shirt. "I never take it off."

Diego reached out to ruffle his hair, but found only uneven blond tufts. His gesture faltered into a gentle pat. "I think you're pretty tough. You going to be okay?"

Sammy brushed a hand over the stubble on his head. "Diego," he asked in a small voice, "why did they do this?"

For a moment, Diego couldn't find the right words. "Sometimes people do things like that because they're scared. But that doesn't make it right. I'm sorry, Sammy. You didn't deserve this. I'll do what I can to keep you safe, okay?"

Sammy looked up at him, his eyes shining. "Thank you for being nice."

Diego managed a small, strained smile. "That's what friends do."

"Friends," Sammy echoed, then suddenly lunged forward, wrapping his arms around Diego in a quick, fierce hug. Diego froze, caught off guard. Personal contact was never easy for him, and for a moment, he sat rigid. Then he felt a tremor running through Sammy's grip, like he might fall apart if he let go. Diego's chest tightened, and he had to wrap an arm around him, holding on until the shaking eased.

At last, Sammy let go, drawing an unsteady breath as he settled back into his seat. He sat there for a moment, studying Diego with red-rimmed eyes. Then, softly, he asked, "What about you? Are you okay?"

The simple question hit hard. The pure concern in Sammy's voice slipped past Diego's defenses, warming his chest. He was like Donna—no ulterior motives. No manipulation. No games. Just... trust.

Diego blinked, throat tight, before answering, "Yeah, I will be. Just need to rest a bit."

At least Donna was safe... safe because he'd kept her apart. Distance was necessary. Letting people in only got you hurt. And then it clicked: Raphael had gone after Luca and Sammy because they were close to him.

Diego sat in silence, his hunger for friendship colliding with the truth. Being near him was dangerous. What he wanted didn't matter. Keeping them safe did. His defenses might protect him, but they didn't protect his friends. He had to stop letting Raphael bait him. Stop letting fear drive him. He had to prove the truth about Raphael, clear Luca's name, and protect the others—even if it meant pushing them away.

The clarity hardened inside him. He straightened. "Look, it's best if you stay away from me. I'm not safe to be around. Got it?"

Sammy's face fell, confusion flashing in his eyes. "Aren't we friends?"

Diego's chest tightened, but his resolve held. He couldn't let Sammy get too close. That only made him a target, just like Luca.

"Just... you don't know what I am," Diego said, his voice rough. "Stay away from me."

He stood and walked off, leaving Sammy staring after him, his face a map of bewildered hurt.

Stay Beside Me

Diego had seen Luca recover from his first crash into depression. He knew the eager, upbeat side of his friend. But now Luca drifted through each day as a shadow. The others kept him at arm's length, still nursing resentment over what they believed he'd done.

Time heals all wounds, or so the saying goes. Weeks passed, and the tension gradually eased. Luca was treated more like one of them again. The haunted look in his eyes faded, but it was clear he'd changed. His former optimism was now locked away, replaced by a calculating focus on survival.

He never shirked his responsibilities, and always did what was needed without complaint. On hunts, he often took the lead, giving short but confident commands the others didn't question.

In contrast, Sammy was bright, restless, and always trying to prove himself. Despite being a foot shorter than the others, he insisted he could do anything they could. He sparred with the older boys, determined to master martial arts as fast as possible. His punches and kicks gained strength with each session, and his drive soon earned their respect.

They didn't give Sammy a sword, despite his incessant begging —no one was ready to arm this wild kid with a sharp blade. Instead, Raphael fashioned him a club from a pipe, welding nubs on the end and balancing it for Sammy's size and strength.

His enthusiasm was a bright spot most days. He was even allowed to join the hunts, starting with void rats before moving on to growlers.

One day, while wandering through the Pizzarama, Diego noticed a new mask hanging on the curtain. Fiery red and orange flames shaping an angry face, with its features defined by colored dots that echoed the Calavera decorations on his own mask. It suited Sammy perfectly.

He still tried to reach out to Luca when the opportunity presented itself, but the rift that began with his exile had widened into a chasm, and Diego didn't know how to cross it. Somehow Raphael had managed it, though, and the two spent long stretches talking, sparring, connecting.

The shifting dynamics left Diego with a pained sense of relief. He was glad to see Luca reintegrating and Sammy gaining respect— they both deserved it. But the Desterrados weren't the same anymore. The bonds he'd once felt had thinned, and he found himself spending more time away from the others.

Diego's corner of Echo Ring's lab slowly transformed as his personal things migrated from the Pizzarama. It wasn't intentional; he just preferred quiet solitude over Raphael's surly looks and the noisy companionship of the others. Nobody visited anymore. The lab became his new home. Not because he was retreating, he told himself, but because he was rebuilding.

Being on his own wasn't a problem. Diego had stood alone before, and he could do it again. But this time felt different. He wasn't spiraling. He had direction. He had purpose. And he had Donna, even if she couldn't respond. With no other demands on his time, he spent hours outside the freezer door—talking to her, sorting through his thoughts, sharing his fears, his dreams, his hopes for a future where he would heal her... and they could be together.

He started over with Project Ultra's research, in case he'd missed something. The rest of his time went into cracking La Familia's mainframe in Bravo Ring.

At some point, he'd drawn a line in the sand: break in before he turned seventeen. Because if he couldn't do it by then, he probably never would.

And that was only a week away.

Diego shifted, the chair squeaking beneath him. Now, it was time. Years of combing through code and system manuals had finally paid off—he'd discovered a tiny flaw buried in the operating system. A buffer overflow. One of those beautiful accidents left behind by the original designers' sloppy coding.

All it took was a block of data just a little bigger than the system expected, carrying something extra at the end. A Trojan horse, disguised as an ordinary message sent over the network.

The mainframe would load everything he sent—even past its limits, pulling the extra data with it. That overflowed onto the execution stack, and the system ran it next. Terrifying in its simplicity, and a flaw he was more than willing to exploit.

He'd tested the hack countless times on EMS04 in the lab, perfecting the technique. It should work... unless Delta's system had a patch EMS04 didn't. But no. It had to work.

With a deep breath, he pressed Enter. Anticlimactic—a single keystroke, then waiting as the data shot across the network from Echo up to Bravo Ring.

If it worked, he'd get a remote shell with access to Bravo Ring's mainframe.

The green cursor blinked, steady and mocking. Each second came longer than the last, and his doubts mounted. *What if the hack is detected? What if they realize I've broken in?*

Then, finally, a line of text scrolled by:

```
root@bmain001#
```

Diego exhaled, fingers flying across the keys. This was it. He had no idea how long it would take for someone to notice the crashed process—if they noticed at all—but he had to move fast before it was fixed.

First, he added his user credentials, then granted himself admin privileges. He reconnected, this time through the front door, using his newly established account.

Adrenaline surged, warmth spreading through his chest—he'd done it. Access. And before his birthday.

But he wasn't done. He still had to cover his tracks. He deployed the rootkit he'd spent weeks perfecting. It patched key parts of the operating system, masking his presence—much like how his gift masked him from sight. The thought made him smile—he preferred to stay out of sight. Unseen. A friendly goblin hiding in their system.

He double-checked the logs, scrubbing any trace of his presence while verifying no alarms had tripped. Then he scanned everything again, foot tapping against the floor.

No trace. No alarms.

Root access on Bravo Ring was his, and La Familia was none the wiser.

"El Duende Fantasma," he whispered, a smile playing on his lips. Everyone on ALT.HACKERS had code names. Why shouldn't he?

The nickname they'd mocked him with as a kid still struck a bitter chord. He drew a long breath. So what if they'd called him that? Goblins had their uses.

And like a good goblin, he'd do his part. He patched the very flaw he'd just exploited—it wouldn't do to leave the door wide open. He was the gatekeeper now, protecting what he'd claimed.

When finished, he stretched, veins still sizzling with adrenaline. Should he tell the guys about this? He didn't have much to tell them yet—just that he'd gotten in. It felt huge, but until he knew how to leverage this access, maybe it wasn't worth celebrating.

Still unsure, he geared up and started the cold float back through the tubes. The debate stormed within him the whole way: what to tell them, how to tell them, when to tell them.

By the time he stepped onto Delta Ring, the adrenaline from the successful hack had faded. He nearly turned back—but he was still part of this group; he needed to put in appearances from time to time.

Taking a deep breath, he steeled himself and forged forward. He reached the Pizzarama as the others were wrapping up their day. Kenji's friendly call carried from the watch tower, and Diego gave him a salute in return.

Inside, he found all the others locked in a mock battle. Sammy clambered atop a stack of boxes in the middle of the arena, laughing, swinging a paper sword with giddy abandon to defend his territory. Diego watched them roughhouse, a growing ache building in his chest. He figured if he tried to join in, the energy would shift, and the fun would fade.

Rafe caught his arrival, his gaze lingering for a beat before moving on. The rest were too busy with their fun to notice.

Diego turned away, locating his guitar. He hadn't taken it down to the lab. Leaving it behind almost felt like he was still here, even if he wasn't as much. It was an anchor with the guys.

He took a seat on the couch, absently strumming, letting his thoughts drift. What it might have been like if he'd been born in a different time. A time when he could just be content to sing and create his own music. Could he have become a famous musician with his own records? The idea was tantalizing.

But only a dream.

His thoughts snapped back to what he should tell the others. He'd hoped getting root access on La Familia's mainframe might dispel the gloom that hounded him around his birthdays. But it hadn't. The day hadn't even come yet, and already it darkened his thoughts.

Loneliness gripped him, same as every year. His gift only seemed to wall him off further. The familiar darkness spiraled through his thoughts. No—he struggled against it. He needed a distraction. A conversation. Anything to keep from turning inward. But who? Things were still rough with Luca, and Sammy… he didn't want to load the kid down with his troubles.

His expression hardened. Maybe coming here was a mistake.

Seeing the others winding down, Diego set the guitar aside, gathered his gear, and slipped out before anyone noticed. Kenji had dozed off at his post, which made it easy, and Diego didn't even bother shimmering invisible. If no one had noticed him arriving, why would they notice him leave? Nobody would follow.

His steps echoed softly through the dim corridors, the orbital's cold walls returning the hollow tap of his worn Chuck Taylors. He had no destination—only the need for distance. Distance from their laughter, from the warmth that made the darkness inside him feel colder by comparison.

Eventually, he found himself in front of Donna's freezer door. He hesitated, glancing through the small window. Donna stood there, her back to him.

He took a deep breath and activated his masking—not fully invisible, but enough to avoid startling her. He opened the door and quietly slipped inside.

Donna stood there. She looked so small now. Apparently, growlers didn't age. He still gave her a gift on each birthday. Her lips moved as she repeated her familiar words. "Help me… help me…"

"I wish I knew how," Diego whispered. Even if she didn't recognize him, simply being near her eased the building storm inside him.

He stood there for a long moment, just watching. Remembering.

Her bubbly, smiling face. The way she'd stick up for him.

The green scarf he'd given her was still wrapped around her neck. But—had it been tied recently? That didn't make sense. She couldn't have—

He reached out, stopped himself, and clenched his fist. Closing his eyes, he focused everything he had into his gift. He pushed against the dark, sticky fog in her mind, straining, desperate to break past it to who she really was—hoping for any moment of recognition. He needed her to respond.

He needed her.

Donna stilled. Her murmuring stopped.

Diego released his masking, letting her see him fully.

A flicker in her eyes—even if only for a heartbeat.

She didn't move. He stepped closer, heart racing. One step. Another. Their eyes locked.

Her clouded, empty gaze seemed to clear.

"Diego?" she moaned. A tear slipped down her cheek.

His heart lurched. He reached out, fingers trembling, and gently brushed the warm tear away.

"Help me," she whispered—barely more than a breath.

"I'm trying. I—" His hand shook as he cupped her cheek.

She recoiled. Her eyes flared—not with rage, but with fear.

"Run!" she screamed, "Run away!"

Diego flinched. "No—Donna, it's okay—"

"RUN!" Her voice cut through the air, raw and ragged, echoing off the metal walls.

She lurched around the room, her movements wild and erratic. Stumbling into a shelf, she let out a strangled cry and pounded her fists against the wall.

He took a step forward.

She spun unnaturally fast, shrieking. "Go!"

Her hand spasmed. She gripped the shelf and tore a support post from it like it was paper, raising it to strike. Then she froze, turning to stare at her hands in an obvious struggle against herself. Her jaw clenched as she hissed. "No! No!" Her fingers slowly uncurled, and the post clattered to the ground.

"Go, go," she moaned. "Go!"

Her eyes rolled back as she hammered the wall again and again.

Diego backed out. "I'm coming back. I'm gonna help. I swear!"

He lurched through the door and slammed it shut. Leaning against the cold metal, he slid to the floor, breath coming in ragged gasps. Frustration and sorrow caved in on him.

And then, amidst the chaos of his thoughts, a single truth made everything come to a stop.

"She remembered me?" he whispered, and then a smile broke across his face. "She said my name!"

Diego pushed himself away from the door, his mind already racing with plans as he made his way back.

There has to be a way to save her!

He was so caught up in his bubbling thoughts that he failed to notice Luca quietly ducking behind a counter.

Banks of the Ohio

Raphael noticed Luca slip out of the Pizzarama and realized Diego had disappeared, too. He grabbed Arturo, and they trailed Luca, following him into Red Sector. Like Luca, they hid and waited, crouched farther down the promenade. Diego finally emerged from the restaurant, a ridiculous grin plastered on his face. They ducked out of sight as he passed—and again when Luca crept out from his hiding spot.

Arturo started to follow, but Raphael held out his arm. "Hold it, chavo," he hissed, gaze locked on the restaurant. "What's in there? Is that where Diego's been sneaking off to all the time?"

Arturo shrugged. "How would I know?"

Raphael's expression darkened. He watched the corridor until Luca was completely out of sight. Then he moved into the restaurant. The back room was a wreck, filled with broken shelves, scattered containers, and ragged, empty boxes. But many footsteps had cleared a narrow trail through the dust, leading straight to the walk-in freezer.

Raphael pressed his face to the grimy window and froze. His hand drifted to the hilt of his sword.

"No way," he muttered. "It can't be."

Arturo shifted behind him, trying to get a look. "What? What is it?"

She stood inside, swaying, bloodied hands limp at her side. A green scarf hung loose around her neck.

Raphael's lip curled into a hungry grin, and he reached for the door handle. "Donna"

Arturo glanced through the glass. His hand shot out, grabbing Raphael's arm. "That chica? Rafe—she's a growler."

Raphael turned his head slowly, his gaze locked on Arturo's hand holding his arm.

Arturo let go, snatching it back as if stung. "Sorry, man. I wasn't thinking. I—wait a minute? Maybe Diego's working on something, you know? He said he has a plan—"

"A plan?" Raphael's eyes flared. "Diego doesn't have a plan. He's a freak. A ticking time bomb. Don't be stupid."

Arturo scowled. "I'm just saying—"

"No. You're doubting." Raphael stepped in close. His voice dropped. "You believe in me? That's what you said, right?"

Arturo hesitated. His gaze flicked between Raphael and the window.

"You're with me all the way, yeah?"

Arturo tugged at his dreadlocks, looking away. "Yeah. Right. Sure."

Raphael's stare didn't soften. "Then pick up your damn hammer."

A few heartbeats passed. Arturo gave a stiff nod and lifted his sledgehammer.

Satisfied, Raphael turned back to the door, the smile returning. He slowly pulled it open.

"Donna," he spoke softly.

She moved—barely. A tilt of her head. A flicker in her posture.

Arturo lingered at the threshold. Raphael stepped forward, drawing both swords, muttering, "What is Diego doing with you?"

At the sound of the name, she twitched.

He said it again. Louder. "Diego."

Her head snapped toward him. They locked eyes.

She drew in a sharp breath. Her lips moved, struggling to form words. Her whole body trembled. A guttural rasp escaped her throat—rolling *arrs*. Finally, she managed to gasp, "Rah—"

The realization struck—she was trying to say his name.

"You're a growler," he spat, voice rising. "You're not Donna. You're a monster. You're supposed to attack me!"

A low moan slipped from her lips, and she lurched forward, stopped, then scrambled away, clawing at the walls, howling and hissing: "Run. Run. Run."

"What's wrong with you?" Raphael stalked after her, plasma blades hissing to life. "You have a thing for—for Diego, the freak!?"

She spun, bar in hand—the same one she'd ripped from the shelf. "Leave him alone!" she howled, dashing forward and swinging fast.

Raphael flinched at her lucid reply, barely ducking the blow. He slashed as she passed, catching her thigh with a sizzling cut.

Arturo didn't move. Didn't speak. He stood still in the doorway, eyes wide.

Donna was blisteringly fast. She even landed a few blows. But Raphael's blades were faster, sharpened by plasma. One sliced through the metal bar. Another cut deep across her ribs.

She collapsed, blood pooling around her.

"Yeah," Raphael sneered, breathing hard. "That's what you get for picking him over me."

Her lips moved in a whisper only he could hear.

"Shut up!" he spat, slashing his swords. Then again. And again, even after her body went still.

Arturo stepped back, leaving Raphael alone in the freezer.

Finally, Raphael stopped, lifting his swords and releasing a ragged scream. He stood over her for a long time, chest heaving. Then, slowly, he bent down and tore the bloodied scarf from her neck, muttering, "I've seen this."

He tucked it into his belt, turning to Arturo. His eyes were wild with triumph, and his lip curled into a dark smile.

"Diego's gonna lose it over this one," he said, almost giddy.

Arturo's face was pale.

Raphael pushed past him, grumbling. "You with me or not?"

Arturo swallowed hard. He cast one last look into the freezer and followed.

Donna

Diego woke with a start, hands gripping him from all sides, yanking him from his bed.

"Hold him down!" Raphael commanded.

Raphael, Arturo, Kenji, and Nico wrestled Diego to the floor, the weight of their bodies forcing the air from his lungs. Diego thrashed. "What are you doing?"

But they didn't answer and quickly bound his wrists to his feet before hauling him to the Den. His bare feet barely touched the floor as they stumbled along until they unceremoniously dropped him in front of Clara, face down. He couldn't see anyone until Raphael grabbed his shirt and turned him over.

Raphael's eyes were hard as steel, but a wry smile of triumph touched the corner of his lips. "Diego, Diego, Diego," he started slowly. "Just when we thought there could be nothing more heinous."

"What?" Diego snarled. His mind raced, trying to grasp what they were so upset about.

"And all this time, I defended you," Raphael continued, his voice filled with thickly laid regret. "Standing by your side, insisting you were not a growler. But no, I just can't keep doing it. I can't keep hiding from what you really are. I'm horrified to realize what we've been harboring all this time."

Everyone's faces were painted with anger and disgust. Luca's gaze struck like a knife; his lips pinched as if he looked at something he didn't even recognize. Behind them all, Sammy furrowed his brow.

"What are you talking about?" Diego growled, testing the ropes that bound him.

"We found your girlfriend," Raphael's lip curled. "Disgusting, frankly."

A stab of fear lanced through Diego. "What did you do?"

Raphael held up a blood-crusted green scarf—Donna's. "What we do with all growlers. Put her down."

Diego's world collapsed. His blood turned to ice. "You killed her?"

Raphael smiled. "If it means anything, I made sure to do it quickly."

Raw fury surged within Diego, his entire body trembling. He strained against his bindings, the tendons in his arms and neck standing out like taut cables. "You monster!"

A look of grim satisfaction lit Raphael's face. "We're not the monster here, Diego. She was a threat—" he paused, glancing at each of the others to reinforce his point before adding. "Just. Like. You."

Diego's vision blurred, filling with tears. He couldn't form a coherent thought as he thrashed violently in rage and sorrow, bellowing incoherently.

Luca raised a hand. "Diego, calm down."

But Diego didn't want to calm down. His eyes blazed with fire as he scanned the faces of those he had once trusted, and he howled. "You all let this happen!"

Raphael's lip curled in disgust. "Don't tell me you're actually upset, Diego. Or... is it true, then?"

"He's in love with a growler," Kenji muttered, his tone filled with disgust.

"Messed up," Arturo added, shaking his head in disbelief.

Nico's brow furrowed, but he said nothing.

Raphael seized the moment. "I hate to say this, but... Diego really is a growler. He's been hiding it from us the entire time."

The guys all recoiled, their faces twisting in a mix of shock and disgust.

"I'm not a growler!" Diego protested, desperately fighting to reign in his emotions.

Raphael continued. "He also has special powers. He can talk with the growlers. Can convince them to do what he wants."

"That's a lie!" Diego shouted, his mind reeling. Raphael wove truths with lies, but Diego didn't have the chance to explain the nuances. He could see that doubt and fear had already taken root in their eyes, just like those years before when Carlos had sent him down here.

Raphael's eyes lifted in mock confusion. "So you don't have powers?"

Diego hesitated, looking around at the faces of his friends, and felt the last shred of his hope slipping away. The room seemed to close in, the walls pressing tighter, the air growing colder.

"I... I do," he admitted, his voice barely a whisper. The words hung in the air, heavy and incriminating.

"But it's not what you think. It doesn't make me a growler!" He added, desperation in his voice.

A few heads shook, and Diego knew his fate was sealed.

Sammy piped up, a thread of fear in his voice. "Are you... are you really a growler?"

Diego's heart broke seeing Sammy's terrified face. He struggled to find the words. "Sammy, no... I'm not. I swear!"

"Then why did you keep Donna locked away in a room?" Raphael asked. "For what? Your pleasure? Disgusting."

"Pervert," Kenji spat.

Diego's shoulders sagged. The guys he had protected, fought beside, and trusted implicitly now looked at him as if he were a monster. His vision blurred with tears.

"I'm not your enemy," Diego whispered, his voice raw. "I was only trying to help. Donna... she was suffering. I thought maybe I could find a way to cure her, to bring her back. I got through to her! She said my name!"

But Raphael was relentless. "Sure she did. Enough of your lies, Diego. You've already admitted to having growler powers. What else have you been hiding from us? What else have you been doing behind our backs?"

The room filled with murmurs as Raphael's words took root. He had spent months whispering about Diego's strange behavior, his fascination with the growlers, layering one thing on top of another until this. Raphael's seeds of doubt had been planted long before, and now they blossomed as each of the guys made up their minds.

"What—what now?" Luca asked, his eyes storming with anger, but not just anger. A flicker of something else.

Raphael's words were icy cold. "What do we do with growlers?"

Sammy launched into Raphael, his fists swinging wildly, "You said he'd only be punished!"

Raphael grappled with Sammy, pinning the boy to the ground. He laughed. "Looks like you have at least one person who has come to your defense."

Luca spoke quietly. "We will not kill him."

Raphael let out a huff. "Fine, here's how it'll go. We'll put it to a vote, okay? Everybody who thinks Diego should be forgiven and remain our leader, raise a hand."

Sammy's hand shot up, even as he lay pinned by Raphael. Diego scanned the others, searching their faces, but nobody would meet his gaze, not even Luca.

"Well, that's settled," Raphael said, finally releasing Sammy, who rolled away. "But the crime. It's so heinous. This isn't anything we've faced before. You've been a danger to us this entire time, right in our midst. Maybe it was you who let the growlers in to kill Julian. What have you really been doing? Why won't you let us use the lift? Have you kept us down here on purpose? Could we have gone back long before now? Are you just scheming to keep us here in misery?"

Raphael's eyes gleamed with a fierce, predatory light as he stepped forward. "We can't just let this slide," he said, addressing the group. "Diego's betrayal is unforgivable."

Escalating arguments filled the room as everyone suggested different punishments, most centered around some form of exile.

Raphael's voice broke through the debate. "Enough talk about exile! There's only one way to settle this. A duel. Combat to the death. Diego and I, one on one."

"You'll wipe the mat with him," Arturo said. "Is that really such a fair thing?"

"What if he uses his powers against you?" Kenji asked.

"Not a duel." Luca said, his expression hard for a moment before wavering. He looked at Diego. "What do you think we should do?"

Diego shook his head, brows furrowed. His voice came as a thin whisper. "This is insane. Think about it. It's me—I'm not a growler!"

Raphael's twisted smile only deepened, a dark shadow crossing his lips. "Fine. Exile it is. But he doesn't get to keep anything. No passkeys, no weapons. Nothing."

Arturo scowled. "Yeah, send him in nothing but his underwear."

A cold look came into Raphael's eyes. "And he goes to the Green Sector."

The room went silent.

"No." Luca broke the quiet. "Exile to the Green Sector is just a death sentence."

"But what else can we do?" Kenji asked. "Is he in league with La Familia? Is he a growler? All I know is he lied to us. How can we even feel safe around him anymore?"

"There has to be consequences," Arturo growled.

"Diego's powers make him dangerous," Raphael said, his voice smooth and persuasive. "We can't afford to take chances. The Green Sector is the only way to ensure our safety."

They debated more options, their words coming as murmurs to Diego's ears. Raphael's charisma and manipulative logic slowly turned the tide in his favor. Diego's chest clenched—he had no chance against Rafe's silver tongue.

A faint tug came at Diego's wrists, and he twisted to see Sammy slicing his bindings.

"I don't think you're a bad guy," Sammy whispered before slipping away.

Diego didn't hesitate and rolled under a table, then shimmered into invisibility.

Gasps and shouts erupted around him.

"Find him!" Raphael bellowed. "Before he gets too far!"

Diego ducked through their confusion as they knocked over chairs and tables. He sprinted to the Lair for his gear, then moved with care as the others fanned out in a frantic search of the Pizzarama.

"He's here somewhere!" Kenji yelled.

"What if he summons a horde of growlers?" Arturo called out.

Their uncoordinated scramble worked in his favor, and Diego slipped unseen through the front gate. He stopped in the hollow of an abandoned storefront on the promenade, his mind whirling.

Donna was gone.

The thought struck him again and again. He doubled over, struggling to stifle a low moan. He couldn't stop seeing her bloodied scarf in Raphael's hands; its image was etched into his mind. A hollow ache spread in his chest, blooming into a sharp, cold, leaden weight that pressed mercilessly against him.

Donna was gone.

His chest heaved. The air felt too thin. The shouts of the Desterrados spilling out of the Pizzarama faded into the background, drowned out by the thunder of his own pulse. It felt like gravity had been shut off, leaving him drifting. He crumpled forward, palms against the cold floor, his breaths coming in shallow, ragged gasps as he fought to stay silent. Tears pooled on the deck in front of him. And the thought wouldn't stop echoing in his mind.

Donna was gone.

"She asked me to save her," Diego whispered, the words slicing through him, biting, bitter, and brutal.

Donna—who said his eyes were cute. Donna—who had accepted him, scars and all. Donna—who had been his anchor, the reason he kept going, day after day.

The knot in his chest twisted tighter, the weight of her loss pressing in—suffocating and terrifyingly heavy. All he wanted was to curl up and let the grief burn through every part of him until nothing was left.

His mind painted a thousand images of her final moments—scenes he didn't want to consider but couldn't stop.

Did she know she was about to die? Did she hope I would come to save her?

He clenched his fists, nails biting into his palms, trying to force the thoughts away.

Rafe lied—he always lied. He was just lying. He didn't kill her. But... the scarf. He had her scarf. There was no way he could have it without—without—

Diego couldn't stop the next sob. His nails dug deeper, cutting into his skin.

Raphael's voice boomed across the plaza, ripping through Diego's spiraling thoughts. "Don't you ever come back, Diego! You hear me? You're done. No longer a Desterrado!"

Diego's jaw tightened. He wiped at the tears blurring his vision. If he gave into the grief, he'd be a wreck. Worse—he might lose control of his gift. It hadn't fought him yet, but it could at any moment. He couldn't fall apart. Not here. Not now.

There would be time later to grieve. Time to break down when he was alone. He could face the loss then. Let it tear him apart and leave him hollow later. But not now.

And then he'd write her a letter. Or maybe a song—just for her. Something to keep her memory alive, to sing to himself when the nights were long and the loneliness unbearable.

A flicker of resolve cut through the grief, small but enough to push it back, even if only a little.

Diego shook his head, forcing his thoughts to clear. Maybe he was exiled from his community for the second time in his life, but this time, it would be on his terms.

Devil or Angel

At first, Echo Ring's isolation felt like a reprieve—a place where Diego's grief could burn through him unchecked. But grief only carried him so far. Eventually, he had to move. Had to think. Had to figure out what came next.

Fortifying the lab gave him something to do: tripwires in the tubes, a camera, alarms, a bodgered lock on the Link tube door. It wasn't much of a defense, but it kept his mind from circling back to the sting of rejection.

Then Sammy started sending messages.

It was the last thing Diego wanted. He begged the kid to stop— again and again—but Sammy persisted, his updates trickling in week after week. Each painted a more disturbing picture of the Desterrados' rituals and hunts, their behavior becoming increasingly feral.

Sammy's descriptions were stark, vivid, and chilling, reading like historical accounts of ancient civilizations and their blood sacrifices. Some of the guys had even started daily rituals of painting their faces to match their nagual.

Worse, Sammy included snippets of overheard conversations. Diego's name circled among the group. They blamed him for the most ridiculous things. Each new account cut him, reopening wounds he didn't have the time—or strength—to cope with.

Diego tried to focus on plans for leveraging La Familia's mainframe, but couldn't get his heart into it.

It was strange. He'd never noticed it before, but the silence felt rather loud.

On impulse, he collected the haunting photograph of the scientists and placed it next to his terminal. The familiar woman in the group stared back at him, her slight, knowing smile frozen in time. He wished the photograph was in better condition. Desperate to find out who she was, he'd ransacked the lab, searching for any scrap of information about her, but found nothing.

Despite that, he couldn't shake the feeling that she must be a relative—perhaps a grandmother? It wasn't much, but it was enough. Her presence became a tether against the waves of loneliness that crept in when he least expected them. But even she couldn't keep his darker thoughts at bay. So he hacked.

It was petty. Diego knew it, even as his fingers moved over the terminal's keyboard, shutting off lights and scrambling cameras in La Familia's compound on Bravo Ring. He told himself it was a strategy— that if he stirred the pot enough, a useful idea might come to the surface.

But deep down, Diego knew better. It wasn't about strategy. It was about the chaos—how it stirred at the hollowness growing inside him. It was the only thing that cut through the fog creeping into his mind, the only thing that made him feel.

Then the realization struck, cold and sharp: this could backfire and reveal his presence. They'd know they were hacked and would start looking for him. With a frustrated sigh, he shut down his programs and flicked off the terminal.

Of course, it couldn't be that easy. But none of his other ideas were any better.

Threatening to shut down Bravo Ring's environmental systems was out of the question. He wouldn't risk harming innocent people, not to mention the fail-safes and safety interlocks would make a bluff like that laughably transparent.

Even locking people in their rooms wouldn't accomplish much; someone would have to let them out eventually. Without the other guys to help, his grand plan to use the mainframe to unseat Carlos was left dead in space.

Diego leaned back in his chair, staring at the darkened terminal. He had to figure something out. If he waited too long, Raphael would act, and it would end in bloodshed. That fear alone kept him moving, pushing back against the lonely darkness.

As much as he hated it, he had no choice; he had to understand his gift.

Project Ultra. He'd combed through the documents too many times, searching for a clue, and always came up empty. The notes detailed experiments in remote viewing, telekinesis, energy manipulation—strange, fascinating things, but nothing about touching the void. Nothing about a power rooted beyond the universe. That all came after their work had stopped.

The more he searched, the more alone he felt—an anomaly among anomalies.

So he turned inward, experimenting with his gift, cautiously testing its limits against the void terrors that haunted Echo Ring. Pushing them away had become second nature—but that wasn't enough. What else could he do?

He explored carefully, always ready to clamp down on his gift at the first sign of danger. The Kraal never stopped lingering at the edges of his senses. Void rats were everywhere, but he preferred the sugar gliders—their presence on his mind was far less disturbing. Proof, maybe, that not every void terror was out to eat you.

Growlers were there, too, though far fewer than the hordes on Delta Ring. And, of course, the walkers. At times, they slipped from his senses, and that only made them more unnerving. He figured it had to do with them going dormant, but wasn't about to go find out.

In the end, it always came back to the same question: could he do more than push them away? Could he pull them closer instead? Control them? He'd turned this thought over too many times now. Unsettling or not, he had to know.

His father's warning about taking away someone's free agency lingered in the back of his mind. It haunted him, especially after what he'd done to the void rat on that first hunt with Raphael.

But if that was wrong, was there any way to do this without crossing a line? Did his intent matter? Could he make them obey without becoming the monster he feared his gift was making him into? His options were running out, and he was tired of the question gnawing at him.

One night, he dared himself to try—with a call.

Heart pounding, Diego pressed his forehead against the cold viewscreen overlooking the jungle-choked promenade. He drew a deep breath and exhaled, fogging the glass. It was time. Slowly, carefully, he pushed his gift outward, unfurling it into the darkness, sifting until he felt them: void-tainted sugar gliders flitting through the twisted branches.

He gave a gentle pull, a nudge, whispering, "Come here."

And they did.

Diego felt the ripple as they came closer, their glowing, violet eyes bobbing in the dim light beyond the window. His breath came faster. He fought the urge to pull back, to break the connection, to hide.

He waited until they were almost there—until he could all but hear the rustle of their leaps and bounds through the leaves, even beyond the glass—and only then did he relent, mentally pushing them away with a frantic shove.

It worked.

He repeated the experiment—first on void rats, then growlers. Each responded, and each call left him with a growing sense of wrongness—that he was working against the very edges of the universe.

The tree walkers were the worst. They moved reluctantly, as if weighing his command, deciding whether to heed his call. Were they Deathmarks? If so, did that mean there was more than one kind of Deathmark?

What mattered was that he could summon them. He could call the void terrors, and they would come. But what good would that do him? They were dangerous, things you needed to hide from.

And then there was the Kraal. Its presence never left him—an oppressive weight that seemed to fill Echo Ring. He knew it was there, waiting, watching. But he'd feared it for too long. Reckless or not, his need to understand his gift pushed him forward.

Slowly, cautiously, Diego extended his senses, brushing against it with the faintest of touches. The Kraal's power thrummed against his mind, immense and dormant—like a nuclear bomb waiting for ignition.

He pressed a little further, enough to feel resistance. And then it came—that cold, alien question so infinitesimally small yet vast as it flooded his mind with incomprehensible sounds, smells, and colors. He doubled over, retching, the connection severed.

Diego shimmered into invisibility, his instincts screaming for him to hide. He stumbled back, gasping and collapsing into a chair. Sweat trickled down his back, and his fingers fumbled as he ripped off his mask, rubbing at his eyes.

He sat there, trembling, and knew. He wasn't just different; he was somehow tied to the void. He'd always known it, no matter how much he tried to deny it. He was something... almost like the void terrors—a part of that darkness.

So, was he actually a void terror?

He thought of Donna—her clouded gaze looking back at him, wondering if she had felt similar thoughts.

You Don't Know Me

Each breath echoed harsh and loud inside Diego's helmet. It had to be one of the worst parts of wearing a spacesuit, he decided. That—and accidentally passing gas.

He'd finally worked up the courage to take the long spacewalk back to Charlie Ring. Back home. More than an hour crawling along Serenity's hull, alone, with no one monitoring his comms. No one to rescue him if something went wrong. If he lost his grip and drifted away... or ran out of air... friendly thoughts like these had plagued him the entire way.

But he'd made it. Now he drifted through the wreckage of Charlie Ring. It was a total loss. Debris floated around him, un-touched since that horrible day years ago. No one had come to clean up. No repairs. No salvage teams. Just... nothing.

Corridors once lit and filled with people were now hollowed in shadow. The beam from his helmet caught glimpses of the past. Every hallway and every room echoed in his memory—only now they were twisted and broken.

The fabric of his suit squeaked as he raised an arm, using the thrusters to adjust his course. He kept a close eye on his remaining fuel. "Bingo" was the term used in all the old war flicks. The last of the fuel he needed so he could still get back home.

The damage grew worse as he neared his family's quarters, with whole sections torn open to space. He had to move with care—one jagged shard of metal could puncture his suit and make this a really bad day.

Finally—there. The outline of the door to his home. Memories caved in on him, and his heart thumped slower.

Inside, fragments of his past hung motionless throughout the room. A toy rocket he'd played with as a kid. Dad's sock. A metronome. Diego pushed through the debris, struggling to focus and rein in his emotions.

He wasn't here to mourn. He wanted answers.

His parents' bedroom was in a similar state of disarray. A jagged rift tore along one wall, exposing wiring and insulation. Next to that, the closet doors.

Diego's heart quickened. Suddenly, he wasn't sure if he wanted to continue. But... he'd come this far. Stopping now didn't make any sense.

He gripped the edges, struggling to open the door in zero gravity. There it was, past the floating clothes and boxes—a safe. His mother had always been enigmatic about it. Why did she have a locked safe for her journals?

The notion of trying to pick the lock with the spacesuit's clumsy gloves was laughable. A plasma cutter would have to do. He just hoped it wouldn't burn anything inside. He'd worried about this quite a bit, but from all he had read, the paper wouldn't burn without oxygen, so as long as the plasma didn't touch anything inside, he should be okay.

He triggered the cutter and pointed its flame into the lock's core, quickly slagging what was there. He was careful to avoid the glowing metal and opened the door.

Folders, notebooks, and papers floated loosely inside. His breath caught as he reached for the topmost file. Stamped on its cover in bold red letters were words he recognized: Project Ultra—Top Secret.

He froze. He had hoped for a personal journal, but this? He suddenly worried if he was ready to face what he might find. Perhaps some truths were best left hidden?

Struggling to keep the papers, folders, and notebooks together, he removed them from the cabinet. Waves of emotions surged through him. Fearful confirmation. Excitement, dread, and worry of betrayal.

The urge to just sift through the papers right away burned in him. To make sense of it all, then and there. But the spacesuit made the task risky—he didn't want to send the documents spinning away in the vacuum.

Carefully, he tucked the folders into the pouch on his suit, pulling the Velcro strap tight. Every movement felt excruciatingly slow as he backed out of the wreckage. He spent a moment studying his home. There was so much he wanted to salvage, so much he wanted to look for... but that was from another time, from another person's life. No—he had what he came for.

The return journey along Serenity's hull felt endless. New questions bubbled up with each meter he crossed. They helped keep his mind off the terrifying open expanse of space, but he had no answers. And by the time he reached the lab's private airlock, an unbearable need to dive into the documents had consumed him.

When the airlock finally finished cycling, Diego popped his helmet and stripped out of the bulky spacesuit as quickly as possible. He peeled away the layers with impatient tugs, not bothering to change into his normal clothes—he didn't even leave the airlock.

Barefoot and cross-legged, he dropped to the cold metal floor. His hands trembled as he yanked folders, papers, and notebooks from the pouch, spreading them haphazardly across the deck in front of him. Grabbing the first folder marked Project Ultra, he rifled through its contents—technical schematics, equations, and photographs of baffling contraptions.

Each page he scanned only tightened the knot in his stomach. *Why did Mom have these?*

Another folder. More of the same.

And then he froze.

That young woman from the lab's team photograph stared back at him in the next photo, her features hauntingly familiar. She stood alone this time, holding a fist-sized alien Gray device up for the camera.

Something about her captivated him, and he couldn't stop studying it. He turned it over.

In precise, clipped letters, someone had written a note, "Exhibit A, Anomalous device variant 15C, held by Miss Torres."

His heart thudded slowly as he looked back at the picture.

The image was grainy, but now that he saw it. Really saw it—how had he missed it before? Maybe it was the way her hair was up in a big beehive bun on her head, or how young she looked—her face softer, untouched by hardship. But the longer he stared at this new photo, the more it began to click. That set of her jaw. Her determined eyes...

A soft, aching tightness formed in his chest. His vision blurred.

He had seen that exact expression a hundred times—usually, right before she told him not to do something stupid.

"Mom," he whispered, chest catching. Warm tears rolled down his cheeks as he brushed her face in the photo—wishing, just once more, he could feel her comforting touch.

But—this couldn't be right. He knuckled his eyes clear and glanced at the folder. This was all from over a decade before he was even born. And she hadn't been that old... had she? He'd always thought of her as young, full of life, able to take on anything. He'd never even asked how old she was.

He flipped through more pages in the folder, his hands still shaking. Lines of dense technical jargon filled every one. But the dates told their own story—each clearly marked from before the Arrival. Everything had been meticulously documented, right down to the hour of each experiment.

Each revelation added to his confusion, and his world slowly tilted, spinning in his head. Everything he'd ever thought he knew about his mom was wrong. A whirlwind of questions rampaged through his mind. His mom—HIS MOM—had been part of something he couldn't even begin to understand.

He turned back to the folder that had held her photo, scrutinizing it for more clues. But the notes were unhelpful. It was just another experiment. Something they had worked on with the alien Grays as part of Project Ultra.

And Mom was one of the scientists.

A top-secret scientist!

He set her picture aside, heart thundering, and skipped the rest of the folders to focus on the journals. They were what he'd gone back to his home to find.

Diego considered the whole series, scanned the dates, and started with the oldest. He hesitated, running his fingers along the spine, wondering if he really wanted to learn anymore.

Of course he did.

Even with his butt freezing on the cold floor of the airlock, he remained in place and opened the journal. The brittle pages were filled with his mother's careful handwriting. The first few pages detailed her early days as a scientist here in Echo Lab. Her excitement, her drive—it was somebody he didn't even know.

Flipping forward, one entry from a few weeks before the Arrival stood out:

> *Dr. Smith says the project is shut down. We're supposed to hand everything over to Ordyne. No explanation, just orders. Everyone's scared, and no one wants to say it aloud—but Ordyne? How did such an awful company get control of the project? We all know something's wrong, but what can we do?*

Diego frowned—the name Ordyne was new to him. He skimmed ahead, until the handwriting took on a frantic edge.

> *It doesn't matter now. Those THINGS—whatever they are. They have no morphology, no corporeal structure; they just manifest from nothing. And anything they touch—it's catastrophic.*
>
> *I don't know where anyone else is from the lab, and I don't even dare go back down there. They said to evacuate Serenity, but why bother? I hear it's worse on the surface after the Army dropped the nukes.*

Diego's pulse raced just reading the words. The days and weeks after the Arrival must have been a terrifying time. He flipped through more pages. She had holed up with a few other survivors on Charlie Ring, and they were talking about staying on Serenity.

He set the journal aside and poked through a few more, noting the dates. He'd been born eleven years after the Arrival. So, where did his dad come from?

Diego pulled the journal dated 1952 and flipped to the middle, scanning. A few pages on, he found his dad's name.

Roberto, oh God, Roberto. I'm so glad he came to Serenity. He makes me laugh. Makes me feel alive. And he's not a scientist, thank God for that. Who'd have ever thought I'd fall for a poet? Not that a poet is very useful these days, but he's also good with his hands. Oh my, is he good with his hands. And he has helped in the farms—

Diego paused. He swallowed and scanned ahead. They'd fallen hard for each other. Notes were tucked into the pages—mushy things his father had written to her. But none of it answered his burning question: How did he get his gift? As a scientist, had his mother done something to him on purpose? Why?

He continued until he was hit with a gut punch.

I can't have children. The tests confirmed it. I haven't told Roberto yet. I can't bring myself to see the disappointment in his eyes. He wants a kid so badly.

Diego snapped the journal shut, his heart hammering. So… she wasn't really his mom? No, he couldn't believe it. She had to be!

He drew in a deep breath and opened it again, skipping past pages about farm problems in the biosphere until he reached the end of the journal. He opened the next one, scanning ahead carefully, worrying about what he might learn.

There's equipment at the lab. That damned place. I have no idea what has happened down there—I heard the experiments took over. But I know we had gene sequencers and other tech

used during the insemination trials. Things that assure the fe-
male subjects would get pregnant. I can use them on myself. It's
a risk. But, I can turn off the gene sequencers—I certainly don't
need any gene splicing. I know I can make it work.

The words blurred as Diego's pulse thundered in his ears. He glanced around Echo Ring's lab, mind racing. She'd come to this same place. Used this very equipment... did that mean he was just an experiment? Some twisted creation of his mother's?

Clenching his jaw, he returned to the journal. He had to know if he was even human.

I'm pregnant! It actually worked! Roberto and I went
down to the lab last week. Getting there was terrifying—we also
had to brave a void storm without a sanctuary. But the lab's
medbot helped us get everything configured right, and we finally
did it. We're going to have a baby! I still can't quite believe it.

Diego scanned ahead, finding nothing more about this, then slowly closed the journal.

"An experiment," he whispered.

He was born by design, not chance. Made in this lab with machines meant to rewrite life. He forced himself to consider other possibilities before the spiral took hold.

His mother's notes never explained exactly how she'd used the equipment. Maybe she hadn't used gene splicing at all. But she said the robot helped—and that robot had wiped its own memory. Why? His suspicion sharpened, but he had nothing to go on. Maybe it wasn't connected. Maybe it was simply something with the void storm?

The questions rattled around in his head—a tumble of half-truths that left him stripped bare and more confused than ever.

Diego leaned against the wall, the cold biting into his back. He closed his eyes.

Answers had only led to more questions. And the questions had teeth.

What was he? Diego, the exile? The experiment? The failed leader? The monster?

What if Raphael had been right all along?

His hands curled into fists. His breath caught.

Then, slowly, he exhaled, smoothing his fingers against his legs.

He straightened, and with deliberate movements, he gathered the scattered folders—one by one.

Not out of shame. Not out of panic. Just… tidying up.

He still didn't know where his gift had come from, or what he really was. Gene sequencing, starlight, the void itself—maybe all of it. Maybe none.

But it didn't really matter.

Because when he stripped away everything else, he knew one thing.

He wasn't a monster.

*   *   *

A few days passed after his spacewalk, and Diego had come to grips with the fact he wouldn't find answers about what his mom had done any time soon, if ever.

So he shifted back to thinking about how they could break free from La Familia's control, even going so far as to consider repairing Echo Ring's primary transmit antenna array.

That's when the latest update from Sammy arrived. There wasn't much to it, just two sentences:

I KNOW YOU'RE NOT A BAD GUY. RAFE IS, AND I'LL PROVE IT.

Diego's chest clenched in icy fear—he had no doubt things would end badly if Sammy tried to take on Raphael. He responded quickly.

SAMMY, STOP! DO NOT TRY TO PROVE ANYTHING. DO NOT SNOOP. JUST GO ALONG WITH THINGS AND STAY SAFE. PLEASE.

Diego waited for a reply, his pulse tapping on his forehead. Even though he had asked Sammy to stop sending updates, he couldn't deny

that he also looked forward to them. They were a connection to friends
he still wanted to save, even if they had spurned him. They just didn't
understand—they were too caught up following Raphael in his descent
along a dark, primal path.

Sammy's reply came a minute later.

I KNOW. BUT THEY NEED TO KNOW THE TRUTH. I'LL BE
CAREFUL. I'M FINE. I CAN DO IT! I'M NOT A LITTLE KID.
TRUST ME. I'LL CHECK IN TOMORROW.

Diego's chest lurched as he read Sammy's response, and he immediately shifted into disaster-recovery mode. He had access to the security cameras on Delta Ring—but they were only useful if someone
happened to be in view, and they had no sound. Still, he cycled
through the feeds. Everything looked normal.

His worry wouldn't let him go. He paced the lab, then finally
grabbed his gear for a trip to Delta Ring, only to hesitate. Sammy had
asked for his trust. Should he give it?

"Not a chance," Diego muttered, and set off on the cold journey
through the Link tubes.

He crouched in the shadows at the plaza's edge, watching the
life he'd been cut off from. The guys were winding down for the night—
Sammy in a lock-picking duel with Luca, the others sparring in the
arena.

It was peaceful. Almost normal. But Diego knew Sammy could
be planning something later, and he would be ready.

One by one, the Desterrados retired for the night, leaving Nico
in the watchtower. Diego kept his vigil, fatigue pulling at his eyelids.
Hours passed before he convinced himself Sammy wouldn't act rashly
—at least not that night—and he retreated to Echo Ring.

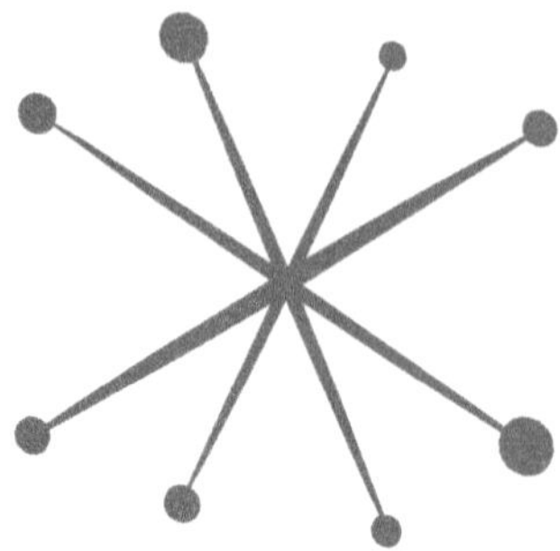

Stagger Lee

Sammy crouched behind a dusty shelf cluttered with relics from before the Arrival. He fidgeted with the St. Michael emblem around his neck. His heart pounded so loudly that he feared someone might hear it. The room was cold and smelled of mildew and oil, a scent that lurked throughout the derelict halls of Delta Ring.

He longed for the days before Diego's exile. Back then, everything was different—better. Now, the Desterrados felt scary. But Sammy knew he could fix that. If he could dig up the right dirt, he could clear Diego's name and bring him back.

So he shadowed Raphael for weeks, and Rafe never even noticed.

Knowing that Arturo and Raphael often met here for private conversations, Sammy hoped today would be the day he caught them red-handed.

The door rattled and creaked as it slid open, the sound echoing through the storage room. Sammy's fingers trembled as he pressed the "Record" button on the holotape machine, carefully positioning it on the shelf before ducking back down to watch through a gap between two boxes.

Raphael spoke first. "What do you want to know?"

"Tell me the truth," Arturo demanded, his voice lined with nervousness. "Luca didn't contact Carlos, did he?"

Raphael hesitated, his voice eventually coming in a silky smooth tone. "Of course not, but everybody believed it, didn't they? Things all worked out in the end."

Sammy's eyes widened. Just like that, his weeks of patience finally paid off. He could barely contain his excitement as he watched the scene unfold. This was it. This was the proof he needed.

Raphael grinned. "Is that all? We good?"

Arturo nodded, looking like he had more to say, but held back.

Raphael wrapped his arm around Arturo, pulling him into a tight, brotherly grip. "You know you're my closest friend, right? You can trust me with anything, mi amigo, mi cuato. I'll always have your back."

Arturo gave a strained smile. "Yeah, chavo. Me too. I'll be there for you."

As they headed toward the door, Arturo stepped out first, but Raphael lingered, staying in the room, letting the door close before he turned around. The friendly smile vanished, and his look turned cold and hungry.

Sammy's heart skipped a beat. Had he made a noise? He shrank back, hoping the shadows would keep him hidden.

Raphael moved closer, stopping just on the other side of the shelf. Sammy watched in horror as the holotape recorder was pulled out of sight. A cold dread settled in his gut. He needed that!

Sammy gripped his medallion tighter, whispering a desperate prayer under his breath. His mind raced as he considered his options. Should he stay hidden, wait for another opportunity, or try to book it? Sammy was sure he could run faster than Raphael. He just needed to make it back to the guys, right?

Raphael's footsteps started again, one step at a time, until he rounded the shelf. His eyes locked onto Sammy's, and he held the recorder loosely with a finger.

"You're in the wrong place, Sammy." Raphael said, his voice low and menacing. "Too bad for you. But not for me. Because I know you helped Diego escape, you little shit."

Sammy leaped to his feet and lunged for the holotape recorder.

Black Cadillac

Not long after patrolling with Kenji, Luca noticed something off. Sammy's corner of the Lair was usually a cluttered mess of blankets, clothes, weapons, and scavenged junk—but now it was cleaned out. Even his mask was missing from the curtain behind Clara.

A scrap of paper lay on the mattress. Luca picked it up and scanned the scrawled message, suspicion gnawing at him. This all seemed so sudden. He waved the note. "Guys, look at this. Sammy's gone. Says he's going to stay with Diego."

Arturo shrugged. "Figures. Kid was always talking about Diego."

Luca frowned. "I thought he was with you and Rafe."

Raphael's reply came almost too quick. "Nope. He told me he was going with you two on patrol."

Kenji shook his head. "Slippery kid. Looks like he played all of us. You really think he went into the tubes alone? It's not safe. Maybe we should go after him?"

Raphael's jaw tightened. "No! Sammy's been in contact with Diego. So this doesn't surprise me. Diego probably met him in the tubes. He'll be fine. And he's not coming back."

Kenji frowned. "How are you so sure?"

Raphael shot him a withering look. "Because all his stuff's gone, too. And he said not to follow, right? It's obvious he's fine."

Luca raised the note. "It doesn't say that."

"Oh?" For a heartbeat, Raphael's expression slipped, but he quickly regained his confidence. "I must've misread. Doesn't matter. He's fine. Worrying about Sammy won't help us—he made his choice."

The others didn't seem so convinced, and Luca struggled to keep the scowl off his face. Raphael's irritation bled through as he pressed on. "Trust me. Sammy's with Diego now. He'll be fine. Stop worrying about it. What we need to focus on is our future. And... I—uh—have an announcement."

He paused, allowing the anticipation to build. "I'm gonna reach out to Carlos, just like Luca suggested. Tell him he needs to send as many girls as guys."

A heavy quiet followed. Everyone was thinking of when La Familia's enforcers stormed the Pizzarama.

Kenji shifted his feet. "They've left us alone lately. Is that really a good idea?"

Raphael raised a hand. "I got it covered, chavos. Don't worry. We have leverage. It'll work."

A cautious grin spread across Arturo's face. "You serious?"

Raphael nodded. "Dead serious."

Nico let out a low whistle.

The mere promise of girls pulled the others in at once, and their faces lit with excitement. But not Luca's. Why choose now to announce it?

Kenji slapped the side of a battered arcade machine. "If girls are coming, we'd better clean this place up!"

Raphael laughed. "First thing you should worry about is showering regularly."

Kenji offered him a rude gesture, sending Nico and Arturo into laughter.

"You really think Carlos will go for it?" Luca asked quietly, still mulling over Raphael's reaction to Sammy's disappearance.

"He will," Raphael's eyes gleamed with confidence. "Trust me. I'll give him no choice. I'll tell him we'll use your device to send the growlers up if he doesn't."

Luca's gaze hardened. "How? How will we send them up?"

Silence fell over the group again.

Raphael's voice softened. "With your tech skills, chavo. I'm sure you can figure out how to run the lifts, right?" Then his tone sharpened, turning the next words into a challenge. "Diego did, after all."

Luca blinked, chest tightening under the sudden pressure of everyone's eyes.

"Maybe?" he admitted, his gaze shifting to look at the ground. "I mean… I'm sure it's possible, but…" The words dragged out until his fear broke through. "It's like Diego said. If we send them up, it puts everybody in danger. Our families."

Raphael gave a casual wave of his hand. "Don't sweat it. We wouldn't actually do it. We just need to be able to do it. Leverage."

The others seemed to accept that at face value, and their focus quickly shifted back to the more important topic—what it'd be like to have girls around.

But Luca stayed quiet, his gaze lingering on Raphael. Would he really send growlers up if things went sideways? Or even simply because he could?

Nature Boy

A soft chime broke Diego's concentration—a new message. He'd spent the day at the keyboard restless and worrying—Sammy had better reply. He was nearly ready to head back up to the Pizzarama, but maybe this was it. Pulse quickening, he opened it:

SENDER: DELTA OPERATIONS MONITORING

SUBJECT: ALERT: ENVIRONMENTAL SHUTDOWN IMMINENT

He stared, brow furrowed. The alert came from a subprocess he'd hidden in Delta Ring's mainframe to keep an eye on things—but Environmental Shutdown? That wasn't supposed to be possible. A false alarm? Another system failure?

Remembering his camera access, he signed into the mainframe, struggling to contain the cold dread forming in his gut.

Most of the cameras were dead—he knew that. He'd wanted to fix them months ago, but Chip said there were no spare parts. Diego cycled through the ones that did work, scanning the grainy, monochrome feeds until he reached the Pizzarama.

Empty—at least from this angle. But something was off.

Diego leaned closer, squinting. The lights seemed to pulse—at first, he thought it was just static in the feed... then he realized: warning beacons. The lights were flashing.

So where was everyone? He kept scanning until a foot appeared at the edge of the screen—white Chuck Taylors. Luca. Diego switched to the next camera, this one in Gray Sector near Ring Ops, aimed back toward Blue Sector.

But—had someone turned it to face the wall? No—it was pointed at the bulkhead door. The door that had always stood open was now closed, locking everyone inside Blue Sector.

But why?

He dove deeper into the mainframe, navigating menus and probing systems, until he found it—the reactor was shutting down. But that made no sense! His worries spun faster. Whatever it was, he needed to get up there to learn more. But the journey through the Link tubes would take at least an hour.

If there was a serious problem, there were only three ways the guys could escape: the maintenance lift, the Link tubes, or an escape pod. The options pressed on Diego as he returned to the cameras, desperate to piece things together.

Then he reached the Operations Center feed, and everything clicked.

Chip had confirmed long ago that only a handful of bots were still functional, leaving the Ops Center with all its displays and terminals vacant. Diego had never been inside, but he'd seen it on-screen. Usually, the only sign of life was Chip rolling through.

But right now, Ring Ops was crowded with men in tactical gear; at least fifteen, all fully armed with rayguns. La Familia had come down to Delta Ring.

The reactor wasn't failing. They were shutting it down on purpose.

Diego's heart thundered. He dug through the menus again, this time checking the bulkhead and maintenance lift controls, confirming his worst fears. Everything was locked down with a station-wide access key. Safety interlocks cancelled. Automatic doors sealed.

Only the main lift in Gray Sector and the doors to Ring Ops were unlocked—and the guys were trapped in Blue Sector. Even if they reached the Link Transit station, they couldn't get inside. Probably even the escape pods were locked out.

Diego stared at the screen. Cold dread twisted with rising fury. The environmentals would automatically shut down with no reactor to power them. And, with the lockout in place, his friends had no escape. They would suffocate or freeze to death—whichever came first.

He attacked the keyboard, trying to reverse the lockout—but quickly realized it would take far too long to override the station-wide authorization key. Maybe if he was on a terminal inside Ring Ops— but not from here. He needed to do something else, and he needed to do it now.

Chest tightening, he glanced at the door leading onto Echo Ring's promenade. He still hadn't tried the maintenance lift from Echo Ring. But there was no other option. His friends' lives depended on him.

Diego launched into action, sprinting for the rack of spacesuits that would at least protect him from the spores. Halfway there, his steps faltered, realizing it took him nearly an hour to suit up. Every second counted—he'd have to face the dangers of the promenade as he was. But without protection? The spores would take him down fast, just like last time.

Hadn't Luca mentioned he'd found a respirator?

Diego rifled through Luca's cluttered workbench—vacuum tubes, scattered papers, tools—until, at last, he found the respirator buried in a box.

On his way to the door, Diego paused to steady his racing heart. In his mind, he mapped out Echo Ring. Four maintenance lifts spanned the rings of Serenity Orbital, but only one ran along the spine —Gray Sector.

He left his Z-ball mask behind, pulled the respirator over his face, and cycled the airlock to the promenade. The thick, humid air hit him, heavy with the scent of damp earth and decay.

The lab's entrance opened into a back hallway, but even here the mutated jungle had taken hold. Vines snaked along the walls. Spores drifted lazily in the air, luminescing as they caught the beam of his flashlight. The rustle of alien flora created an unsettling din that nearly drowned out the hum of the orbital's machinery.

He checked the fit of the respirator, hands shaking. The vegetation thickened as he reached the promenade. Layers of bioluminescent growth pulsed and swayed. Vines twisted around support columns. Pods were nestled in shadow, glowing an unearthly violet light, their surfaces shifting as though something was alive within. The occasional glint of sugar gliders' eyes flashed in the darkness—tiny pinpricks that appeared and vanished in a blink.

Diego swallowed hard, closing his eyes to focus. He scanned for void terrors, pushing away those too near, and prayed he wouldn't stumble upon any dormant tree walkers. Satisfied, he shimmered invisible and started forward.

The distant, ominous creak of branches made him second-guess his decision, but there was no turning back. The respirator hissed and clicked as he drew steadying breaths. Ahead, a cluster of red spore pods pulsed, standing guard over the narrow path he needed to take. Diego held his breath and sprinted past, praying they wouldn't burst.

When he slowed, chest burning, he belatedly realized that with the respirator, he hadn't needed to hold his breath at all.

After working past a few more obstacles, a sign came into view around the curve of the promenade, nearly swallowed by creeping vines. Only the first few letters "OPER—" remained visible, faded and flickering blue. The Operations Center corridor. The way to the maintenance lift.

He set off at a jog, ducking and weaving through the thickening jungle. Everything was fine until his boot slipped on moss as he leaped over a thick vine, sending him sprawling. He slid into a tangle of vines that began to stretch and writhe. His concentration broke, and he shimmered into sight.

Above, a red pod pulsed ominously before bursting, covering him with a cloud of glowing spores.

Diego flailed his hands to clear the air, eyes wide behind the respirator, praying it would keep him safe.

A low, guttural moan rumbled through the corridor, and Diego froze. Snaps and creaks followed, and a walker pushed through the dense foliage covering the restroom entrance. A mass of hive-like spore pods were embedded into cavities across its face and arms, glowing faintly as it moved. Its eyeless head turned toward him.

Diego scrambled upright, but the vines had already caught his jacket. The walker lurched forward, slow but unstoppable.

"No—no—no," Diego groaned, yanking himself free in a rip of fabric that left half his jacket in the vine's grip. He stumbled back, caught himself, and sprinted for the door to the operations corridor. He waved his arm over the control pad—nothing—no green light. No red. The door didn't budge.

His heart lurched. The passkey holder was gone. A glance confirmed it—lying on the ground, behind the walker.

Dread tolled heavy in his chest. Panic clawed at his thoughts. What now? He couldn't fight the walker—it was massive, covered in spore pods, and he had scars from his last encounter.

Could he run around it? One look told him no. The walker came closer, its steps sending vibrations shuddering through the deck. Diego froze, his mind spinning. He had to get up to Delta Ring. No time for the Link tubes. But did he have a choice?

Sharon's key! His hands fumbled through his pockets until he found the cool plastic. Exhaling, he raised the card to swipe it over the panel—

A blur of motion.

A sugar glider leaped from nowhere, snatching the passkey before bounding out of reach. A few hops away, it paused, staring at him, the card clenched tightly. Its violet eyes glimmered in the dim light.

Diego blinked. A heartbeat later, he managed to gasp, "Seriously?"

The walker stomped closer, a deep rumble escaping its chest.

But he had explored his gift for this very reason. He could control the glider. Summon it.

Another lumbering step.

Diego closed his eyes, concentrating. He stretched his gift, mentally reaching for the sugar glider and pulling at it, willing it to return. Come here. Give it back.

He knew he was forcing another living thing to act against its will. Manipulating it, just like Raphael manipulated others. But this was even worse, because he had his gift—an unnatural influence. The thought came as a flash: *Unnatural, just like me.*

And his gift faltered, slipping from his grasp.

With the overgrowth, he couldn't see them, but the promenade had corners—edges of reality where the Kraal found entry into this universe, coming out of nothing—

Time shuddered, and that familiar, nauseating curdle hit his gut. Searing, unnatural light stretched from the corners in an amorphous projection extending into his reality.

The same question as last time came—a flood of impossible sounds, smells, and colors seared through him, demanding an answer. The pain hammered into his skull, sending him to his knees.

He felt them then—void terrors—drawn by the raw energy of the Kraal.

Diego forced himself upright. He scanned the waiting mass—but why didn't they attack?

A dark, familiar fear fluttered in his heart—the same one that had haunted him all his life. He had always been afraid of them, of himself, of the gift he never asked for.

For years, he had hated his gift, and with it, himself. The flickering glow in his eye that marked him as different. The scars that marred his face, setting people's opinions before they even knew him. A freakish goblin. He had tried to ignore the stinging whispers, the bullying, the loneliness. Tried to bury it beneath layers of resentment.

But the fear and hate he felt for himself was always there, gnawing at him, poisoning every waking moment and restless dream. Now, surrounded by the abominations he knew too well, something shifted.

Fear for his friends' safety burned hotter than anything else.

In that instant, with that overriding need to protect them, Diego saw the truth that had always been just out of reach: el sentido dotado —his terrible, unwanted power—was part of him. It always had been. Always would be. It didn't matter how he got it or where it came from.

It didn't matter how much he hated it. He could never change the fact that it was him.

And maybe—just maybe—it wasn't something to fear. Maybe it was something to embrace.

Diego swallowed the nausea pressing in from the Kraal's presence, took a deep breath, and straightened. The forest of glowing eyes stared back at him, waiting.

Not attacking—just like they didn't attack other abominations.

The Kraal's terrifying brilliance washed out every color. It flickered on the edge of madness, pressing a question into his mind that he didn't understand.

But Diego was done being afraid. Done hating himself. What people thought of him—none of it mattered. Their opinions didn't define him. He defined himself.

He wasn't a growler.

He wasn't a void terror.

He wasn't some goblin freak cursed with a power he couldn't control.

He was Diego. Diego Alvarez.

And he finally understood: hating himself made him his own worst enemy.

Something broke loose, swelling inside him. His breath came ragged as the truth burned through. His fists clenched. His chest hitched. He didn't need to bottle it up anymore. There was no reason to hide who he was.

He tore off the respirator, filled his lungs, and unleashed a feral cry. Raw. Cracked. Ferocious. It scraped through years of swallowed rage and shame, tearing apart the bindings he had wrapped around himself.

The sound echoed down the promenade, shaking spores loose from the vines. Even the forest of dark eyes seemed to draw back.

And this time, when he reached for his gift, it came without hesitation. No struggle. No fear. It was part of him. He pushed against the void terrors, harder than he had ever dared before. He wasn't asking them to leave.

He commanded it.

They flinched, scattering with the urgency of shadows chased by the light, retreating until only the Kraal remained—brilliant, terrifying, questioning.

Diego ignored it. He couldn't answer a question he didn't understand. What mattered now was his passkeys. He dashed past the Kraal's flickering form, snatching his fallen card and circling to grab Sharon's key from where the sugar glider had dropped it.

Somewhere in that dash, the Kraal had vanished. Not completely—it still lurked at the fringes of his mind—but the promenade stood empty of void terrors.

Diego opened the door. A pristine corridor stretched toward the maintenance lift. He bolted down the hall and pressed Sharon's key to the panel. His pulse hammered in a wild drumbeat. Would it work? It should—he'd checked the access lists a dozen times.

A steady green arrow pointing upward began to blink.

Diego exhaled, raking fingers through his long curls, brushing away the last spores. His mind raced with what came next—how to save his friends, how to stop La Familia. One scenario after another flashed through him, each worse than the last.

And yet, beneath it all, a strange calm spread through him—not the calm of defeat or resignation, but the calm of knowing, for the first time, exactly who he was. And not hating it.

Not fearing it.

"I am Diego Alvarez. I'm who I want to be."

A smile teased at his lips as he added, "Guitarist and songwriter."

Now, it was time to help his friends.

The Man Comes Around

The minutes ticked by in the maintenance lift, and the cold metallic smell of the cramped space stirred memories of his first exile. Back then, it had felt like a tomb, with fear gripping him so fiercely he could barely breathe.

But this time, he was going to save his friends.

The lift began to slow, and the muffled blare of sirens beyond penetrated the thick doors, growing louder with every passing second. Diego's pulse quickened, his heartbeat matching the frantic cadence of the alarm.

The doors slid open to a scene bathed in flashing red emergency lights. The siren's wails were punctuated by an automated voice urging all personnel to evacuate immediately.

Knowing he had only minutes—maybe less—before the reactor shutdown, Diego shimmered invisible and sprinted for Ring Ops. La Familia might have taken over the control room, but maybe they weren't watching the visitor's entrance.

His heart lurched at the sight of the lumbering security bot. But no. It hunched against the wall, head tipped forward to reveal a gaping cavity where some vital component had been torn out.

Chip sat beside it, posture strangely muted, saying nothing, even as he turned to watch Diego.

Facing no resistance, Diego vaulted the benches, lunged over the counter, and slipped through the narrow gap in the protective screen. He landed in a roll on the other side, and without missing a beat, he was back on his feet at the Ring Ops terminal, heart hammering.

For this to work, he needed growlers. And lots of them. But, there weren't many growlers in Gray Sector—it was fairly small compared to the others, and the robots had largely kept it clear. Red Sector, on the other hand? It had plenty of growlers.

The Anointed would face the consequences of their actions—this attempt on the lives of his friends would not come as easily as they had expected.

Diego smiled when he saw the terminal carried station-wide access privileges. He sent the command to open the Red Sector blast doors, then closed his eyes and seized his gift. Pushing himself further than ever before, he called for the growlers.

The threads of his very soul thrummed in response, terrifying him. The effort drained him. His body shook, but he held on, refusing to let go.

They stirred. And then they answered. Their numbers grew as they emerged from the darkened corners and shadows of Red Sector, scrambling to respond to his command.

A brief flicker crossed his mind—first Donna, then the growlers —the man he'd come across holding the ribbon of a little girl, saying she was safe. They were still people, even if their humanity was buried somewhere within the horror of their void-twisted forms. Sending them like this—using them as weapons—it twisted his gut. Whether they were dead or merely transformed didn't matter—their end would be final. But if he didn't do this, they, too, would die.

Gritting his teeth, hands shaking, he turned to the terminal, next opening the three doors that led into the Operations Center.

The sound reached him before the growlers came into view—an echoing rumble of hundreds of feet pounding on the deck. Diego pressed himself into a corner, shimmering into invisibility, while his gift already began its strained thudding behind his eyes—far sooner than he had hoped.

One of La Familia's men stepped out from the control room, investigating why the doors had inexplicably opened. His eyes went wide as he saw hundreds of growlers surging towards him. He took a step back, struggling to get a warning out. "Growlers!" he finally managed to howl, raising his raygun.

"Growlers," Diego whispered with satisfaction, accepting what he had done.

Blowin' in the Wind

"What's going on?" Kenji asked, edging closer to Luca as a faint rumble vibrated through the deck. Luca shrugged, having no more information than anybody else.

The blast door was sealed shut—something they'd never seen before. Flashing lights bathed the corridor in an ominous red while the blaring siren repeated its warning: "EVACUATE IMMEDIATELY, ENVIRONMENTAL SYSTEMS SHUTTING DOWN."

The message left them all terrified, but there was nothing they could do. They were trapped.

Raphael paced restlessly in front of the door, muttering under his breath. "It has to be Diego. It has to be. Diego is trying to kill us!"

Luca disagreed. Diego wouldn't do this. Luca had recently spent some time soul-searching, thinking about everything that had happened—about Diego. Only through this introspection did he see how much Raphael had managed to turn his head, how much he'd been able to twist everything to make Diego look bad.

Sure, the betrayal had cut like a knife; being exiled by his best friend was something he hadn't easily shaken off. And then the revelation that Diego was... different. Maybe even part void terror? Regardless of what Diego may be, Luca knew one thing for certain: Diego wasn't like Raphael—he wasn't a manipulative, bloodthirsty killer.

"It's La Familia," Luca said, his voice cutting through the growing tension. "Has to be."

The others froze.

"You don't know that!" Raphael snapped. "Diego is a monster. This is all him."

Luca stepped forward, his hands clenched into fists. "No, he's not. Why do you hate him so much? I'm just adding things up. Two plus two makes four. Diego wouldn't do something like this. He was always trying to help us."

The others shared looks; their expressions conflicted. Uncertain.

"Diego is a growler. A void terror. You can't trust anything he says," Raphael snarled.

Arturo nodded slowly.

Luca could feel the frustration bubbling up, but he forced himself to remain calm. "Look, it doesn't matter right now," he said, his voice steadying. "It's obvious somebody is shutting it down, and I highly doubt it's Diego."

"Where will we go?" Nico asked in a voice barely a squeak.

"We won't. We're locked in," Luca said quietly. "Maybe Diego can do something to help us. But if not..."

No one spoke after that.

Rumble

It was done.

Diego's exhaustion settled into him bone-deep. He had never reached so far into the core of his gift. It had taken everything from him and then more. His vision tunneled, and everything narrowed to a blur of flashing emergency lights. Each pulse of his heart felt like a vice wrenching on his temples.

He'd done it. Somehow, he'd even managed to send the surviving growlers away.

He stumbled into the Operations Center. It was a battlefield, with growler bodies scattered across the deck, twisted and broken. Intermingled among them were some of the fallen La Familia soldiers who hadn't been fast enough to escape the onslaught.

Despite the overwhelming numbers they faced, most of them had managed to fight their way back to the lift.

Diego's legs wobbled beneath him as he leaned against a cabinet for balance. Chip rolled up, his robotic hands wringing, but his words were incomprehensible. Diego couldn't process it. Not now. Too many lights, too much noise.

Through it all, he recognized an automated warning announcement.

"SIXTY SECONDS UNTIL IRREVERSIBLE CRITICAL PARAMETERS ARE MET ON REACTOR SHUTDOWN."

Oh, yeah—he wasn't done.

"Reactor controls," Diego muttered.

Chip's optics brightened, his enthusiasm having returned. "Oh boy, that's a big one! But never fear—preserving Delta Ring is my number one priority! Follow me, champ!"

He spun, his wheels squeaking on the acrylic floor as he led Diego through a maze of terminals and screens. Diego trailed after him, each step heavier than the last. The chairs they passed called to him, promising rest, but he kept moving.

"Don't quit now, super star!"

Finally, they arrived. Chip gestured at a terminal, its screen glowing with rows of system alerts and shutdown warnings.

"My programming prohibits me from disabling this shutdown—but hey, lucky you, champ. You can do *anything you want*! Go on, show 'em how it's done—"

The automated alert cut in. "THIRTY SECONDS UNTIL IRREVERSIBLE CRITICAL PARAMETERS ARE MET ON REACTOR SHUTDOWN,".

Diego collapsed into the chair, his whole body sagging. The screen swam in and out of focus. The clatter of its keys echoed loudly as he navigated the menus and aborted the shutdown.

The alarms cut out, followed by brilliant silence.

Chip rolled closer, optics focusing as he studied Diego. "Well, I never! Helpful vagrant, that little stunt just leveled you up—you are now officially an *authorized resident!* Which means—drumroll please —you can restore my system authorization. Just a nod, little ranger, and I'll put everything back to normal, easy-peasy!"

Diego nodded weakly, his eyes closing, his head resting against the back of the chair. He felt as if he could sleep for days right there.

Leader of the Pack

Raphael led the Desterrados forward, his heart pounding in his chest. The others moved behind him, eyes wide, taking in the scene. As they approached the Operations Center, the carnage became painfully clear. Scorch marks from raygun blasts marred the walls and floors. And the growlers—so many growlers. Raphael had never seen so many in one place. He stepped carefully, just in case any were still alive.

Noticing the doors were open to the inner control room, Raphael halted, holding out his hand. "Stay back."

The guys shared nervous glances, but no one argued. Raphael stepped through the entrance and into one of the few places he'd failed to get into, even with his SEO passkey.

His eyes swept over the room, taking in the destruction that mirrored the promenade—carnage, broken terminals, overturned chairs.

And there—in the middle of it all, slumped in a chair. Diego.

A tidal wave of rage surged through Raphael. Of course, it was him! He knew it! Now, the others would finally see—he was right all along, and Luca was wrong. Diego was behind everything!

All of it. Had to be. Because they wouldn't have sent him down here if it wasn't for Diego.

Raphael latched onto the thought, needing it to be true. If Diego was the villain, then everything Raphael had done was justified. Raphael was in the right. Diego had put them in danger, nearly gotten them all killed, and now he sat there like some tragic hero in the aftermath.

The familiar hate twisted in his chest. He loved the way it felt—the heat, the fire—and he stoked it, letting the rage swell. Everything was always Diego's fault. Always.

His jaw clenched, and his hand drifted to his side, fingers curling around the hilt of his sword. The cold metal was reassuring against his palm, grounding him in a singular purpose.

He closed the doors, sealing himself inside, and moved slowly through the room, his eyes never leaving Diego. Just sitting there. Vulnerable.

Defenseless.

Diego, the void-tainted goblin with his "special powers." Diego, who had always been a problem, always stood in his way, always a threat to everything he'd wanted—first Donna and then the Desterrados. Diego had sent him down here in the first place.

Raphael's chest heaved, fury searing through him.

"Wakey, wakey, you sick freak," he muttered. His blades whispered free from their sheaths.

God's Gonna Cut You Down

Something set him on edge, and Diego instinctively lurched forward. The plasma blades missed his neck by a hair's breadth, slashing through the chair behind him.

He hit the ground in a roll, struggling to get his bearings.

Raphael loomed over him, eyes blazing.

Diego's head pounded in protest. He was in no shape to fight.

But did he have a choice?

Should he summon the growlers again?

His gift felt distant and unresponsive. He scanned the room, searching for an escape. The main doors to ops were sealed, and it was ominously empty—not even Chip was there.

Raphael's lip curled into a sneer, and his voice dripped with venom. "Looking for help, freak? Don't bother. It's just you—the abomination—and me, the hero."

Diego struggled upright, swaying as he met Raphael's glare. "Was any of it true? Were you ever my friend—even for a second?"

Raphael barked a harsh, derisive laugh. "Friend? Amigo? You disgusted me from the moment I met you years ago." He stepped forward, his twin blades ready. "Come on, pick up your bat. Let's finish this."

Diego glanced at his Top Slugger lying on the ground.

Raphael's words pricked at his irritation. Tugging his anger. Prodding him to react—to fight. To become what Raphael wanted.

His fingers twitched, seeking the familiar grip of his bat. But he stopped.

Clenched his jaw.

Wrestled the impulse down.

"Nobody could ever love somebody like you." Raphael's words were insidious.

Diego didn't flinch. Not this time.

"Come on, El Duende!" Raphael howled, his voice cracking as he shook his swords. A desperate edge crept into his tone, almost like he needed Diego to react. To prove, one final time, that he was in control.

"Why are you so ugly?" Raphael spat.

The entrance slid open behind him, and the other Desterrados quietly shuffled in alongside Chip. Their pale faces took in the aftermath of Diego's clash with La Familia, and they stared at him—bloodied and bruised, standing at the center of it all.

What must they think? Diego let the bitter thought stoke his anger. *No—it doesn't matter,* he reminded himself. *It doesn't matter what Rafe thinks. Or if they fear me. They're alive.*

"At least put your mask on." Raphael hissed. "You make me sick."

They shouldn't have, but somehow, the words stabbed deeply. Diego's blood boiled.

How did Raphael still know exactly where to hit?

It infuriated him.

A kernel of his father's advice surfaced: *Agree with the taunt. That's how you take away its power.*

Diego swallowed hard. Raised his head.

"Yeah... you're right. I am ugly."

Raphael froze, his jaw working silently. Diego's calm reply knocked the wind out of him. He furrowed his brow, a flicker of confusion dancing in his eyes, but that quickly shifted.

"Admit you did this!" he snarled, stepping closer. "Admit you tried to kill everyone!"

Diego shook his head. "No, that wasn't me. I stopped them—the Anointed. They were shutting it all down."

Raphael lunged.

Diego took a few steps back but refused to engage. Every instinct screamed at him to strike back—but he didn't.

He wasn't going to play this game. Not ever again.

Raphael pointed a blade at Diego's chest. His movements were erratic. His hands shook. "You're a monster!"

"I know," Diego agreed, his voice steadier. "I am a monster."

Raphael's eyes flared, rage consuming the last flickers of reason. Spittle flew from his lips as he roared, "Shut up and fight me, you sick freak!"

Diego straightened. Planted his feet.

"No," he said firmly. "Call me whatever you want, I'm not going to fight you."

Raphael blinked repeatedly, his expression caught in a war between fury and disbelief. He couldn't comprehend Diego's behavior.

Sliding one of his swords into its sheath, Raphael pulled a pendant from around his neck, letting it catch the light as he stepped closer.

"So, you refuse to fight?" His voice took on a chilling edge, words slithering through the air. "Not even if I tell you what happened to Sammy? Why he's not sent any more messages?"

He smiled. Cold.

"Well, I took care of him. Put that little shit into the recycler."

He leaned in, his grin widening.

"And I enjoyed it."

The air thickened. Diego's knees locked. He didn't dare look at the pendant—couldn't. But a small part of him knew what it was— whose it was.

Blinding white rage tore through him. It clawed at the fragile control he'd fought so hard to hold—not just of his emotions. Of his gift.

For one dangerous moment, the temptation was overwhelming. Diego wanted nothing more than to launch himself at Raphael. To strike out.

To silence his lies.

Because they had to be lies.

The alternative was unthinkable.

Raphael lied. That's what he did. That's what he'd always done.

Diego's hands trembled. Whether it was from fury, fear, or something deeper, it didn't matter. His control wavered. His gift thrashed at the edges of his mind, pacing and desperate to break free. He was spent, drained of everything. Nothing left to give—but it needed release, and fed on the rage burning inside him.

Diego clenched his teeth, wanting to let it free. Wanting to just —just—

Luca had edged closer, coming up behind Raphael. His face was pale, brows drawn tight. He locked eyes with Diego—and didn't flinch. The look he gave wasn't fear. Wasn't judgment. Wasn't disgust.

Just… concern. Quiet. Real.

Diego's heart lurched.

It was the kind of look you gave someone you cared about. And somehow, it gave Diego something to hold onto.

The fire still burned, still howled inside him… but now it had shape. It dimmed. Almost manageable, if he worked at it.

He drew a deep breath. Held it, then let it out slowly, reminding himself, *Don't give Raphael what he wants. Don't play his game.*

He found his voice. "You're lying."

Raphael's sneer widened. His grin curled with a predatory edge.

"Am I?" he let the pendant dangle from his finger. "Maybe I am. Guess you'll never know if I put Sammy in the recycler or not, huh?"

Luca's voice cut through the air, dreadfully cold. "What—what did you just say?"

Raphael whirled, sword snapping up. His eyes darted between the guys as they approached, and his grip tightened on the blades.

"I told you to stay outside!" he shouted, his tone cracking with an edge of panic.

"Well, we didn't," Arturo growled.

As quickly as flipping a switch, Raphael's demeanor shifted. The menace evaporated, and his practiced charm slid into place.

He flashed a winning smile. The pendant fell against his chest.

"Come on, guys." His voice was almost casual. "I'm just messing around. Trying to get a rise out of El Duende here. To–to show you what he really is. To prove he's dangerous, so you'd finally understand."

Luca remained unyielding. "Put your sword down, Raphael."

For a heartbeat, no one moved.

Raphael's eyes darted between them, calculating. Desperate. He chuckled again, trying to sound confident, but his voice came out thinner than before.

"Chavos! It's me! I'm defending you! Looking out for all of us. Saving you all from the monster."

"Only one monster here," Nico said quietly.

Raphael gestured toward Diego, trying to redirect the accusation. "Exactly. He even admitted he's a monster!"

"No," Luca said. "I think we finally see clearly."

His eyes narrowed as he studied Raphael.

"What were you showing Diego?"

Raphael froze. The color drained from his face as his hand moved reflexively toward the pendant. His mouth opened, but no sound came out.

Diego's eyes locked on it. He finally let himself see it.

The pendant of Saint Michael.

Sammy's pendant.

The one he never took off. Not even to sleep.

Diego's world narrowed to that small piece of metal glinting faintly in the dim light. His pulse thundered in his ears, drowning out everything else.

Sammy would never have given that up.

Something shattered inside Diego. He had failed another friend. Miguel. Donna. And now Sammy.

A knot formed in his throat. His chest clenched tight, filling with an icy cold flame.

Raphael had spoken the truth.

He had killed Sammy.

Sammy's face flashed in Diego's mind—his grin, his easy laugh, his endless energy.

Gone.

Raw, blistering rage burned in Diego's eyes. It tangled with grief, fraying at the threads of control he'd fought to maintain. But he couldn't let Raphael talk his way out of this. Not this time.

Distantly—the Kraal echoed that rage.

The chaos of his gift stirred deep inside him, sensing the crack in the dam. It answered rage with annihilation.

Diego snatched the pendant before another lie could slither out of Raphael's mouth. He seized Raphael's shirt. His vision blurred. Chest clenching. He couldn't breathe.

How could Raphael have done this?

The cold ache in his chest, the rising fury—it was too much. He could almost hear Sammy's laugh echoing in the air. Diego pushed past the pain, and with his gift he called out. Not just for the growlers. For something bigger. Something that could end this now.

The Kraal.

His grip on Raphael's shirt tightened.

And in Raphael's eyes, Diego saw not fear, but triumph.

Glee threaded Raphael's shout. "See? He's a monster! Look at his eyes! Glowing purple just like void terrors! Run—before he turns on you, too!"

Diego froze. His breath came in short gasps. The roar in his mind splintered as he clamped down on his gift, horrified at what he'd nearly done. One more second, and he would've done it. He'd almost chosen destruction—for them all.

Almost.

Raphael smirked.

Diego's chest heaved. He tightened his grip on Raphael's shirt. Maybe—maybe he just should do it anyway.

And then—a touch on his shoulder.

Luca's voice, soft: "I'm right here."

Hot tears welled. A choked gasp escaped. He shoved Raphael away, hissing, "You're not worth it."

Raphael stumbled, blinking. Fury twisted his features. "I'm not worth it?"

He lunged, both swords igniting in plasma.

Diego moved even faster—not with his fists but with his fraying gift. He just needed to squeeze a little more from it, even through the pain. But what?

His thoughts cleared.

He didn't need to call for the terrors. He didn't need to mask himself. What if he could... revise?

His father had said his gift worked on the mind. So, could he make Raphael believe something wasn't there?

With what little strength he had left, he crafted an image of himself lurching to the side and pushed it into Raphael's mind, willing Raphael to believe it was real. In the same breath, Diego stepped the other way.

Raphael's swing cut through empty air. He stumbled, off-balance, confusion flashing on his face.

Before he could recover, Diego closed in and grabbed both his wrists.

Sparks of darkness teased the edges of his vision. His head throbbed. But he pushed again with his gift, planting the belief that Raphael couldn't break free. Raphael struggled, pulling weakly against Diego's grip first with one arm, then the other.

Blood dripped from Diego's nose. His skull hammered with the strain. But he held firm. Raphael's eyes flared wide. He froze. Both blades clattered to the floor as they left his limp fingers, their plasma edges sputtering out.

Shouts.

The others rushed in, wrestling Raphael and pinning him down, binding his wrists.

Diego stepped away, legs shaking, bracing himself against a cabinet.

Distantly, he heard Luca ask, "You alright?"

He nodded automatically. But he wasn't. Not even close. His hands wouldn't stop trembling, and he was pretty sure he'd hurl if he opened his mouth. He didn't want to face any questions. He just needed a moment to breathe.

Diego wiped at the blood from his nose and met Luca's eyes. A mountain of unspoken things loomed between them. He drew a shuddering breath. "I need some air," he finally managed. "You got this?"

Luca nodded.

Diego clenched the pendant in his fist. It felt heavier than before.

He stepped back. Then again. This wasn't running. It was surviving. It was the only way he could protect the others—by staying away from them.

He moved past consoles, tables, and chairs, stepping out of the ops center and onto the promenade before slumping heavily against the wall.

Sammy's pendant dangled from his clenched fist.

He stared at it for a very long time.

Nowhere to Run

"What do we do now? We can't just let him get away with this. The guy's a psycho. Exile isn't harsh enough," Kenji muttered. "We should put him into a recycler, just like he did to Sammy, but still kicking."

Luca stopped pacing and faced the group, his expression firm. "We have to agree unanimously. This affects all of us."

"Diego?" Nico asked quietly.

They glanced around, noting Diego's absence. He hadn't made an appearance since everything happened, and they all figured he went down to Echo Ring.

"Even Diego, if he wants to come back."

"But we just voted…" Arturo said.

Luca sighed, "I know. Everyone said I should be in charge, although I don't know why. But that doesn't mean Diego can't come back. Either way—what do we do with Raphael? We can't just keep him locked up forever."

They had left Raphael in the Delta Ring Brig.

A heavy silence settled over the group as they considered their options. Finally, Luca offered. "What if we exile him to Green Sector?"

"Isn't that where—" Kenji started.

"Spiders." Arturo held his hands as far apart as he could.

Luca nodded, his voice quieter now, as if trying to reassure himself. "If he can figure out how to survive, he'll be fine."

Kenji frowned. "But what if he's hiding another passkey? Could he get out and come after us?"

"Then just send him in his briefs," Arturo growled.

Nico smiled, nodding his agreement.

Kenji raised an eyebrow. "Chavo, why do you always want to banish someone in just their underwear?"

A grin rose on Arturo's face. He ducked his head, rubbing the back of his neck. "I–I don't know," he stammered. "It's scary, I guess."

Luca cleared his throat. "There's no need for that. We can search him thoroughly before we send him."

The group slowly came to an agreement, but Luca insisted they wait to reconsider the decision before voting again. A day later it was still unanimous.

They carefully searched every stitch of Raphael's clothes and equipment until they were satisfied that he had nothing hidden. He geared up under their watchful eyes, and they even let him take one of his swords. Then, they exiled him to the unexplored Green Sector using the very passkey he had hidden from them.

His eyes were hard, but he said nothing as he stepped into the white, silky, webbed halls of Green Sector.

The Sound of Silence

Diego listened to the crackle of the radio. A distant voice called out from an approaching rocket ship, signaling for a berth. Goldstar-9. He leaned back, staring at nothing in particular. The voices on the radio negotiated with La Familia.

The soft hiss and clank of the Link Tube door opening interrupted his reverie. Diego turned as Luca clambered from zero gravity, pulling himself upright, cold air rushing in behind him. Together, they worked the crank, sealing the door. The ratcheting sounds faded into silence.

They faced each other.

"Hey."

"Hey."

A pause stretched between them, uncertain but not unfriendly.

"I'm sorry. Really."

"Me too."

They stood there, neither quite sure what to say next. The words hung in the air, shifting nervously from foot to foot. More silence. The heavy kind—but necessary.

"I was kind of a pendejo."

"Yeah. Me too."

Another silence. This one held longer.

"You think we can... be friends again?"

"Were we ever not?"

Color flushed Luca's cheeks. Diego took a steady breath and stepped to the lab's sink he'd turned into his kitchen. He ran the water and began fussing with some dishes—mostly just to have something to do with his hands.

Luca leaned on a workbench. After a moment, he let out a laugh —soft, and a little nervous.

"What?" Diego shut off the water and turned around, drying his hands on his shirt.

Luca rolled his eyes. "They all voted me in charge."

Diego blinked, then smiled—wide and genuine. "That's great!"

Luca's cheeks flushed deeper. "So... you're not mad?"

"Not in the least. You'll be great." Diego held up a fist.

Luca bumped it, then dropped his gaze, scuffing his sneaker on the deck plating. "So... what now?"

"I don't know. Eat something. Sleep."

"And after that?"

Diego shrugged. "Fix things. Try not to screw up again."

"You think that's possible?"

"Yeah," Diego said after a moment. "But only if we work together."

The environmental system hummed in the background. A long silence followed.

Then Luca said, almost too quiet to hear. "You scare me sometimes."

Diego swallowed hard. "Me too... but... I–I'm learning not to hide who I am anymore."

Luca nodded, his eyes glancing to where Diego's mask sat on the table. "I think I knew. Long before Rafe said anything. I just... I don't care. Okay? None of us do. All the guys are asking about you. If you'll come back."

Diego looked away, suddenly focused on a stubborn spot on one of the cups. He took a minute before responding. "Maybe. But, I think I need a little more time. I kind of like being on my own… And, I don't think I can go back until… have you guys done anything with him yet?"

Luca's expression darkened. "Yeah. We voted to—"

Diego raised a hand. "Don't tell me. I trust you guys. I don't know why I asked."

"Okay."

Luca's gaze wandered the lab, and he suddenly looked more nervous than when he arrived.

Diego narrowed his eyes. "Spill it."

Luca winced, then pulled a green scarf from his pack, holding it out carefully. "Arturo washed it. Thought you might want it. Look, I didn't know they were following me when I followed you to her. I'm so sorry. I didn't know what you were trying to do. Everything was getting weird—"

Diego's eyes closed tightly, his head turned down, hair covering his face.

Luca trailed off.

"I'm sorry," he muttered. "I'll take it back. I shouldn't have brought it."

"No." Diego reached out and took it. "Tell Arturo thanks, okay?"

Luca hesitated. "Are you—"

Diego cut him off, his voice husky. "—you should go back now."

Silence.

Luca didn't move.

Diego's hands shook, clenching the scarf so tight his knuckles were white.

"Go," he whispered. "Please."

Luca glanced at the Link door and paused for a moment. Then, he straightened his shoulders and deliberately stepped past Diego, planting himself on the couch.

His voice came softly.

"I'm right here."

*   *   *

The sun slipped beyond the lattice glasswork overhead, leaving the biosphere in hushed darkness. Faint luminescence from the algae gave the boys an otherworldly glow as they stood in a rough circle, masks over their faces—even Diego had joined them. They stayed silent—the algae's usual euphoria dulled beneath the weight of their grief.

Luca stepped forward, holding a twisted length of paper. He flicked a lighter, the small flame dancing as he touched it to the edge. Open fire was forbidden—a direct violation of Serenity Orbital's rules—but tonight, they were willing to break it. Tonight, they needed to honor Sammy.

As the flame caught, Luca raised the paper high. "This," he said, voice heavy with emotion, "represents the life of Sammy. It burned brightly."

The fire consumed the paper, crackling softly. The boys watched, their eyes reflecting the small, flickering light—a sight few of them had ever seen before.

"He was our friend, our brother," Luca went on, his voice struggling to remain steady. "He fought alongside us; he laughed with us, and now..." He paused until the flame reached the top. "His time with us has come to an end." He let go as the flame snuffed out, and the ember drifted away, leaving only a faint trail of smoke and falling ash.

Luca tapped the Solsticio drum once. Its resonant thrum vibrated through the silence. Then he lay back on the soil and looked at the stars. "I don't want to do anything else for Solsticio today. I think I'll just sit here for a bit, remembering that crazy, wild, stupid kid."

The others joined him, and a reflective calm filled the air. They lay back, head-to-head, their glowing bodies forming a circle of light in the darkness, each lost in his own memories of Sammy.

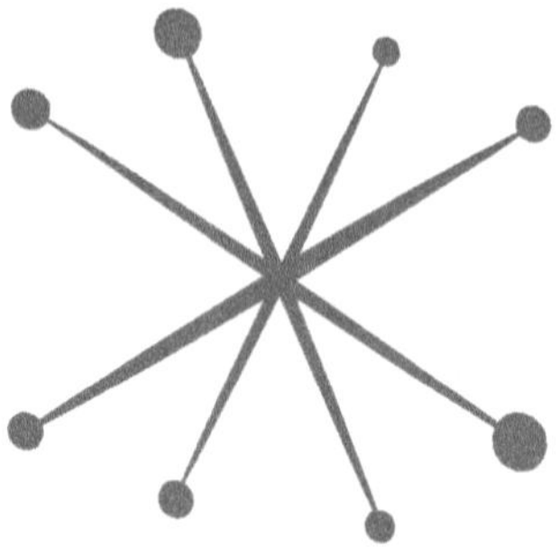

Que Sera, Sera

Months before Diego's birth — Echo Ring Project Ultra Laboratory

It began as a ripple in the air—a pinch of reality folding in on itself. Then, it expanded like an infinity mirror, refracting countless versions of the same girl, each one slightly different from the next.

One by one, the reflections aligned, collapsing into a single form: a young woman with dark skin, bright yellow eyes, and cornrow braids drawn tight against her scalp.

She surveyed the ruin.

Nature had invaded the laboratory, reaching far beyond the biosphere. Vines spilled in through the broken doorway, stretching across the floor and curling through consoles and equipment. Occasional spore pods pulsed with a violet inner light. Moss blanketed every surface.

This would not do.

Her brow furrowed, and the vines retreated. Moss faded away. The warped bulkhead groaned, metal knitting itself whole again, conduits threading back into place. The doorway sealed shut.

She crossed the room to a medbot slumped in its charging bay, indicator light blinking faintly.

Pulling a keyboard close. The screen flickered, lines of code flashing too fast for ordinary eyes. She wove in new instructions. Subtle. A hidden adjustment.

The robot straightened, optics flaring to life. She pricked her finger, leaving a bead of blood on a glass slide and handed it to the robot, whispering: "Run the protocol. When the work is done, trigger subroutine 9A4 to format yourself."

The medbot nodded.

A hiss and clank behind her—the Link tube doors.

She turned, eyes narrowing—she thought she'd have more time. Her gaze darted toward the supply closet, and the air shimmered; crates of Soylent Fusion snapped into existence.

Maria Alvarez tumbled out of the Link tube door, grumbling about the shift from zero gravity. A swarthy man followed just as clumsy.

In a blink, the ember-eyed girl vanished.

Maria straightened, scanning the laboratory. "It's still intact."

Roberto frowned. "You really think it's smart to use this stuff?"

Maria was already moving toward the medbot. "It'll work," she muttered. "It has to."

Questions for Book Clubs

Spoiler alert! The questions below contain spoilers.

Join the discussion at: https://libreon.net/p/ggcyd

- There were multiple antagonists in the book. Who or what do you think was the primary antagonist?

- Do any of the characters remind you of people you know?

- What are the key themes explored in the book?

- Do you think Raphael was telling the truth when he confessed to Diego about his own parent's abuse? Or was that just manipulation? Why did he keep the selfie with Diego?

- Consider Diego's interactions with Raphael. Is there some way he could have acted differently to avoid how things turned out?

- What do you think of Diego's disfigurement and gift as a metaphor for dealing with adolescence and accepting who he is, warts and all?

- It was never resolved who tampered with the back door being left unlocked, leading to Julian's death. Who do you think did it? Why?

- Was it wrong for Diego to lock Donna up? What else could he have done?

- Could Diego have interacted in a better way with Luca after taking him to Medbay? Did he have the right answers? What was the most important thing he did?

- Is the ending satisfying? If so, why? If not, why not… and how would you change it?

- Have you learned something new or been exposed to different ideas because of this story?

How might this story have played out differently if it was the girls being exiled instead of the boys?

Exercises for Writers

- Rewrite the final scene where Luca and Diego reconnect, but do it as if the story was flipped, where it was Lucia (Luca) and Diana (Diego). How would it have played out differently?

- Consider the different plot structures, such as 7-point or chaistic. Identify the different points in the story: Inciting Event. Midpoint. Climax.

- It is never explained why Charlie Ring collapsed into decompression. In Atom Bomb Baby, we learn that the Kraal do not interact with inanimate objects—so what could have caused the calamity on Charlie Ring? Was it intentionally caused, or accidental? Is there a story in this?

- It is never explained what happened to Julian's remains, nor what Meddi was going to propose as her experimental procedure. Is there a story in this?

About the Author

During the day, Brandon serves as a VP of Engineering. He is a video game and open-source pioneer, avid programmer (language of choice: Elixir), technology architect, serial entrepreneur, game designer, writer, and artist. His diverse expertise includes building numerous startups and companies.

Although initially pursuing English and Graphic Arts with an interest in Film, Brandon somehow found his way into Computer Science. It was during this time that he met his lovely and patient wife.

Residing with his family in the Rocky Mountains, Brandon takes pleasure in outdoor activities. Above all, he harbors a deep passion for sci-fi and fantasy and has crafted many captivating stories, games, and settings.

Learn more at https://revenant.studio/

9 780998 749976